CROOKED WINDOWS INN MYSTERIES

BOOKS 1-3

VALIA LIND

SKAZKA PRESS

ONCE UPON A WITCH

CROOKED WINDOWS INN COZY
MYSTERY #1

Valia Lind

1

There is a slight possibility that my life is a complete disaster. Okay, maybe only a mild disaster. Oh, who am I kidding? Today has proven that no matter how much I would like to have my act together, I have a tendency to tumble headfirst into a mess. Or multiple. At the same time. Go me!

Granted, cleaning up messes is kind of my specialty. Being an interior decorator requires a certain finesse of organization. Normally, I can handle myself. But today, the one thing that I've been keeping under wraps this whole time has decided to unravel.

"Cassandra, I understand that you had good intentions, but I do not see how any of this is good." My boss, Laura Jingle, waves a hand at the apartment in front of her. Don't let her jolly name fool you. She's anything but a good spirit. Especially today. You see, I had this huge project, an enormous client, and everything was going according to plan. Until my magic went on a downward spiral and ruined every piece of furniture and art in the room. It's as if the paintings melted off the walls and right into the thousands-of-dollars sofa. Among other things. The table, the lamps, and the—it might be good if I stop listing items.

It's been so long since I've used my magic, I couldn't even stop what was happening. And then Laura walked in on me trying to push the paint back into the painting with my bare hands. It was not a good look. I've literally been caught red handed.

I glance down at the red paint staining my palms, and I wonder if magical paint will be harder to scrub off my skin.

"What will I tell Mr. Richards? He is paying us a huge amount of money to make this livable for his daughter. You made it look like a rundown art studio from one of those indie b-rated movies that are so popular right now!"

Her voice keeps getting higher and higher as she talks, and honestly, I don't pick up much of what she's saying there at the end. At this point I'm just hoping and begging that nothing else happens. Because if I suddenly start setting the tables on fire with my mind, I'm pretty sure I will never work at another firm ever again.

Although, at this point, I fear that's my fate anyway.

"I'm sorry, Laura, I don't—"

"No, I don't even have time for your apologies. I need to call a cleanup crew. Maybe by some miracle we can do this before—"

Just then, the front door opens. Mr. Richards walks in, talking in that incredibly loud voice of his.

"Where is my favorite interior designer? I brought a special guest! We could not—" he stops mid-sentence as he gets his first good look at the room. His daughter peeks out from behind his shoulder, her eyes narrowing.

"Mr. Richards, we apologize. There was an accident and—"

"An accident?" Mr. Richard bellows, cutting off Laura's apology. "This is a disaster. Thousands of dollars' worth of disaster!

How could you? Who did this? Is this a joke? You were supposed to be a reputable firm?"

"Sir, I am. My assistant had a mishap. But we will take care of it."

Mr. Richards spins around, his eyes on me. I stand my ground, because my aunt didn't raise a coward, but I have to admit that he is a little scary.

"You." He points, and I almost giggle at the slightly comical way his cheeks puff out. "I want you out of here. Now!"

"Sir—"

"No, out! In fact, if you want any of my money," the man says, turning back to Laura. "You will fire her on the spot."

My world drops out from beneath me, because even before Laura turns to me, I already know what her response will be.

~

"Are you sure you have to go?" my roommate Meg asks as she watches me zip up my suitcase. We've been having this conversation for the last two days, and the answer is still the same.

"You know I don't have a choice."

"Yes, you do. You can come work at the office. They're always looking for a reliable assistant. And you're nothing if not reliable!" We've been living together for the past year and have become friends as well as roommates. She did a two-week stint with Laura's firm, and that's how we met. We were both in the market for a new place to live.

"I appreciate the offer, Meg, but you and I both know I need to be designing living spaces, not filing paperwork. And Laura made sure I won't be doing that around these parts anytime soon."

Needless to say, the woman fired me on the spot and then made sure to make a point and tell me that I'm not welcome in any of her friend's firms. And she has a lot of friends. She has to, to be successful in the business. But this also means I'm completely out of luck unless I take a few steps backward in my career and take a job completely out of the field, which I really refuse to do.

"So, going to stay with your aunt is your best idea?"

"It is." I sigh because I know what staying at Crooked Windows Inn will do. Auntie Grace is a witch through and through and she has been trying to get me on the right side of the tracks for years. Her words, not mine. But I have my battles with magic, and it has cost me more relationships than I care to admit. Instead of dealing with all them rules and such, I chose a life of normalcy. Look where that has gotten me.

"Plus, her hip has been bothering her with all those stairs. She also said I can help her renovate some of the upstairs rooms, and I can't pass up an opportunity like that. It'll be good practice."

I know I sound like I'm still trying to talk myself into it, and maybe I am. My roommate watches me with a look of concern in her gaze, but I'm not budging.

"I'll come visit!" Meg finally says, catching me in a long hug.

"You better."

There's not much to say after that, so I get into my little Toyota Corolla and head off to Monroe Cove. It's the one place I never truly wanted to return to.

It's not like it's a terrible place to live. It's near the water, and the town is adorable enough to be on a postcard. That means there are plenty of tourists to keep the place afloat. The economy there is not struggling, that's for sure, which is why Auntie Grace has never understood my need to get away. But it wasn't like I thought I couldn't make a living there. I just needed to be somewhere else to do so.

Now, as I begin my ten-hour drive, I wonder if this is how it was always going to end. Was there was some part of me that just expected to return to Monroe Cove? Or was it my magical blood that always thought so?

My mother was one of the greatest witches to ever live in Monroe Cove. Too bad I never knew her. She led the coven with compassion and understanding. I never knew my father, and honestly, from what I've heard from Auntie Grace, that's probably for the best.

Mama disappeared when I was just two years old. I'd be lying if I said I haven't thought of that more than once in my lifetime. A part of me doesn't want to be anywhere near Monroe Cove because that part of me thinks Mama chose to leave me behind.

But Auntie Grace says she never would have done so, and I have no choice but to believe it.

Even though, after twenty-two years, no one knows what happened to her.

As I pull onto the highway, I click the button for the radio and let my playlist fill the space around me. I've always been a fan of driving, so I plan to use this trip to help me figure some things out.

Like what in the world am I supposed to do with my life now?

2

———

When I finally park in front of Crooked Windows Inn, my first thought is that it looks exactly how I left it. The building is the biggest contradiction in Monroe Cove. I'd be lying if I said I didn't love it.

The mansion is large and dark, housing thirty-two rooms, a huge kitchen, a big dining room that's open to the public, a ballroom, and two sitting rooms on the first floor. One of those rooms is my favorite place in all of Monroe Cove—the library. There's also a smaller sitting room between the bedrooms where Auntie Grace lives, and where I'll be staying. I love it. Everything in Monroe Cove is bright and airy, and Crooked Windows Inn looks like it's inhabited by witches.

As I get out of the car and rearrange my black mini skirt, I can't help but smile at the large plaque hanging over the front entrance.

Crooked Windows Inn is named after its crooked windows. You'd think it was some play on words but nope. The place is actually built to be asymmetrical, and it's one of my favorite things about it. The dark wood and the mismatched shapes, which light up at night, make the atmosphere here top notch.

A loud horn makes me jump where I stand. When I turn around, my eyes zero in on the dark blue pick-up truck idling behind my car. The man behind the wheel honks again before waving his hand out the window. Instead of moving my car, which he clearly wants me to do, I fold my arms in front of me and wait him out. I know for a fact that this place is reserved for Auntie Grace. And since she doesn't drive anymore, it's mine for the taking.

The man jerks his truck into park, before jumping out of his vehicle. I've met plenty of intimidating individuals in my life, so I don't even flinch when he marches over to me.

"Ma'am, I'm not sure what you think you're doing, but you may not park here."

That voice. I'd know that voice anywhere.

For a second, I freeze as the six-foot-two gorgeous specimen of a man stops in front of me. But only a second. I ain't a thirteen-year-old girl anymore, and he is not my number one tormentor.

"I'll have you know, Dean Harvey, I am allowed to park anywhere I please on this property."

It's his turn to be struck dumb, but he's always been a quick one. He rips off his baseball hat, which shielded most of his face from me up until this point, and I prepare myself for the impact his eyes have always had on me. They're dark blue like the ocean down the road right before a storm rolls in.

"Cassandra?" he mumbles. Only then do I take my sunglasses off and give him a nice long look.

"Still as rude as they come, I see," I reply, meeting his gaze.

"You're the mystery assistant Miss Mary Grace has been talking about?" he asks, bewildered. I can't help it; I roll my eyes. Of course Auntie Grace has been telling anyone who'd listen that I'm coming home. Not exactly sure why she had to mention it to Dean.

"Wait, assistant?"

Dean shifts to the side, pointing back to his truck. "Harvey Construction, at your service." Now I notice the large white lettering on the side of the door. This time, I roll my eyes *and* groan a little. Auntie Grace and I are about to have some words.

Without a response, I spin on my heels and march my way up the driveway, the stairs, and straight into the inn.

This building has been in our family for generations, but it's only been about seventy years since it was converted into a public inn. Grams decided it would be a good use of our talents, apparently. And Auntie Grace kept it up.

Now, as I make my way inside, I'm assaulted by the smells of my childhood. The same wood that never seems to lose its freshness, the same lavender and rosemary in the air.

"There she is, my gorgeous niece. Welcome back, sugar plum."

I'm barely inside before Auntie Grace swallows me into her embrace. I was determined to be upset with her, but the moment her arms close around me, I feel at home. Hugging her back just as tightly, I breathe in the basil and fresh-baked-bread smell she carries around with her. The tension evaporates.

"Let me look at you, sweetheart. It feels like ages since I've seen you." She places her palms against my cheeks, examining me closely. I know better than to interrupt while she gets all of her emotions out. In this place, emotions come with a lot of words. "Sugar plum, you look exhausted. Doesn't she look exhausted?" Auntie Grace directs the last question at the man who came in behind me, but she doesn't wait for a response. "But also, as beautiful as the rising sun. Your hair is so long, I don't even know what you do with all of it. And that outfit. Goodness me, you look like a big city girl. But I know you still gots all that small town blood in you," she pinches my cheeks, reminding me just why I left in the first place. The feeling of suffocation begins to surface, but I push it down. "Well, you're here now, and that is all that matters."

She hugs me again, and I don't resist. Regardless of my feelings for this town and the magic that flows through my family line, I am glad to be in her arms again.

～

"YOU'RE LOOKING WELL, AUNTIE GRACE," I say when she finally releases me.

"Of course I am, Cassandra Duke. There's good blood flowing in these veins." She winks at me, and I try to suppress a smile. I'm sure all the herbs don't hurt either. That's something I carried with me even though I don't practice magic anymore. The knowledge doesn't go away, so why not use it?

"Oh, and Dean, I see you remember Cassie."

"Yes, Auntie. We are acquainted," I reply, being sure not to make eye contact with Mean Dean. That's what Pen and I dubbed him in seventh grade when he spilled a whole pie down my shirt at some school function. I can't even remember which one. Up to that point, he tormented me, but once I was covered in peaches and whipped cream, it became war from both sides.

"Good afternoon, Miss Mary Grace," the deep voice drawls behind me. "I'll see myself upstairs."

I refuse to look at him as he leaves, but Auntie has other ideas.

"All my southern cookin' made him good lookin', wouldn't you say?" Auntie mumbles, giving me a small wink as she heads to the counter.

"You've been feeding him too? Now he'll never leave."

"Oh, hush you. I know you have your differences, but he is a respectable young man, and a handyman, and we need one around these parts."

I shake my head but don't take the bait. Auntie may know a lot of what happened when I was a kid, but I haven't told her everything. And I don't want to open up that can of worms right now. Instead, I focus on the inn.

"It still looks just as good as I remember," I say as I follow my aunt into the hallway toward the kitchen. The large dining room is bursting with activity. It always is, since it's open to the public. Families come for lunch, old ladies come for gossip. Dinner is a more romantic affair at times, but no matter the time of day, everyone comes for Auntie Grace's cooking.

Auntie does a quick check of the place, making sure everyone is where they need to be, before heading to the front desk once again. I follow after her like a little puppy. She always seems to be moving, and I've learned to roll with it.

"I can't believe you're still manning the front desk," I comment as I lean against the counter. The long wooden stand stretches across the foyer. Stairs lead up to the rooms on one side, and a hallway and double doors lead to the dining room on the other. It's as if time stood still here. Except for Dean. He has definitely changed in the time I've been away.

"It's my small pleasure, and I will do it until the day I die."

The simple words bring a tinge of sadness to my heart. Finding an occupation that brings you real joy isn't a normal occurrence. I left friends in the city who are at their jobs because they have to be, not because they want to be. I thought interior design was my calling. I thought working for Laura was going to give me that dream. Yet, here I am.

"Don't look so glum, honey. You'll find your footing once again."

"Are you magic analyzing me, Auntie Grace?" I ask, narrowing my eyes immediately. It's a family trait, being able to pick up on people's emotions. It's not something I retained, but Auntie has always been good at it.

"I don't need no magic to know my baby girl is sad." She reaches over, placing a soft palm against my face. "It's okay to be a little lost."

"Why do I think you're talking about more than just my job?"

"Because you're a smart girl, and you always have been." I smile at that, because she always knows how to make me feel better but also make sure she works her way into the conversation with all of her opinions.

"I'm sorry to disappoint, Auntie Grace, but my magic is near nonexistent." There's no use telling her about my work mishap right now, especially with all the busybodies walking through the inn.

"Magic is part of who you are, sugar bun. Ain't no fuss about that. Just because you decided to stop exercising, doesn't mean it went away. It just went a little dormant." Auntie Grace pats my hand, much like she used to when I was a child. But then, with her, I always will be.

"Did you bring me here for interior design or magic spells?" I narrow my eyes while Auntie gives me one of her winning smiles.

"A little bit of both, honey pie."

Just then, one of the servers comes out from the kitchen, waving Auntie over. I stay at the front desk, mulling over her words. It would probably be wise for me to figure out a little more about my magic. It's not like I want a repeat of what happened. But if I open myself up to that, I'm not sure what will happen.

A scream shatters the pleasant quiet. I hurry to the dining room, following the commotion. Auntie is right beside me coming out of the kitchen. The moment we step inside the dining room, my heart drops.

There, at the table near the bay windows, a woman is slumped over in her chair. You'd think she just passed out, but there's blueness to her and not a sign of life.

Even after all the time I've suppressed my magic, I can still see the woman's spirit stand up from her body, looking completely lost.

"Someone killed me! You have to find them!" she exclaims before she poofs out of the room. Auntie and I exchange a look before she hurries over to check on the woman. I watch as she meets my eye, shaking her head sadly.

Well then. What a lovely day to be back at the Crooked Windows Inn.

3

___

After that, the whole place becomes a whirlpool of activity. The sheriff is called. The dining room is cleared out and taped off. People are ushered back to their rooms. Servers are running up and down the stairs carrying teas, most likely filled with extra chamomile. Auntie Grace handles all of it with complete calm, ordering everyone around. I do what I can, but mostly, I just stay at the front desk where she places me.

I've never seen a ghost before or any kind of a spirit. Auntie's cousin specializes in that sort of a thing, but I've always stayed away. Granted, I've stayed away from the majority of my extended family. But this? It's a strange experience and one I don't want to repeat. Ever. My skin is still covered in goosebumps.

I've tried to stay away from magic most of my life because it's never brought anything but trouble. Look at that, I was right. Take that, Auntie Grace.

"Honey bun, the phone might start ringing any minute. You know them busy bodies are already spreading all kinds of rumors. You just politely decline any conversation. And while it is very inhospitable of me," Auntie Grace takes a deep breath, placing a hand over her heart. "You have my full permission to hang up on anyone who decides to raise their voice at you."

"Auntie, don't you worry. I know how to handle unhappy customers." I give her hand a small squeeze before she reaches over to pat me on the cheek. And then she's gone.

"Trouble still follows you around, don't it?" a deep voice says over my shoulder. I only just barely manage not to jump. Slowly, I turn to give Mean Dean one of my cool stares.

"Pouring salt into a wound is still part of your daily routine, hmm?"

His chuckle takes me by surprise, and I suppress the shiver that wants to run up my spine. I am not having this reaction to Mean Dean. I am not! Have I been so deprived of human contact I'm going to start melting at the sound of his laugh? I absolutely will not.

"How are you holding up?" He stops near the counter, placing one big hand on top of it. Shifting my gaze away so I don't stare, I take a deep breath before finally meeting his eyes. It surprises me when I find real concern there. Whatever I was going to say dies on my lips.

"Cassie, are you—"

"I'm fine." I nearly jump when he moves closer. "Just fine. Shouldn't you be more broken up about it? Did you know the woman?"

"I'm saddened and concerned," he replies, narrowing his eyes a little, as if he's trying to figure me out. "But accidents happen. And Mabel had health problems. I'm not surprised."

Now it's my turn to study him suspiciously.

"How well did you know her?"

"Just as well as I know most people in this town." He shrugs, completely unbothered. "I've lived here a long time."

For some reason, the way he says it makes it seem

accusatory, but it's not like I actually know the man well enough to pick up on his moods. I'm not sure why I should even bother.

Before I have to make a decision one way or the other, Auntie Grace makes an appearance.

"Oh Dean, you're here. Good. Would you be a dear and run over to Loretta's and pick up the food?"

"Food? Auntie Grace, you have a kitchen," I say, looking between the two of them. Dean is already reaching for his keys.

"Yes, and people will want dinner soon."

"Don't worry, Miss Mary Grace. I've got it."

Dean gives me one long look before turning and walking out the door. Just then, another man steps in. Even though I've been gone for years, I know Sheriff Bernard on sight. Not that I'd admit to it out loud, but I may have had a few run ins with him growing up. I saw him arrive earlier with the doctor, so I assume they finished up in the dining room.

"What's the prognosis, Sheriff?" Auntie asks as the man stops by the counter. He spares me a quick glance and a nod before turning to my aunt.

"I'm afraid we'll have to keep the room cordoned off until we can sweep through it a few times."

"Oh, but—"

"I understand it is inconvenient for your business, but we have no choice. We may not have had a death like this in years, but we still remember how this works."

"Death like this?" I ask, my mind on the ghostly form of Mabel yelling at us to find her killer. It's not like the sheriff can see ghosts.

"A suspicious circumstance, Miss Cassandra," the sheriff replies. He clearly knows exactly who I am, not that I thought he'd forgotten.

"What's suspicious is that she'd decided to pass to the other side in my inn," Auntie Grace mumbles. The sheriff opens his mouth but decides against whatever he was going to say. Clearly, he's acquainted with my aunt's attitude well enough.

"We'll be in touch, Miss Mary Grace," he replies before heading back to the dining room.

"And that is why, honey bun, I sent Dean to pick up some food," Auntie Grace announces before patting my hand and hurrying off in a flurry of skirts.

Another shiver runs up my spine as I'm left standing in the foyer. I give the room a brief once over, almost expecting to see Mabel floating a few feet away. Thankfully, there's no one there. I have no idea how I'm going to be able to sleep in this house now. Not when I keep expecting a phantom to jump out at me at every turn.

LET'S BE HONEST, I barely slept. Every time the house made any kind of noise, I sat up in my bed, waiting for Mabel to appear. Let me tell you, an old house like this makes many, *many* noises during the night. I don't think I've pulled an all-nighter like this since my slumber party days, and this feels very different than that. There was no fun involved.

Even though it's only five o'clock in the morning, I get out of bed and head for the bathroom. I've never been a morning person, but I'm feeling way too awake to lay in bed any longer.

The inn has many uses, but one of my favorite things about it is the area on the west side of the building that's entirely away from the guests. The main library opens up to a small hallway that leads to a smaller library and the rooms on the opposite sides of the main one. My room is on the far west side of the small library. It's spacious, with a queen-sized bed, a dresser, and a vanity mirror setup straight out of a regency romance. I have my own bathroom with a full-sized tub.

When I got old enough that Auntie Grace gave me permission to redesign anything in the room, I thought about it but never could bring myself to touch anything in here. It made me feel like I was stepping back in time. And while I do have a television and a desk with my computer here now, it still feels like that. For the longest time, this was where I went to escape from all the family drama. Now, I'm once again looking for an escape.

After a quick shower, I don my black mini skirt and a green sweater before I sit down to brush out my hair. I swear the red hues look more reddish since I've come to town, but maybe it's the light in here. Leaving my locks to air dry, I rearrange them over my shoulders as I step into my boots. The weather is still cool outside, but I don't mind it.

Leaving my room behind, I head out into the library when something stops me. Glancing over my shoulder, I try to figure out what made me pause. I don't see anything. Maybe it's just a feeling. When I turn back to the library, I'm shocked to see a few of the books levitating off the table.

Walking over slowly, I wave my hand above and below the hardback, but it stays midair. Grabbing the book, I place it on the table, but it just makes its way back up again. I have no idea if I'm doing this or if something else is causing it. But it would probably be best if I could make it stop.

Closing my eyes, I take a deep breath in and out. It's just like I used to do when Auntie Grace made me practice my magic. When I open my eyes, I concentrate entirely on the intention, willing the books to settle. They don't budge. I hear a creak behind me, making me jump. The books fly straight across the room and right into the opposite wall.

"Well, good morning to you, sugar plum," Auntie Grace greets me with a grin. I can't help but groan. I was hoping to make the magic disappear before she saw any of it.

"Please don't get any ideas, Auntie Grace," I say, marching

past her toward the hallway. She's right on my heels, of course. That display just gave her all the ammunition she needed.

"Cassandra Duke, don't you be taking that tone with me. Clearly there is something going on with your magic. Why didn't you say anything?"

I stop and turn to face my aunt, feeling exhaustion in my very bones. She looks concerned, of course, but there's also that glimmer of hope in her eyes.

"That," I point at her face, "That is exactly why I didn't want to say anything. You'll start plotting, and I'm only here to help you around the inn."

"And to help Mabel. You know now that she asked us for help. We have to do it or bad things will happen."

I sober up instantly.

"Yes, and to help Mabel."

I really don't have a choice in that matter, do I? I just wish I knew where to start. It feels like this thing will get worse before it'll get better.

4

———

I spend the morning helping Auntie with breakfast. By the time eleven comes around, I'm ready for a nap. We're at the front counter once more, and I think maybe now is the time for me to ask about Mabel.

Suddenly, I jump back as a small gray form lands on the counter.

"What's that?"

"It's a cat, dear," my auntie replies, speaking a little slower than usual. I can see it's a cat, and a pretty one. If you're into that sort of a thing.

"I don't like cats."

"Ah!"

I glance between my aunt and the cat because I'm pretty sure they both just gasped at me. In unison.

"What? I know, it's very un-witchy of me. But they've never been friendly."

"That's because they can tell you're not friendly, my dear." Auntie walks over and gives the gray furball a rub. "Birdie is a lovely companion."

"Auntie, that's a cat."

"I thought we established that."

"You call him Birdie?"

"Her, sugar plum, Birdie is a she, and she loves her name."

"Well, I suppose it could be worse. You could've named her Dog." The cat hisses while Auntie laughs.

"I thought about it." Auntie continues to chuckle as she moves around in a flurry of activity, straightening the papers and pens at the front counter. I narrow my eyes at her agility, my suspicions confirmed.

"That hip is feeling mighty fine, huh, Auntie?" I ask, side-stepping the cat still perched at the counter as I give Auntie a look. She stops immediately, realizing her mistake, before slowly turning to me.

"Oh pash, Cassandra Duke, don't you be giving me that look now. You and I both know you are needed here, even if it's not for the hip."

I shake my head, but I can't exactly deny it. The ghostly form of the woman from the dining room enters my mind once more. I give the room a quick scan.

"And don't you worry, honey bun. Mabel Smith won't be visiting you any time soon." I open my mouth to ask how she knows that, but we're interrupted.

"Is it because you made sure of that fact, Miss Mary Grace?"

All three of us—Auntie, Birdie, and I—turn at the sound of the deep voice coming from the front door. Sheriff Bernard is right in the doorway with Dean to his left. I give both men a thorough glare before I reply.

"Are you accusing my aunt of murder, Sheriff?"

The older man has the courtesy to look uncomfortable for a moment before he takes a step forward.

"This is an active investigation."

"So basically, what you're telling me is that there *was* foul play and it was not a natural death?" I glance at Dean briefly.

"So now my aunt is a suspect?" I may not be in control of my magic, but I know a thing or two about life.

"You know how these things go, Miss Duke." The sheriff squares his shoulders, clearly not liking the fact that I talked back. "Your aunt had the means to the end. A witness came forward stating she was seen arguing with the deceased to the point of telling her to, umm," he glances down at the notepad in his right hand, "'go and die, you old witch.'"

I twist around to look at Auntie, but all she does is shrug, completely unbothered.

"I bet my bottom dollar that witness was the no-good busy body Sue Lynn. And of course I argued with Mabel. She was a witch!"

"Auntie!" I'm completely shocked.

"Oh, not that kind, sugar plum." She pats my hand, like it's nothing to be talking about magic in front of people. "She was an honest to goodness, bless her heart, monster of a woman. Everybody knows it. Her name may have been Mabel, but she was anything but lovable," she directs that at the sheriff, her finger pointing. "Don't you be telling me you don't know that. You've been around these parts long enough, Marcus Bernard."

This time the sheriff looks chided, and it's very hard not to smile. Auntie has always been a force to be reckoned with, and this isn't stopping her, that's for sure. I could use a few pointers.

"Miss Mary Grace, you know the protocol. You need to come with me."

"And leave my place of business during the day?"

This time, four pairs of eyes turn toward me. I really need Birdie to stop looking like she knows what's happening around her. It's freaking me out.

"Fine," I say, throwing my hands in the air. "I'll watch the inn. And I'll call Lucy to come help. But please behave." I'm concerned Auntie will end up getting herself in more trouble than she already is in.

"I haven't behaved in 63 years, and I'm not about to start now. Don't you worry about that apparition problem we were discussing earlier. The battery needs a recharge." She throws the words over her shoulder as she marches to the door. Thankfully, I understand exactly what she means, which makes me feel a little better. "Well, lead the way, sheriff!"

I'm shaking my head when the door closes behind them and then I realize Dean is still standing near the door. He's been a silent statue this whole time, watching. Which is kind of unnerving. It doesn't help that he's intimidating, even with the staring.

"Don't you have a table to saw or paint or something?" I ask, walking around the counter, if only to put some distance between us. I shoo at the cat, but she gives me one of those "you've-got-to-be-kidding-me" looks and then proceeds to lay down on the counter. She also makes sure to lay facing both of us. I watch as her eyes follow our every move. This cat is character, but I heard they all are. I think she just winked at me. I turn back to the bane of my existence.

"I actually have a door to paint," Dean replies, giving me a smirk. That brings back all kinds of memories. I inhale slowly, keeping my heart rate down before I pull an Auntie and go off on the Mr. Tall, Dark, and Annoying.

I can still feel his eyes on me, so I look up, meeting that gaze head on. We're locked in a battle of wills, and I'm no longer just his younger brother's best friend. I'm a grown woman, and I can handle looking into his deep ocean-blue eyes.

Okay, brain. Less descriptive adjectives would be nice.

"Well, carry on then." I wave my hand in the direction of the stairs before looking down at the papers in front of me. Dean stands there for another moment before heading for the upstairs rooms. The moment he's out of sight, I breathe a sigh of relief. He really does have me in all kinds of knots. There's not much I can do about a physical response. I'm not magical.

"It's not my fault," I say out loud, looking at Birdie. "And it's not Auntie's fault either. We just have to make sure the sheriff knows it too."

~

I DO the best I can at the inn, but I'm still relieved when Lucy arrives.

"I can't believe the sheriff actually thinks Mary Grace had anything to do with this!" Lucy announces, setting her stuff behind the counter. The woman is only about ten years older than me, but she's always had a sense of an old soul about her. She's been Auntie Grace's right-hand woman for a few years now, and I'm thankful.

"I can't either. Did you know Mabel well?"

"I'm not sure anyone knew that woman well." Lucy continues moving around the counter, reminding me of my aunt. "She would take her tea here every two days, and she would always made sure to make her rounds and spread whatever the daily gossip was. Let me just tell you, Cassie, no one is surprised she's gone. She made plenty of enemies with that big mouth of hers."

There's a note of bitterness in Lucy's words that I hadn't heard previously. But before I can comment on that, she continues.

"Come here and give me a hug first. Then you can go do whatever you need to do to get the sheriff to see the light of day."

Lucy envelops me in her arms before shooing me away. Hiring her on was Auntie Grace's best business decision. No one commands a room like she does. Me-thinks the sheriff will be calling her in as a witness soon. She seems to know every-one's business. Comes with the territory, I suppose.

I leave the counter and head to my room to grab my purse.

I'm barely inside the library when Mabel appears right in front of my face.

I jump back, swallowing a scream.

"Someone killed me!" she yells, getting even closer.

"Yeah, I heard you the first time."

That stops whatever else she was about to say. She stares at me with her mouth open, as if she can't believe I heard her.

"Wait, you can hear me?"

Oh, that's *exactly* what she can't believe. Fun stuff.

"Yes, I can hear you. And see you. Well, mostly," I move around her and fully into the small library while she follows behind. Way too closely. Also, she's giving me a headache. "Could you take a few steps back or something?"

She looks completely confused before she kind of floats two feet back. It's strange, and that creepy feeling at the back of my neck is back. I'm pretty sure there's a reason I stayed away from all things ghostly before this. It's definitely the creep factor.

"How is it you can hear me? Who are you?"

"Cassandra Duke, at your service," I reply, rubbing my temples. The headache is coming on fast. I can't tell if it's because I'm stressed or if it's actually her presence that's affecting me.

"You're Mary Grace's niece?"

"One and the same." How lucky am I that my reputation precedes me? I wonder if there is anyone in this town who doesn't know who I am. Small towns are a whole different world, and they definitely like to talk.

"But you can see me. How can you see me?"

"Well, I suppose I can tell you now. I'm a witch, so you know, magic exists."

There's a moment of silence and then. "I knew it!" She shouts the words, even though I'm right in front of her. I'm amazed how such a small woman can make so much noise.

"I knew there was something funny about that Mary Grace. A witch! That makes all the sense in the world, that woman."

I roll my eyes because I can't help it. With the evidence presented, I definitely don't disagree with Auntie Grace about Mabel being a horrible woman. She looks like a cat who just caught a canary. She should not be looking this peppy, considering her situation.

"While I appreciate your enthusiasm, could we please get back to the part where you're a ghost because you think someone killed you?"

She sobers up immediately, narrowing her eyes at me.

"Of course someone killed me."

"Do you have any proof of that?"

"Don't you think I know what happened to me? I am not senile." Wow, that went zero to fifty fast. Maybe I should tread a little lightly. But it's not like I have a book on how to talk to ghosts. Actually, Auntie Grace might. I should probably look around this library eventually.

"If you know what happened, can you tell me? Then I can tell the sheriff, and he can arrest the guilty party." I'm using my best customer service voice on her, and it seems to be working. She opens her mouth in excitement but then stops.

"No, I can't. I... I don't remember. Something is off."

Great, just great. If I knew more about ghosts, maybe I could talk her through it? No, I can't be wishing to know more about magic. That won't lead anywhere good.

"But you know someone murdered you?" I try a different approach, keeping my voice gentle.

"Yes, I know it. I tasted the weird tea right before everything went black."

Poisoned. That would make sense. It's the easiest way to kill someone when you're trying to stage it as a natural cause. But most poisons are traceable. Wouldn't the killer know it wouldn't work?

So many questions swirling in my mind. I'll need to make a list. I glance up, getting ready to ask Mabel another one, when she suddenly blinks out of existence.

"Mabel?" I call, but there's no answer. My headache lifts instantly, which proves the fact that it was her causing it.

"Great," I say out loud as I head for my room. "More questions, and no answers. So helpful."

5

I reach downtown in about seven minutes flat, and wow, this town really has not changed. Parking across the street from the sheriff's station, I get out of the car and stare at the building.

Coming here was an impulse. I couldn't just sit around the inn doing nothing. Lucy insisted I get out and so I did. But not before I made a phone call, of course.

"Cassie!" the voice exclaims from behind me. I turn to see my five-foot-two, baking goddess of a friend, who grabs me with all of her might. I hug her back just as hard, excited to see a friendly face.

"Penny, I'm sorry it's taken me so long to come by." We were supposed to see each other last night, but that obviously didn't happen.

"Oh, don't you worry. It's crazy what happened at the inn. Is Auntie Gracie okay?"

"You know auntie. She's taking it all in stride and causing more problems than helping."

Penny and I have been friends since we were both put into a

Christmas pageant when we were ten years old. Since I stopped coming to spend my summers here, she has visited me in Chicago, and we kept up with biweekly FaceTime calls. But it's definitely not the same as seeing her in person.

"That sounds like Auntie Grace." Penny hooks her arms through mine, steering me toward her bakery. Even though it's across the street, I can already smell the delicious scent of freshly baked bread and frosting. Penny is a master at all things sweet and fattening, which is why opening up her own place was a natural business choice.

"I do have a bone to pick with you," I comment, settling at the bar-like counter as she steps behind it. There are a few tables and chairs in the room, and people give me a quick glance when I walk in. Most don't look familiar, telling me they're tourists.

"Here, have a cupcake and tell me all about it." Penny places a plate with a pink and white frosted cupcake the size of my fist in front of me.

"You can't bribe me with sweets."

"I can always bribe you with sweets." She gives me a look, and she's right. I do have a weakness.

"Fine, but why didn't you tell me Mean Dean was working at the inn?"

She has the courtesy to look chastised for about half a second before she shrugs.

"You would've gotten all weird."

"I got all weird when I saw him anyway." I sigh.

"I haven't heard you use that nickname in ages. That bad?"

"Well, it wasn't good."

We get quiet for a moment as Penny helps another customer.

"How are you holding up with everything?" Penny asks as she moves around the counter. I turn around, watching as she delivers a plate of baked goods to a couple sitting by the window. It puts a smile on my face.

"This place is fantastic, Penny. You've done such a great job here." Even the sign out front that simply says *Penny's* is perfect. The marketing is very on point. I may have helped but only a little.

"Thank you, I know. Now, don't change the subject."

There's no getting around her questions. I sigh, before replying, "Honestly, not well. I never even thought I'd come back here. And now all this? It feels like a fever dream or something. I'm still trying to wake up."

Penny reaches over, taking the cupcake and replacing it with a piece of cheesecake in front of me.

"Are those raspberries I see?" My voice sounds a little pitched even to me, but my excitement is genuine.

"Of course they are. Try it. It's a big hit."

"And officially my new favorite," I say around a mouthful. Not exactly ladylike, Auntie Grace would say, but the joy on Penny's face is worth it. "You've got a gift, girl." I continue, this time after swallowing.

"It's not a hard recipe—"

"No, I mean it. This whole place. You wanted it, and you got it. I'm so proud of you."

"And I'm proud of you!" she replies with a grin. "I know you'll bounce back from all of this. I know it."

"Well, that makes one of us."

I turn to glance out the window at the people mulling by. A few come in, and Penny moves down the counter to serve the newcomers. It's the perfect location to catch the eye of every tourist in town, and it makes me so happy to see my best friend thriving.

Taking my time with the cheesecake, I let my mind wander. When staging an apartment, I begin by making a list. Things that are absolutely necessary go at the top. Then, I move through the client's wants. After that, I pull out a blueprint of the space and rearrange the items, pulling from both parts of the list. At the very bottom I make a list of all the things that will make the space even better.

It's a specific type of a process and it works. This is exactly what I need to do with this problem.

Obviously, Auntie Grace had nothing to do with Mabel's death. But the ghost did appear to us, so it is our responsibility to see this through. The whole if-a-ghost-tasks-you-with-a-job-and-if-you-don't-do-it-then-everyone-suffers? Not a fan. It's basically the only thing I remember about my ghost lessons. See, magic is nothing but trouble.

Penny comes back just then, so I lean over, lowering my voice.

"What can you tell me about this Mabel?"

Penny pulls back, giving me a long thoughtful look before leaning back in.

"Are you making your lists again? Are you scheming?"

"I am in a position where I have to." I raise my eyebrows a little, to emphasize a point. It's takes her a split second to realize exactly what I mean.

Out of all the people in this world, Penelope Sharks is the only one who knows my magical secret.

When we were eleven years old, I wanted to add a special type of art to my room. So, I made the crayons draw on the wall without touching them. The mural was beautiful, but Penny caught me right in the middle of my masterpiece. At that point, I wanted and needed someone to talk to, and I knew she would keep my secret.

Which she has, all these years.

"You can't be serious, Cassie."

"I'm dead serious."

Okay, no pun intended. But Penny makes sure to give me a look before giving in.

"Mabel was... a special kind of a woman. I don't think I need to explain in detail what that means. She was in everyone's business, and she didn't care about her reputation."

"Does she have family here?"

"A nephew comes and goes, but other than that, she lived in that big house all by her lonesome, and that's how she liked it."

I shift my focus back to the outside, wondering if there's a way I can get into the house and have a look around.

"Don't you dare, Cassandra Duke." Penny's words pull me back toward her.

"What?"

"Don't *what* me!" She lowers her voice and leans in closer, "We've been friends long enough that I can practically see the gears turning in your head. You can't go to that house. Your aunt is already in trouble with the law, no need to add yourself to that list."

"Come on, Pen. I have to do something. For some reason that sheriff is determined to keep my aunt behind bars. Whatever is driving that, I need to put a stop to it."

"Well, can you at least wait until I close up so I can go with you?" A note of pleading enters her voice, and I can't say no now. She's worried. I could see that the moment I saw her, and now I'm adding to it.

"Okay, we'll go right after closing."

"Ah! Perfect! Now go do what you need to do and come meet me here at six."

"Yes ma'am." I chuckle as I slide off the stool and reach for my wallet.

"Don't you dare," Penny threatens.

"Oh, I dare," I reply as I drop a ten-dollar bill on the counter and book it out of the bakery. My lifted spirit carries me down the street, toward my car, but that's where it ends.

Glancing across the street, I watch the sun glimmer off the glass doors in front of the sheriff's office. My aunt is in there.

Being interviewed about a crime she clearly didn't commit. This is definitely not the homecoming I pictured, but there's no use crying over spilled milk. There's something amiss in this town, and it all started with Mabel.

"Ma'am, I will ask you to move along now. No loitering allowed." A voice comes from behind me. I'm ready to give the guy a piece of my mind when I turn, but then his voice registers in my mind at the same time his face does.

"Finn!" Without hesitation I launch myself at the man in front of me. He catches me easily. Just like he's always done. I'm lifted off the ground and given the best kind of a hug before he gently places me back on my feet.

"Look at you, officer!" I exclaim, getting a good look at his uniform. "You look good, my friend."

"So do you. I see you still prefer the dark skirts and tall boots." I glance down at my black mini and gray boots with a smile.

"A girl knows what she likes."

And this girl has always liked Finn Harvey. We used to say he was a gift to me from my fairy godmother because I met him on my twelfth birthday. We've been incredibly close since then. Of course, he doesn't know fairy godmothers actually exist, and I never had the courage to tell him. Outside of family, Penny is the only one who knows. It's better that way.

"Finn, you did it. You really did it."

My friend grins, nearly blinding me with his polished good looks. The uniform seems to have been made for his six-foot frame and not just because it was tailored. He looks right in it somehow. His blonde hair and light blue eyes add to the whole package. I bet he makes all the ladies swoon around here.

"Didn't think that was going to happen, what with all the shenanigans we used to get into."

"My thoughts exactly." But I'm grinning, because if anyone was ever going to make anything of themselves, it would be Finn. We may have been a headache for our guardians, but this man has always had the most determination of anyone I know.

Just then, his radio cues up with a disturbance at one of the booths down main street.

"Ah, Cassie—"

"Go do your thing. We'll catch up later."

He gives me a long look before backing away. "It's really good to see you."

"You too!"

He clearly wanted to talk about Auntie Grace, but I'm a little glad we got interrupted. I need to think this through on my own. Now that he's an officer, I don't think he'll be as keen about getting in trouble with me.

I watch him retreat with a smile. I also don't miss how a couple of the ladies follow him with their eyes. He's a charmer, that one. If Penny is my best girl friend, Finn has always been my best guy friend. He's like a brother I never had. He, however, has a brother. My very own thorn at the side. Even at the thought of Mean Dean, my blood boils.

Yanking my car door open, I get into it with a little more heat than I intend to.

"Focus, Cassie," I say out loud once the door is shut. "You have a job to do."

There's no use thinking about Mean Dean. I'd probably see him soon enough as it is. He seems to be planted at the inn. But I've worked through other distractions, and this is no different. I'm an adult for goodness sake. I can handle my childhood nemesis.

Driving through Main Street, I give myself a moment to appreciate this town. My friends have obviously done well for themselves. I probably would've too if I stayed. But I needed to get out, and I needed to get away. The magic was too much and too close. A therapist would probably tell me to deal with my emotional trauma. But I'm just going to push it down and deal with the problem at hand.

Like how in the world I'm supposed to find Mabel's killer before her ghost becomes my personal poltergeist.

6
—————

Six o'clock comes around slowly, and Auntie Grace never returns to the inn. Lucy got tired of me asking a bunch of questions, so I retreated to make some sketches. I pick Penny up, ready to finally do something about the current situation.

"So, what exactly are we looking for?" Penny asks as we pull up to the old Victorian house. It's a lot smaller than I expected, only two stories high, even though Penny called it a mansion. It looks like it could be on the cover of those old children's books about hauntings. The windows are long, the wood is dark, and the whole thing gives off scary movie vibes.

"I have no idea," I reply honestly, but I still don't get out of the car.

"What is it, Cassie?" Penny asks when I continue staring at the house without moving.

"I'm not sure," I say, fighting the goosebumps that are breaking out across my flesh. "I'm getting a bad feeling about it, that's all."

"Well, maybe we shouldn't be going in there then," Penny

says, glancing at the house and then back at me. "Your family isn't exactly wrong when they get one of those feelings."

"I'm not my aunt, Pen," I roll my eyes. "You know I don't have the same sensitivity."

"Just because you've never had it before, doesn't mean you won't develop it now."

I turn my head sharply, but Penny isn't looking at me. I don't have to have witchy powers to know she's acting suspicious.

"Pen, don't tell me you've been talking to Auntie Grace." I groan, and because I'm watching her closely, I know I hit the nail on the head. "Penelope!"

"Don't be getting mad at me!" She turns to face me, her eyes big, "You know I never want to get between you and your magic, but your aunt is not wrong. Maybe all the weird stuff you've been experiencing is because your magic is growing."

"Great, I never would've told you about this if I knew you were going to take my aunt's side!"

"I'm not taking sides! I'm just saying."

"And I'm saying a seed won't grow if you don't water it, and I haven't done anything with my magic for years."

"Except that's not true, and we both know it."

I grunt, swinging the door open and getting out of the car. Penny doesn't hesitate to follow. I might slam the door a little harder as well.

"This is what I get for telling you anything," I mumble, marching up to the house.

"You have to tell me. One, because you need someone to talk to. And two, because you know I'll always be honest with you. Right now, that means telling you there might be something to this idea Auntie Grace has mentioned."

"Pen, you don't have magic. I don't think you can speak on how it works."

"I may not, but an outside opinion is sometimes exactly what one needs."

"Okay, Dr. Phil. I'm not here for a therapy session."

"Can I help you?" The voice makes us jump. We turn in unison as a middle-aged man steps out of the front door of the house. He's dressed in a dark suit, his hair stained with grey at the temples.

"Oh, Penelope, I didn't recognize you."

"Hello, Carl. We're so sorry to hear about your aunt."

So, this is the nephew? He seems...so opposite of what I pictured. Maybe because Mabel carried with her a sort of chaotic energy, this man seems the exact opposite. He's polished and put together and definitely doesn't seem like he fits into this small town.

He gives me a confused look, and that's when I realize I'm staring.

"I'm sorry, this is Cassandra Duke." Penny hurries to introduce me. "She's Miss Mary Grace's niece."

"Ah the prodigal. I've heard about you."

The way he says that doesn't comfort me. I give him a small smile anyway before replying,

"I'm sorry we've met under these circumstances." He sobers up right away, hanging his head for a moment, like he needs an extra breath.

"Yes, I knew Aunt Mabel was having health issues, but I didn't expect this," he finally says, looking up. Clearly, the sheriff hasn't said anything about it being foul play to him, and I'm not about to break the news. His eyes glisten. My heart goes out to him. I can't imagine what I would do if something happened to Auntie Grace.

"Is there anything we can do?" Penny asks, her face full of compassion.

"No, but I appreciate you asking. I just... I have to head to the sheriff's office to see..."

"We understand." Penny reaches over and gives Carl a pat on the upper arm. "Let us know if you do."

"Of course." He moves past us but then stops. "Was there something I could do for you?"

That's when I realize how this looks. Two random women show up at the deceased house. Not exactly a great look.

"We were in the neighborhood and wanted to check on you," I hurry to say, trying on one of my customer service smiles. It seems to work. The confusion leaves as he gives me a firm nod. Without another word, he's down the stairs and to the car parked on the driveway. It's new and shiny, an SUV of some sort, and he looks like he belongs inside of it.

"Now what?"

"Now, nothing. If we don't leave while he's still here, it'll be suspicious."

There goes that idea.

~

WE FEEL STRANGE WAITING AROUND, so Penny and I head back to her bakery and the apartment she lives in upstairs.

"You didn't tell me you own the whole building," I say when she opens the door to her beautiful living room. The top floor has been converted to one big living space and it's amazing.

"It's pretty recent. I was going to tell you when I saw you and then—"

"And then all this happened."

Penny grabs some iced tea from the fridge while I grab glasses, and we head for the couch. Just like old times.

"It's so crazy, Cassie. You're here. Mabel is dead. Your aunt is in jail! I can't even imagine what you're going through."

"You and me both, Pen. I feel like I've stepped into a Twilight Zone episode, and I can't get out." Penny hands me a glass, and I take a long sip before I continue. "I know I have to figure this out, but I'm not a detective. I don't know how these things work."

"Well, figure it out!"

I scream, jumping in my seat and spilling the tea all down my shirt.

"Cassie, what?" Pen hurries to her feet, racing to grab a towel. I glare at Mabel, standing in the middle of the coffee table as my head begins to pound.

"Could you at least stand somewhere else so your legs aren't cut off below the knees?" I wave one hand in her direction as I take the towel from a very confused Penny.

"Cassie, are you okay?"

"Yes, sorry about the couch. Mabel here decided to drop in for a visit."

Penny stands up straight, giving a room a three sixty, but of course she can't see the woman who still hasn't moved. It's very unnerving. I blot the spilled tea off the couch and then my shirt.

"Let me get you another one," Penny says, slowly backing out of the room. Even though she can't see Mabel, the fact that she's here is probably freaky. I mean, it creeps me out, and I'm used to magic. Somewhat.

"You're sitting there, drinking iced tea, while I am dead. Shouldn't you be out looking for my killer?"

This woman is truly getting on my nerves now.

"Don't they say death is quiet?" I mumble, but there's nothing wrong with Mabel's hearing.

"You are just like your aunt. No good Duke women, just in everyone's business. Meddling, meddling—"

"Okay!" I get to my feet, waving my hands, my head ready to explode. "If you don't have anything nice to say, don't say it at all. I can't believe I am arguing with a ghost!"

I throw my hands up in the air, as Penny walks back into the room. Taking the shirt from her hands, I head to the bathroom, needing a moment. My headache is the worst, and my emotions are ridiculously heightened. The moment I reach for the faucet, the water turns on, even before I touch it.

"Stop it, stop it, stop it," I tell myself, taking big breaths. I have to calm myself down. Magic is fueled by emotions and mine are all over the place. I count down from ten, then from twenty, then from thirty, before I finally feel better. Quickly pulling the shirt over my head, I exchange it for Penny's t-shirt and then step back out into the living room. Penny is right where I left her.

"What are you doing?"

"I don't know where to go!" she replies. "What if I walk into her?"

I give the room a once over, but I already know it by my lack of head pounding.

"She's gone."

Thankfully. I'm not sure how much more of this I can take. It's not like her visits are helpful either. They just ruin my mood and then she disappears. But from what I'm learning, that's how she was in life too. Lucky me.

"Wow, Cassie, that's intense." Penny plops back down on the couch, and I follow her.

"You have no idea."

7

After Penny and I drank our fill of iced tea and caught up on most of the gossip, particularly things that don't include the murder, ghosts, or Mean Dean, I head home. The moon is out and it's full. I've always thought it looked closer to earth here somehow. It has always taken up more of the sky.

Tonight, I don't find comfort in that. Or in the small town that has always felt a little too safe. There goes that thought, right? Nothing is what I thought it was anymore. Not my life, not this place. All I can do is keep moving forward.

When I finally pull into my spot at the inn, the place is quiet. Glancing at the clock, I see it blinking nine thirty at me. I guess everyone has turned in for the night. Not that I blame them. The guests have to sleep at a crime scene. I'm sure their rooms are looking mighty fine to them right now.

The inn does seem a bit menacing as I step inside into the silence. Birdie is the only one there to greet me, her violet eyes staring at me as I shut the door behind me.

"What? Is it past my curfew?" I mumble as I hurry to our

wing of the house. The cat makes almost no noise at all as she jumps off the counter and follows close behind me.

"You know, I really don't like cats," I say as I step into the library.

"She's determined to make you like her," Auntie Grace says from her spot on the love seat. I hurry over immediately, reaching down to give her a long hug.

"When did you get back? I was afraid they'd keep you overnight. Are you actually a suspect? Do they know what happened?"

"Slow down, sugar bun, and take a sit." She pats the space beside her. I drop down right away, happy to just have her here. "They couldn't hold me overnight because they are just interviewing all the people who may have been involved."

"They can't honestly think you had anything to do with this, can they?"

"It is my inn, and Mabel did drink my tea."

"You didn't put the poison in there!"

"But someone did, and I had the best opportunity." She pats my knee, her face a picture of serenity, as if we're discussing the weather and not a murder investigation.

"How can you be so calm about this?"

"There's no use making a fuss about this one way or the other, honeybee. Sometimes these things happen."

"Sometimes these things happen?" I jump up to my feet, the nervous energy inside of me too restless to sit still. "I don't think murder just happens, Auntie Grace. Or people being haunted by the victims. Or—" Before I can finish the sentence, all the books on the coffee table in front of me lift right up and drop back down. I yelp, jumping back, one hand on my heart and the other on my forehead.

"That, my darling Cassie, is exactly why keeping your cool is important." Auntie Grace smiles at me as Birdie jumps up and takes up the seat I vacated. I take a few deep breaths before my heart rate slows down enough that I won't cause more damage.

"Would you like to talk about it?" She's still watching me, and I can't hide from it any longer. I have to tell her the truth.

"This has been happening a lot lately. My magic is completely out of control, Auntie." The words tumble out of me as I sit down on the edge of the coffee table, facing her. "I didn't even know it caused any problems at my last job until after it was all said and done. It's like it has a mind of its own, and it wants to ruin everything for me!"

"Oh, my darling girl," Auntie Grace reaches over, taking one of my hands in both of hers. "Magic is a part of you, just like this skin of yours. You cannot separate from it. I don't think it's trying to ruin anything. I think it's trying to steer you in the right direction. There's no shame in not having control. Sometimes it's exactly what needs to happen to open yourself up to more possibilities."

"I'm not sure I'm ready to deal with my magic," I reply honestly, the memories still too fresh in my mind. Auntie Grace squeezes my hand. When I look at her, her eyes are full of compassion.

"You'll be ready when the time comes. But don't run from it. Don't try to push it away. It will guide you."

Birdie meows then, as if agreeing, and Auntie Grace chuckles.

"Now, I have a trip to take with the sheriff tomorrow," she announces, getting to her feet.

"What?"

"Don't you worry. Lucy will take care of the inn. You should spend the day with Dean in the upstairs rooms. The restoration is coming along nicely."

Just the mention of that menace has me grimacing.

"Oh, sugar plum, he's not so bad you know."

"Maybe not to you," I grumble, getting to my feet as well.

Even though he's not here, he's still making me feel like I'm thirteen years old again.

"All will be well," Auntie Grace says, giving my cheek a squeeze before heading to her room. "Tomorrow, be a dear and see to the remodeling upstairs. That project needs a woman's touch."

I watch her retreat, not sure what that was all about. She's calm, yes, but it's like there's something else under the surface. And then this mysterious trip with the sheriff? What is all that about? I realize I didn't even mention Mabel to her, but that's that. I'm not bothering her with this right now.

Once her bedroom door shuts, I head to mine. Birdie stays on the couch, thankfully. I don't think I can deal with her in the room with me. What a strange witch I am! Most witches I know love animals, especially cats. But I guess I've never been normal.

Plopping down on my bed, I lean back and stare at the ceiling. Tomorrow I need to get some answers. There is mischief underfoot, and I need to find out exactly what's going on. Before someone else ends up in trouble. Or, you know, dead.

Following my aunt's instructions—well more like demands—I make my way upstairs to the east wing. The house has undergone plenty of upkeep over the years. Some of it magical. But Auntie Grace wanted a bit of a different approach this time around. I think part of it is just her heart for the community. She would hire the local handyman, for example, instead of whipping up some spells and calling her family.

I pull back the tarp over the door and enter carefully. Immediately, I can see what the plan for the room is. It's a gift of sorts. I can picture the place vividly, the way it will look once it's all done.

The walls re-papered to look fresh but similar to the original. The large window, crooked in parts, covered by the light curtains.

What I would love is to visit some antique shops to find some knickknacks for this space. A vintage silver mirror would look amazing against the green of the wallpaper. Once the bed is put in place, I'd love a hexagon shaped, stained glass bedside lamp.

"Are you hiding?" the voice says from behind me. I glance over as Dean fills the doorway. He's always been a large guy, and now, he's become a large man.

"Just inspecting the handy work." I'm determined to be civil. Even if it kills me. Okay, maybe not the best choice of comparison. Either way, I school my features to appear pleasant when I turn to face Mean Dean.

The man looks like he just stepped off of one of those fundraiser calendars the fire house used to sell every year. Probably under the caption of Hot July and Holy Smokes.

Wow. Calm it down, Cassie. What is happening in my brain right now? We hate him, remember?

But when he gives me that half smile, casually leaning against the doorframe that appears smaller in size somehow, I can't help it. I blush.

Now I *am* reverting to my thirteen-year-old girl ways and that needs to stop. I am a professional. I can manage to keep my emotions reined in and get the job done. When the wooden boards on the other side of the room start to float, I almost scream. Clearly magic is out to get me.

"Is there a compliment in there somewhere?" Dean asks, still watching me with that half smile. I force my eyes to focus on him while mentally willing the boards to settle back down.

"I wouldn't go that far," I reply, keeping my tone even. "There is still plenty of work to be done, and therefore, plenty of work to mess up."

"Wow, a harsh critic. Why am I not surprised?"

"I'm not sure. It's not like you know me." That comes out a little sharper than I intended, and he narrows his eyes, not missing a beat.

"I probably know you better than you think." The deep voice sends goosebumps up my spine, so I square my shoulders in defense.

"You, Dean Harvey, are a lot of things, but not someone who is capable of figuring me out."

"You really don't like me, do you?"

"Oh, and here I was trying to be subtle about it." I give him a small pout and the laugh that rings out takes me by surprise. I've never intentionally made Dean laugh before, and there is something to be said about a man who laughs with his whole heart. The boards float a little higher, so I stomp my foot in frustration, forcing my magic into place. The boards drop, snapping Dean's attention to them.

"What was that?"

"I have no idea." I turn my back to him, getting back to business. "Are you planning on rebuilding this whole wall?" I point to the partially torn down wall to the right of the doorway.

Dean gives me a questioning look, as if he knows what I'm trying to do, but he answers anyway.

"The other room was too small for guests, mostly just a glorified closet. So, Miss Mary Grace asked if I could combine the two. This wall will have an opening, with an arch, and the smaller room will have a sitting area."

I can see it. A standing lamp should go in the sitting area, with a green velvet chair. The image of it forms perfectly in my mind. This is why I love interior design so much. It comes as naturally to me as magic does to Auntie. Glancing over my shoulder, I make sure the boards are still on the floor before I take a step toward the wall. A rug would look nice in there as well, once the wooden floors are in place.

"You're really good at this, aren't you?" Dean's soft question surprises me. I glance over at him and find him watching me.

"What do you mean?"

"It's just, I can see it. On your face. You're scheming with that small smile on your lips. You enjoy this."

I'm not sure how I feel about him noticing such a thing about me, but I manage a nonchalant shrug.

"You can't judge someone by their enjoyment of a thing. I could be terrible at it."

"But you're not." That quiet conviction does something to my insides. Before I can reply, there's a commotion downstairs. Dean and I exchange a look and then we're both racing for the stairs.

8

———

We barely reach the stairs when a couple beats us to it. They hurry down, carrying their suitcases in their hands. We're right on their heels. When we turn the corner and glance down into the lobby, we see what all the noise is about. There are couples and families filling the whole front desk area while Lucy and Auntie Grace try to keep some sort of order. Dean manages to push us through the crowd as the noise gets louder.

"What's happening?"

"Oh, good, you're here." Lucy is first to notice me. "Could you see if you can organize this mad house into some kind of order?"

"Everyone is trying to check out, my dear. Word has gotten out about the cause of Mabel's passing," Auntie Grace calls out, answering my question. "We need a bit of help with the madhouse."

"Weren't you supposed to be leaving?" I ask.

"That clearly is not the case now, sugar bun."

I glance over at the crowd, everyone bunched up together

and trying to talk over each other. Immediately, I get an idea. Turning to Dean, I study his tall frame and smile.

"Why do you look like you're planning something?"

"Only because I am," I announce before motioning him with me. "Stand here and get everyone's attention."

Dean doesn't even hesitate. He steps up the stairs, right where Birdie is perching, watching the madness. I stand a step below. One sharp whistle from Dean and the crowd gets quiet immediately. I grin up at him before turning to the crowd.

"Everyone, listen up. If your last name starts with A through M, please stay where you are. If your last name is N though Z, I need you to move into the sitting room." Everyone exchanges a glance, as if I'm speaking a different language. "In order for everyone to be checked out in a timely manner, we need order. If you don't follow these instructions, you will be moved to the back of the line."

That does it. People start moving immediately, even if they grumble while doing it. Satisfied, I bounce down the stairs. Auntie Grace and Lucy both look at me like they've never seen me.

"What?" I glance between the two of them. "Please stop staring at me like that. If you have a clipboard, I can go around the room and write down the names of the families in there. You can deal with those in here. Divide and conquer?"

Lucy hands me a clipboard, and I don't wait for a response before I head to the sitting room. The moment I step inside, I can feel it. The nervous energy in the room could be cut with a knife. Not that I blame anyone. It's not every day a person drops dead in the dining room of your bed and breakfast.

I start on one side of the room, asking for the name and any other information that's needed for check out. It takes a little longer than usual because I have to stop to reassure each individual as I go along. A few minutes later, I notice Dean coming in and out of the room. When he returns the next time, he's carrying a pitcher of lemonade. Catching my eye, he gives me a quick grin, and I have no strength in me to resist it. I return it. He stares at me, as if surprised by my response before the little girl beside him catches his attention. I watch him smile down at her, mesmerized by the ease with which he does...well, anything. Shaking myself mentally, I turn to the couple beside me and continue taking down names.

It's about forty minutes later that the last guest finally leaves. Birdie has moved to sit on the counter, observing the happenings around her. I make sure to keep my distance.

"I can't believe they all just left," Lucy says when the door shuts behind the last family. There are only about four guests left in the whole of the inn, and I'm not sure how long they're going to stick around. The atmosphere has definitely changed from cozy to crazy and no-one wants that on vacation.

"It is what it is, my dear." Auntie Grace sighs. I know it hurts her that so many people left. "People are scared. Now that word has gotten out about Mabel being murdered, it is perfectly reasonable for people to want to put distance between them-selves and a bad situation."

"Auntie—" I begin, but she waves me away.

"Don't you fret, my sweet Cassie. This is nothing but a small setback. We, Dukes, don't take these things laying down, and I'm not about to start now."

Even though she sounds determined, I can see the sadness in her eyes. Taking care of people is what she's all about. It's why this place is so popular. There is genuine care in the way Auntie Grace runs it.

"Oh, sweetie pie, how about you take that friend of yours and see if you can run down to the antique shop for some new-to-us gems?" Even though it sounds like a suggestion, I can tell Auntie Grace needs me to do this. Maybe if only just to keep me busy. I glance at Dean, who's near the stairs, and I almost have the urge to thank him for helping out. But I don't. Instead, I pull out my phone.

"Are you sure you don't need me here?" I ask as Auntie Grace shakes her head.

"Oh pash, Lucy and I are mighty fine here. You go work your antique shopping magic. I know how much you enjoy it. We'll be just fine. Right as rain, sugar plum." She sounds cheery, but she's not all that convincing. Still, I don't see another choice.

"I'll call Penny," I say, dialing the number.

TRINKETS AND THINGS is on the other side of Main Street, and thankfully, there is a parking spot right in front. Penny and I get out of the car as I continue my little tirade.

"I don't understand why she won't just talk to me. Not about Mabel, not about—other things." I lower my voice as we head for the front door. "She says she wants me to learn, but then she's constantly so secretive. She basically nudged me out of the inn, like me being there is the last thing she wanted."

"You know I can't speak on these... other things," Penny whispers, stepping inside the store after me, "but I know your aunt has never done anything in her life without a reason."

"Ain't that the truth?" I mumble, getting my first good look at the shop in front of me. Or shall I call it antique enthusiast's heaven? Holy moly, this place is filled to the brim.

"Is that Penelope Sharks I see?" A short, stout woman appears between the stacks, heading in our direction. Her silver hair is arranged in tiny curls around her head, and she's got a gold chain with her glasses dangling around her neck. She looks like she belongs in this place.

"Hello Mrs. Tootsie, how are you?"

"Tootsie?" I mouth at Penny. My friend tries to suppress a smile.

"You are looking mighty fine, Penelope. And who is this? Is this Mary Grace's girl?"

"Hello, Mrs. Tootsie," I say with my customer service smile as the older woman gives me a once over. Even though I lived here until I graduated high school, I'm still a stranger to many of these people. I had a specific policy when I was younger. Stay away from strangers so they don't discover your wayward magic. I still stand by that exercise. But this means I'm only familiar with places and not many of the people.

"You don't remember me, do you dear?"

"I'm sorry," I shake my head, deciding to be honest.

"That's probably because your aunt and I haven't spoken in twenty years. That woman sure knows how to get under someone's skin."

Her words take me back a little because most people seem to sing Auntie Grace's praises around here. Well, I guess besides Mabel. And now Tootsie. I glance at Penny, but she seems as confused as I am.

"You two don't get along?"

"Of course not." Mrs. Tootsie spins on her heels, motioning for us to follow. "Your aunt can't tell one chandelier from another. She told me once that I had fake tiles for sale. Fake! Pfft! As if! I do the inventory myself. Nothing sneaks past me."

I open my mouth to reply but stop myself. It's true, with Auntie's magic, she probably could find fakes if she tried to. But I don't think I'm supposed to tell Mrs. Tootsie that. Doesn't matter anyway because she's already switching subjects.

"I have a lovely painting for you, dear. It would look magnificent in that inn of yours, not that many will be staying there. I heard what happened this morning. All those people running away? That would've been a sight to see. A mass exodus."

Narrowing my eyes, I follow the talkative woman farther into the shop.

"And here we have a crystal with brass accents sconce. They come in pairs. I think they would look grand in the first sitting room, by the front doors. It's a tragedy what happened to Mabel. We were friends, you know?"

"Friends?" I dare to ask because I didn't think that woman had any friends.

"Of course. We go way back. Back when her family still lived in these parts. Now there's just her poor nephew, Carl. Such a darling boy. Always tried to take care of his aunt. But Mabel and I, we were two peas in a pod. Always talking antique mirrors. She loved them, you know."

This woman is giving me whiplash, but in a good way. I have finally stumbled upon someone who is willing to talk about her. Although, I can see that I have to tread carefully. Talkers can clam up real fast if the wrong thing is said. I know that from working with some of the gossipy clients back in Chicago. They liked the sound of their own voice and having information to share, but they did not like to be interrogated.

"It was such a shame," I say, keeping my tone sympathetic. "I didn't even get to meet her. I would've loved to get to know her."

"As you should. So many people in these parts were afraid of her, but that's only because she had a strong personality. We were alike, me and her. Always talking about paintings I found at estate sales. She loved them too, you know."

Mrs. Tootsie thrusts a serving tray at me, and I grab it before it falls.

"This would fit so well in the dining room. It would be like olden times, when serving trays were a thing. Mabel loved taking tea in that Crooked Windows Inn of yours, not that she would admit it. She loved to people watch, knowing who came in and who was leaving. We always talked about traveling one day, like one of them businessmen who were always coming to the inn."

"Businessmen?" Penny asks, keeping her tone inquisitive as well. I see why it's an odd clientele for the inn. Mostly, it's families and couples on their honeymoon or second honeymoon. Businessmen rarely come through these parts. And if they do, they usually stay in the Holiday Inn off the highway.

"Oh yes, there were some coming in and out in the last few months. I can't tell you how many conversations Mabel overheard. They were looking to build some sort of business venture in these parts. Even approached me once."

"You?"

"Oh yes. This shop is prime property. I wouldn't sell for anything and neither would Mabel. She owned the land beside me, as you know. She never wanted to do anything with it, just preserve it for future generations, and here we are. She won't even see it come to pass."

Penny and I look at each other, and I notice she's just as surprised as I am. Just then, the door dings. Mrs. Tootsie hurries to help her next customer.

"I will be right back, girls. Peruse, peruse!" And then she's gone.

"Did you know about the land?" I ask as soon as Mrs. Tootsie is out of earshot.

"Not at all and I've lived here my whole life. I wonder why it was kept secret."

"Well, from what I heard, Mabel liked to share other people's secrets but not her own. You know what this means, don't you?" I ask, looking intently at my friend as she shakes her head.

"It means, we found a very good motive for her murder."

9

______

We leave Trinkets and Things with only one purchase, despite Mrs. Tootsie's sales pitches. But I did promise to come back, and that seemed to pacify her for the moment.

"Cassie, are you sure about this?" Penny asks as we deposit the mirror I bought in the back of my car before heading down Main Street.

"Finn will talk to me. You know he will. And I need more information. Not only is my aunt still a suspect, but this investigation is affecting everything, including my—you know what," I finish, as a family of tourist walks past us. I've told her about my recent magic flairs, and of course she knows about Mabel's ghost. "I can't live like this, Pen."

"Okay, but what exactly is Finn going to do?"

"He's going to tell me if there were some shenanigans happening around the land Mabel owned."

At least, I hope he will. I'm not sure how willing he will be now. I pull out my phone as we reach Penny's bakery. She has someone covering for her today, but she steps inside to get us coffee as I dial Finn's number. He answers on the first ring.

"Cassandra Duke, to what do I owe the pleasure?" I can hear the grin in his voice.

"Get your butt outside and have a face-to-face conversation with me, Officer Harvey."

"Wow, demanding. Where are you?"

This time, I smile. "Across the street by Penny's."

"I'll be right out."

I hang up just as Penny comes up carrying two cups of coffee. I reach for the cup eagerly, realizing with all the craziness of today, I didn't have my morning dosage.

"What? I don't get one?" Finn calls, coming up to us in the next minute.

"You have to pay for one," Penny replies, grinning before she takes a sip. He goes to grab her cup, but she dodges him like a pro. I watch, narrowing my eyes a little, because there's definitely something going on here. Penny and I will have a talk. She catches my look and sobers up immediately. Oh yes, we are definitely talking.

"If I give up my coffee, will you answer my questions?" I ask when Finn finally turns to me.

"Depends on the questions," he replies, cautiously. Because of course he does. Finn maybe my best guy friend, but he's now an officer of the law. He's not just going to provide information. But maybe, he can let some things spill. Mostly, I'm curious about Mabel and the fact that no one wants to talk about her.

"Well, I've been gone a long time, and I didn't exactly come back to a warm welcome. And no one tells me anything." I give him a little pout. "Do you know how frustrating that is?"

"Put that pout away, Cassandra." Finn rolls his eyes, suppressing a smile. "I know what you're doing, and it won't work."

"What do you mean?"

"Don't try the voice either," he says, but I can tell he's softening up. He could never resist my puppy eyes. Which is exactly what I'm giving him now. "You play dirty."

"I play to win. Tell me about Mabel."

"Cassie—"

"Come on, Finn. Everyone is being so secretive. It's like she was in the midst of some royal scandal or something. Give me something."

"You know better than to ask me to break the rules."

"You used to break rules all the time."

"And then I got a badge."

I try the pout again, but I can tell he won't budge. I almost ask Penny to try, but she's standing to the side, enjoying this as if it's her own personal theater show. I have to try another tactic.

"Okay, then don't tell me about Mabel. Tell me about the town. Any new developments coming through?"

"Where did you—" He stops himself, but it's already too late. "Cassie—"

"I've heard there have been businessmen at the inn."

He sighs, and I can tell he's giving in but only a little.

"Yes, there has been a lot of activity around these parts." He glances around, as if making sure no one is close enough to overhear. "The lot of them have really enjoyed Dan's Diner, I hear. And Sue Lynn is a waitress there."

My eyes grow big at the realization, and I launch myself at Finn. He returns my hug, right before I thrust the coffee cup at him.

"Here, you've earned it," I say before grabbing Penny and dragging her behind me. Even though I've been gone for a while, I know all about Sue Lynn Alcott and what I know is that woman loves to talk.

∽

MY PHONE PINGS with a text just as we step inside Dan's Diner.

You owe me.

From Finn. I text him back.

I gave up my coffee. We're even.

I put the phone away as Penny leads me to a booth away from the front entrance.

"I can't believe I didn't think of Sue Lynn before. That woman knows everything," Penny comments as we slide into the booth.

"I know, I haven't thought of her either, and my aunt even mentioned her. This should've been our first stop."

"Cassandra Duke!" The woman in question half squeals as she rushes over to our booth. Reaching down, she gives me half a hug, grinning. She looks just like I remember her. I think she's been fifty for thirty years or so. For as long as I've known her, she's been serving tables at Dan's Diner and talking up a storm.

"It's about time you came by to see me!"

"I'm so sorry, Sue Lynn. It's been a crazy couple of days." That's all the opening she needs. Her voice gets a little quieter as she leans down.

"Ah, yes, of course. How are you holding up, honey? It must've been such a shock!"

"It really was. I didn't even know the poor woman, which is such a shame."

"Well, that depends on who you ask." Sue Lynn winks before she glances over her shoulder and leans down farther. "That woman could and would steer up trouble anywhere she went. Never met anyone who enjoy chaos as much as she did."

Someone calls Sue Lynn's name right then, and she straightens immediately.

"I'll be back with some of Dan's special for you in a jiffy." And then she's gone.

"Okay, so this may have been a good idea," Penny comments as we watch the woman hurry off.

"Maybe. As long as she gives me something useful to go off of. At this rate, I feel like everyone is just sharing three pieces of information with me, and the rumors are filling in all the interesting bits."

"That is how Monroe Cove operates." Penny shrugs. She's right of course. It's that small town, everyone in everyone's business, deal. It's something I did not miss in Chicago.

"Here you are, honey." Sue Lynn comes up, depositing two steaming bowls of stew in front of us and a plate with bread piled on high. "I'll grab some drinks as well."

"If you have a moment to sit, I'd love to catch up." I smile up at her, and she beams back.

"Smooth." Penny chuckles as I shrug. Taking a small sip of the stew, I realize one thing I did miss about Monroe Cove is Dan's Diner. The man can cook, that's for sure.

"Now tell me all about you," Sue Lynn calls out, placing two cups of water in front of us and taking the seat next to Penny. "I have a few minutes."

"You haven't aged a bit, Sue Lynn," I comment honestly, because it is truth.

"Oh, honey!" She gushes, her cheeks getting that rosy color at the compliment. "Thank you. Makes an old woman happy. You grew up pretty. Your hair is so red and long!"

It really is getting a bit out of control as I push over my shoulder. I smile in response. Just like with Mrs. Tootsie, I don't really have to nudge Sue Lynn into talking. She continues on her own.

"It is such a tragic thing for you to come home to a murder." She whispers the last word, quickly looking around as if the murderer will jump out at her right here and now.

"Do you have any idea who could've done it?" I also lower my voice.

"Well, it wasn't your aunt, that's for sure. Mabel has been a bit under weather lately, but she was just as fierce as ever. Even with all the new faces coming through here, she never budged in her stance. A fiery woman, that one."

"What do you mean?"

"Oh, haven't you heard? Some big corporation arrived just last week, looking to buy up some property. They came incognito, but of course, I know my own neighbors. I could tell." She looks very proud of the fact, so I make sure to compliment her on it. "That's just how we are around these parts. We take care of each other. Mabel had started to feel sick, so she couldn't come to the town meetings like she used to. Such a shame. She may have been a tough woman to be around, but she got stuff done. I'm curious how many people will show up to the memorial."

"A memorial?"

"Oh yes, honey. The memorial is tomorrow at the big church on Fourth. It will be very interesting to see exactly who darkens the church's doors. Maybe the shady businessmen who have been hanging around." She winks.

A male voice calls out to Sue Lynn, and she hurries to her feet.

"It was lovely seeing you, Sue Lynn," I say as the woman goes back to work.

"Did we learn anything?" Penny asks once she's out of hearing range.

"I learned that I have a memorial service to go to tomorrow."

10

Auntie Grace is out when I finally return to the inn. I haven't seen Mabel yet today, but I'm thinking she could appear at any moment. I need more information, Since it seems my aunt is avoiding me at the moment, I'll have to get that information myself.

First stop, the small library between my room and hers.

Standing in the midst of Auntie Grace's library, I try to figure out where to start. She has papers on every surface. And books. There are books everywhere. For someone who is beyond organized in the kitchen, it looks like a hurricane came through here.

"I don't suppose you have any idea?" I glance down at my new shadow. Birdie has been sticking close by, always watching, always following. Since my experiences with animals have always ended badly, I'm really hoping this one is better.

As if she understands me, she walks over to the love seat on the opposite end of the room, jumping up on the table beside it. She turns and stares at me, as if daring me to call her out on it.

Seeing no other choice, I make my way to the table. There

are a few stacks of papers, a journal, and three books. I leaf through all of it and it's the last one that finally yields some results.

"The Ghost and You." I read the title out loud, chuckling to myself. I remember witch books always had the strangest and the most straightforward titles. I'm not sure if it was to hide the truth behind it, or if it's just that witches enjoy playing around with hiding things in plain sight. Either way, right now, I'm thankful. Heading for my bedroom, I don't bother to shut the door as Birdie follows me in.

Settling on my bed, the cat doesn't hesitate to make herself a spot in the corner, laying so she can watch me. It's still unnerving, but I'm trying to deal with it.

Opening the book, I begin to speed read the pages. I look for anything that deals with the little information I remember and that Auntie Grace has given me. When I come across a passage about hauntings, I slow down and read over it again.

"It is said that when a witch is tasked with a job from a ghost, they are bound by laws of magic." I read out loud because it helps me remember it down the line. "They have a connection that can amplify or diminish the witch's magic, depending on the circumstance. Once the witch has performed the task, the spirit is released to cross over and the bond between them is separated. For witches who are unable to perform the task, the binding becomes stronger. While the ghost will fade with time, the presence will turn unkind and follow the witch for all of her days, or until the task can be completed. This is the standard curse."

I stop reading, taking a deep breath. So, I remembered correctly, I really don't have a choice. I'm not sure why Auntie Grace isn't the one who's bound to Mabel, but then I remember that the ghost made eye contact with me when she told the room to find her killer. That's got to be it.

"I was basically at the wrong place at the wrong time," I say, glancing over at Birdie. She raises her head a little, holding my gaze steadily. "Okay, can you blink or something? You're creeping me out."

The cat puts her head down, but she doesn't move her eyes away or close them.

"Fine." I shake my head before looking at the pages again. It doesn't say anything about another way of breaking the bond. I have to figure out who killed Mabel, or I'll be stuck with her forever.

There is still her house I haven't been inside of, which might give me some clues. Although, I'm not sure how. This whole investigating thing is very new to me, no matter how many shows or movies I've seen. And I've seen plenty. But it's worth a try, I suppose. It's better than sitting around here.

"Are you staying?" I ask Birdie as I head for the door. This time, the cat doesn't even bother raising her head. That's my answer, I suppose. Grabbing my keys, I head back out to my car.

I DRIVE over to Mabel's house, parking far enough down the street that I won't be instantly recognized if someone sees the car. The moon is out, and the trees cast shadows on the sidewalk as I walk. I'm not exactly sure what I'm doing here, only that I need to do something. The book's information sits heavily on my shoulders. I'm afraid that I'll fail, dooming myself and Mabel to a very unpleasant life. Auntie Grace was once again gone when I was leaving the inn, so I have to figure this out on my own.

When I stop at the side of the house, the place is completely dark. I have no idea if Carl is staying at the house or not. A part of me wants to get inside and look around, but I can't come up with a scenario where I'd get out of it if I'm caught. I can't exactly tell the police, or Carl, that I'm here on Mabel's behalf.

The memorial service for her is tomorrow, so there is a possibility I'll meet someone who will have more information on her. For a woman who was in everyone's business, she sure kept hers to herself.

A light flickers on across the street, and I retreat immediately. I don't need anyone calling in a prowler. One Duke in trouble with the law is plenty enough.

So, I pivot, heading toward the Trinkets and Things store. It's only about a block down from the house. I wonder how much of the land I'm walking on belonged to Mabel. There has to be some type of a record of it, even if it was a guarded secret.

When I come to the place near the store, I realize that the space is a park, or a sitting area with some trees and flower beds. It's not big. It's about the size of two buildings off Main Street. But if a developer was looking to build, I can see how this would be prime real estate, especially since they asked Mrs. Tootsie to sell her place as well.

It's darker here. The town clearly decided against spending money on some street lamps, or maybe it was Mabel who wanted to keep it dark. Either way, as I make my way into the park, I realize how quiet the night has become. The trees are large, blocking off most of the view from the street. Here's where having my magic not be on the fritz would be helpful, because I could whip up a protection spell to carry with me. But since magic and I are not friends right now, I can only wish for it.

There's so much I don't understand about the whole Mabel thing. For one, it's been a full day without a sighting of her and that's strange all on its own. Now that I know how the whole ghost thing works, it's making me even more nervous. I have a lot of questions as well, but it's not like I've had the time to sit down and have a conversation about it with Auntie Grace.

That's another thing. Killing Mabel at the inn may have been a way to make it look like an accident, but just because it looks like one, doesn't mean the toxicology report wasn't going to provide information about the murder. So why wait until she was at the inn? Only to make Auntie Grace the main suspect? But then, who's going around holding a grudge against my aunt?

So many questions and absolutely no answers in sight.

When a noise comes from behind me, I freeze.

Fight or flight. Pick one, Cassie.

But I can't seem to make a decision fast enough before the noise approaches closer. I realize it's footsteps. *Fight it is*, I think as I twist around to face my attacker, fists raised.

"Okay, Rocky." Dean's voice reaches me right before his face comes into view.

"Seriously, Harvey? Are you trying to give me a heart attack." I drop my arms to my hips, staring the man down. It's difficult, considering how much taller than me he is.

"I called your name. You didn't hear me?" I narrow my eyes because, no, I absolutely did not hear him.

"What are you doing here?"

"I was across the street at the hardware store when I saw you creep in here. No one really hangs out here at night, considering there are no lights." He waves his hand around, as if I can't see that.

"No kidding. The town decided to be stingy or...?"

"I'm not sure, actually." Dean looks around, a line forming on his forehead. "The main park is across the street from the police station, as you know. It has everything a park needs, a carousel, park benches and tables, even some barbecue pits. No one comes out this way. Most people just cut through to get to the other side." He points into the darkness, and I notice a few lights coming through the trees.

"It comes out on Second Street?"

"Yes."

"Hmm." I'm not sure how I've never noticed that before.

There are three streets that run parallel to each other, Second Street being on the north side of Main Street, and Fourth Street being on the south. The streets are almost identical, in that they house the commerce of the town. Second Street is more floral shops and tiny specialty boutiques, like Tata for Teas and the herbal apothecary. Once upon a time, Auntie Grace thought I'd open up a shop there, full of witchy things to sell to the tourists.

Fourth Street has more mainstream attractions, like the museum and the library. Speaking of which, I bet the library has blueprints of the town for me to look at. There has to be a record somewhere.

"Earth to Cassie. Where did you go just now?" Dean's voice reaches for me, and I force my attention to him.

"Just thinking."

"More like plotting. You get the same look on your face when you're thinking up a design for a room."

His words take me completely by surprise, I don't even have time to hide it.

"What? I do pay attention, you know." There's that disarming grin of his and disarm me it does. I have no retort. So I do the mature thing. Mumble a goodbye and briskly walk away from him.

11

The next morning, I beeline for Auntie Grace before she can leave her room and dodge me all day. I can see she was planning just that when she opens the door, dressed and ready for the day.

"My, Cassandra, aren't we peppy this morning?" Auntie says, stepping out of her room. I don't let her go far.

"Auntie Grace, we need to talk."

"Oh, we do, honey bun. But I have so much work—"

"What work? Most of the guests are gone. Please stop avoiding me and have a conversation with me." I'm putting my foot down on this because I'm tired of all these secrets. My aunt gives me a long look, and I can see the moment she gives in. Walking over to the love seat, she settles down as Birdie jumps up onto her lap. The cat has been sticking extra close to me anytime I'm in the inn, but thankfully, still not in my bedroom. Except for that one time. I'm still deciding how I feel about her.

"I haven't been avoiding you, sweetie."

"Yes, you have," I interrupt before Auntie comes up with a million excuses. I'm sure she can because she's the smartest person I have ever met. "And I need you to explain why. You keep sending me out there, away from the inn, but I'm floundering. It's the whole reason I came home in the first place. And yes, I'm supposed to be helping you out, but clearly you don't need that physically. So why am I here? I don't understand, and I need to understand because I'm tired of all the secrets."

The words tumble out of me, and I feel a little out of breath as I finally stop. Auntie Grace gives me a sympathetic look, but it's not patronizing. She's truly feeling for me and that makes me feel better immediately.

"What a mess this is, honey pie." My aunt sighs, patting the space near her. I walk over, settling down while Birdie rearranges herself so that she can watch me. I try not to meet the cat's eye, but it's difficult when it feels like she's staring right into my soul.

"I won't lie, I was happy to hear you needed to come home because you've been gone such a long time. Your place is here, within these walls and amongst these people. This town fuels your bloodline and your magic. It is the best place for you to learn about who you truly are."

"I thought I knew who I was," I confess honestly, because isn't that the whole reason I left? I figured myself out. I wanted to go out there and see the world, away from the prying eyes of the town. Yet, here I am, in the midst of a murder investigation by association, with the whole town watching us.

"Just because you knew who you were before does not mean you are the same person now. People grow and evolve. It's the natural flow of things. Your magic was bound to bring you back to me."

I glance at her sharply, never having heard her put it quite in those terms before.

"Auntie—" I'm not sure how to form the words, but I try anyway. "I didn't abandon you. You were never the issue. This town, after what happened—"

"I know, sweetie pie. I know. I never thought you left me on purpose. It was a byproduct of something that you had to do. But my dreams have been telling me for a while now that you needed to come back, and I have been patiently waiting."

Her words surprise me because she hasn't mentioned her dreams in a while. Many witches have gifts that pertain to their personalities. Witches who are sensitive to the world are more open to receiving premonitions. Considering Auntie Grace's whole brand is helping people, I'm not that shocked she's open to those.

"Something is wrong with me, Auntie," I whisper, afraid to speak the words out loud.

"Oh, sugar plum, nothing is wrong with you. Your magic is just out of practice. It happens even to the best of us."

That doesn't seem to comfort me at all. I feel out of sorts. I feel like everything I do is a big mess. When Auntie is out of the spotlight, and this murder is finally put to rest, I'm going to ask for help. Because I can't keep running from my own magic any longer.

"I'm dead and y'all are just sitting around, shooting the breeze!" Mabel pops into existence out of nowhere, right in front of the couch. Auntie Grace and I both jump, and I swear the ghost of the woman grins.

"Mabel Smith, you watch your tone. If you want my help, you better rail in that attitude," Auntie Grace says, not missing a beat.

"That's assuming you didn't have anything to do with my death." The other woman raises her chin, not backing down. I may not have known her in life, but I can see how she would be a difficult person to be around.

"You know better than to be accusing me of any ill doing." Auntie Grace levels her with a pointed look, and I know for a fact there's a story there. "Now, have you seen anything on your wanderings?"

"Wanderings?" I glance at my aunt, but her attention is on Mabel.

"Nothing. Not a thing. I pop in and then pop out, only catching glimpses of conversations. It is very frustrating."

I notice my aunt trying to suppress a smile. I bet it would be frustrating for a busybody to finally have a way to spy on people without them noticing, but then not actually be able to control it.

"I hope you—" She pops out existence then, while Auntie Grace chuckles and stands.

"That woman can make a saint curse," she comments, standing up. That's when it hits me. There's no headache this time, no pain after Mabel's visit. Birdie meows, catching my attention while giving me a pointed look.

"Auntie Grace?"

"What is it, dear?"

"I'm not sure. But typically, when Mabel is around, I get an excruciating pain in my head. Also, when I use my magic. But there's nothing now." She's already smiling even before I finish my explanation. She reaches down, giving Birdie a quick scratch behind her ear.

"One of the reasons witches keep cats around is that they are a filter of sorts. Birdie helped the energy in the room balance, therefore, balancing your magic output. And Mabel's."

I guess there's some good at having Birdie around after all. The cat gives me a look as if to say *no duh*, and not for the first time, I wonder if she can read my mind.

"Now, I have a meeting with the sheriff this morning. Would you like to drive me?"

～

I DROP my aunt off at the front of the police station before driving over to the main public parking lot. Since I'll be all over downtown today, it'll be easier to just leave my car in one spot. This morning keeps replaying in my mind as I think of my magic and Birdie's balancing act. There's so much I still don't know about magic. It truly is about time I learned.

But first things first.

Having Auntie Grace meet with the sheriff for the second time this week is not sitting well with me. Not at all.

Either they're planning a town takeover, or he's still determined to pin this murder on her. I have no idea how that would work without a motive. Isn't that what all detectives look for first? Motive and opportunity. The opportunity is pretty obvious. Auntie Grace could've slipped something in Mabel's tea while serving it. No one would know any better.

But there's no motive. And motive is important.

The one thing I do know is that there is someone who has a motive, the businessmen and the developers I've heard whispers about. I keep wondering if there is someone else I can talk to about Mabel, but I've been away for so long, I don't even know who the gossip mill consists of. Well, besides Sue Lynn. That woman has always been the president.

Once I park, I head toward the bakery, ready for a good cup of coffee. Penny is behind the counter when I enter and greets me with a smile.

"You're up early. How big of a cup of coffee would you like?" She doesn't even hesitate.

"The biggest you have. I will need all the caffeine today."

Thankfully, the place is completely empty considering it's not even eight in the morning, so we can talk freely.

"What are you scheming, Cassie?"

"Why is it everyone automatically goes to *scheming*? Maybe I'm simply thinking or wondering or—"

"Scheming?" Penny chuckles, placing a to-go cup on the counter in front of me. "If anyone thinks otherwise, they don't know you very well."

That brings up the last person who called me out on it. I grimace.

"What?"

"I ran into Mean Dean last night, and he also told me I was scheming." How many times in a row are we going to use that word? The world may never know.

"Mean Dean, huh?"

"What? What is that tone, Penelope?" I ask before taking a sip of my coffee. The warm liquid hits my taste buds just right, and I sigh with happiness. My best friend grins at me before moving back down to the pastries display.

"Penelope."

"I'm just thinking."

"Thinking what?"

"That for someone who doesn't like the man, you end up around him quite often."

"Not on purpose! He followed me into the trees."

"Trees?"

"I went to see that piece of land by Trinkets and Things."

"Cassie! You're not supposed to be wondering around by yourself. What if the killer got you?"

"Well, we just established, I wasn't by myself. Unless you think Mean Dean had anything to do with it?" I raise an eyebrow, but Penny is already shaking her head.

"Of course not. That man couldn't hurt a fly. Okay, he could. But only if someone he cared about was in trouble."

Narrowing my eyes, I lean over the counter while Penny suddenly focuses all her attention on the shelf in front of her. She said a little too much, and she knows it.

"Pen. Penny."

"Did you want a scone to go with that coffee?"

"Don't change the subject. Are you and Dean friends? Like actual friends?"

"I wouldn't say that." She hurries over to stand in front of me. "But I mean, we live in the same town so we see each other. He helped me rebuild some shelving units in the back, so we have talked. Once or twice."

I should've been expecting this, of course, but I wasn't. She smiles at me carefully, as if I'm going to blame her for being a decent human being.

"Penny, it's okay. You could've told me. We're not thirteen anymore. I don't expect you to hate someone just because I do."

"But do you?" she asks way too fast, as if she's been sitting on that question. One thing I have always been good at is glaring, and I let her have the full effect now. "Sorry, but I have to ask."

"Fine, that's fair I suppose. I don't think I hate him. But I also don't like him or trust him or... something. I'm not sure. He unnerves me."

"I mean, he's gorgeous enough that he does that to a lot of people."

"Penelope!"

"What? I'm not blind. And neither are you. You can't tell me you haven't noticed he grew up good." She wiggles her eyebrows at me, all tension forgotten. I let myself laugh, because this, this right here is what I missed so much about Monroe Cove. No one has truly made me feel at home like Penelope.

Just then, the bell over the door dings and a couple with two children walk in. I drop a ten-dollar bill on the counter, refusing to accept free stuff from Penny, even as she protests.

"I'll see you later!" I call out before slipping out the door.

With my coffee cup in hand, and my heart lighter after spending a few minutes with my friend, I head for the library. It's time to see if I can figure out what Mabel was up to before she died.

12

———

The building looks and smells exactly how I remember it. It's funny to me how some things truly never change. The walkup to the front doors is only five stairs, and they don't look as menacing anymore as they did when I was a kid.

There are two large pillars on each side of the entrance and a statue of one of the first mayors of Monroe Cove on the right. Unlike the building itself, the bronze monstrosity is just as odd and intimidating as I remember. I hurry inside without meeting the eye of George George.

I'm not making it up. His first and last name were the same. The little plaque says so.

The moment I'm inside the double doors, the front desk is there. The library is one huge room with walkways on each side for extra shelve space. The desk is situated in the middle and there is a small barrier at the back to it, to help separate the main space from the entrance. The woman looks up when I step inside, a pleasant smile on her face. The smile broadens as she realizes who I am.

"Cassandra Duke, it's about time."

"Hello, Miss Loretta," I say, my own smile as genuine as the morning sun. This woman has always been a friend to me. She even hid Finn and I from trouble a time or two. She's in her sixties, her hair is cut short and curled around her head, and her clothes are comfy but professional. She hasn't changed at all.

She steps out from behind the desk, reaching over to wrap her arms around me. I hug her right back. Seeing all these people reminds me that even though I had a rough time, there are still a lot of good people that stayed behind.

"I'm sorry it's taken me so long to come by."

"I've heard all about what's been going on at the inn. Don't you worry."

"That's right. You cooked the meals for the guests."

"I like to help out at Dan's Diner when I can. He can use a feminine touch."

I don't comment on the fact that Sue Lynn works there, and Miss Loretta glazes over that fact. This is not the time to pry about that drama. Maybe later. I have other questions.

While I know Miss Loretta has bent the rules for me before, I don't think I have the same pull nowadays, so I'll have to tread lightly.

"You are not here to visit an old lady, are you?" The woman beats me to the punch. She never really misses anything. I realize I can't lie to her. I'll need to tell her as much as I can.

"I'm not. I was hoping to look at the plans for the town. Any blueprints of Main Street or even the setup of the three streets?"

"What are you looking for, Cassie?" Miss Loretta asks as she motions for me to follow her.

"I'm hoping to see if I can find more information on that small park near Trinkets and Things," I say, keeping my tone casual. I'm watching Miss Loretta closely, and I can tell my words bring a bit of tension to her shoulders.

"Why is that?"

"I think you know why," I dare myself to say. The woman turns to look me in the eye. "My aunt didn't do this, but it's like the sheriff can't see past the obvious evidence. I have to do something."

Miss Loretta watches me for a moment longer before sighing in defeat.

"You've always had a good heart in you, Cassie. So, I will tell you this now and you listen carefully. Mabel may have been a harsh woman, but she has always had this town's best interests in mind. Everything she did was to protect our heritage, no matter how many enemies she made."

Grateful someone is finally talking to me about the woman, I can't pass up this chance. But I know I have to be careful.

"Can you tell me about her, Miss Loretta? I feel all I've heard are bad things, but you seemed to have seen a different side of her."

Miss Loretta gets a faraway look in her eyes, and I have no choice but to wait her out. She travels to another time and place for a moment before she blinks and focuses on me.

"It's true, Mabel Smith had her share of enemies in town. They were mostly newer people who didn't know the kind of a woman she truly was. We go way back, you know, back when we were friends in high school. She was sweeter back then but still as stubborn. Once she had an idea in that head of hers, nothing could stop her. It only got worse the older she got. We all become more stubborn with age."

Miss Loretta smiles a sad smile before turning to continue down the small hall. I've never been in this area of the library before. When we come to a set of stairs, I glance back to see that we're completely out of sight here.

"Can you tell me about the property at the edge of Main Street?" I ask as we descend down.

"You mean Mabel's property." This woman doesn't miss a thing. "It wasn't the only piece of land she owned in town. There are a few that no one, not even I, know about. We all have our secrets."

The way she says that, I can't help but ask.

"Do you have land in town as well?"

Miss Loretta doesn't reply as we come into a small room with a large table right in the middle of it. There are shelves on each side. She heads to the left, pulling some tubes out.

"Here are the town's blueprints. You can look at anything you like down here. I'll be leaving for the memorial at eleven, so you have until then."

I don't miss the fact that she hasn't answered my last question, but I don't press.

"Thank you, Miss Loretta."

"You're welcome, Cassie," she replies before heading back up the stairs. I glance back over at the tubes. There are six of them. It's only eight o'clock now, so I have some time. Taking a sip of my coffee, I get to work.

THERE IS a lot of information on these blueprints, a lot more than I expected. Whoever kept record of the town's development took pride in their job. I have to be thankful for small favors.

So far, I've found three other places across town that belonged to Mabel Smith. She owned a lot of property, and as far as I can tell, almost no one knew about it. There are a few properties with nothing but initials on them, DF. I can't think of anyone in town with those initials. At least not any of the older families that live here.

"Cassie, I'm closing up. Are you ready?" Miss Loretta calls down, pulling me away from my research. I glance at the clock, surprised to see that three hours have gone by.

"I'm coming up," I call back, quickly rolling the papers back up and into the tubes. When I reach the main floor, Miss Loretta is waiting by the front doors. "Thank you for letting me down there."

"Of course, dear," Miss Loretta says as we walk out together.

"Would you mind if I came to the memorial with you?" I ask, since I was planning on going anyway. The woman smiles. Then, we set off toward the church, which is only a few buildings down from the library. That's Fourth Street for you. All the important buildings are close together.

When we reach the church, people are already filling in. Truthfully, I'm surprised by the number of individuals present. So far, the one sure thing I know about Mabel is that she was not that liked. Yet, here is a crowd of people who show otherwise.

Once inside, Miss Loretta moves to greet some people. I walk over to lean against the wall. It's not as if I'm part of this as I didn't know Mabel personally. I want to observe, but I'm not participating.

I notice Auntie Grace at the front, sitting with Lucy. I assumed at least one of them would be here but not both. But I suppose with most guests gone from the inn, it doesn't require full time care like it usually does.

This time, a headache comes a split second before Mabel materializes beside me. It's different than any other time, as if she can tell where she's at before she becomes visible. Well, to me. No one else can see her. She gives the room a quick once over before leaning against the wall beside me.

"I honestly did not expect this many people," she comments. I don't have to look at her to know she's crying. I give her the small privacy she craves and keep my eyes on the crowd.

"This town shows up for its people," I mumble, but I know she hears me.

"I tried to protect it. I tried to do what others couldn't."

"What did you do?" It's hard to ask questions, while I try to appear like I'm not just standing here, talking to myself. Not that it matters. Mabel seems to be lost in her own head at the moment.

"It's getting harder to come back, to remember the good. I keep getting lost." She's still crying, and this time, I risk a glance. She's looking out into the congregation, tears on her cheeks. But she also looks worse somehow. She's not as bright as before, more muted in color. It's not a good sign.

"If I don't—" she begins, and then she's gone. Every time it feels like she's actually going to say something significant, she poofs out. It's very frustrating.

My eyes shift over to the entrance right as Finn walks in. Dean is two steps behind him. Finn's eyes find me immediately, as if he's been looking for me. He beelines for where I'm standing. Dean sees me as well, but someone stops him, and he turns his attention to the elderly man in front of him.

"Hey there, Cassie." Finn takes the spot Mabel vacated, a quick smile on his lips. "Staying out of trouble?"

"Never and you know it." He bumps my shoulder with his, and I lean into the move. It's been a while since Finn and I hung out, and it feels like I've barely seen him since I've been back.

"Did you find anything?" he asks, lowering his voice. Rolling my eyes a little, I lower my voice as well.

"Are you trying to jump in on my investigation?"

"Come on, Cassie. You've always had a knack for seeing what others don't see. I'm curious if you found anything interesting."

I give our surroundings a quick glance, but most of the people are out of earshot as they settle down for the service. Turning more fully toward Finn, I lean over so I can keep my voice to barely a whisper.

"What I discovered is that this town is owned by only a few families, and they hold properties all around. Most of those properties don't connect."

"Families?" Finn gives me a look as if he's hearing about this for the first time.

"You can't tell me you didn't know."

"Honestly, Sheriff Bernard has been keeping a pretty tight leash around this whole investigation. And I think he still struggles with me being on the right side of the law."

That earns him a smile from me, because we were real troublemakers growing up. Not really illegal, mostly just local nuisances.

"So, you didn't know Mabel had property?"

"I knew she had a chunk near her house, and of course, the house itself. You're saying there's more?"

"It's not hard information to find. The archives at the library carry the blueprints."

Finn pauses as the pastor gets up and walks to the front. The rest of the crowd settles down as well, but Finn and I aren't the only ones left standing. Sheriff Bernard is on the other side of the church, at the front, standing next to a man who looks like a lawyer.

Dean also stays standing on the opposite side of the entryway, with a few ladies nearby. He's got himself a real fan club, even though most of the women are old enough to be his mother. There are a few other stragglers, but thankfully not near Finn and me.

"If you could find that information, then so could someone else." Finn's voice turns my attention back to him. I glance over because I haven't thought about that.

"You're right. All they'd have to do is be nice to Miss Loretta and they're in. So, who would need that information?"

The obvious answer would be the developers, but wouldn't they already have that information on hand? There has to be someone else in town who would benefit from it. I just can't think of who.

"Is there a way to check and see who had access to the information?" I ask as the pastor begins speaking.

"I was thinking of that, but I doubt Miss Loretta keeps records. And if the individuals knew where to look for information, they wouldn't even need to go through her."

We grow quiet as the service starts, each of us lost in our own thoughts. I didn't exactly come to Monroe Cove to play private investigator, but the job has fallen into my lap. I don't see a way out of it until the murder is solved. I'm a little surprised Finn is talking things over with me, but at the same time, this is why we always got into so much trouble growing up. When we put our heads together, we're pretty unstoppable.

"Finn," I whisper as Carl stands and begins his eulogy. "Do you have any idea what DF might stand for, in terms of a family name that's from these parts?"

He thinks it over before shaking his head. "I'll have to go down to the library and see these blueprints for myself. Maybe I'll notice something you didn't."

I nod and then get back to the service. Carl speaks with a clear but heavy voice and my heart goes out to him. I can't imagine what I would do if I lost Auntie Grace.

My eyes roam over the crowd, trying to pick out any naysayers or bad wishers, but there's nothing. If I was a stronger witch, maybe I could sense some of the emotions. But I can't. So, I settle in and listen.

13

O nce the service is over, I'm sad to report I've learned nothing. Only that no matter who dies, people in this town will show up for your family. Carl is getting a lot of support right now. Maybe I've misjudged this place a little.

I suppose in retrospect, that's not nothing.

Mabel hasn't appeared again, and the headache she left behind is almost gone, thankfully. I really need to figure out this whole headache thing when Birdie is not around. Can't say that I'm enjoying the knowledge that I have to rely on a cat to make me feel better.

"Are you coming?" Finn asks as people start filing out of the sanctuary and toward the adjacent building for some finger food and fellowship. At least, that's what the pastor called it. There's no graveside service yet, considering Mabel's body is still with the police. I wonder how long that usually takes.

"I don't know, Finn. I'm not exactly family or friends."

"Yes, but if you're going to play detective, you should *make* some friends. You haven't been gone so long that you've forgotten who you are." He winks at me, reading me like a book. Of course he can tell exactly what I've been trying to do. It's foolish of me to keep this from my closest friends. I shake my head at him, pushing him a little so he walks in front of me.

"I've missed you, Cassie," he says, leaning over to tip the bottom of my chin up. The smile that blossoms on my face is genuine because I missed him too. I really left a lot of good things behind. It's only hitting me now.

I might be slightly more melodramatic about the whole thing considering a death occurred the moment I stepped into town. But it still makes me want to hold my loved ones closer.

Finn's name gets called then, and I wave him off, following the crowd to the hall. Keeping my ear's on alert, I wander around, trying to see if I can glimpse some information. When I notice Mabel's nephew sitting alone by the window, I head his way.

"Miss Duke." Carl Smith greets me when I stop in front of him.

"I'm so sorry for your loss, Mr. Smith."

He motions for me to take the seat beside him, and I do.

"Oh, please call me Carl. Mr. Smith makes me sound so old." I realize we're not that far apart in age, he's probably only about ten years my senior.

"Only if you call me Cassie." I smile, and he returns the gesture, even though his eyes are sad.

"Thank you for coming, Cassie. I know you didn't know my aunt well."

"Sadly, I didn't know her at all, but I've heard some lovely things about her."

He chuckles then, but there's no humor in the sound. "I'm sure those aren't the only things you've heard about her. She may have been tough, but she was a great aunt. The best." His eyes pool with tears. I have the urge to reach out and take his hand, if only to offer a bit of comfort. My heart truly goes out to him as I think about my own aunt. Before I do, a couple comes up, and he stands to speak with them.

Just then, my eye catches movement beyond the door across the room. I stand to follow the movement. I'm not sure what I saw exactly, but it looked like Mabel. She seemed to be in a hurry. Since I'm trying to catch as much time with her as possible, I should see if she'll stick around for some questions this time.

When I step outside and look around, I don't see anyone suspicious immediately. There are still groups of people out here, and everyone seems to be talking at once. I can hear the low buzz of conversation. Glancing back into the building, my eyes find Carl again, and I realize I have a perfect opportunity right now. No one is at Mabel's house.

This is my chance to see if I can find more information about what's been going on with her in days leading up to the murder. But more so, Finn gave me an idea. Even though he doesn't know it.

I do remember who I am. And who I am is a witch. It's about time I start using that to my advantage.

HEADING toward where I left my car, I quickly calculate everything I will need. It's been years since I've tried anything magical on purpose. Maybe the smarter choice would be to go back and ask Auntie Grace specifically, but at this point, she's a little too involved with the investigation. If I get caught, she needs to be as much in the dark as she can. She won't like it but tough luck. If I'm going to do this, I need to do it right.

It takes me about ten minutes to get back to the inn. I park in my regular spot, quickly noticing that Lucy and Dean's vehicles are both still gone. Good. I didn't see either of them in the hall after the service, but if they're not here, it works to my advantage.

One of the younger girls is at the front desk when I come in. I wave in her direction, heading directly for my aunt's and mine residence area. Birdie appears beside me when I hit the small hallway. I glance down to see her looking inquisitively up at me.

"What? You've got something to say?" I ask as I step into the library. Last time I was snooping in here I found a few of Auntie's spell books and journals. They appear like regular books to outsiders but show their true content to me. Now, which one will have what I need?

"I don't suppose you want to be helpful and steer me in the direction of a spell that'll help guide me inside of Mabel's house?" I look over at Birdie, perching on the coffee table. She stares at me for a long second, before jumping down and heading for the table near the window. Her movements are effortless, that of a cat. When she lands on top of a stack of books, she proceeds to balance there as she looks back over at me.

"I'm going to assume you're giving me that evil stare because I'm not moving fast enough," I say, walking over to the table. The top book is a Tolstoy volume, but the one under it shimmers the moment I touch it. There's no writing on the cover, just vines and flowers. When I open it, I see that it's an herbal encyclopedia of sorts. There are potions and pouches for everything.

"Birdie, we might've just become best friends," I mumble as I leaf through the pages. The cat makes a small noise. It's not quite a meow, more like an agreement grunt, and I smile. She's grown on me, y'all. This is very unexpected.

Heading to the couch, I speed read as much as I can, looking for any words that might jump out at me. I learned this trick in college, and it has been very helpful. I'm about halfway through the book when I see it. An "open your mind" pouch.

"Okay, Birdie, this is where you come in." I glance up to where the cat has been sitting. She's watching me as if she's waiting for instructions. "I have a clear quartz crystal, but any idea where I can get rosemary and peppermint?"

The cat gives me one of her "you are so helpless" looks before jumping down and heading for the bookshelves near Auntie Grace's bedroom door. I follow closely behind. When Birdie stops in front of it and reaches up to stretch, I squat down to see where her paws landed. Many of the bookshelves here have glass casings, but I haven't explored many of them. I see that this one houses a number of herbs used in spells.

"I definitely think we're becoming friends." I smile at the cat before reaching over and grabbing what I need. The spell is very simple. It's fueled by intention and assisted by a few natural ingredients. I don't even need to wrap them or put them into a glass jar. I just need to carry them.

Placing a pinch of rosemary in my left pocket, and a pinch of peppermint into my right, I stand, heading for my bedroom. Even though I haven't been a practicing witch, I've kept the crystals I've collected over the years. There's no way I could've parted with them. I have a few on a necklace, so I select the one with the clear quartz, pulling it over my head.

It's not much, but this will help me think more clearly. If I'm lucky, it'll open up more possibilities. Closing my eyes, I focus on that intention and on clearing my mind. I stay like that for a full minute before I dare to open them and look around. Nothing seems to be floating or melting, so my magic is working. For now.

"Wish me luck, Birdie," I throw over my shoulder as I race for the front door. I really am talking to a cat like she's a human. I suppose that just finally makes me a real witch, don't it?

14

Sneaking into the house is a lot easier than I expected. I make sure to park down the street again and then look around to see if any of the memorial service goers have returned yet. There are a few houses on this street, but it seems quiet. But I'm not about to trust appearances. That'll just get me in trouble. I remember that from my youngling days.

I circle the house on foot, keeping to the bushes. There are quite of few of them around the front and side, so it provides ample shade. The back has a porch, like most of these old Victorian houses do. After a quick glance around, I hurry to the back door. It feels like I'm being watched, but when I do another scan, I don't see anyone.

Hoping Mabel wasn't a stickler for locking her back door, I turn the knob. It opens easily, and I breathe a sigh of relief. If I had to try and use my minuscule lock picking skills, this would've taken forever. There was a client once who was notorious for locking the door with the keys still inside. I had to learn a trick or two. So sue me. Actually, don't. I'm trying to do a good thing here.

Not sure that'll fly in court if I get arrested, but there are too many secrets, and no one is talking about any of it. I can't shake the feeling that this has something to do with the property, or properties, Mabel owned around town. After my many hours of watching crime shows, I know there are really only a few motives for murder. Usually, they're narrowed down to love or money. After everything I've learned about Mabel, I can't really picture the love thing, but I'm not about to rule it out.

"What are you doing in my house?" Mabel materializes, bringing with her a sharp headache. I rub my temples as I glance up at the woman who is slowly fading from existence. There's no doubt about her coloring here. Not that she would actually disappear. She would just become one of those mean looking things movies are made about.

"I was hoping to have a conversation with you, without you disappearing on me."

"Well, it's not like I can control it," she snaps before pointing at my hands. "What are you doing that for? Am I that much of a bother to be around?"

"From a magical standpoint, yes," I reply, glaring at her. She really hasn't slowed down on the attitude train, and I'm going to need her to be a little less... squeal-y.

"You are just like your aunt, aren't you? Always throwing her knowledge in people's faces. Always—"

"Okay!" I hold up my hands, stopping the sudden attack. "I know you're turning into a real-life poltergeist here, but I need you to focus. Do you have an office in the house? Or any place that you kept confidential information?"

"Are you going to snoop about in my life?"

"Yes. Please stop yelling." We're still in the back hallway, barely past the laundry room. I'm not exactly sure how much time we have left.

"Shouldn't you be trying to catch my killer? Why are you in my house?"

"Because," I turn to face her head on, "someone did kill you. And there has to be a reason. But no one knows what that reason is, and I think it might have something to do with the property you owned. Can you tell me anything about it?"

That shuts her up immediately, and that's all the proof I need that something was going on with that land. She scrunches her face as she thinks deeply, but even before she speaks, I can tell she won't be any help.

"I remember talking to that businessman at the inn, but I can't remember what we talked about. Or when it really happened. It's so fuzzy." She sounds distressed at that last word. I feel inclined to reassure her.

"It's okay, Mabel. That happens. We'll figure it out."

It's the most inconvenient thing about becoming a ghost. Her recent memories disappear first because they're the freshest. So, whatever was going on with that land, she'll never be able to tell me. So, let's go back to the original tactic.

"Mabel, can you direct me toward an office?"

She seems to snap out of it for a moment. I hurry after her as she walks farther into the house and turns to the right. The double doors in front of me are open. I step inside to find myself in a sewing room.

"This was my place," Mabel says. I turn to watch her look at the room with sadness. I can't imagine being in her shoes. "Cross stitching was my thing. I would make all kinds of decorations and Tootsie would sell some in her store."

"The owner of Trinkets and Things?"

"Oh yes, we've been friends for ages. She has always had such a good eye for decor."

I don't agree or disagree on that one. Some of the items in her store were definitely good, others not so much. But I'm not here to argue with a ghost. While this definitely looks like a place Mabel spent a lot of time in, it's not the conventional office I was looking for.

I leave her behind as I wander through the house. She seems to need a moment. The house has two stories instead of the typical three around these parts. It's so much bigger than I expect it to be. The floor plan is pretty open, and for someone who was in her late sixties, Mabel did have a good eye for furniture that was more modern and lively. I think, despite her reputation, I might've liked her.

"Mabel," I call out softly when I come back to the sewing room. She's still standing where I left her, but she turns at my voice. "You had a beautiful house. I'm sorry I didn't meet you under normal circumstances."

"Oh, but you did. You were only ten years old back then, but I remember your pigtails. You went through a whole pigtails stage. Mary Grace would always say she missed the time when you let her braid. But you were getting to be a big girl and you wanted to do your own hair."

The words completely baffle me. I don't remember Mabel, much like I don't remember a lot of the people in town. But this is such a specific memory, something that makes it sound like Mabel and Auntie Grace were more than just two ladies who lived in the same town.

"Mabel—" I start again, but just then, the front door opens and she poofs out of the room.

Seeing no other choice, I rush for the closet. A moment later, I hear a voice and recognize it immediately. Carl is back, and he's not alone. Another voice reaches me, and while it's familiar, only when Carl says sheriff do I realize it's Sheriff Bernard.

Great, just great. Not only did I break and enter—well, technically only enter— the owner has now returned as well. And he brought police with him. There's a possibility I'll get lucky and they're only picking something up? But no, I'm not that lucky.

"Sheriff, would you like some coffee?" Carl asks, shattering my idea of them getting out of here soon.

"Actually, your aunt loved her chamomile and citrus tea. I would love to have a cup of that."

"I believe she said something about needing to get more the last time I talked to her. I can check, but I think she was out."

"That's a shame. Coffee will be fine."

They continue farther into the house, and I realize I have no way of getting by them without being seen. The kitchen has a full view of both the front and the back doors. It's that open floor plan I was just admiring. Now, it's the bane of my existence. I can't exactly hide in the closet the whole time. Carl might be back for the night.

"Is there any progress on my aunt's case?" Carl's voice reaches me, and I instantly stop looking for a way out. Maybe this will be good for me.

"It's an ongoing investigation, Carl. You'll know something when I do."

Come on, sheriff. Give me more than that to work with. This whole entering the house fiasco cannot end with me leaving empty handed.

"I did have a question for you." The sheriff continues, as if he heard my silent pleas.

"Of course."

"Have you been approached by any of the developers that have been scouting the town?"

There's a moment of silence and a clink of cups before Carl answers.

"A few. They approached my aunt and me before her passing as well. Something about building a commerce center in town."

"Yes, big corporations have been begging for a foot in the

door at Monroe Cove for years. They say we can't stop the progress. But part of the charm of the place, and why so many tourists come to these parts, is because of the small-town feel. That and all the undeveloped forests that allow for hiking and camping and such."

The way the sheriff speaks makes me think he's tired. This investigation, looking for someone in town who might've done this, would have to be draining. But it seems he's also been dealing with the vultures. That's something I will never miss about the big city. Everyone is out to make that money. Not that money is bad, but the love of it, that's where the real problems start.

"Did your aunt mention anything about wanting to sell?" The sheriff gets back to business.

"Honestly, no. She was pretty set on never giving those developers the time of day."

"Will you sell?"

There's a moment of silence, and I hold my breath as I wait for Carl to answer.

"I wouldn't. But sheriff, I'm not sure what I'm getting in the will. It's not being read until the investigation closes."

"Isn't that a little strange?" The sheriff seems surprised, and so am I. I thought the will is usually read right away. Sometimes it can even provide motive.

"It was a stipulation my aunt added recently." There's not bitterness in Carl's voice, but there's something. I'm sure sheriff picks up on it too, but he doesn't push. There are a few more clunks of china and then sheriff speaks up again.

"It must be difficult, not knowing."

"The most difficult part is having her gone. Please catch whoever is responsible. Then I can rest."

"What ya doing in my closet?" Mabel mock whispers, appearing beside me. It's only because she's been doing this a lot that I don't yelp in surprise. I point in the direction of Carl and the sheriff, afraid to even whisper. She doesn't hesitate, walking over to see what they're up to.

"They're facing the back door right now," Mabel says, coming back a few minutes later. "With your witchy powers, can't you make some noise in the backyard or something and escape."

"No," I mouth before I point at her and then the backyard.

"What? I can't move stuff around."

I raise my eyebrows at her as if to say "have you tried?" She looks thoughtful.

"Okay." She shrugs finally. "Here goes nothing."

She disappears into the hallway. I stand there, completely still, waiting for some kind of sign. Suddenly there's a big bang, and I hear Carl and the sheriff jump to their feet.

"What was that?" Carl exclaims before I hear the door slam. I step out of the closet, and then the sewing room, daring a look down the hall. Both the sheriff and Carl are now outside, so I don't hesitate. I race for the front door, slipping quietly outside and down the stairs. It's only when I'm a few houses down that I stop to take a breather.

I have no idea what that accomplished, but I might want to take up running again, because boy am I winded.

15

———

On the way back to the inn I realize there is a very important piece of information I did learn from being in that house. And that is the fact that Auntie Grace and Mabel were friends, once upon a time. That is something Auntie Grace forgot to mention.

"Lucy, is my aunt back?" I ask when I walk through the front door. She told me someone from the station would drop her off, so I didn't have to wait around.

"Yes, she's in the kitchen," the woman replies without looking up from the computer. I thank her before marching over to the back. When I step into the kitchen, the aroma of baked goods hits me right away. Auntie Grace always starts making cookies when she's anxious. It's either that or practicing spells. I find her in the corner, near the mixer.

"Ah, sugar bun, you're back. Would you like to sample some of the cookies? I know how much you used to enjoy that."

I'm tempted, especially since they smell amazing, but I'm not about to be deterred from my mission. The longer I'm back, the more I think something is going on underneath the happy-go-lucky cover of Monroe Cove. And since I've dubbed myself an investigator, this falls under my jurisdiction.

"Auntie Grace, we need to talk." She stops what she's doing immediately, surprised by my serious tone.

"What is it, sweetie pie?"

I take a deep breath, preparing myself for what I need to say. I'll start slowly.

"Why didn't you tell me Mabel and you were friends?" Her face remains completely neutral at my question, which I recognize as a defense mechanism. She starts stirring the mix again, turning her attention to the dough.

"I'm not sure what you mean, my dear," she finally says as I narrow my eyes.

"I mean that Mabel has a distinct memory of me in pigtails and how much you loved braiding my hair at that time, so you were sad you couldn't." That gets her attention. "And if your next question is if I remember this, I don't. I seemed to have forgotten a lot more about my childhood than I realized."

For a split second, Auntie Grace looks guilty, and that solidifies every half thought I had in my mind.

"Auntie Grace, did you alter my memories?" My voice comes out controlled instead of angry, and for that I am grateful. She doesn't answer right away. That makes me even more nervous. "Aunt Grace?"

It's the 'aunt' part that finally gets to her, I think. She puts her baking down and turns to me. A somber look falls over her features as she reaches for my hands.

"It was an accident, Cassie."

"An accident?"

"When you were fourteen, you started getting these nightmares about your family and your parents. Nothing would work and nothing would help you sleep. So, I went to my cousin and asked her for help. She was a much better witch than I at that time. She gave me some herbs to put into your tea before bed, and you started to sleep through the night."

"I don't remember this."

"That's because the spell backfired. I'm not sure if it was your own powers coming into play or if Ronda didn't mix the potions as well as she should've, but you began experiencing side effects, some of which were losing memories and not just memories from when you were younger. Sometimes it'll be something that happened two days ago. Of course, I stopped the potions, but the damage was done, and even to this day, I can't find a way to undo it."

I stay quiet for a moment, letting the words settle over me. This makes so much sense when I think about it. This explains much of my magic going haywire.

"Is that why my magic control is so... unbalanced?"

"I think so, honey bun. You've forgotten some of the basics. With the gaps in your memory, you wouldn't know how to deal with an unbalanced spell."

"Why... why have you never told me?" There are tears in my eyes now, as I finally realize that what's been happening to me has a reason. I'm not as messed up as I thought I was. Well, I still am. But there's a reason now.

"I was hoping I could fix it. But, my love, I did tell you. Once."

I shake my head, one part in anger, one part in disappointment.

"Is that why I left? I always felt like something happened, but I couldn't put a finger on it."

"You were angry. As you had every right to be. I failed you, and I am sorry."

I retract my hands from her grip, taking a step back. This is not what I expected coming in here. I need time to process. I can't do this with her watching me.

"Cassie?"

"I need to figure this out."

And for the second time in as many days, I turn, and run.

I DRIVE to Main Street on autopilot. So many thoughts twirl in my head. So many questions. I started out this week trying to prove my aunt's innocence in a murder. But now I find out she's not so innocent after all. I don't believe she murdered anyone, but what happened to me? There should've been a better way to handle it. Now, I'm not sure how to feel about it.

When I pull in front of the park, I get out and head straight for Penny's bakery. There are only two people inside, and they don't bother looking up when I come in. Penny takes one look at me though and shoos them out.

"I'm sorry for the inconvenience. The bakery must close immediately."

They take their coffee and a free cookie and leave. Penny shuts and locks the door before turning to me.

"What happened?"

I can't even put it into words, but tears come and then she's hugging me as I babble on about everything that happened. Penny guides me over to the table. I sit while she rushes over to grab me some tissues. And some tea. I clean up before wrapping my hand around the warm mug.

"That's... I don't even know what to say, Cassie. I never even thought... I mean I wondered why you didn't remember some people, but you've been gone long enough that it wasn't as weird."

"I bet you would've realized it was weird the longer I was here. I mean, I was bound to say something that threw off some red flags."

"I can't believe Miss Mary Grace didn't tell you when you explained to her about your magic."

"A part of me understands." I sigh because I can't stay mad at the only living relative I have. "She wanted to protect me, even from myself. Because you know I'm going to do everything in my power now to restore my memories. That's going to be tiresome and maybe dangerous."

"But?"

"But I wish I knew it wasn't me who was broken. It was something I had no control over."

"You are not broken, Cassandra Duke." Penny slaps her hand on the counter, her tiny frame completely outraged on my behalf. "Look at all that you've accomplished, even with this, umm, situation. You have overcome so many obstacles, even without your full memory and without your full magic. Now that you have this information, you'll figure it out. And I'll be there to help."

There isn't a person alive that could keep a straight face after that speech. I grin at Penny, my heart full.

"You are one amazing friend, Penelope," I say, reaching over to squeeze her hand.

"I know. Now what are we going to do about this?"

"Well, before we do anything about this, let me tell you what I did earlier today."

Penny narrows her eyes, cocking her head to the side. "Please tell me it wasn't illegal."

"I can't."

"Cassie."

"Do you want to hear about it, or would you like to continue to scold me?" I raise my eyebrows at her and she caves.

"Tell me."

After I finish, there's a thoughtful look on Penny's face.

"What are you thinking?"

"The whole will thing is so weird. They're waiting to read it? Why would Mabel make that stipulation?"

I shrug before replying. "That's what I'd like to know as

well. Do you think Carl actually knows, and he's just not saying?"

"I'm not sure. He's never been very active around here. He lives two towns over and only came in to see his aunt once in a while. He came over a little more lately since she hasn't been feeling as well. But I have no idea. I only know him because he loves the coffee here."

"Everyone loves the coffee here," I comment, and Penny grins. "I guess I could talk to Carl and see what he says. He seems nice enough."

"Just be careful, okay? And if you're doing more breaking and entering, at least bring me along as a lookout."

"I only entered! There was no breaking."

"Same thing."

Penny stands to grab us more tea, and I let my mind wonder. The whole thing with my aunt overshadowed it for a second, but it's true that the will situation is strange. Penny mentioned Mabel feeling sick before she passed away, and that's the second time someone mentioned it. I wonder if there is someone I can ask about that. Finn won't talk to me, but he would be a good source. If he decided to help me. But I don't want to get him in trouble, so I'll have to figure this out on my own. Mabel is fading fast. I'm running out of time.

16

––––––––

After making plans with Penny to finally have a girls' night with no murder talk and a lot of nachos, I leave her bakery and head for my car. Halfway there, I pause, because something has been nagging me. It's the blueprints. There's something there, I'm sure of it. It's been in the back of my mind. Maybe having another look will help.

When I turn around, the sheriff is coming up on the sidewalk toward me. His eyes are on me, so I have no choice but to wait and see what he wants.

"Miss Duke, out for a walk?"

"Visiting my friend." I nod toward the bakery, and the sheriff smiles.

"That Penelope sure knows how to bake, doesn't she?"

"Yes."

I'm not sure where this is going. I haven't spoken to the man since he took Auntie Grace into questioning almost a week ago now. He's watching me in that sheriff-like way of his, waiting for me to be the first to break the sudden silence. But I worked for Laura for almost three years. I can wait out awkward silences and intimidation tactics. When it appears that I won't be the first to speak, Sheriff Bernard sighs.

"It seems you have been getting into the middle of my investigation," he comments.

"Just making conversation with the locals," I reply. He narrows his eyes, as if he's trying to figure me out.

"I know all about how you Duke women make conversation. I would advise you to stick to your circle of friends."

It doesn't sound like a threat, but it definitely sounds like a warning. Not that I'm going to listen to it anyway. I think he can tell that just by looking at me.

"I'm only trying to get reacquainted with my hometown, sheriff. There's nothing wrong with that, is there?"

He shakes his head, not missing a beat.

"You and your aunt are such a pair. If you're not going to stop asking questions, at least be careful about it. And maybe let your friend in on whatever you find."

I cock my head to the side, surprised by him giving in so easily, which is why I don't hesitate to ask him about it.

"I've learned that you Duke women always get your way. So, it's better if I'm in your good graces," he replies before turning to go. "Don't play a hero, Miss Duke. That's all I ask." He inclines his head and then he's walking back to the station.

I watch him go, wondering, what was the point of that? Maybe to let me know that he knows what I've been up to and that's he's watching me. But I also think there was an undercurrent of... something there. Has Auntie Grace told him about our family's heritage? Does he know we're witches? Maybe he does and maybe this is his way of letting me know he'll keep our secret.

Or maybe it's been a long day, and I'm reading into every little thing.

Deciding against going to the library, I get into my car and head home instead. Before I play detective any more than I already have, I think I need to take a nice long bath. The combination of water and aroma therapy has always been able to clear my mind.

Right now, that's exactly what I need.

THE NEXT MORNING, I wake up rested but also a little disturbed. Sitting up in bed, I try to remember the dream I had, but there's nothing. All that's left are feelings of uncertainty, and I don't like it. Everything seems to be up in the air right now. I might just be reacting to that.

Either way, after I take a shower and get dressed for the day, I choose one of my necklaces as an accessory. This one has three black tourmaline crystals at the center of it. Hopefully, the extra protection helps me get through the day without any problems.

I head to the kitchen first, grabbing a cup of coffee and toast, before I make my way upstairs. Thankfully, I haven't run into Auntie Grace since I ran out of here yesterday. I'd like to keep it that way until I find my footing a little better. Of course I still love her, and she's still the most important person in my life. But I'm also still mad at her.

When I reach the upstairs room, I walk through slowly, letting my mind wander as I drink my coffee. Imagining how a room will look is the easy part. Mentally, I create my lists, with the necessities on the top and the wants on the bottom. Once I have the time to sit down and write it all out, I'll sketch the room as well, so I need to take down the dimensions. The precise nature of work calms my mind.

There were a set of four candlesticks at Trinkets and Things that I think will look perfect on the shelf created by the cutout in the wall. I might need to purchase some air plants to go in the candlesticks, to fill in the space. I also need to find some better curtains, for every room, if I'm being honest. Crooked Windows Inn needs to breathe a little, and lighter curtains will bring in that breath of fresh air.

Noticing a tape measure, I set my coffee cup down and begin the measurements. Pulling up my phone's notepad app, I jot down the information I need and the few items I want to pick up at the antique store. Last time, I was too preoccupied with asking questions to really look around, but there were a few things that caught my eye. Some will need refurbishing, but that's just part of the fun.

"How long have you been up here?" Dean asks when he finds me an hour later. I'm sitting on the floor now, rearranging tiles and screws into a mini layout of the room. Walking all the way downstairs to grab my sketchbook seemed like too much of a risk.

"Oh good, you're here. I had a question. Since you're making an opening in the wall here," I point to the makeshift wall I made on the floor, "do you think you can add another one up here?"

"Good morning to you too." Dean chuckles, setting down his toolbox. He looks good this morning. Not that he ever looks not good. The jeans fit him like they were tailor made and the black t-shirt stretches over his biceps just right. I tear my gaze away before I start drooling and glance back down at my masterpiece.

"Good morning. Now can you do it or not?"

Dean chuckles, but he walks over to where the wall is being rebuilt and looks up.

"You mean here, right?" he asks, pointing to the space above the cutout. I nod.

"Yep, and it needs to be a rectangle. I'll write down the dimensions." I move to stand and am met with an outstretched hand. At first, I almost refuse it. But deciding against it, I place my own into his instead. He lifts me effortlessly and then we're standing a few inches apart.

"Any other commands, I mean requests?" He grins down at me, and I can't help but smile back.

"Not yet, but it's still early."

Then, I'm the one moving away. I pick up my now-cold cup of coffee and head for the door.

"Leaving so soon?" I glance over my shoulder to find him watching me, that smirk still in place.

"Don't miss me too much," I throw back and then I'm through the doorway. I have no idea what possessed me to suddenly be all flirty with him, but it felt good. Not that it should. He's still Mean Dean. Although he hasn't displayed many of those attributes since I've been back.

I chalk it up to the bath last night. It put me in a good mood, despite everything that's been going on around here. Or maybe it's the fact that I'm finally working on this design project. Designing rooms has always been a passion. I'm happy to know that hasn't gone away, no matter what I discover about myself or what's happening in my life. It's my creative outlet, and today, I'm going to focus on it.

17

By the time afternoon comes around, I have been all over town. This time, it has nothing to do with me trying to find out anything about Mabel. I was rediscovering all the places I need to make sure the redesign goes as smoothly as possible.

The hardware store is bigger than I remember and has a whole section dedicated to colors. I was a little nervous they would have five or six and the rest I'd have to order in from the big city, but that's not the case. Same goes for the wallpaper.

I guess the developers really know what they're doing. Monroe Cove has grown and expanded in ways I didn't imagine. It's always been such a small town in my mind, but it really isn't as small as I made it out to be. The tourism has definitely picked up in recent years and commerce followed. While it still feels cozy and adorable, there's real potential here. Getting a business here would make someone a lot of money.

Maybe I can't go a day without thinking about the murder. I haven't seen Mabel yet today, but I'm sure she'll be by eventually.

After I finish up at the flower shop, I head to Penny's. A late afternoon sugar snack is what I need to get me to dinner. I may have forgotten to eat lunch.

The place is full when I get there. As I get in line, Penny waves to me. She looks completely in her element, throwing orders around and moving behind the counter with the ease of a dancer. She may be small, but she is fierce, that's for sure. The girl behind the cash register takes one order while Penny fulfills two. When it's finally my turn, Penny doesn't even let me order. She places coffee and a piece of her raspberry cheesecake in front of me and motions toward the end of the counter.

"You read my mind."

"Of course I did."

I move over and watch as she finishes up with the rest of the customers. It's amazing to see her doing what she loves. Her passion for this place hasn't diminished a bit.

When she finally makes her way to me, the place has mostly cleared out. She leans against the counter, taking a swig from her water bottle.

"Is it always this busy around this time?" I don't think I've ever been here in the mid afternoon before.

"Two to three is usually pretty busy," Penny replies, throwing me a grin. "The kids adore the extra chocolate chocolate chip cookies. A huge fan favorite, even though it has dark chocolate in them. This is that perfect time to grab something sweet while browsing around town with enough time that it doesn't ruin dinner."

"That last part sounds like you've heard it somewhere." I smile.

"Almost every parent utters a variation of that sentence to their kid, but it works."

The door jingles again, and we both turn to see Mrs. Tootsie rush into the bakery. She seems a little frazzled and maybe a little paler than the last time I saw her.

"Hello, darling girl. Could I have one of those strawberry danishes to go please? Oh Cassandra, dear. I didn't see you there." She looks right me, like she saw me the moment she walked in, but I give her a smile anyway.

"Hello, Mrs. Tootsie. I was actually coming to see you later today."

"Oh, you were? Was it because of the sconces? I kept them in store just for you. I knew you'd come around. It's been such a whirlwind of a day, I thought I deserved a little sweet snack, don't you think? Those developers came by again. Two this time." She lowers her voice as she leans in closer. "They think they can take my shop and the park next to me and build a mall of sorts. They said I could have a spot inside of it for my trinkets, but they don't appreciate antiques like we do, dear." She pats my hand, not missing a beat. "They would stick me in some corner and then no one would be able to find me and what a tragedy would that be? Don't you worry though, I sent them on their way. I ain't selling, no matter how much money they throw at me. This town will keep it's dignity, I tell ya."

"Here you go, Mrs. Tootsie." Penny hands her a little baggy with a smile. "Take care of yourself."

"Thank you, sweet girl," the older woman replies before hurrying back out the door. We watch her go in silence before I turn to Penny.

"Did she seem off to you?"

"Maybe a bit, but then, she's usually a little off."

"Hmm. I wonder if the sheriff had a chance to talk to the developers. I saw a man in a suit come by flower shop when I was leaving. They're really just creeping all around here, aren't they?"

"Not that it'll do them any good. This town will take care of its own. Always does."

I let that be as Penny moves off to help another customer.

My mind is still on Mrs. Tootsie, and I decide that I will go see her today for sure. Maybe even look at those sconces.

I HAVEN'T SEEN Mabel in almost a day. I'm afraid the next time I do see her, she'll be in full-poltergeist mode. It seems like the sheriff hasn't made any progress on her case. Or maybe he has, and she's gone because it's closed.

But I know that's just wishful thinking. I can feel the heaviness of her still, just beyond reach. I have no idea what to do about it.

I make it to Trinkets and Things near closing time. There's almost no one at the store at that point, and Mrs. Tootsie beelines for me the moment I walk in.

"It's so nice to see you, darling. Come this way. I saved a few things for you to look at. I know how good they'll look in that inn of yours. Or should I say your aunt's? I guess it's both of yours, isn't it? Maybe you'll be nicer to my tastes because you and I both can see I have a good eye for these types of things."

I'm starting to get used to her rambling style of conversation, and her enthusiasm for antiques really rivals my own. She does look more tired than the last time I saw her, even from this morning.

"Mrs. Tootsie, are you feeling alright?"

"Oh, you're a sweetheart. You know how these old bones are, sometimes they're working fine, sometimes they're not. Now let me see what we can find. I'm loving the silver collection that was delivered this morning. I think you will too."

"Can I ask you a question? Will you really not sell this place to those developers?"

The old woman turns and looks me straight in the eye before replying. "This town is my home, and I want to keep it that way. Bringing in a big corporation will disturb the way things are, and we can't have that. Monroe Cove is thriving without the need for big money. The only way those vultures are getting this property is over my dead body."

I've never heard her be so assertive before, and I truly believe that she will stand by every word.

"Now, let's see those trinkets."

I follow her to the back, letting her talk. She truly has a lot to say. About thirty minutes later, I leave with a basket full of items. I'm not sure about this rivalry she mentioned with my aunt, but Auntie Grace won't be making a fuss either way when I decorate the room with these goodies.

It's gotten dark outside, and the street has cleared out of tourists. After I place the items I bought in the trunk, I go to get into my car, but something stops me. The mini park, or over-grown walkway, on the other side of Trinkets and Things seems to be staring at me.

That probably sounds crazy, but I can't think of another way to describe it. I feel a pull toward it, so I close my car and head that way.

When I step into the area, the air seems to fill with tension. I've never been sensitive before, but maybe now that I'm more open to my magic, I am developing other gifts. Being away from the prying eyes of town, I take a deep breath and let myself walk.

It's dark here with the trees looming over me. I let my mind wander over all the information I have gathered. Something is there, right beyond my reach, and I can't quite put my finger on it. So, I make a list in my mind.

Mabel was poisoned, but she was feeling sick even before then.

There have been businessmen coming in and out of town, approaching various businesses in order to purchase land.

Mabel owned land, much of which no one knew about. Only a few trusted friends.

The logical conclusion would be that one of the corporations sent someone to take care of Mabel, in whatever way possible. But while it's happened before in other towns, it doesn't seem that such a convoluted scheme would come to Monroe Cove.

No, this town is all about the small community and the personal touch. It's about knowing the people next door and meeting your neighbors at the store for a chat.

That's when I realize something. The person who had the most to gain if something happened to Mabel isn't a businessman sent from a big corporation. It's someone much closer to home.

A noise comes from behind me, and when I turn, I'm not surprised to see who it is.

Carl steps out of the shadows, but it's not his face I'm looking at. It's the silver revolver in his hand, pointed at me.

18

"You couldn't just leave it alone, could you?"

I try to play it cool, try to keep Carl talking.

"I'm not sure what you mean."

"Don't play stupid with me, Cassie. I overheard you asking Toots in there about her property. You've been asking a lot of questions. Snooping around where you don't belong. I've installed cameras at the house, did you know that? I know you've been in there."

Well, there's no reason to deny anything now. I figured it out, but I did it too late. Maybe I can stall him until I figure out my next move. Don't the villains in the story like to talk? I'm about to test that stereotype.

"You were poisoning her for a while, weren't you?" I ask, keeping my eyes trained on him and on the gun he's holding.

"How could you possibly know that? She loved her tea, you know. Or maybe you didn't since you didn't actually know her."

"You seemed so sad at the memorial service."

"I should get an Oscar for my performance, don't you think? Tears of frustration, baby. I just found out the will was being held back until the murder was solved. I had to figure out a way to speed up the investigation. It's why I agreed to speak with the sheriff."

"But it backfired, didn't it?"

"I don't know what you mean."

"He asked for tea, and you lied. I bet Mabel had a lot of tea on back order. I bet if the sheriff contacted the store, he would know. You lied straight to his face, and he'll figure it out."

"I don't think he will. I covered my tracks. Now I just need to figure out how to make it all fall on you. Maybe you were protecting your aunt. Maybe her and Mabel were in some secret war, and you did the dirty deed to help your aunt out."

"Do you hear yourself? You actually think someone will believe that?" Maybe antagonizing him isn't the best idea, but he's spiraling. I need to rein him in before he loses his mind completely and shoots me on the spot. "Was it all about the money?"

"You make it sound like the money is nothing. Twelve million dollars, Cassandra." He spits my name out like a curse. "You know what I can do with that money? Live like a king!"

"She was your aunt! Your family!"

"And she was a nasty woman who didn't listen to anyone. She did her own thing and expected everyone to bow down to her wishes."

"He's right." Mabel appears beside me, her eyes big as she looks at her nephew. There's no remorse in her face or voice though. "But he was a nasty child who needed discipline. He didn't like rules, and he didn't like me."

"She would never sell!"

I'm trying to follow both conversations at the same time. With Mabel's presence, the headache is back. I feel like I'm going to pass out before Carl figures out what to do with me.

"Protecting the town." He mocks me, his voice full of bitterness. "She could've protected me by providing for me!"

"If you stopped betting on the wrong horse, you wouldn't need the money!" Mabel shouts to be heard over his ramblings and everything falls into place.

"You have a gambling problem." It's not a question. My soft words stop his tirade. He blinks at me, stunned into silence.

"How could you possibly know that?"

"Mabel told me." I smile before she and I launch ourselves at him. The momentary distraction gives me the upper hand I need as we tumble to the ground. I may not be a self-defense queen, but I know the main areas to aim for. I jam my knee into his groin before scrambling to my feet. I have no idea what happened to the gun, but I'm not about to stick around and find out. Mabel has disappeared again, so I push off the heels of my feet and run.

Carl walked me about halfway into the park. I can't see where I threw my phone. Maybe if I get to Trinkets and Things, I can call the police. If Mrs. Tootsie is still there.

"Where do you think you're going?" Carl appears behind me, grabbing me around the waist. I kick and squirm and realize I haven't screamed yet. So, I do just that. His hand slaps over my face in the next moment, and he tosses me against the tree trunk, making my head ring. I might've also scratched my temple because a little bit of blood drip onto my cheek.

"Now I have to get messy," Carl says before he grabs me around the throat and begins to squeeze. He's full of rage. If I don't do something right now, I'm a goner. Surprisingly, even with my head bruised, I'm still thinking clearly. That's when I realize I have an upper hand that he knows nothing about.

I reach for my pockets, the rosemary and peppermint still in each one. I crush them in my hands, rubbing them over my fingers. My active magic hasn't been in proper use in ages, so I have no idea if I could do anything about it. But I can make him squirm.

His only strength here is his anger, so I do the opposite and stay calm. The next moment, I thrust my fingers into his eyes, my mind full of intention. He immediately drops his hands and starts screaming. I hold my intention, push him away from me, and once again run. I'm not two steps away when a body steps into my path. I'm ready to fight for my life here too, but then I recognize who it is.

Carl recovers long enough to launch himself at me, but Dean is there to catch him. Mean Dean is a whole head taller than Carl. With his large shoulders, he could probably stop a mob of Carls. One punch and the smaller man is out for the count. I don't even pretend to be a strong independent woman and sag against Dean in relief. He catches me, holding me up, concern etched over his features.

"Want to tell me what happened?"

"First, call the sheriff."

EVERYTHING HAPPENS SO FAST after that. The sheriff comes in flashes of blue and red. He might've already been heading this way because it only takes him two minutes to get there. Dean leads me to one of the two benches in the park area, holding a rag to my bleeding temple.

"Is that thing clean?" I ask, because of course I focus on the important things. Dean chuckles, his large hand gentle on my skin.

"Brand new from the back of my truck."

I nod, which makes my head throb more. We're sitting incredibly close, and I don't mind it. Dean makes me feel safe. The world truly did turn upside down.

Just then, Carl walks by us in handcuffs, his eye already forming a shiner. He glares at me, and I can't help but smile. He really went after the wrong woman. His first mistake was thinking I'd take any of this laying down.

"Miss Duke." Sheriff Bernard comes to the bench, his face somber. "Are you okay?"

"I'll be right as rain in no time, sheriff." I manage a smile, and I think it actually comes out somewhat decent. My body feels exhausted. I would like my bed. At least my head has stopped bleeding, thanks to Dean.

"Are you up to answering a few questions?"

"Is this necessary right now, sheriff?" Dean speaks up, and I place a gentle hand on his arm. While I love seeing him in the knight in shining armor role, I do understand how police work. After all, I'm a professional crime TV show watcher.

"You can ask me what you need right now, but I can come down to the station tomorrow, when I'm feeling better." The sheriff smiles but sobers up quickly.

"I'm sorry you were put into this situation."

"Everything happens for a reason, Sheriff." I mean to be comforting, but the moment I say the words I believe them to be true. Me coming home when I did, everything that happened with Mabel and even my aunt. All of it was needed somehow. I feel it in my bones.

"Can you tell me what transpired here tonight?"

I don't hesitate, going into detail about everything. I only leave out the part where Mabel appeared and helped me to get away. I haven't seen her since then. I wonder if that means she crossed to the other side. But that's a question for another time.

"I got a call about half an hour ago from a guy I know in Memphis. He found information on Carl's gambling."

"That's why you were heading this way?" I ask, and the sheriff nods. "Did you suspect him at all before this?"

"I did. I wasn't sure if it was my genuine dislike of the man or something else. When he told me his aunt was out of her tea, I started looking into it a bit more fully. That woman would never be out of her tea."

I smile because I knew that would raise red flags for the

sheriff. I love being right. The EMT comes over then, kneeling in front of me.

"I'm okay, really."

"You may be, but I still have to check," the woman says, her face kind. I've never seen her before, but she appears to be in her forties, and she has a mother's touch. She cleans the wound, checks my eyes and sensitivity before placing a bandage on the cut. She also looks over my throat, but Carl wasn't strong enough to do any real damage.

"I was told you hit the tree pretty hard, so I would watch for a concussion. You might develop a few bruises on the neck, but you're not experiencing any discomfort?"

"None at all," I reply truthfully.

"Then you are free to go. If you have any symptoms, give the station a call. I'll come take a look." She gives Dean a pat on the back and smiles at the sheriff before walking away.

"Should I know her?" I ask as she retreats.

"You mean my cousin Mara?" Dean asks, looking a bit confused at my question. The moment he says her name, it falls into place. She used to babysit Penny and me. I should've recognized her.

"I knew she looked familiar; I'm just a little fuzzy." I place my hand against my temple, and Dean looks pacified. I'm really going to have to figure out this memory thing soon or people will start to wonder about my mental health. Don't need any of that going around.

"Let me take you home now," Dean says. I don't argue when he helps me stand.

"What about my car?"

"I'll have Finn bring it," the sheriff calls out. I was wondering where my friend was. I'm sure I'll be getting an earful from him tomorrow about hanging out in the shady part of town. I hand over my keys and then follow Dean to his truck.

Giving the area one last look around, I still don't see Mabel.

19

My aunt is in complete uproar when Dean pulls up at the inn. The sheriff must've called her. She's standing at the front entrance, hands on her heart.

"My Cassie," she calls out when Dean helps me out of the truck. She rushes down the stairs. "My sweet child, are you okay? I'm so sorry. I'm so sorry—"

"Auntie Grace, I'm okay. You have nothing to be sorry about."

"I have everything to be sorry about. I knew Mabel was having issues with Carl for years, I should've seen this coming."

"Okay, we're going to talk about that later, but for now, could I change out of my dirty clothes, please?" Dean stays quiet beside me as he leads me inside. It's not that I'm feeling super lightheaded, but it's that I kind of want him playing nurse.

He's growing on me, fine. Don't yell at me.

"Hey." I look up at Dean as we come up to my bedroom.

Auntie Grace is already inside, pulling out clean clothes for me. "Thank you for coming to my rescue tonight."

"It seemed like you had it well under control but glad to be of assistance."

The way he smiles at me erases many of the misgivings I've had about him. His dark eyes are intense on my face, a general sense of care all around him. Maybe I've been too harsh to judge him based on the past. I might be open to the possibilities now.

"I'll see you tomorrow, okay?" he says, stepping backward out of my bedroom. I smile and nod before he shuts the door, leaving me with my aunt. She stares at me for a split second before we both reach for each other at the same time.

"Oh, my sweet, sweet girl, I don't know what I would do if anything had happened to you."

"I'm really okay, Auntie Grace." But I hug her back just as tightly. Seeing the way bitterness ate away at Carl and what a huge wall it built between he and his aunt definitely gave me a new perspective. I wouldn't want to become like him.

"Mabel helped me, Auntie Grace," I say, pulling back as she leads me to the bathroom. "But I haven't seen her since."

My aunt turns on the water, then deposits my clothes on the counter.

"I'm not sure what to tell you, sugar plum. Every ghost is different. She may have passed over the moment she received justice. She might be back in two days to get closure with you. No one can predict these things."

"You really were friends?"

"Once upon a time. Before we became frenemies. This town used to be a bit more accepting of the kind of a woman I am."

"You mean a witch?"

Auntie Grace smiles, but there's a touch of sadness there before she wipes it away.

"Let's not worry about such things. You get your pretty butt in the shower and shout if you need anything at all. I'll make you some warm soup once you're out, to help your vocal cords with some healing."

She hurries off in a flurry of skirts as I get into the shower. Thankfully, I stay upright the whole time. Once my pajamas are on, I head for my bed.

The moment I step into my room, the ping of a headache comes and then there's Mabel.

"You did it. You actually did it. Maybe you Duke women aren't as useless as I thought."

I can't help but smile at her grumbled voice. Even giving out a compliment, she's still sour about it.

"You're welcome, Mabel," I say with a smile. She huffs and puffs as I get into bed.

"My own nephew. Can't say I didn't see it coming. I'm pretty sure he's been putting poison into my tea for months."

That's what I figured when sheriff mentioned the tea. It'll be an easy check. If he had any of it left over and didn't think to get rid of it, they'll find the poison easily. He seemed a little frantic about everything, so maybe he wasn't as smart as he thought he was.

"You never really know about people, do you?" I say. Mabel grunts in agreement.

"I suppose this is where I say goodbye. I heard I get to leave this wretched in-between place now and finally move on."

"Heard? From whom?"

But Mabel isn't here to answer questions. She's giving herself, and me, the closure we need.

"Tell that aunt of yours this inn isn't half as bad of an idea as I made it out to be all those years ago. And tell her to keep Monroe Cove as safe as possible, in whatever way she can."

It's cryptic, but I'm not getting any clarification because Mabel is already starting to fade.

"It wasn't half bad meeting you again, Cassandra Duke." I

smile at her and then she's gone, the headache dissipating immediately.

"Goodbye, Mabel," I say into the empty air.

IF I THOUGHT I was being fussed over last night, I hadn't seen anything yet. Penny arrives even before I'm out of bed. She sits on my bed, her hands all over my face.

"Could you like not touch me?"

"I have to! You're alive. When Dean told me what happened I yelled at him for a good minute for keeping that quiet until this morning. You should've called immediately. We're soul sisters, I should've felt you in danger."

"Pen. Penny! Calm down. I'm okay, I promise." I grab her arms, holding them down as I peer into her face. She's paler than I've ever seen her, so I reach over and give her a hug. She holds me close, her little body exhaling in relief.

"I can't say that I imagined your little investigating would actually put you in danger, but I should've. I mean, Mabel was murdered!"

"Penny, it's fine. It's over and done with."

"You mean," she gives the room a quick scan as if she could actually see the ghost before, "she's gone?"

"Yes ma'am. Now, help me out of bed."

I grab a cardigan and put on my slippers before following Penny into the sitting room. Auntie Grace is already there, a tray full of food in her arms. As I take a seat on the couch, she places the tray in front of me with a smile.

"Good morning, sweetie pie. I wasn't sure what you would be in the mood for, but here is an array."

"You really didn't have to, Auntie Grace," I say, reaching over to give her arm a quick squeeze.

"I know sugar bun, but I wanted to. I have to get back to the front. Are you going to be okay?"

"Of course. I'm here to keep her company," Penny announces, reaching over to grab a piece of bacon off the plate. Auntie Grace slaps her hand, but she's chuckling.

"I'll be back to check on you later." I grab the coffee cup off the tray and take a sip.

My aunt leaves, and the next moment, Dean walks into the room.

"Good morning." He gives Penny a nod of acknowledgement, but his eyes are on me.

"Good morning," I reply, pulling my legs up beneath me. I look a mess, but Dean doesn't seem to mind. He gives me a once over, as if making sure for himself that I'm truly okay. He opens his mouth to say something else as Penny and I look up at him from the couch. But then, he seems to decide against it.

"I'll see you later," he says before turning and walking back out the door. Penny and I exchange a look before we bust out laughing.

"What did you do to poor Dean?" Penny asks between gasps of breath.

"Me? You're the one who yelled at him this morning!"

I shake my head, taking another swig of my coffee. That was definitely a little strange. Everything seems a little strange right now. I can't believe Mabel's killer was caught, and I was a part of that. Life really hasn't turned out the way I planned.

"You're really okay?"

"Yes."

We grow quiet, and I snuggle closer, placing my head on her shoulder. She leans hers on top of my head. We stay like that for a while. Each of us enjoying the other's company. It's been too long since I felt like I belonged anywhere, and maybe, everything I've been looking for is where I left it behind.

"So, what happens now?" Penny finally breaks the silence. I

sit up, reaching for the food on the tray. Taking a bite out of the perfectly buttered toast, I give her a look.

"I suppose I help Dean with the remodel like I was supposed to do from the beginning."

"Does that mean—" There's a flash of hope on her face. "Does that mean you're staying?"

A week ago, I would've said no. A week ago, I would've had to really think about it. Now, the answer comes easily.

"Yes, I'm staying."

EXTRA CHOCOLATE CHOCOLATE CHIP COOKIES

INGREDIENTS

- 3 cups all-purpose flour
  - 1/2 teaspoon salt
  - 3/4 cup brown sugar
  - 1/2 cup granulated sugar
  - 1 teaspoon baking soda
  - 1 and 1/2 teaspoons cornstarch
  - 3/4 cup unsalted butter (melted)
  - 1 large egg
  - 1 large egg yolk
  - 1 teaspoon pure vanilla extract (or 2)
  - 1 cup semi-sweet chocolate chips - dark chocolate
  - 1 cup - milk chocolate chips
  - 1/2 cup - white chocolate chips

INSTRUCTIONS

1. Mix flour, baking soda, cornstarch, and salt in a bowl. Set aside.

2. Mix melted butter, brown sugar, and granulated sugar together in another bowl. Add egg and then egg yolk. Pour the mixed ingredients in with the dry ingredients and stir. Add in the chocolate chips (dark and milk), then chill for 2-3 hours or overnight.

3. Once ready, take out and allow to chill to room temperature.

4. Preheat oven to 325F

5. Separate the dough and roll into balls. Press a few chocolate chips (the white chocolate ones) on the top.

6. Bake for 12-14 minutes.

7. Allow to cool for about 10 minutes before transferring off the cookie sheet.

8. Enjoy!

INSPIRED BY VARIOUS FAMILY RECIPES

TWO CAN WITCH THE GAME

CROOKED WINDOWS INN COZY
MYSTERY #2

Valia Lind

1

———

S pring has come to Monroe Cove and so has allergy season. The amount of sneezing that's currently going on within the walls of Crooked Windows Inn is making me very uncomfortable. It's not that I'm a germaphobe or anything. Germs are a part of life; I get that. But I am conscious of the fact that some people don't know how to cover their mouths when they sneeze. It makes me rethink touching any of the doorknobs.

Which is probably why I volunteered to help outside of the inn.

"Birdie, do you have to?" I exclaim, walking out of my bathroom to find the grey cat spread out on the bed, right over my black skirt. The cat gives me a look as if I'm bothering her, not the other way around, and proceeds to stretch.

"You know, I thought we were going to be friends, but I take back everything I said. I don't like you."

Birdie gives me another look before meowing once and then continuing to lick her paws. I really did think I got over my dislike of furry creatures, but nope. This cat is going to get on my last nerve. She's already nearly there. I don't care how strange it is for me to be a witch who dislikes cats. Birdie and I are inching toward an all out war.

When I pull my skirt from beneath her not so tiny body, it's covered in fur. I give the cat another strong glare before marching to the bathroom and the lint roller I purchased a few weeks ago. The sticky part is almost gone, so I make a mental note to pick up another one.

Glancing at the clock, I realize I'm running late.

"Thanks for nothing, Birdie," I mumble, pulling the skirt over my hips before rushing into the bedroom to grab my boots. It might be warming up outside, but I'm going to wear these babies for as long as I can.

"Sugar plum, are you a little late?" Auntie Grace greets me as I speed walk out of our own hallway and into the main foyer of the inn. Having my own and Auntie Grace's side of the inn all to ourselves is heaven sent. I love our small library and spacious rooms.

I'll never get over just how beautiful and authentic this place is. The wooden accent has been preserved wonderfully over the years, still carrying that fresh smell. The last part is no doubt Auntie Grace's magic's doing, but I don't mind. It makes me feel at home. Which is something I didn't think was possible.

"That cat decided my black skirt was her favorite lounging place." I grunt while Auntie Grace chuckles. "It's not funny."

"It is too, honey pie. That cat, as you so affectionately call her, has got your number."

"Cats don't do that."

"You can do magic, honey bunches. And you think cats can't find which buttons of yours to push?" She gives me a look which I try very hard to ignore. Talk of magic isn't my favorite, okay? Sue me. I haven't exactly had the best go of it lately. I lost my big city job because of a mishap. And even before "lately"

I've had more problems with magic than any sane person should. Auntie Grace keeps telling me it's in my blood, and I'll learn how to control it. All *I* want is to push it out of my mind.

"Well, I'm off to help Penny. I'll see you later."

I turn with a little wave and slam right into a hard chest. Air leaves my lungs in a woosh. I would've fallen backward if the arms attached to the said hard chest didn't grab onto me, pulling me forward. I land right against him, my hands planted between us. When I raise my head up, I meet the amused face of none other than Mean Dean, childhood nemesis turned handyman.

Okay, I'm trying really hard to stop calling him that, I promise. But it's a process. Rome wasn't built in a day.

"In a bit of a rush, are we?" Dean says. I can feel his chuckle under my fingertips. The movement is quite intimate, and that's when I realize I'm still plastered to him.

"I have places to be," I hurry to reply, taking a step back. I also ignore the way my body instantly wants to be back in his arms.

Stupid, traitorous body.

"Have you had your coffee yet? You're a little dangerous without it."

My shoulders snap back, all thought of intimacy forgotten, as I give Dean my best glare.

"I am a grown woman. I am perfectly capable of functioning without coffee."

This time, it's my aunt who chuckles. I turn to throw her a look. When I meet Dean's eyes again, his haven't lost the amusement.

"That's it. The nickname stays," I mumble, receiving a quick confused look before I push past him and out the door. Most of the time, I can give as good as I get. But when it comes to Mean Dean, my tongue decides to stop working. Which makes me a nutcase in his presence.

So impressive, I know.

Whatever and whatever. Penny and I used to say that when we wanted to move on from a topic, and I'm bringing it back.

"Oh no." I glance at my phone, seeing what time it is. I should've been at Penny's by now.

Pushing all thoughts of Dean out of my head, I get into my car and drive toward Main Street.

OF COURSE, all I'm doing on the way to Penny's is thinking about him. My day would start like that. I couldn't just, you know, have a good morning. But, no, I get a run in with Mean Dean. Well, and a fur covered skirt.

Okay, okay, I'm back to thinking maybe I shouldn't call him that anymore. He did kind of help me out last time. But I still can't shake off my childhood or the memories that I carry with me. Especially after Auntie Grace decided to drop a huge truth bomb on me and told me there are memories of my childhood that have been erased by magic.

Yes, I have to live with that information like nothing is wrong.

Anyway, that has nothing to do with anything, and today is not about me, it's about Penny. Since spring has come to Monroe Cove, so has the annual Bake Off, and Penny, being the baking goddess that she is, of course, has to participate. That's putting it lightly, she's basically in charge of making sure the event runs smoothly because of said expertise. It's a lot. I am determined to help her do—well—everything so she can focus on the baking. I'll be helping out during the day and running her bakery when needed while she preps all the baking stuff for the bake off.

"Good morning, sunshine," I say, when I step into Penny's bakery a few minutes later.

Penny, my poor friend, is already running around like a crazy person trying to serve the customers. Monroe Cove has always been a place for tourists. The quaint little town holds enough charm to attract singles and families alike. Close enough to the water for boating adventures and such, yet far enough away to be isolated by the forest on every side. It's a unique experience. The minute it starts warming up and spring break and family vacation time comes, it is filled with new people and families.

"Oh, good. You're here," Penny says. "Can you please make sure the coffee is ready and being served?"

"Wait. What are you talking about?" I ask. "Don't you sell coffee here?"

"Yes," Penny says. "We do sell coffee here, but there's also a table outside with free coffee, so that we can advertise the bake off."

I came in through the back, so I clearly missed an important new feature.

"Oh, wow. That seems like a good idea," I say scrunching my eyebrows. Not that I don't love free coffee, but that seems like a less than smart business decision. I don't want Penny to be missing out on customers.

"Don't look at me like that, Cassie," Penny says. "It is a good idea, and plus, it wasn't really my idea. It was the mayor's."

"Yes, of course, the mayor." That man has been a special kind of a thorn in a lot of people's sides.

"Oh, that's right." Penny doesn't miss my tone. "You haven't met Mayor Moore yet."

"Wait, Mayor Moore. Are you serious about this?" I ask. "What happened to old Mister Gary the Rude Mayor?"

Yes, I have a nickname for everyone. Even though they're not very original.

"He got nudged out, very nicely and firmly." Penny says. "Of course, there's a woman in charge now. We are very progressive around here." She winks at me.

I laugh at that because Monroe Cove has always been big on tradition. As far as I know, they have always had a male mayor, from the same family mind you, mostly because of that said tradition. We've had some really awesome women candidates in the past, but nothing ever stuck. At least not when I lived here. Huh. I guess things really do change.

"Okay, fine," I say. "I'll go outside and make sure people get some free coffee, so they can come in here and not buy it."

"Cassie, they'll come in here and buy some baked goods to go with that coffee." Penny smiles. "Don't worry. I'm still making a profit."

"You better be."

She smirks at me as she hands me a clipboard.

"Also, please try to get people to sign up for the bake off. We're having a bunch of different booths, and it will be great to see a big crowd participating."

"Okay, okay." I glance down at the empty sheet. "I'll just do my part, and shut my mouth. Ha."

"You have never just done your part and shut your mouth, Cassandra Duke," Penny says. "And I love you for it. Now please, get to it?"

"I'm gettin'. Am I allowed to have the free coffee?"

"You can have as much as you want. Wait—" She raises her hand, realizing her mistake. "You can have some, with enough left for the majority of the customers."

She smirks again, and I roll my eyes. I love coffee, okay? No crime in that.

Leaving Penny to her pastries, I head past the busy line and step outside. The table has already been set up with two coffee dispensers. Justin, one of Penny's few employees, is standing in front of it.

"Oh good, you're here."

"I'm here."

Without another word, Justin turns to the table, flipping up the sign that says "Free Coffee" and walks toward the bakery's door.

"It's all yours."

I reach over to grab a cup, ready for some deliciousness. But before I can pour myself one, two women walk up, chattering away, and ask for one. Then a family is there, and I realize—it's going to be a long day.

2

By the time lunch comes around, the coffee dispensers have been refilled five times. Surprise, surprise, it has nothing to do with me drinking it like water, as Auntie Grace likes to put it. I only had one cup, and it was mostly warm. People really do flock to the freebies. I have to begrudgingly admit it was a good idea. If Penny isn't losing out on money, I'm good to go. And she isn't. Almost every single person I helped went into the bakery afterward and bought a pastry. I've also managed quite a few signups for the bake off, which is slightly surprising. I guess people really do enjoy a good pie.

"Hello there. You must be Cassandra Duke."

The woman who stops in front of the table is the most put together person I have ever seen. Her button-down blouse and pencil skirt look pressed while her polished heels click against the pavement. Her blonde hair is shoulder length, and it's so smooth and shiny I wonder if it's magic. My own red hair hangs past my back. It's more than unruly at times and always just a little bit frizzy because it is not a fan of humidity.

The fact that she knows my name is a little unsettling, but then I realize who she is.

"You must be Mayor Moore. I've heard great things."

"Likewise."

She smiles, and I have to say, she seems nice. I'm not used to thinking that about Monroe Cove's political...individuals. But I'm not getting any bad vibes from her, and that's interesting.

"If the information came from Penny, it's only half true." I return her smile.

"Actually, Mary Grace speaks very highly of you. As do Finn and Dean Harvey."

Finn I understand, but Dean surprises me. What does that mean exactly? It's not as if Dean and I were ever friends, so why would he be speaking highly of me to the mayor? He was the bane of my existence growing up. We've only recently started to mend our—do I call it friendship? I'm not sure what it is, to be honest.

Ugh, Dean. Always invading my every breathing moment. That pest.

Quickly, I push all those thoughts away, hoping the mayor doesn't notice my distraction.

"I have also heard that you are quite the interior designer. I would like to speak to you about that when you get a chance."

A job? Outside of the inn? Abso-freaking-lutely. Is pumping a fist into the air considered unprofessional? Asking for a friend.

"Of course. I can come by your office Monday morning," I say instead, keeping my voice fully professional.

"Sounds great."

"Would you like a cup?" I ask as the mayor begins to move toward the bakery.

"Yes, thank you."

After she leaves, I try very hard not to do a happy dance. It may not seem like a lot, and while I love renovating the inn, there's something special about an interior designer job for an outsider. It challenges me, and I love a good challenge.

Seeing someone else's vision and then making it come to life has always been my favorite part of design. Not that I don't enjoy making my own vision come together. It's just that right now, renovating the inn, my vision is very limited, considering I want to keep the majority of the inn as is. This feels like what I was looking for—a fresh start. A way to let my imagination soar. I'm excited, to say the least.

The door to the bakery opens again, and this time, Justin steps out.

"What's up?" I ask, giving him a brilliant smile. He blinks for a second, as if I've shocked him, before clearing his throat.

"Penny said we can put the table away for the day. I'll help you clean up."

"Thanks!"

Picking up the tray with the leftover cups, I place the clipboard on top and head for the bakery. Lunch time is usually a little quieter, but then Penny gets hit with a crowd an hour or so after. All those healthy meals must be followed up by a yummy dessert. It's a pattern.

I use my back to hold the door open for Justin just as Penny comes over to help. She takes the clipboard from me.

"Oh, wow. That's quite a few participants. People really do like free coffee."

"People like free anything," I smile, placing the tray on the counter. Justin gives me another long look before disappearing in the back with the dispensers.

"You should really stop flirting with my staff," Penny comments, walking around the counter and pulling out a danish for each of us.

"What? Me? Flirt?"

"Oh please. That smile blinded poor Justin here into stupor."

"Poor Justin there is barely out of high school," I point out, but that makes sense. I was probably way too excited when he came out, and he might've thought it was about him.

"Mhmm." Penny places a plate in front of me as I take a seat at the counter.

"Never mind that, Penelope," I say, leaning forward. "Guess who I met?"

"Mayor Moore?" My friend doesn't even hesitate. Oh, that's right. The woman came in here after she left me.

"Yes, smarty pants," I reply, unable to contain my excitement. "And she invited me over for a consultation. I'm meeting with her Monday."

"That's amazing, Cassie! No wonder you're beaming."

"Oh, Pen. If I get this job, if I do a good job at it, maybe people in this town will take my interior design seriously, and I can finally start doing jobs again." The wistful note in my tone is impossible to miss.

"It'll work out. You know it and I know it. Now don't you have a lunch date?"

I glance down at my phone, realizing what day it is.

"I completely forgot!" I jump down from the seat, stuffing the rest of the danish into my mouth in a most unladylike fashion before I race for the door. "I'll be back before close!" I call out. Penny's laughter follows me out.

"You forgot, didn't you?" Finn Harvey greets me when I reach the diner.

"I could say no?" I reply, shrugging. My friend shakes his head before reaching over to give me a hug. I've known Finn for almost as long as I've known Penny, and he's the closest thing to a brother I have. He knows me too well for a lie of any kind. Also, his hugs always make me feel grounded somehow.

"I thought you were off duty?" I ask, pulling back and glancing down at his uniform.

"The sheriff called me in because of all the extra people traffic." Finn holds the door open for me and I step into the diner. No kidding on the extra people traffic. The place is packed.

"Has it always been this popular?"

"In the last few years, the bake off and everything that goes with it has really taken off. A big thanks to Penny and her creativity with it all." I glance at him as Finn waves at Dan and the man behind the counter points to the side of the room.

"Better grab it now." Sue Lynn hurries over, handing us two menus before she's off to deliver the plate she's holding in her other hand.

Finn leads me to the table Dan saved for us, and we take a seat. Since coming back, I've been trying to work on my friendships. Especially with Finn. I let a lot of it go when I moved away. But he seems to have forgiven me for it.

"How are things at the bakery?" he asks once we've looked over the menus. Not that I'm not just going to order Dan's special. In small diner fashion, he changes it daily, and it's always the best thing. I trust him. What I don't trust is Finn's way too innocent sounding question. I noticed this earlier, but now I'm wondering if I should press it.

"Things are good," I reply, leaning over the table to stare him down. He doesn't even flinch at my antics, mirroring my motions until we're staring at each other very intensely. It's like we're thirteen years old again, seeing who will win the battle of wills.

"What ya doing, Cassie?" Finn asks, not moving from his position.

"Seeing if I can stare into your soul," I reply, completely serious. But he laughs, and that makes him move. "Ha!"

He laughs harder, leaning back. I smile. This may be

beyond silly, but it makes me feel like the good old days where I didn't leave, and we didn't have a care in the world.

"Ask me what you want to ask me, Cassandra," Finn comments, pinning me with his gaze. This time, I mirror his posture, folding my arms across my chest.

"What are your intentions toward Penelope?"

There's a pause in the air, as if the whole diner just heard my question. If I wasn't watching Finn so closely, I would've missed the little twitch at the corner of his mouth.

"I knew it!" I spring forward, pointing my finger at him.

"I didn't say anything."

"You didn't have to."

Before he can reply, Sue Lynn is there, and I stop my probing. If she hears anything, it'll get back to Penny before even I do. I forgot that little part about small towns, so I need to be more careful. After she takes our orders, she doesn't linger, being called back by another table.

"Cassandra Duke," Finn leans over to whisper. "Did you forget where you are?"

"For a second. But she didn't hear anything. Not that there was anything to hear, but now that you're doing this," I wave my hand between us, "it makes me sure there's something there."

"Okay fine," my friend gives in. "But don't say anything. I think Penny is great, but it's not like that between us. I don't want to ruin our friendship."

A part of me thinks he has nothing to worry about, but I'm not about to spill Penny's secrets either. I love them both dearly and would actually love for this to happen. But I'm an interior designer, not a matchmaker. I'm not pulling any Auntie Grace shenanigans on them. Even though I kind of want to.

"Don't you be thinking things, Cassie," Finn warns, knowing full well I'm thinking things.

"I don't know what you mean."

"Sure you don't. As if I haven't been a part of enough of your schemes to know better."

That makes me grin. Finn really has been such a huge part of my life. And then I ran away. Maybe I shouldn't say it, but it feels like I must.

"I *am* sorry, you know." I lean back over, my features somber. "I never meant to abandon you."

"Ah, Cassie, don't do that. You needed to leave. I will never fault you for chasing your dreams."

He makes it sound so noble. But now, I'm not sure if I was chasing my dreams or just running from my demons. Sue Lynn brings over our food then, and we dig in without hesitation.

For the longest time, I thought of this town as a place full of bad memories. But now I realize, I left a lot of good behind. It's nice to have a second chance at it.

3

———————

"**P**enny, I'm here!" I call out as I step into the bakery right before closing. After lunch with Finn, I ran a bunch of errands for the inn, but now I'm back as promised.

The bakery is empty. There are only a few tables that still need to be cleaned up. Glancing at the clock hanging over the counter, I realize it is closing time, so I lock the door behind me and flip the sign to "Closed". I'm a little concerned that Penny left the front of the bakery like this, so I hurry to the back.

Penny is standing beside the table, covered in flour and something else that's a little gooey. She looks up when I enter, giving me a panicked look.

"Penny? What's going on?"

"I don't know, Cassie! I went to put the flour into the mixer and when I turned around the mixer it—it just turned on!"

"Turned on by itself?" I ask, carefully. My friend looks like she's either about to pass out or scream. I'm not sure which one I prefer, to be honest.

"Yes, exactly. I was way too far away to have accidentally bumped it, but it just turned on, spraying flour everywhere.

And the jelly custard I made is now dripping down my apron." She sighs, glancing down.

I step closer, giving Penny a once over. She is covered in baking things. Maybe I should've cut my errand run short and came back sooner. But it is what it is. Now, let's deal with the issue at hand.

"Okay. Don't panic. It's okay. Let me take a look while you go clean up. Okay?"

"Okay."

Penny disappears into the bathroom off the side of the kitchen area, while I approach the mixer carefully, considering my options.

I'm a witch. I know things can be made alive by just a few little words of a spell. Taking slow steps toward the mixer, I try to reach out with my magic and see if I can sense anything. I don't pick up any malicious spirits or any black magic, which is my first concern.

Black magic is a nuisance in the magic community. Even though I've been out of it for years, I still know how black magic witches affect all the good regular witches can do. There is something here, an energy, but I can't tell if it's just Penny's essence or something else.

Granted, I'm not the best at this. Auntie Grace would have much better luck trying to figure out if there is any magic use in the shop. But I will give it my best try. When I don't sense anything, I reach over and unplug the mixer.

Carefully, I pick it up and turn it over to see if there are any stripped wires or anything that could've jolted the mixer. But there's nothing. It really does seem like the mixer came alive and threw the flour all over Penny.

"Well?" she asks, as she steps back in, this time cleaned up.

"I don't know, Pen. I don't see anything that would have caused it. Has it ever happened before?"

"No," she replies.

But there's a slight hesitation in her voice, and I pick up on it.

"Penelope. What are you not telling me?" I ask.

She takes a second to reply as if thinking it over first.

"Well, I don't know if this is anything but, yesterday I had problems with the oven."

"What do you mean?"

"Well, when I went to turn it on, it wouldn't turn on at all. I tried everything, unplugging it and plugging it back in. When I did finally manage to turn it on, it kind of made a weird noise. And there were rocks inside of it."

"What do you mean inside of it?" I ask.

"Umm, when I opened the top. There were rocks inside. Right under the top rack. And I swear they weren't there when I first opened the oven to check. It's like they appeared later."

That's concerning.

"Okay, so how would that happen?" I muse out loud. Penny leads me to the other side of the kitchen where the oven stands. I reach out with my magic, trying to see if I can pick anything up off it. But still, I get nothing.

"I don't know, Cassie, I have no idea what's going on, but it's like, I don't know, maybe I'm cursed or something. Are curses real?"

I don't want to alarm her, but I do need to be honest with my friend. So, I nod.

"Yes, curses are real, and hexes can be placed on basically anyone. Even a new inexperienced witch can make someone's life a little more difficult if she wanted to, but I don't know. Who would do that to you, Penny?"

"I have no idea, Cassie. I don't know any witches besides you and your aunt. Are there any other ones in town?"

"Oh, well, maybe? I have no idea, Penny. I've been gone for so long. I don't know anything about the coven. When I left, I left all that behind. I know Auntie Grace is all involved in it so I suppose I can ask her, but I've never heard of another witch living in Monroe Cove."

She mulls that over.

"Okay, so if it's not another witch then what is it? Bad luck?"

"I'm not sure, Penny. How about for now, we just go and make those pastries you were planning on making tonight, and I'll see what I can find out on my end."

"You think the mixer isn't going to attack me again?" Penny asks, eyeing the machine.

"Well, if it does, I'll be here to protect you." She gives me a tentative smile. "After all, what are best friends for?"

THE NEXT MORNING, I'm up earlier than usual because I decided I have research to do. When I told Penny I would talk to my aunt, I meant it. But she's also been a bit busy with all the extra people coming into town, so I didn't get to yet. My best plan of attack is to do my own research, while I wait for Auntie Grace to come out of her room.

"Cassie, what are you doing?" Auntie Grace asks as she steps into the small library that separates my room and her room at the back of the inn. But she doesn't come from her room. She's already been up and cooking in the kitchen by the looks of her apron.

"I'm reading," I reply, happy that my plan worked somewhat. She's intrigued. She can't escape me now.

"Yes, I can see that, honey bun. But you're reading a magic book."

I understand where the confusion is coming from. I have been actively trying to stay away from magic for a while now. But now that I'm back in Monroe Cove and trying to learn more about the crazy that's been going on with my magic, I've been trying to sneak in some magic study just so that I don't get

Auntie Grace too excited about being, you know, involved again.

"Yes, Auntie. I am reading a magic book, but it's not for me."

"What do you mean?" she asks, coming over to the love seat to glance down at the pages.

"I mean there is something weird going on at Penny's, and I need to figure out how to help her." I sigh.

"You want to tell me about it, sweetie pie?"

"I do actually. "

I take a deep breath, putting the book down and turning to face my aunt. She takes the seat opposite of mine, folding her hands over her lap with and inquisitive stare. She always has a way of making me want to tell her everything and also not tell her anything at the same time. It's a weird kind of a gift.

I'm not sure if others would call it a gift, but it doesn't matter. My mind is still in the process of figuring out if it's a good idea talking magic with my aunt. She's kept so many secrets from me over the years. But this isn't about me. It's about Penny. So, I'm diving in.

"Auntie Grace? Is there another witch in town? Or you know, a coven or something?"

"Why do you need to know?" Auntie Grace asks. Her voice is completely innocent, but I can tell there's something underneath.

"I'm gonna take that as a yes," I say, giving her a long look.

"Maybe, maybe not. I'm gonna need more information than that, sweetie pie."

"Well, something's been going on at Penny's, and it's a little weird, but it seems like she's been—cursed. Her oven ended up with rocks in it, and then last night, a mixer attacked her."

"What do you mean attacked her? Like Maximum Override attacked?" she asks, surprising me. I had no idea Auntie Grace knew anything about horror movies.

"No, more like it turned on by itself. It didn't actively come alive to murder her. She ended up covered in flour, so it's more of a nuisance than anything. But it's strange. There's no way she could have done that accidentally. She was too far away to bump it, or anything." I raise my eyebrows, as if to drive home a point.

"Yes, that does sound a little bit suspicious."

"A little bit? It's not like normal people are used to appliances just turning on around them."

"I suppose. But I don't know of any of the witches in town who would do such a thing."

That makes me pause.

"What do you mean, any? There's more than one?"

"There are a few of us who have stayed around. The official coven has made its home in Williams. The few who still live here don't really practice in the open, more like in the background, guiding the town in the right direction."

Williams is two towns over and is a bit more populated than Monroe Cove. Also, it's closer to the water. I know witches take it upon themselves to look out for whatever town or city they live in. I guess I shouldn't be surprised Monroe Cove is like that. What I am surprised by is the amount of information my aunt keeps hiding from me.

"Ah, I see, and I feel like you are keeping way too many secrets from me for my liking. I'm going to need more information than that."

"Oh, honey bun. I don't think you're ready for more information. But I will tell you what. I will talk to them and see if anybody has felt any disturbances in the magical world. How about that?" She stands then, without giving me a chance to reply, and I know that it's the best I'm going to get from her.

"Okay, Auntie Grace. Thank you."

I want to ask her another million questions, but it's going to be of no use. Plus, magic talk isn't exactly my favorite topic. Right now, I'm still trying to deal with the fact that my whole childhood has been affected by it in a way that I didn't even know about until very, very recently.

"Oh, and Cassie?" Auntie Grace calls as she reaches her room. "Dean is looking for you."

I groan while rolling my eyes. Of course he is because I just need another issue on my plate full of issues right now.

4

There's a possibility that Dean and I will never see eye to eye but we kind of have to when it comes to this project. I mentally prepare myself for him as I head upstairs and toward the wing of the inn we're renovating.

"Well, good morning there, Cassie," Dean says as I enter the room.

"Good morning, Dean," I reply, keeping my smile in place. Yes, I may be using my customer service smile on him, but it's better than the grimace I want to have on my face. It's not that I don't appreciate what he did for me, or how nice he's been or how helpful, but there is a certain kind of a memory that just won't let me go. And so instead, I am stuck being professional and...cautious around him.

Yes, cautious is a good word, I am going to stick with it.

"So, what do you have planned for us today?" Dean asks as I continue walking around the room and study the walls and the progress he's made while I've been helping out Penny.

"I was thinking we really should get some wallpaper on this one wall."

"Just this one wall?"

"Yes." I turn, giving him a cold look. "Is there a problem?"

"No, no problem, but I just thought you wanted to keep this as close to the original as possible."

"Well yes, which is why I think the wallpaper that goes here should be the original wallpaper. The rest of the walls can be painted a color to accent it, and the sitting chair will go right here." I point to a spot in front of the wall that will rest in front of the wallpaper.

"We can add a lamp and a table, and this can be the perfect sitting area for guests."

"Okay." Dean looks around, studying the walls, and then the spot that I pointed out. "I think I can see it."

"Well, technically, you don't really have to see it because I'm going to make it happen." I grin at him, this time, my smile is entirely genuine. He blinks a few times, as if coming out of a fog before he smirks.

"Ah yes, I get it. I'm the muscle. You're the brain."

"Okay, I don't think I appreciate that tone of voice, mister." I say, my tone more teasing than I'd like it to be, placing my hands on my hips.

There's another moment of silence. Now that I'm paying attention, it seems like something is bothering him. I'm expecting him to speak up, make a joke, but he says nothing.

"Is there something you want to say to me?" I ask folding my arms in front of me.

"There's a lot that I want to say to you," Dean replies. I have no idea how to take that or the soft way he delivered those words. He gives me another long look as if he's trying to see inside of me. And then he turns away.

"I'll get that wallpaper for you. And I can start on the colors. They'll need to be mixed to match exactly. They don't sell this shade of green in town anymore."

The sudden shift in energy throws me through a loop.

"Dean," I call out as he turns to leave the room. He stops, slightly inclining his head to the side, as if he's listening.

"Thank you." The words come out before I can think too much of them. There are a million questions on the tip of my tongue, but I settle on the simple two-word sentence.

It's not like we're friends. If it's something personal, he's not going to want to tell me. And I still don't know how I feel about being around him, not when I carry too many memories inside of me.

Too many bad things happened in my life, and I don't know if I can really truly trust that he has my best interest at heart. Although, if I'm being fair, I should remember that he did kind of help me with a problem I had when it came to a little murder mystery. But I don't know, I don't trust anybody right now, least of all Dean. He gives me another nod before he leaves me with my thoughts.

Focus, Cassie. You have things to do. People to see. I take out my phone, trying to make a few notes of the things that I need to get, when I look at the time. Oh no. I have to go. What is it with me being constantly late all of a sudden? I have to meet Penny at her bakery.

And I need coffee.

I SPENT the whole day running errands for Penny. Mostly because her unreliable worker decided not to show up again. Justin was there, of course, and took care of the front while Penny multitasked. But she's had a bunch of deliveries today, and since Mary didn't show up, that's what I did. It's closing time now, and I'm ready for some rest and relaxation.

I walk into the bakery just as a scream reaches my ears.

"Penny!" I call out. "Are you okay?"

There's another loud bump, and then another yelp. I place

the coffee—yes, I'm drinking coffee at night—on the table on the counter and rush for the kitchen. I freeze right inside the doorway, my eyes taking in the whole room and the mixer next to Penny, which is currently smoking.

"Penny?" I approach cautiously as my friend continues to stare at the mixer.

"I don't know what's going on, Cassie. I don't understand. I went to turn this on, and it just went up in flames. And then smoke and then—"

"Okay, okay," I say, "Let's take a step back."

I pull Penny away and approach the mixer.

"Is this the same one that gave you problems last time?"

"No, this is a different one."

When I take a closer look, I do see it's a little bit bigger and the shade of turquoise is a little bit darker.

"How many of these do you have?"

"Cassie, I run a bakery." A little bit of my friend's humor returns to her voice. "I have at least," she pauses, "ten." The tiny smile on her face makes me feel better about her state of mind.

"Okay. All right. So you use different ones for different things, such as?"

"Yes, for example, my cakes get the turquoise mixer. The cookies get the yellow one. And so on. I was just trying to see if maybe I shouldn't use the other turquoise one since it was giving me issues. And now, I don't know, it's like everything I touch seems to just crumble in front of me." Her voice rises as she speaks, the panic clearly setting back in.

"Hmm. Something is definitely going on. All your appliances can't go up in flames just because. There has to be a reason."

"Well, that's what I think, too, but I can't even imagine what the reason could be." She looks worn out, and I can't blame her. The last few days have been trying. Considering this place lives off freshly baked goods, not having those readily available is difficult.

"And there's more."

That stops me. "What do you mean?"

"I think I'm missing some supplies. I've been so distracted I can't be sure though. Maybe they just weren't delivered."

That is curious. She's panicking a little, and who can blame her?

"So, let's figure it out," I begin, keeping my tone calming. But my voice of reason isn't working anymore.

"How, how are we going to figure it out? I don't even know how these things are happening. It's not a normal —occurrence!"

I study my friend. I can't find a way to disagree with her. The poor thing has been having way too many issues, and my aunt still hasn't given me any indication that she talked to the witches in town. Or out of town. Or wherever they may be hiding.

"I'm cursed."

"Pen, we talked about this. You're not. Someone is doing this."

"How can you be sure?"

That's the thing. I can't. But...

"Maybe...maybe there's something I can do." I say.

"What do you mean?"

"Well, I can't exactly feel if there is any magic at work here. That's beyond my powers. But I might be able to put together a protection spell of sorts."

My friend stands up a little taller at that.

"You can do a protection spell for this?"

"Actually, I don't know," I reply honestly. Considering I've been so hesitant about all things magic, I don't even remember the basics at this point. It's frustrating that I don't remember much of what I learned when I was younger, but that's very much been explained now that Auntie Grace told me the truth about my childhood. But I digress.

"I don't know, Penny, but I can try. First, I need to figure out if there is any kind of magic in play here. I don't want to mess with what's here but maybe?"

I know I keep saying that a lot, but I don't want to give her false hope. Yet, I do want to help. It would be easier if I didn't have such an aversion to all things magical. But my childhood has really proven to stick around. One of these days I'll deal with it all. But for now, one problem at a time.

"Thank you, Cassie. For even offering."

Penny is the only other person, beside my aunt, who knows everything now. She understands how nervous I am about opening up the magical wounds. But for now, I smile at my friend.

"Let's just get this cleaned up, shall we? And we'll go from there. I'll stay and help."

"No, you don't have to," Penny hurries on to say, but I wave her off.

"Penny, I'm not going anywhere. I'm helping. And then we can figure out our next step after."

She looks like a weight is lifted off her shoulders. I smile. Approaching the mixer carefully, I make sure it's unplugged before I move it off the counter and by the back door. Somehow the flour got everywhere, so Penny and I clean off the countertop and the floor first before Penny carries everything outside. Picking up the mixer, she gives it a long stare.

When she notices my look, she shrugs.

"It was the first mixer I bought when I bought the place."

Ah, that makes sense. Penny worked for years to earn enough with her baking and other odd jobs to finally be able to afford the building. I remember what a big deal it was. She came out to the city to see me so we could celebrate. It would've been the only reason for me to come back. But Penny, being the saint that she is, refused. She wanted to celebrate in a "big city style", as she put it. I don't have to be a genius to know she did it for me.

I lean against the doorway, holding the door open as Penny carries the mixer out to the back dumpsters.

"It's just a mixer, right?" she comments. And then she screams.

"Penny?" I rush over immediately. She holds the mixer to her chest, staring at something in the darkness. Without hesitation, I move past her to get a better look, and my heart sinks. Then, her small voice utters what I'm looking at.

"Cassie, is that a dead body?"

5
___

We don't hesitate to call the police. I make sure to push Penny back inside, and away from the crime scene before we do. She's a little shell shocked.

"Miss Duke," Sheriff Bernard says as he comes up to me. "How is it that you always seem to find yourself in the middle of these...issues?"

Issues is a nice word to use but I don't comment.

"Oh, Sheriff. I am just here to support my friend."

"Right. And last time you were just here to support your aunt. Two murders, and you are at both locations. To find the bodies nonetheless."

The urge to take on a defensive pose almost overwhelms me, but I know he won't respond well to that. So, I keep my arms at my sides, trying to appear as harmless as possible. Not that I should have to prove anything.

"What is it you are trying to say?" I ask, giving the sheriff a long look. He pauses but doesn't answer. I realize he might actually think I had something to do with this. Or maybe he suspects something about my magic and thinks I am bringing a curse on his town.

Welp, not exactly sure where that last thought came from. It's a pretty big stretch, considering Sheriff Bernard has no idea about any of this magic. I really shouldn't put my "issues" with magic on other people.

But I can also understand why he is suspicious. I have been at the scene of two murders in this town in the last couple of months. That seems like a lot.

I'm a little concerned myself.

"Do you know the woman?" the sheriff asks. A few minutes ago, I saw the coroner head to the back where the victim is propped up against the dumpster, so I'm assuming they don't know much either. Yet.

We saw the blood though, on her temples, so I'm assuming it's a head wound.

"No, sir," I reply.

"I think I know her." I hear Penny's little voice speak up as she comes up to stand beside me. She's a wreck. I can understand why. But her words take me by surprise. Sheriff too, although he's probably better at not showing it.

"What do you mean, Miss Sharks?"

"She's been visiting here for the last couple of spring semesters. I think maybe she is a teacher or something like that and there is a Spring Break during this time of the year. She always comes up, and she comes in and gets a dark coffee and a lot of cream, no sugar, but she always buys three of the danishes, and then goes and sits outside and explores the town like she's never been here before." The words rush out of Penny all in one breath.

"Miss Sharks, you really know your customers, don't you?" Sheriff Bernard says, cocking his head to the side.

"Yes, Sheriff. Dark roast, a pinch of cinnamon and whole milk, right?" Penny replies, a little more fire back in her gaze. I can tell the sheriff feels put in his place. That's my best friend right there. I try not to cheer out loud.

"That's part of why Penny's is so popular," Penny continues. "I try to be very personable with the customers who come in. Especially familiar faces."

"That makes you a great host," I say, rubbing my hand up and down her arm. She smiles, leaning into me a little.

I just wish I could protect her from all of this, my little five-foot-two best friend is not made out for murder. Not that I am either or want to be for that matter. But I've always thought of Penny as a sister, and I'd protect her if I could. From all the bad in the world.

"Has she been in this spring season?" the sheriff asks.

"No, actually," Penny replies. "I don't think I've seen her since last spring. But I don't know, with the bake off being a huge event this year, we have been a little busy, so I haven't been at the counter as much as usual."

"Do you know who has?"

"Well..." Penny looks off into the distance, trying to think. "Justin has been working a lot. He covers the counter for me. And I think that's about it. Oh, Cassie has been in the shop a lot too, but other than that, I don't think anybody else has been by to really help out."

The sheriff makes a few notes in his notepad, very old fashioned, but I kind of like it.

"Don't you have another employee baker?" he asks.

"Yes, Mary. She helps out with cookies. And deliveries. She's been a little flaky lately. I'm not sure... " Penny gives me a quick look as if she's looking for my help, but I'm not exactly clear on what she wants me to say here. Having mind reading powers would come in handy in this situation, and actually in the whole "looking for a killer situation," but I'm digressing. Again. "I'm not sure what's been going on with her," she finally says.

"What does that mean?" the sheriff asks.

"I don't know, she's just been a little weird lately. She's been dropping dishes and breaking things, and I just didn't want her around the place after everything that's been going on."

Ah, there it is.

I'm the only one who knows about her little mishaps lately. She's not about to go around saying she's cursed. But I suppose if we truly believe someone is behind this, the sheriff needs to know.

"What has been going on?" the sheriff prompts, looking between the two of us.

Penny gives me another side glance.

"Oh, just tell him," I say, finally, because it feels best not to keep any information from the police at this point.

"What is it that you're not telling me, Miss Sharks?" Sheriff turns his full attention to my friend. She shrinks into herself a little, so, I jump in.

"Sheriff, I think Penny has been sabotaged."

"What does that mean?"

"It means that her appliances have been bursting into flames, and she's been missing orders, and I don't know, supplies have gone missing." I point in the direction of the kitchen. "We were cleaning up one of these messes when we stumbled on our discovery."

"Why haven't you said anything?" There's genuine concern in Sheriff Bernard's voice now and that's small towns for you.

"I don't know," Penny replies. "I was just hoping that it was going to go away."

"Well, whatever is going on, now we have a murder to add to that list of problems."

Penny hangs her head, and I glare at the sheriff. He was just showing concern. What happened to that? He could be a little more sensitive.

"You don't think Penny had anything to do with whatever

has been going on here?" I ask, going a little mama bear over my friend.

"Maybe not," Sheriff replies. "But maybe if Penny had said something, we would have investigated sooner."

"Investigated what? A toaster that didn't toast the bread correctly?" I say all full of fire. My emotions are rising, and with them, my magic. I have to keep control of it.

It's not as if I'm the only one with heightened emotions. Sheriff Bernard isn't exactly accustomed to all these murder investigations. I need to be more open minded and attuned to others. That's one magic lesson I do remember.

"Penny has done so much for this town, for years." I try again, this time keeping my customer service voice in place. It's better not to rile up the authorities. "I think she's earned a little bit of respect."

"You're right. I'm sorry, Penny. I'm not trying to cast blame on anyone. I'm just trying to find the answers."

"I know, Sheriff."

"We'll do what we can. Just please tell us if anything else happens."

"I can do that." Penny nods. I can tell she's feeling slightly better knowing the police are in the know now. However, she's still shaky, and I can't blame her.

"Sheriff, if there's nothing else, could we possibly get out of here now?" I say, wrapping my arms around my friend who is shrinking into herself at this point.

"Yes, if we have any more questions—"

"You'll know where to find her and me," I say, because we all know the sheriff will have questions for me again.

I lead my friend farther into the bakery, and up the stairs to her living space. It's usually convenient, having her apartment in the building. But at the moment, it seems like the opposite. With the police still moving around downstairs, it feels anything but safe.

"Now, we're going to get some tea. And then we're going to relax." I guide Penny to the couch, pushing her gently down when she continues to stand there. Hurrying over to the kitchen, I turn on the kettle and pull out two mugs. When I finally make it back to the couch, Penny hasn't moved.

"Hey," I say softly, as if not to startle her. She looks up at me, and I hand her a mug. "We'll figure it out."

She nods, but I don't think she believes me. At least not at this moment. But it's okay. I believe myself. There is no way I'm leaving this up to the sheriff. Not when he thinks I may have something to do with it. I guess I have another mystery on my hands, and I am going to solve it.

I'M NOT GOING to lie, I had a restless night. I'm sure Penny didn't sleep well either. Thankfully, since the crime didn't seem to have happened inside the bakery, we can open it right up on time. Penny made sure to call in Justin this morning. I leave her upstairs as I head down to give him the scoop.

The guy is barely out of high school, but he seems like a good worker and is always on time.

"What's all the secrecy about?" he asks, after greeting me. I glance up, wondering how much I should tell him, but this is Monroe Cove. He'll probably have all the information in a matter of two customers.

"A dead body was discovered in the back by the dumpsters last night. There'll be some activity around the bakery while they investigate that."

"Dude, that's crazy. Penny okay?"

"I'm fine," my friend announces, walking into the kitchen. She looks like she had as bad of a night as I did. Her skin is a little pale, and there are bags under her eyes. But her smile is in place. "No worries about me. Let's get to work."

Justin doesn't hesitate to start pulling out whatever it is Penny needs. I walk over to her as she picks up the freshly brewed coffee. Clearly, I need to invest in an automatic coffeemaker. That seems useful.

"You'll be okay if I leave?"

Penny turns to me instantly, reaching to give my upper arm a squeeze.

"You are the bestest friend ever, but please get out of my kitchen. The bake off is only days away, and we're about to get slammed."

Penny is in work mode now, which means I can leave and get down to my own business. Like talking to Aunt Grace about the whole magic angle.

Before I leave, I grab a cup of coffee. Then, after giving Penny and Justin another thorough study, I let them be. Having Penny be the front man of the bake off seemed like a good idea, but now I'm just worried about her.

First things first, I need to see if my aunt will have that promised conversation with me.

I find her in the kitchen of the inn. Apparently, I only know people who spend their time in kitchens.

"Auntie Grace, we have to talk," I say by the way of greeting. My aunt grabs a towel immediately, wiping her hands as she hurries over to me.

"Oh, sugar plum, I heard all about that poor woman. Are you alright? How is Penny?"

Of course Auntie Grace knows. I hug her back, not even a little surprised.

"She's shaken up, as you can imagine, but that's not even the worst of it. Those troubles I told you about? They haven't stopped. And now I'm worried she's in even more danger. Have you talked to your...friends?"

I give the room a quick scan, hoping it's too early for anyone to eavesdrop, but you never know in this town. The walls have ears.

"As far as I know, there have been no major disturbances." Auntie Grace is also careful in the way she phrases her answer. But she's been at this a lot longer than I have. She's a pro.

"Is there a way you can check for sure?" I take a step closer, lowering my voice some more. "There has to be something we can do. Penny won't show it during work hours, but I know she's not exactly feeling the safest in her place of business. And home."

Auntie Grace is quiet for a moment, mulling over my words. This is the most serious I've seen her. I wonder if there's more she isn't telling me. I mean, would I be surprised? I wouldn't. She's notorious for keeping secrets.

"I think there's definitely something we can do. I'll look into it a little more. But honey bun, please be careful."

"What do you mean?"

She gives me a "really now?" kind of a look as I try to appear innocent. I don't think it's working.

"I know you, Cassandra Duke. You've got a sparkle in that eye of yours, and my mischievous tendencies running through that blood in your veins. Whatever you are cooking, you better keep an eye out."

"I think, Auntie Grace, you should take your own advice," I reply, pointing to the stove, where the water is now boiling. She half grunts, half chuckles, as she hurries over to deal with that. I slip out of the kitchen before she can look any deeper into my brain.

She's right, of course. I am cooking something up. I just wish I knew what it was.

6

___

"Are you sure this is no bother?" Penny asks as she walks into my bedroom later that night, still holding onto her duffel bag as if it's her lifeline. I walk over to take it from her.

"Of course it's no bother! Penny, I don't want you to be alone right now. And I don't want to be alone either."

I know it's that last part that really gets her. She gives my room another quick look and then finally relaxes enough to walk over to my bed and take a seat.

"Thanks so much for doing this, Cassie."

"Pen, this is what best friends are for." I smile before walking over and giving her a quick hug. Her little body trembles as she hugs me back. I know it's because of all this murder business. She's not exactly used to finding dead bodies, although apparently, this is something that I'm getting used to now. Not sure what to do with that information, but here we are.

"So, is there anything you need specifically?" I ask, stepping back. She just shakes her head.

"No, I think I'm good. If it's okay, can I take a shower?"

I almost joke that she's not allowed, but instead wave her toward the bathroom.

"Yes, absolutely. I'll be in the library if you need anything."

She reaches over to grab her bag from where I placed it on the bed and starts pulling stuff out. I leave her be as I head to the library.

Auntie Grace did say she'll think it over, but I've gone through a whole day without her saying anything to me, and I'm getting impatient. If I can figure this out on my own, it will be much quicker. My go get them attitude is really helpful right now.

I jump slightly as a big grey fur ball lands on the table beside me. Birdie. My fourteen-pound nemesis.

"Well, are you here to help?"

The cat gives me a glare, that I return, before she jumps over to the couch and curls into a ball.

"We're going with *not* help then," I mumble, turning my back to her.

I turn my attention back to the bookshelves, scanning them, trying to see if there's anything that I can see to pinpoint anything that might be helpful. Reaching for my magic, I try to set an intention, looking for information, but it's hard when I have no idea what I'm looking for. Or you know, how to actually use my magic properly.

I mean, I know the basics. Magic is a lot of things, and if I was just to look for something magical or a magical direction, I'd find plenty. It's the specifics that get ya.

Specific types of magic and specific types of spells require precise concentration and a whole bunch of other stuff I don't really know about. The best I can do is use my magic sort of like a metal detector and hope that in all the little scraps I pick up, one will be useful.

Slowly, I walk through the room pulling out book after book as my magic notices the small beacons they set off. Birdie proceeds to watch with both eyes open, but she's completely relaxed in her spot.

No help, as usual.

Not sure how long I've been walking around like that when Penny comes out, wrapped in a bathrobe.

"What are you doing?" she asks as I place another book back on the shelf.

"Research, of course. Without any help from Auntie Grace, which is, you know, frustrating." I roll my eyes, puffing out a gust of air.

"Okay, cool. I'm glad we're handling this like adults." Penny chuckles, and I turn to send a glare her way. Yes, I sound a little bitter but that's life right now.

"Is there anything I can actually help you with?" Penny asks, settling on the couch.

"Honestly, Penny, I wish there was, but I don't even know what I'm looking for."

"Isn't there like a magic spell you can say to find something you're looking for?" Her voice is very nonchalant.

I turn around, giving her a look, and I notice Birdie is sitting up now, also giving her a look.

"Is there something you're not telling me?" I level her with a piercing gaze.

"No, no," she hurries on to say. "I mean, okay, when we were younger, and you first told me about the whole witches thing. I did a lot of research and then kind of just continued doing so as time went on."

There's a pause while I process that.

"Wait, so you're like a magic expert?" I ask slowly, a smile blossoming on my face.

"Oh, I thought you'd be mad."

"Why would I be mad?"

"I'm not sure. I don't know. And I'm not really an expert, but I kind of like knowing what you can and can't do."

That earns me a good laugh.

"Penny, I don't even know what I can and can't do," I say, throwing my hands up in the air for a second.

"You know it's because you haven't been practicing and it's just like a muscle."

"And now, you sound like Auntie Grace."

"Well, I mean, I know we're a little mad at her right now but she's not wrong, when it comes to that."

"Fine. You're right. But don't tell her I said that."

Birdie makes a little grunt sound, and I give her a look, pointing a finger down.

"You don't tell Auntie Grace anything either."

The cat yawns and then raises a paw to give it a good lick before settling her unnerving eyes back on me.

Penny glances between me and the cat but doesn't comment. I'm sure she wants to. There's something on the tip of her tongue.

"Let's not worry about that. Now," I say, "how about we just focus on this secret that Auntie Grace is keeping from me."

I told Penny earlier that I'm having inklings about how much information my aunt is actually sharing with me. She keeps dodging my conversations, and when we do have one, it's so minimal, it's like we're strangers.

"Are you sure it's really a secret? Maybe she just really doesn't know anything."

Penny and I glance at each other in unison.

"Really? Auntie Grace not knowing something, is that even a possibility?" I ask, but it doesn't require an answer because we both know it's very unlikely. Penny appears deep in thought for a moment.

"There has to be something right?"

"Maybe a spell?" I say, but nothing comes to mind.

"Well, I mean, you don't usually use spells, right?" Penny

does seem to know a lot about this, but I kind of like it. It's nice to have someone besides Auntie Grace to talk to about it.

"Correct," I reply. "Spells are more precise magic. Mine is based on emotion."

"Isn't all magic based on emotion? It's like the fuel that makes the gears work?"

Once again, I give Penny a look.

"What? I love magic! And I watch plenty of stuff on TV that covers the basics. Auntie Grace said they seem to put at least some thought into their research."

"My aunt watches TV?"

"Sometimes," Penny shrugs. Well look at that, miracles do happen. I didn't think Auntie Grace had ever turned on the TV in her room before. That might explain her knowing what Maximum Overdrive is.

"I guess you never know until you try, right?" I say and receive an eager nod from my friend. My heart feels a little lighter because this is more like the Penny that I know and love instead of the scared little girl who was standing earlier in my bedroom.

I'm worried for her. A part of me wants this to have a magical solution because it can be magically fixed. But also, there's a real murderer on the loose now. If her unlucky streak has nothing to do with magic, then it's just a murdered body in the backyard and a person with all the bad motives out to get her.

I'm not sure I like either odds. But I'm not about to say that out loud.

I do have to say that Penny and her eagerness and excitement over my magic is actually making me want to be eager and excited about my magic too. Which is not something I've been in a very long time.

I remember when I was younger, there were times, especially when Auntie Grace was good about teaching me, I got excited that I could do things. But then magic just started being a nuisance and something that made me weird and different and secretive. It became too much.

Having a person who knew what I was, outside of my family, kept me sane. Penny made me feel seen as a person, not just a witch in training.

Wow, I'm getting all kinds of sentimental and emotional. Maybe I need a nap. I thought I left all those weird little girl emotions behind. But maybe it's true what they say. Nothing is ever forgotten, and every little part of our past makes up our future. Or something like that.

Now I'm emotional and philosophical.

Focus, Cassie.

I wish I knew where to start.

"Birdie," I glance over at the cat. "You got any ideas? Maybe point me to a book that might be helpful?"

The cat watches me for a full five seconds before opening her mouth wide and yawning. I roll my eyes.

Penny is trying not to laugh as she watches the two of us.

"I'm glad you find this amusing."

"I said nothing."

Birdie gives me another look before getting up and stretching, and then proceeding to walk out of the room.

"What did you do to offend her?" Penny asks, chuckling.

"I'm not sure. Probably breathed too loud."

My friend laughs at that, and I smile.

"Well, if the cat isn't going to help you, let's see if I can."

WE SPEND much of our evening going through books on magic. Around eight o'clock, Auntie Grace makes her way to her room. She studies Penny and I and gives us a quick wave before saying something about needing the bathroom. Then she nearly ran into her room. It's been two hours, and we haven't seen her since.

"Should we check on her?" Penny asks as I get up to grab another book.

"Not when she's hiding from us," I reply as I take my seat once more. Because that's exactly what she's doing. She's been avoiding me for days, which you'd think be the opposite. She's been trying to push me back into the magic world, and here I am, actually wanting to learn, and she's nowhere to be found. I have no idea why, but that's a problem for another day.

Just then, a noise catches my attention. Penny and I both look up to see Birdie scratching at one of the bookshelves. I didn't even see her come back into the room. Penny and I exchange a look before I get up and walk over to the shelves.

"Yes?" I ask, glancing at the cat. She gives me one of her signature stares before leaping up to the table beside the shelves and then onto the third shelf up. I never realized how deep the shelves were, until this moment. I wonder if it's because of this exact reason: Birdie needs a place to perch.

Ha. I'm hilarious.

The cat makes sure I'm watching before she rubs her face on one of the books. Without hesitation—I learned my lesson —I pull it down and walk back over to the couch.

"What is it?" Penny asks.

"We're about to find out," I reply as I open the book and begin leafing through the pages. At first, it looks like a history book, but after the first two chapters, the pages turn into recipes.

"Wait, is that what I think it is?" Penny asks, looking over my shoulder.

"I think so," I reply, glancing up to where the cat is now stretching out on the rug. I swear Birdie gives me the smuggest of smiles before she proceeds to lick her paw. I shake my head and then look back down at the pages.

"These are new to me," I say after a few minutes. "They use herbal magic. More than I'm used to. A lot of jar and pouches work."

"How is that different from regular spells?"

"From what I remember of my earlier lessons, every witch has her affinity. I have no idea what mine is," I hurry on to add, before Penny can ask. "But whatever it is, it amplifies the magic. Some witches are stronger when they create a physical representation of a spell in the form of a pouch or a jar. Some are powerful enough with just words."

"What about witches who don't need either?"

"Those are rare," Auntie Grace says, stepping out of her bedroom. Penny and I glance up as she gives us a smile. "I would check between pages 170 and 178. There might be something there. I'm going to get a cup of tea. Would you like one?"

"No, thank you," Penny and I reply in unison, our noses already buried in the book. A part of me really wanted to ask Auntie Grace more questions, but she seemed like she was just passing through. And since I have something tangible to do, the conversation can wait.

I find what I'm looking for on page 176.

"Penny, I think this can work."

"What is it?"

"It's a protection pouch. From what I can tell, it works sort of like a sponge. It sucks all the bad magic out of a place. If there is something at work at the bakery, this should be able to detect it."

"Can you make it?" she asks, sounding as excited as I feel.

"I can." I read over the ingredients before standing up and walking to the glass cabinet on the opposite side of the room. "And everything I need is here."

Penny visibly exhales, slouching against the couch. I grin in response, hugging the book to me. Birdie gets up, jumping onto the couch and snuggling against Penny, so she can get a few scratches.

"Yes, thank you, Birdie," Penny says, laughing.

I roll my eyes—I do this a lot where this cat is concerned—but I'm still smiling. This is a start. It's something I can do and that makes me feel better already.

7

———

I'm still worried about Penny, but she nearly pushes me out the door this morning.

"An opportunity like this doesn't come around often. Especially in this town," she says, and she's right. So I listen. It's something I do on occasion. But first, I made sure to put together the protection pouch and placed it at Penny's before opening.

Now, I'm walking into Mayor Moore's office at eight in the morning. My black pencil skirt would look so much more professional if it wasn't covered in cat hair. I should see if there's a magic repellant for this kind of a thing. I mean, shouldn't there be? Since witches and cats are friends, and all that. Not in my case, of course. But that's why there should be a spell for sure.

Wow, my mind is really grasping at randomness here. I must be nervous. I didn't think I'd be, yet here we are.

"Good morning." The pretty brunette at the front desk greets me with a smile. She looks about Justin's age. I wonder if they know each other. Maybe they should date. He's been a little more friendly with me after I blinded him with my smile, as Penny put it. I could probably set them up.

Okay, brain. *Stop it and focus.*

"Good morning. I'm Cassandra Duke. I have an appointment with Mayor Moore?" Not sure why that last part came out as a question, but the girl doesn't seem fazed.

"Yes, I'll let her know you're here," she says before reaching for her phone. Before she replaces the handle, the woman I met at Penny's steps out of the door to the right.

"Good morning, Miss Duke." She greets me with a firm handshake, and I respond in kind. It feels good to put my businesswoman hat on. I feel like since coming home, I've been wearing many, but not this one. And just like always, it feels right.

"Please follow me."

She leads me back through the door she came through, which opens up to a small hallway and into the first door on the right. Instantly, I'm impressed by how spacious the room is. For some reason, the outside doesn't quite match up to how I pictured it.

"You're not the first one to be amazed at this room." The mayor chuckles as she points to the chair in front of her desk. She doesn't walk around to sit behind it. Instead, she takes a seat beside me, in the chair opposite of me.

"It is a bit strange, the layout of the building."

"It was converted from a store, believe it or not. The whole building was a giant room, with smaller storage areas pushed out to the sides. When they decided to convert it, I'm not sure how this office ended up so large. But I kind of love it."

She smiles at that last part, putting me at ease. I can see how she got elected as mayor. She has that approachable attitude about her.

"What is it that you're looking for from me?" I ask, deciding to dive right into it. She gives me a small smile. I knew she'd appreciate it.

"You might be surprised to know that it has nothing to do with this office. Although, it could definitely appreciate your expertise too. What I'm looking for is help with my house. We've just remodeled, recently. But while the inside looks prim and polished, it also looks very dull. I have absolutely no interior design experience, and trust me, it shows." She laughs, and even that sounds like it fits her role.

"Do you have layouts or pictures of the place?"

"I was thinking we'd walk right over. It's only about a block or two away. If you have the time?"

"Absolutely." I stand immediately, more than eager to walk to the place. I can't tell if that was unprofessional of me or not, but the mayor doesn't comment with anything but a smile. She picks up her phone and then leads me back out to the lobby.

"I'll be on my cell," she tells the receptionist and then we're out the doors. Mayor Moore turns right, heading toward the main shops. My mind tries to mentally map out the town, to see what area she could possibly live in. There are a few alleyways that split off Main Street, and then the parallel streets of Second and Fourth in sort of an off the beaten path kind of a residential area. But I don't know of many people who live there anymore.

When Mayor Moore takes a left, I realize I guessed right.

"You look surprised," she comments, as she leads me down an alleyway between two shops. The atmosphere is immediately more somber somehow. As if this area is in shadows, and we left all the light behind. I'm not sure why I'm being so melodramatic, but my mind is conjuring up all kinds of unfavorable scenarios.

"I thought the houses beyond Second Street were mostly abandoned. The residential areas are closer to the main road, no?"

"You're correct. They were for a while, but that's where I come in." She glances at her phone before continuing on. "Monroe Cove is a beautiful town, full of lovely people and their traditions. But there are parts that have been forgotten with time. Areas of town that are right on the other side of the well walked paths that haven't seen a person in weeks."

"How does that happen?"

Mayor Moore shrugs. "Places fall apart, and people move on. The forest is thick in this part of town, so it's easy to forget that this used to be a lively neighborhood. I want to bring some of that liveliness back."

It's quite a walk, but I'm wearing my comfortable boots. It's another ten minutes before I see the end of it. When we come out on the other side of the alley, I understand exactly what she means. The houses here are few and far between. They've been battered with age and elements and the neglect of human nature. But the beauty and the history are still there. The buildings remind me of Crooked Windows Inn. Eccentric enough, and can be made even more beautiful with a little tender love and care.

"Are you the only one who lives on this street?"

"No. There are two other families down that way." Mayor Moore motions farther down the street but turns in the opposite direction. "I won't lie. I kind of love being away from the prying eye of the public."

She smiles, and when I realize which house she's walking toward, I almost stop in my tracks.

The beautiful Victorian structure is straight out of my childhood memories.

Finn and I used to dare each other to sneak over to the abandoned parts of town and see if we could find the coolest knickknacks. Auntie Grace usually knew and made us return the items to wherever we found them. But it was the principle of the thing. I liked being the winner.

This house is one of the ones we visited often.

It's three stories up, which is unusual for this street. Most of the houses here are only two. And the attic. So, I suppose this building is four floors instead of three. There are large wooden shutters around each window, painted red. The rest of the house is a light brown, which makes the shutters look like blood shot eyes. It's a very striking contrast.

"You seem to know this house," Mayor Moore comments halfway up the stairs. This woman is either super perceptive, or my facial expressions are over the top obvious today.

"I did grow up in Monroe Cove." I follow her inside, shaking myself out of my trip down memory lane.

"Why did you leave? If it's not too personal," she adds quickly, and I smile.

"It's a pretty standard reason actually. I needed to go somewhere where no-one knew me, to make something of myself."

"And did you?"

She's not unkind in her question, but it makes me pause. Did I?

"I'd like to think so," I reply honestly. That seems to satisfy her.

Inside, the house is just like I remember it. The downstairs has a wide-open floor plan with mostly sitting rooms. All the bedrooms are on the second and third floors. I can see what the mayor meant about not having a designer's eye almost immediately. The off purple-colored vases mixed with the salmon-colored tablecloth on the table is basically a scream for help.

"Where did you get this?" I ask, walking over to a dream-catcher hanging against the wall in the foyer.

"That was a find at the bazaar in Hastings. A lot of those vendors will be here for the bake off. It's a great place, if you've never been."

I nod, still studying the dreamcatcher. There's something about it that seems familiar somehow.

"Well, do you think you can work your magic?" she asks after a few minutes. I turn, giving her my best smile.

"Oh, I definitely can."

I'VE BEEN HUNCHED over my drawing pad for hours. After doing a thorough walkthrough of the place and jotting down a bunch of notes, I came straight back to the inn and my sketchbook. When my phone rings, I'm so deep in my zone, I almost let it go to voicemail.

"Cassie, something is not right." Penny's voice sounds over the speaker as I push connect.

"Hello to you too." I try for humor, but I can tell instantly that Penny isn't having any of it.

"Today hasn't been all that great, but nothing bad has happened, but now, I think there's something wrong with your pouch thingy."

I sit up a little straighter, rolling my shoulders back as I focus on Penny's words.

"What do you mean?"

"I think—" She pauses, as if collecting herself. "it's crispy at the edges?"

"Wait, what?"

"Hold on." She disappears for a second and then my phone rings with a video chat invitation. I click accept and Penny's worried face fills the screen.

"Tell me what's going on."

"Here, look for yourself." She takes the phone over to the corner I left the pouch in and when she's close enough, I can see what she means. The edges of the bundle look blackened.

"When did you notice it?"

"Just now. We've been pretty swamped all day, and I've been

mostly at the front. Mary came in. I had her bake the cookies today, so I could coordinate for the bake off."

"And nothing crazy has happened today?"

"Not your kind of crazy," she replies, her face once again filling up the screen. "What do I do?"

I think it over for barely a second.

"Wrap it in a paper towel and bring it with you tonight. You sure you don't want me to come get you?"

"No, I need my car. I'll be over in a bit."

We disconnect, and I sit on my bed thinking. None of this adds up.

Not the weird sabotage at Penny's. Not the murder. Not the burned up magical protection bundle.

There has to be a way to figure this out, but I have no idea where to start. Pushing the sketchbook aside, I stand and stretch, my mind racing. There's probably more information in the library, but how much can I really find out in a night? I need months to read through all the books in there. I feel an ever-present stare at the back of my head, and I turn to glare at the culprit.

"You know, *cat*," I say, looking over to where she's reclining against my bedspread. "You don't always have to be around."

She gives me a look as if to say, "Yeah, I do. You clearly can't handle things on your own." And then rolls over and stretches.

I can't help it, I want to smile. It's cute. Not that I'm going to say it out loud.

"Okay fine, if you're going to be here, how about you help? Help me figure out what in the world is going on with these protection spells."

I walk over to the dresser and pull out the spell I found and read over it one more time. I created the protection spell exactly as written, but for some reason, it had a weird side effect. It doesn't say anything about the edges burning, so I'm not exactly sure what could cause that. Bringing the book back to the bed, I start leafing through it.

Birdie does another slow stretch as she gets up, stretching her spine out and yawning.

"Really? You're so tired?" I mumble as she gives me another look before carefully walking across the bed and toward the book. She glares and then butts my hand away from the book I'm reading.

"So what? This isn't the correct book?"

She makes sure I'm paying attention to her, paws at my hand, and then she jumps off the bed.

"Let's do this, I guess," I say as I follow her out of the room. She goes into the library and then walks over to the opposite side of the room before jumping onto the bookshelf, three shelves up. Okay, well, she's clearly, way more agile than I gave her credit for considering she sleeps all the time, but I'm also not gonna say that out loud. I do have a feeling she seems to know what I'm thinking, so maybe I should be a little bit more careful with my thoughts as well. Because if the look that she just gave me is any indication, I'm in trouble.

"Well, Birdie," I begin. "What am I looking for?"

I walk over to the shelf and scan the books on it, but nothing jumps out at me or stands out in any way. They're just typical spell books. But then Birdie pauses at a book on the end. I pull it out, giving it a once over, but still nothing special. I flip through it, not seeing anything that would be out of the ordinary. When I give Birdie a questioning look, she just continues to stare.

"Okay then. Let's have a closer gander," I say and then take the book back into my room.

It takes Birdie all of thirty seconds to follow me in and settle back down on my bedspread.

"You really like that spot, don't you?"

She gives me a "stop asking stupid questions and read the

book" kind of a look before she closes her eyes and goes back to sleep. I'm getting good at deciphering her glances, and I'm not sure how I feel about that.

Sighing, I open the book that she made me choose and start flipping through it. It's about ten minutes before I come to a passage that makes me pause. There is a spell to nullify other people's magic, but not like one I've seen before. This one is more of a hex.

That is something we good witches don't use but something that is definitely used by black magic witches. I'm going to go ahead and assume this is exactly what she wanted me to find. I glance up at Birdie, and she opens one eye to give me a small look.

Well then.

Is this what's been happening to Penny? She's had a hex put on her? There's something here about energies mixing, and how one witch's magic can affect another. I'm not too sure on the specifics.

I don't understand who would do such a thing to Penny. I continue reading, making sure that I'm paying attention and making notes because I know Auntie Gracie is not about to give me all this information on her own. But I also know that I have to talk to her about it.

I have to be very specific about the questions I ask her. Something is definitely going on here, and it's not just the murder. Penny might not be unlucky. She might be cursed. And I'm not about to tell my best friend that if I don't have all the information in front of me. Penny's voice comes from the library, and I jump off the bed.

Pushing the books under a blanket, I head to greet her. Before I leave, I stop and look over my shoulder at the cat.

"Thanks, Birdie."

I'm at the diner the next day, picking up lunch for Penny and me, when I hear it. Sue Lynn is doing her gossip session with one of the local ladies. When Penny's bakery comes up, my ears perk up. I'm not even stealthy about taking a seat at the counter while I wait for my food. When Dan places it in front of me, I open up the bag to check it over, even though all of my attention is on Sue Lynn. Dan doesn't even comment as he chuckles and makes his way back to the kitchen.

"That poor woman they found behind Penny's, she was a regular. I, personally, don't remember her well. I serve so many customers every day. But she's been around. And to have her life snuffed out so brutally. And dumped behind a bakery, in a strange town. What a way to go."

"You have no idea who she is?" the other woman asks. Sue Lynn leans a little closer, keeping the coffee pitcher on the counter.

"I heard she was staying at the inn, but that's all I know. All I know." She raises her hands up in the air, but I heard everything I need to. Grabbing the bag with food, I make my way to the door. Maybe I'm slightly upset.

So what if nobody decided to tell me this woman stayed at Crooked Windows Inn. Granted, the only person who should've mentioned it was Auntie Grace, but she's just full of secrets these days. I was already thinking of bribing Finn into giving me some intel on who this woman was, and if there's anything that can tie her to Penny. But instead, she's tied to me. By default.

I have to find a way to discover this information without giving away the fact that I already know it. Auntie Grace won't tell me, obviously. And I'm not sure I can sneak into the computer system without anyone seeing me.

My only option is Lucy. Maybe she'll be a little bit more willing to share information if I play my cards right. Penny and I eat our lunches, and I do a quick walk through her bakery before I head back to the inn. Maybe sticking my nose into this murder business isn't the best idea, but I can't help it. My friend is involved. Somehow. I need to figure out how before anything else happens. Like Penny getting hurt.

Thankfully, when I reach the inn, there are no guests at the front desk. My aunt is nowhere inside, which is also helpful.

"Hey, Lucy." I greet the woman with a smile, coming up to the counter.

"Oh, hey there, Cassie. How are you doing?"

I don't even have to ask what she's referring to because small towns and all that. Obviously, everybody within the boundaries of this county already knows exactly what happened. Sue Lynn was blabbing about it for everyone to see, so I'm sure the tourists are also in the know.

And the fact that I'm involved, of course.

"Oh, you know, kind of getting used to this being my new thing." I shrug and smile, hoping to lighten the mood. Lucy chuckles but sobers up real quick.

"Oh, Cassie. It is such a crazy situation, you and Penny finding that poor woman."

I try not to show the excitement I'm feeling because she totally just gave me an opening.

"It's crazy, you know, I thought I saw her here. Or I thought somebody mentioned that they saw her here, but I couldn't remember." I pretend like I'm thinking.

"Now that you say it, I believe she was here."

"When was that?"

"Maybe four days ago?" Lucy replies, her eyes focused on something far away. "It's kind of surreal. I would've checked her in, and now she's...gone."

Lucy goes back to typing away at her computer, only partially paying attention to me, so I push it a little further.

"What was the name she used?"

I immediately know that was not the right question to ask.

"Cassie, please tell me you're not getting mixed up in this." She stops typing, turning to focus completely on me. "I know that you find yourself this little detective but getting in the middle of this investigation will put you in a bad light."

While she's not wrong, I'm not changing my mind. I need to say something to convince her.

"I know Lucy, I get it. It's just—it's Penny, you know. I can't let it go."

"I understand." She's instantly sympathetic, "But you have to be smart about this."

"Which is why I came to the smartest front desk manager I know." I smile, leaning against the guest's counter. Lucy shakes her head. She knows exactly what I'm trying to do. But she's also known me long enough that she understands I wouldn't do it unless it was important.

"Cassie." She leans forward. "All I can tell you is her name, but you have to promise that you will be careful. As in, really careful. Your aunt will never let me live it down if anything happens to you."

"Why is everybody so worried about my wellbeing?"

"I don't know, Cassie, maybe because last time, you ended up almost shot. By another killer."

Oh, that. That's right. Not sure how I keep forgetting that fact, but I guess I should probably be a little bit more careful, but I'm only now getting used to this detective thing, so you know, sue me. Still learning here, and it's not like anybody's giving out free lessons.

"I will be careful, Lucy. I promise," I say and I mean it.

It's not like I want to put myself in danger, but I also have a feeling that sometimes these things happen for a reason, and the fact that I have found myself in the middle of this investigation again means that maybe my reason is to help solve it.

While I'm having my moment, Lucy scribbles something on a piece of paper.

"Just don't say you got it for me."

"I never reveal my sources." I smile with a little wink before I head upstairs. I don't even look at the paper until I reach my room, like a true professional.

Tamara Weber.

The name does not sound familiar at all. Her face didn't seem familiar either, but I mean, I only saw her, you know, not alive. So maybe a good idea would be to look up and see what she looked like before she died. I pull out my phone and type in her name. There are a few individuals with that name, surprisingly enough, so I have to scroll through some pages.

It takes me a little while, but I finally stumble upon a picture that looks like her. When I click on it, I see that it is a photograph taken at an outdoor market event. An announcement follows it, saying she had a booth. That's when I see it. The same type of dreamcatcher I saw at Mayor Moore's house. Tamara Weber has a smaller version around her neck. I'm almost positive the necklace was there when Penny found the body. It's what made me pause at the mayor's house, I just didn't realize it until now.

Scanning the information, I see that the outdoor market is a town over. This must be the same one the mayor mentioned. I guess Tamara was a vendor there, so that would make sense.

Perfect. I finally know exactly what my next step will be.

AFTER CHECKING to make sure Penny is still all set at the bakery, I head out. My mind is already calculating a to-do list in my head. Obviously, I'm being watched. By the sheriff, by other people in my life. They're worried, and I can't blame them. Birdie is probably the only one not concerned about my wellbeing.

As I walk, my feet take me where I need to go even before I think too much about it. At least my instincts seem to be guiding me. Go me. There's a second where I hesitate, but then I push right through the doors and walk into the police station. The woman at the front desk isn't familiar to me, but she greets me with a warm smile. I officially know less of the town's population than I think.

"How can I help you?"

"I'm here to see Officer Harvey," I reply with my own smile in place. She motions me in the direction of the bullpen without hesitation.

"Go right in."

With a quick thanks, I enter through the archway and am met with four desks and a lot of windows. Instantly, my mind goes to ways I could open up the space even more and rearrange a few things for maximum productivity. At the moment, everything just looks cluttered, even though the room is large with big windows. Even if I rearrange a few of the desks, moving them to the—

"Cassie?" Finn's voice snaps my attention away from the décor and to where he's coming in from the side hallway.

Right. Focus, Cassie.

I march right up to him. "I need a favor."

"Nice to see you, Finn. How are you today?" my friend says, taking a seat at what I assume is his desk. I roll my eyes but oblige.

"Nice to see you, Finn. How are you today?"

"Well, it's mighty kind of you to ask, Cassie. I've actually been experiencing this pain in my lower back. Right here." He leans forward, pointing to a spot, but I don't have time for his antics.

"Okay, grandpa. Are you ready to get down to business?"

"You're no fun," Finn grumbles as I take a seat next to his desk.

"I am plenty fun, and you know it. But this is beside the point." Something in my voice must clue him in because he leans forward immediately.

"What is it, Cassie?"

"I need you to do something for me. And not ask too many questions."

He looks a mixture of suspicious and worried but nods.

"I need you to watch Penny."

This time, there's no mistaking the determination that washes over his features. He's in his police protective mode.

"Is she in danger? What's going on?"

"I'm not sure, honestly," I reply, because it is after all, only my speculation. But if I'm driving over to Hastings, I can't leave her alone. "But I would feel better if you're around."

"What is it that you're not telling me, Cassie?" It's not only his police training that's making him suspicious. He's always been a good friend and perceptive. He can tell something is up.

"Remember the minimal questions clause?" He just gives me a look. "Fine. I have to go out of town, and I don't feel comfortable leaving Penny alone. That's all."

He narrows his eyes, as if he's trying to see through me. Sometimes I do wonder how much about me he truly suspects. He's observant, always has been. I can't even count how many times Finn almost caught me doing magic, back when practicing it was a regular occurrence. But I'm not ready to tell him that part of the truth, so I stick to the basics. I open my mouth to try and convince him when he speaks up.

"Cassie, are you meddling?"

I'm instantly on the defensive.

"I will have you know, Finn Harvey, I don't meddle. But—I might be doing a bit of researching." I know he doesn't like that, but he deserves at least some kind of explanation.

"I don't like this, Cassie."

"What? I'm not disturbing any police investigations. I promise. I'm just going to be listening a little more closely when I go to the market."

"Market?"

Cheese on a cracker. I need to be more careful. I slipped up. I'm sure Finn knows Tamara had a regular booth at Hastings Outdoor Market. My mind races over how I can get out of this. But maybe I don't have to.

"Cassie, don't tell me—"

"I'm not telling you nothing," I interrupt, giving him a brilliant smile. "That way you can have plausible deniability."

He shakes his head, but he doesn't argue farther. He knows better. There's no way he's talking me out of it.

"Just be careful, okay?"

I nod. "And you?"

"I'll watch over Penny."

That's all I need. I stand, giving his shoulder a quick squeeze as I turn to go.

"Oh, and Finn?" I glance behind me as he meets my eye. "This place could really use some sprucing up."

I wave my hand in the direction of the tables, and Finn's chuckle escorts me out of the building. One problem down, one to go. I just need to figure out how to be inconspicuous when I go to the market. As I pull out my phone to check the market's website, an idea strikes.

9

———

I'm brilliant. Self pat on the back time because I know exactly how to make me look completely inconspicuous. Rushing into the inn, I head for my room to grab my bag. And my sketchbook.

"Where off to, honey pie?" Auntie Grace asks as I reach the front desk.

"Hastings. They apparently host a lovely outdoor market and there are a few vendors I'd like to check out. For the new remodel I'm doing."

"At the mayor's old place?" Lucy speaks up, and I roll my eyes. Seriously, small towns.

"Yes, actually. Mayor likes some of the items there. I want to be there and gone before it gets dark," I say, already halfway out the door. "I'll be back soon."

I don't wait for them to question me any further as I power walk to my car. But of course, I shouldn't have celebrated my victory prematurely.

"What are you doing?" I hear the voice come from behind me, and I turn slowly to see Dean walk up to me.

"I'm getting in my car." I point at it. "Is this unusual for you? You should know what this is, you do have a variation of this yourself." I point to his truck.

"You're hilarious, Cassie."

"Thanks?"

"So?"

"So what?"

"What are you doing?"

Maybe Dean has had too many beams fall on his head at a construction site or something.

"We've been over this. I'm getting in my car."

"And then?"

"I'm going for a drive."

"A drive to where exactly?"

What's his deal? I study him as he questions me. If I didn't know any better, I'd think he's a little concerned. But I know better. So I call him out on it.

"Dean. Don't tell me. You're worried about me now?"

"I wouldn't take it that far, Cassandra," he levels me with a look, and it's one of those where I have to really fight to stand my ground, or I might swoon. "I do think you could use a little bit of help."

"With?"

"With whatever it is you're doing at wherever it is you're going."

Pigs in a blanket, he can make a saint lose their cool. I used to think I was good at this, but Dean is another level. I'm trying to figure out how I'm going to shake him off when he takes a step forward and leans on top of my open door.

"Cassie, where are you going?"

He's not going to let up, but it's fine, because I already prepared a cover story.

"To the next town over to look around their open market." I think he's about to let it be, but then he surprises me. Again.

That jerk.

"Oh, perfect. Then I'll drive."

He shuts the door he's leaning against, making me take a step back from my car. How exactly did that backfire so quickly? I did not mean for him to volunteer to come along.

"You don't have to," I say, but he waves me off.

"Of course I do. Especially if you decide to bring back some of the furniture they're so famous for." He gives my tiny Corolla a once it's over. "I don't think any kind of furniture could fit in there."

I'm immediately protective of my little car baby. She has seen me through some crazy times.

"I will have you know that I can fit a lot of things in this little car."

He gives me another look, as if waiting me out, and I see no other choice. He'll probably block the driveway if I argue with him any longer. I'm losing daylight here.

"Fine, let's go." I walk over to his truck, but he beats me there, just by a second, pulling open the passenger door for me. There's a slight moment when I'm completely dumbfounded. Not that nobody has ever opened the door for me. But for some reason there's something different about this. Shaking my head, I force my mind to focus. When something suddenly occurs to me.

"Wait a minute. Did Finn send you?"

"I have no idea what you're talking about."

I narrow my eyes at his all-too-innocent tone of voice.

"Of course you don't," I grumble, but I get into the truck anyway. Officer Harvey is going to get an earful from me when I return.

Dean begins backing out of the driveway slowly. I try not to notice how close his arm is resting at the back of my seat as he turns his body to look out the back window. There's something incredibly appealing about a man backing his vehicle, don't come at me.

"Where exactly am I going?"

"Oh, that's right." I pull my thoughts away from staring at his very defined biceps and grab my phone. I pull the address up and turn the phone his way.

He glances over and then nods.

"You don't even look surprised," I comment.

"I figured when you said outdoor market. They have the best one across the few towns in this area. Great selection."

I nod but don't comment further. My attention turns to the passing scenery as I try to figure out how I'm going to do my sleuthing without alerting anyone. Including Dean.

IT ONLY TAKES us about forty-five minutes to reach Hastings. I always forget how close all these small towns are. But it's also a weekday, so less traffic.

Thankfully, the only thing Dean and I have talked about is the inn. I've thrown so many ideas at him, he probably thinks I'm a little nuts. But I am a little nuts, so that's fine.

Once Dean is parked, I jump out of the truck and take a full look at the setup in front of us. The open market isn't quite what I pictured it. They have them in the city, and usually they're individual tents set up with a table and items displayed. But these are actual wooden stations, with a table and an over-head roof. Some have shelves built in, while others have a setup with hooks, for hanging items. The booths are evenly spaced out and permanent.

"Pretty fancy," I mumble as Dean comes up beside me.

"It's why it's so popular," he comments as we start forward. "Most who come here know exactly what and who they're looking for." Dean gives me a side glance, that I ignore. I don't have time for his side remarks.

I let myself wander for a bit, just amazed at all the beautiful work I see. This place carries everything from artwork, to plants, to wood carvings. To be honest, I could probably spend days here, just admiring the work. And making lists of all the items I'd like to purchase.

"So, are you going to tell me what's actually going on?" Dean asks after being a silent shadow for the past ten minutes. I glance at him, but he's not done.

"Or are we going to continue to pretend that we are here on some interior design errand?"

That stops me in my tracks. I turn around, giving him an innocent smile.

"I don't know what you're talking about," I reply. "We are here to look at some items for my next remodel."

"At the mayor's house?"

"Seriously, I just barely accepted the job. Is there anyone in town who doesn't know?"

"I doubt it. I heard Sue Lynn talking about it at the diner."

That makes me groan out loud. I should be expecting everyone to be in my business by now, but it's still slightly annoying.

"That woman can't pass up a good gossip session," I comment, moving forward.

"Cassie," Dean's voice stops me once more. "Come on. I've worked with you for a month now. I know how your brain works, and I know that you wouldn't be here just 'trying things out.' You have a plan for everything."

"Okay, did you just use air quotes on me?" I ask, fighting a smile. He cocks his head to the side, but his gaze doesn't budge. He's calling me on my crap.

I have to say that I don't know how I feel about him. About him knowing that about me. A part of me feels kind of good and the other part is a little scared that he can read me so well. But all I can do is kind of shrug, because there's no way I can just admit to him that we are here to find out who this woman was.

"Cassie." Every time he says my name, a shiver goes up my spine.

"Dean," I reply, trying to mimic his tone.

His face lights up with a smile at my attempt, and that smile disarms me.

Of course it does because Dean is gorgeous and he's always been gorgeous. My stupid hormones don't think it matters that he was the bane of my existence when I was a teenager. Granted, my teenage hormones were also aware, because I'm not stupid. But all of this is beside the point. I need to chill.

"Look, just tell me what we're doing here. And then I can help you instead of hinder you with all my questions." Now the smile that he gives me is a little more mischievous and a little bit more like the old Dean that I remember.

"Well," I start out slowly, "we're here to look at some knick-knacks. And possibly furniture," I say again before I turn and march through the market. He doesn't make a sound, but I feel like he rolls his eyes at my back.

I'm absolutely not allowed to turn and look because I might be getting to a point where I give in. If he gives me one more of his mind melting smiles, I'm done for.

He really does have an effect on me, and I don't like it.

We come up to a stall and look over the trinkets that are displayed. Dean keeps pace with me. His presence is calming, even though I won't say that to him. We move on. When we reach the furniture section, I actually have to do a double take. There are so many beautiful pieces here, for a second, I forget that I'm on an entirely different mission.

"Is there anything I can help you with?" A woman steps up, giving me a kind customer service smile.

"You have a beautiful selection, I must admit," I say, stepping closer to her. "It's my first time here. Have you been coming here long?"

I can feel Dean's presence at my back. He's probably trying to figure out where I'm going with this line of questioning.

"Oh yes, I come every single season. This really is the best place to find anything you may be looking for. The selection is always splendid."

"That's amazing!" I say, completely genuine, because I'd have to be blind not to appreciate the talent on display here. "Furniture is your business then?"

"Absolutely." The woman doesn't hesitate.

"Mine too, you could say," I chuckle, leaning closer as if I'm sharing a secret. "I'm in interior design."

"Oh, then you absolutely understand what a difference a chair or a table can make."

"I do." I don't have to encourage the woman any further. She's found a kindred spirit in me, and it's her turn to share.

"I love going to estate sales to see what kind of gems I can uncover. People are hoarders by nature, as I'm sure you're aware. It's amazing what you can find. Coming to the market, I've been able to meet so many interesting people as well. So, I always have a new estate to explore."

"You do have a great eye," I say, giving the love seat in front of us a thorough study. She's clearly the perfect person for me to talk to, but first, I need to get rid of Dean. He's already way too suspicious.

"Hey, could you do me a favor?" I ask, turning to him. "I didn't have much coffee this morning, could you possibly go grab us some while I bargain for this deal?" I lower my voice at that last part, but both he and the woman hear me. He gives me a solemn look, and I have a feeling he knows exactly what I'm doing, but he's not going to call me out on it. Yet. I'm sure the ride back home will be a different story.

"Sure, Cassie, I'll be right back," he says before leaving me alone with the woman.

I turn, giving her a bright smile.

"Perfect, now we have all the time in the world to talk."

"Your boyfriend is quite protective, isn't he? Handsome too." She winks, and I open my mouth to contradict her but decide against it.

"Yes, he's a bit of a bear when it comes to these places. But a teddy bear with me."

I'm pretty sure Dean would lose his mind if he heard me talking like that, but it comes naturally.

She laughs, solidifying our rapport. I began asking her about the furniture, like any good customer would. It doesn't take long until she's talking before I even ask the questions.

"Oh yes, this place is full of such characters. There was a woman here for about five years. She would come in, sell rocks, and people would actually buy them because she would tell them all this crazy mystical information about them."

"Oh really?" I ask, actually interested because maybe this woman is a witch. I obviously have no idea about any of the covens in the area, but I wouldn't be surprised if one was selling trinkets to tourists. We've done that at Monroe Cove before. It's kind of a tradition.

"Can you believe it? Yes, she would just spin some tale, and people would pile them up. I've never bought such a rock, but there were some for luck, some for protection."

"Like crystal?"

"Some looked like crystals, others just looked like rocks."

I am more than intrigued now. Maybe if this rock-seller is a witch, she could help me find more information on Tamara.

"Have you ever met the woman?"

"Oh yes. She and another vendor here have this whole huge feud going on. I, of course, never get involved, but I've watched them go at it."

"So, she's a regular?"

"Absolutely. Every year. Well, I haven't seen her this season. She was on the registry though."

"Registry?"

"Oh yes, there is one at the front of the market," the woman says pointing toward the opposite side of where we walked in. "There's a registry of all the stalls and everybody who was registered to come. Some of the people that don't show up, just get an X next to their booth."

"That's very useful," I say. "Well, thank you so much. I'm going to have to discuss this with my partner." I give the love seat a longing look and the woman simply winks as Dean comes up to me, carrying two cups.

Taking a cup from his hands, I lean towards him just a bit with a grin on my face.

"Thank you, darling," I say before taking a sip of my coffee and wave in the woman's direction. She's watching us both like a hawk, and I stay close by Dean's side as we walk away.

"Darling?"

"Don't get your knickers in a twist. She thought we were sweet on each other. And she was willing to talk."

I take another sip of my coffee, savoring the perfect taste. I know I only used this as a ruse to get him away, but the coffee is heavenly.

"So, Cassie, did you get what you came for?" Dean gives me another knowing look. I'm really starting to not like the fact that he knows me this well.

"Maybe. Stay close."

10

———

I'm being as nonchalant as I possibly can, but let's be honest. All I want to do is race straight for the announcement board and see who the crystals and rocks vendor is. I'm also trying to see if she's here somewhere, but no dice.

"Are you going to tell me what got you so excited?" Dean asks, and I'm being truthful when I say I forgot he was there for a second.

"I don't know what you mean. Just enjoying my coffee." Which is actually ridiculously good, I don't have to lie about that.

"No one likes their coffee that much."

That makes me stop in my tracks, and it's a second before Dean realizes I stopped. Turning to face me, he's already raising up his arms in surrender.

"My bad. You and coffee have a very special relationship."

I'm ready to give him a piece of my mind, but his words disarm me. There's a gleam of amusement in his eye. He looks incredibly handsome. Yes, more than usual. I'm pretty sure I'll be dreaming about that half smile later, but that's beside the point.

"You've redeemed yourself. For the time being." I point a finger at him. "Don't disrespect this vital relationship again."

"I wouldn't dream of it."

There's that freaking grin again. I'll definitely be dreaming of it.

Thankfully, the bulletin board is now in front of us, and I have something tangible to focus on. I scan the map, a bigger version of the printout they gave at the entrance. There are numbers correlating to the booths, but in this case, there are also names. I search for the booth the sales lady mentioned—I probably should've gotten her name—and when I finally find it, I take a step back.

"What is it?" Dean is so attuned to me, that even the slightest expression in my body language has apparently alerted him that something is wrong. Or maybe I look how I feel inside.

Tamara Weber.

The murdered victim and the crystals booth vendor are the same person.

This raises so many questions.

"Cassie?"

"I'm good. Just a little tired. It's been a long week." I turn to him, hoping he doesn't notice what booth I was looking at and give him a sweet smile. He's not fooled, of course, but I don't feel like explaining. Because how do I explain to him that I think the woman who was murdered behind Penny's bakery is a witch? Well, possibly. That would open up a can of worms I am not ready to deal with. Especially with Dean.

"Give me a second, would you?"

I head back toward the vendor with the furniture, and this time, I don't play a part of a customer. I decide to ask her direct questions.

"Back so soon?" The woman smiles, and I smile back.

"Yes, actually. I had a question about the crystal's vendor and the feud. I think I might actually know one of the women."

"Oh really?" The woman's eyes light up with the possibility of gossip.

"Yes, I didn't connect the two before, but of course it makes sense. Tamara was always here." The moment I say the woman's name, I know I got her. The vendor takes a step closer, lowering her voice.

"You didn't hear it from me, but I heard Betty, that's the woman feuding with Tamara, say that Tamara was a witch, full of black magic." I try not to show any outward surprise besides what a normal person would show. "They were always in competition. Last year, Betty went off on a crazy rant and even threw some crystals at Tamara. I assume that's why neither of them showed up this year."

"Wait, Betty isn't here either?"

"No, I heard she may have taken her show to that Monroe Cove for their festivities, but nothing is sure. I can't confirm my sources. How is Tamara?"

"I believe she was going to Monroe Cove as well," I reply, noticing the gleam in the vendor's eye. At that moment, I know this woman believes that information alone was worth the price of admission. I figured she'd find out soon enough anyway, but this way, I can at least offer her something. I ask a few other questions, but she has nothing more to offer.

After I promise to get back to her about the couch, I head back to where Dean is waiting for me. I don't wait for his questions.

"Do you think we can head back now?"

I can see he's confused, but there's also an underlying worry in his features. My heart squeezes in awareness. He's not supposed to be worried about me. That's not who he is.

He's Mean Dean. He's the enemy.

Except, of course that's not the case anymore. I just can't

seem to accept it.

But he's not a friend either, and that's the part I focus on.

I'm preparing myself for another bout of questions, but he simply nods before motioning for me to take the lead. In the direction of the truck.

If I'm being honest with myself, I have no idea how to handle him. The once very obnoxious boy is now a strong, handsome—and kind—man. Even so, I'm not spilling my deepest and darkest secrets. No matter how much I want to when he looks at me like that.

Goodness gracious, eggs and bacon, Cassandra. You've got more pressing matters at hand.

Which is true. I have to find a way to get the truth out of Auntie Grace. She is my only source of witch knowledge, and now, more than ever, I think she's keeping loads of information from me.

It's a contradiction, I know. She wants to teach me, but only on her terms. Well, it's about time I changed those terms and took the matters into my own hands.

Forget subtlety. I'm conquering this head on.

"Can you drop me off at Main Street?" I ask Dean half an hour later as I look up from my phone. I texted Lucy to see where my aunt was, and apparently, she's serving apple cider at one of the already-set-up booths at the bake off.

Honestly, why they keep calling it the bake off and not spring festival is beyond me. There's so much more to it than just pies. Although, that is still the main event. Maybe I should come up—

Okay, brain. *Calm down.*

"Sure. I have to stop at the hardware store for that paint anyway."

I nod, tucking my phone back into my purse. Dean and I were almost overly cordial to each other on the way back. We talked only about the remodel, and while I can tell he has questions, he kept those to himself.

This man keeps surprising me. I don't like it.

Dean drops me off at the front of the park. With a quick thanks, I bail from his truck like my skirt is on fire. He's dangerous to my emotional state, and right now I need my mind clear.

When I finally find Auntie Grace, she's all smiles as she serves up the apple cider. She's a natural at this, which is why she's been the successful innkeeper that she is for years.

But I do have to say, the town is kind of extra on the whole entertaining-the-tourists thing. I know that's what tourist towns thrive off of, but I'm not really used to all this hospitality. Not anymore. I do like all the free food though.

"Auntie Grace, we need to talk," I say as soon as the tourists she's been serving leave.

"What is it, honey bun?" she asks, giving me a quick once over to make sure I'm in one piece before she smiles.

I return it but only briefly.

"It's a conversation we can't exactly have out in the open," I say, hoping she understands what I mean. When she pauses, I know that she does. I also know that she's about to backtrack and completely ignore my request because I am learning to see the signs. It's like she puts on her "fussing aunt" hat and turns up the southern.

"Oh well, sugar cookie, I can't exactly leave. There are all these darling people to hydrate." She smiles at a couple coming up to the booth, already pouring them a drink. "We'll just have to talk about this later."

Normally, I would give in, but I think I'm finally learning to take a stand. In a nice way of course.

"No, Auntie Grace." She pauses immediately at those three

words, glancing up at me. "We're not going to talk about this later. We're either going to talk about this now, in front of everybody, or we're going to talk about it in private." I smile at her before I give the couple a smile as well. They exchange a knowing glance before the woman chuckles and accepts the offered cup.

"What has gotten into you, honeybee?" Auntie turns her attention to me, and I shrug.

"Years of watching you, I suppose." I shrug. Auntie Grace clearly wants to smile but doesn't. "Auntie, I need your help. Can you understand that?"

Maybe it's something in my voice that finally reaches the point of giving in, but she slowly nods.

Turning in the opposite direction, she calls out to the booth beside hers. I didn't even notice Loretta setting up over there, but the woman comes over with a smile.

"Cassie, how are you sweetheart?"

"I'm well, Loretta. You?"

"Oh, you know. Old and springy."

I smile, but I have no idea what that means.

"Loretta, can you take over my spot for a few? I just have to take care of something really quick."

"Of course."

I follow Auntie Grace over to the back area as she wipes her hands on her apron. This is where most of the supplies for the big party are kept, behind the tents set up for the tourists. We both give the area a quick scan, but no one is in sight.

"What's so urgent, sweetie pie?"

"Auntie Grace." I take a deep breath because I know I have to be firm on this. "Please tell me, was Tamara Weber a witch?"

There's a split second where I think she might actually tell me the truth. But then it's gone.

"Oh, I don't even know who you're talking about."

"Yes, you do." I raise my eyebrows at her. I am definitely

learning how to tell when my aunt is lying to me. In this case, it's not that difficult, but the signs are there.

"You know who she is because she came to Crooked Windows Inn as a guest. And you, my dear aunt, know every single person that crosses that threshold. Not only that, but I also think she came here because she needed help. Your help. Am I getting any warmer here?" I cross my arms in front of me, waiting her out. My aunt has been at this secret-keeping business for a long time, but I'm not budging.

"Honey pie, I'm getting up in my years. I don't remember everyone who comes through my inn."

That almost makes me laugh out loud.

"Oh, come on, Auntie Grace. You are the springiest chicken around. Are you honestly expecting me to believe you don't remember?"

"Cassie—"

It's the use of my name that finally gets to me. She doesn't call me by my name often. And the way I've been feeling—overwhelmed and scared—everything starts to pour out.

"Auntie Grace, I can't do these half-truths anymore. Are there other witches in this town? You never told me. Well, you said yes, but who are they? Is there a spell that was put on Penny? You never told me. I can't keep protecting my friends without having all the information laid out in front of me. It's making me very frustrated and sometimes scared. And I'm feeling very unbalanced. In every way. Including my magic."

"Oh, sugar plum, you got to be careful about letting those emotions out unchecked."

"What? What do you mean?"

She points over to the table near us, and I see that all the napkins are floating in the air.

"Sweetheart, you have to calm down."

The napkins continue floating, even as I try to force them to come down. But it's not working. My aunt is right. I need to control it.

Work through my breathing exercises.

I'm fine.

Everything is fine.

I count to five and the napkins settle back down. This is what I did as a child. I'm not an expert, but I'm getting better. I turn to my aunt, tired.

"Will it always do that?"

"No, sweetie pie. And I'm sorry I'm not telling you everything but it's not exactly easy for me to talk about."

"What do you mean, Auntie Grace?"

"Magic is more unpredictable than you expect it, sugar plum. And your emotions are just as volatile. The combination is dangerous."

"I know you want to protect me, but Auntie Grace. I'm already in danger. I just need to know if my friend is in danger and if whoever killed Tamara Weber will be coming after her next."

That makes my aunt pause. "Why would you think they'll come after her?"

"Well, they're clearly targeting her. There's no way Penny suddenly has a case of bad luck out of nowhere."

"Good point."

"What is it you're thinking?" I ask as my aunt turns pensive.

"This competition does bring a lot of people into town."

"You think somebody is trying to take Penny out because they want to win a baking contest?" That sounds absurd even saying out loud.

"Well, this isn't one of your big cities. It's Monroe Cove. There are no big conspiracies here."

"Yes, but a woman was found murdered behind Penny's bakery. We're not exactly the safest town in the county anymore." It's sad, when I stop and think about it. I take a deep breath and try again.

"Auntie Grace, was Tamara a witch?"

"Yes." I really almost thought she wouldn't answer. Then she continues before I can ask anything else. "She did come for help. But I can't tell you what kind of help she was looking for because we never got that far."

"What do you mean?"

"She checked in, spent a day in her room and then went into town. I never saw her again. The next time I heard about her was when you found her."

"So where was she for three days?"

11

———

After promising Auntie Grace that I'd stay safe, I leave her to her apple cider booth. My mind is spinning with half answered questions and even more possibilities. I should be working on the remodel, or the new project for the mayor, but I can't focus on anything. Instead, I grab a cup of coffee and a danish and head to Trinkets and Things.

Tootsie and I have become sort of friends since the whole Mabel ordeal. Tootsie's shop also sits on some nice property, and she was definitely in danger of the delusional mister murderer from my first ever murder. And investigation. Never thought there'd be more, but here we are. I think we're just bonded for life, considering she played such an important part in that huge life event I experienced. And here I am again, in the middle of a murder investigation. I should just accept it as my lot in life.

Tootsie is helping a customer when I come in. I wander off to look at the antique mirrors section, since I've been looking for one for the inn. Well, not actively looking. I have a different job nowadays, apparently.

"Oh sweetheart, it's so good to see you. Did you see the mirrors? I knew you'd love the selection, especially this newest edition, just came in yesterday. Doesn't it look lovely?" Tootsie is standing before the mirror, showing it off, even before I can process her words.

"Hello, Tootsie," I greet her, smiling. Since we're friends now, she told me to drop the Mrs. from in front of her name.

"This is for you."

"Oh, you darling child," she says, taking the small bag from me and glancing inside. "You know I love them danishes at Penny's. How is that sweet girl? It is awful what has happened. And finding that woman like that! How are you doing? I can't even believe it."

"Does everyone in town know about that?" I mumble as I follow Tootsie to the counter. I'm not sure why I'm still surprised by that. The customers have left, so it's just the two of us in the store now.

I'd be lying if I said I didn't find Trinkets and Things the sweetest antique shop I've been to. And as an interior designer, I've been to plenty. Tootsie has excellent taste. Although, that's not always seen by the items she displays here. She has a whole storage room full of beautiful things. But that actually just makes her a good businesswoman, considering those awful-in-my-opinion items do sell.

"Of course not everyone. Most of the tourists are completely oblivious. We do know how to keep our mouths shut when it is required of us." She winks at me. "But you know me, I like to be appraised of all the happenings around town. Plus, that hunky Deputy Harvey has been by to see if I have noticed anyone suspicious hanging around."

I suppress a smile. Just wait till I tell Finn she called him hunky.

"That makes sense. Everyone stops by your place. Have you?" I have to ask, and she doesn't even hesitate.

"Yes, there have been quite a few of them hanging around. The town is full of strangers. But I do what I can to keep the friendly smile in place. You know me."

I pull the cup to my lips to hide the grin.

"And the woman Penny found?" Tootsie lowers her voice, leaning closer. "She was in just the other day, asking all kinds of questions."

That perks me up better than the coffee.

"What kind of questions?"

"Oh, you know, about the old families and who's still around. That sort of thing. Of course I didn't tell her anything. It is no one's business but our own who resides in Monroe Cove. You know we take care of our own here. I didn't tell her nothing. She tried to pretend like she was buying up some paintings for her kitchen, but I can tell a snooper when I see one."

This time I do smile.

"You can always tell who's who, Tootsie."

"That's right. I know my own, and I will protect my own," she says proudly. She's such a contrast to my aunt, who is now notorious about keeping her mouth shut.

"Tootsie?" I start, not sure where I'm going yet but suddenly desperate to have this conversation.

"What is it, dear?" She can instantly tell something is up. Instead of her usual waterfall of words, her attention is on me.

"You've lived here your whole life, right?

"Yes."

"That means—you knew my mother?"

"Oh honey..."

"Could you tell me about her? Please. Auntie Grace won't talk about her, and I don't have any other family I can go to. But being here—coming back—I have so many questions."

"Oh, that Mary Grace, never did know what was good for

her. Always with her secrets, as if the whole town isn't on her side."

"Tootsie?"

"Your mother was the kindest woman I have ever met, child. And she was just as beautiful as she was kind. She doted on you, completely. You were her pride and joy." Tootsie reaches over, placing her hand over mine on the counter. "She loved you more than anything."

"Then, what happened? Where did she go?"

There's a moment of silence, and I can't tell if it's because Tootsie needs the time to compose herself or if it's because she's finding the right thing to say. Not sure when I've become this suspicious of people, but here we are.

"No one knows, honey. I wish I could offer you some sense of closure, but we just don't know."

The way she says that it seems like there's more to it. But before I can ask another question, the bell over the door dings and a customer enters. Tootsie gives my hand a quick squeeze before she chatters up a storm and a sale.

I smile to myself as I wave in her direction, heading for the door. I've never seen her serious before, but I guess my mother's disappearance sobers up anyone. Even though I didn't really learn anything new about her, I did learn that Miss Tamara Weber was looking not for something but someone. Somehow, I feel like Penny might be right in the middle of it all.

THAT NIGHT, while Penny is in the shower, I pull out the ruined protection pouch I created for her. Carefully, I unwrap it, making sure not to touch the burnt edges. None of this makes sense. Not that I'm an expert at magical mumbo jumbo. Give me paint samples and flooring options, that's a different story. But this? It's freaking me out.

"Cassie?"

I glance up as my aunt enters the small library, her eyes on the pouch in my hands.

"You created a protection pouch?" She takes a seat beside me on the love seat.

"I did. Birdie helped me find the spell." We both glance over at the cat curled up on the seat across the table. She opens one eye, as if she heard her name, before getting back to sleep.

"She's good for that." Auntie Grace smiles, turning back to me and the ruined spell in my hands.

"This is what I was going to ask you about. I placed it at the bakery, but it looks like it's burnt at the edges. Any ideas?"

She doesn't take the pouch from my hands, her eyes still trained on it. But it seems like her mind is somewhere else.

"We've been afraid of this."

"Who's we?" I'm nervous to push her, in case she decides to clam up again, but I also need to push her because I need answers. It's a rock and a hard place kind of a deal.

"The coven. There've been talks around these parts of dark magic rising up to counter all the good we've been doing. Weird energy has filled the air."

"The coven?" I'm still on that. "You're still part of one?"

"Of course I am," she replies with a bit of that fire I'm so used to. "And so are you. It's in your blood. Your legacy."

"Auntie Grace, you shouldn't be so surprised I know nothing about this." I give her a look, and she reaches over to pat my hand.

"I'm not, honey bun. I'm just a bit saddened. Your Mama was a good witch, and she wanted to give others a place to practice their magic for the good." My heart skips a beat at the mention of my mom. I'm almost too nervous to breathe, as to not prevent my aunt from talking about her. But she seems lost in her memories and continues without hesitation. "Monroe

Cove has grown tremendously because of all the work we've put into it."

"So, there are other witches here?" I prompt, gently.

"There are and there aren't. The coven isn't in one place. All the towns in this area have at least one witch in residence, to do our part in keeping the place protected."

"Not to be the bearer of bad news, but Auntie Grace, I don't think whatever you're doing is working. There have been a couple murders since I've returned."

My aunt sighs, defeated.

"Yes, sugar plum. We've felt the bad in the world outweighing the good. It affects the people, regular folks with no magic, playing on their shadow natures. We think black magic is at work, giving evil deeds a place to rule."

We sit quietly for a few minutes as I let that sink in. It makes sense in a weird roundabout way, I suppose. If black magic is affecting regular people, then people with bad intentions will be drawn to this town and will act on those urges much faster than they would if they were in a place of good influence. It's not much different than parents protecting their kids from hanging out with bad influences. It's an open-door invitation to do things that you wouldn't normally allow yourself to do.

But then, there's magic. So, it's a little worse.

"Why didn't you tell me? Don't I have a right to know?"

"I'm sorry, honey pie. You've been through so much. All I want to do is protect you."

This time, it's me who reaches over to give my aunt's hand a squeeze.

"I appreciate that. But for me to stay safe, I need information. I need to know what I'm up against. I wasn't raised to sit on the sidelines. I like going into battle knowing what's required of me."

That makes Auntie smile, just like I hoped it would, but I'm not making stuff up for dramatic effect. That's how she raised me. She should know I'll charge headfirst into any situation.

"I will try my best, honey bunches. I have to remember you are not a little girl anymore." She smiles, giving my nose a gentle tap with her finger. Then, she sobers up. "If we are right about the dark magic, you should do a protection spell, which is a little bit different than a pouch. You need to charge some crystals and then place them in the four corners of the bakery. That should keep the energy flow clear while we figure out who's doing this."

I nod, eager to get started. But Auntie Grace stops me.

"Let me look into it. Spend some time with Penny. She needs you right now." Auntie Grace stands, taking the pouch with her. I watch her retreat to her room, thankful we've finally come to some kind of an understanding. There's definitely a lot I still don't know, but it's a start. Doesn't mean I won't be doing some research on my own.

Tomorrow.

12

"Cassie, what are you doing?" Penny asks as she comes into the room next evening and finds me sitting on the floor, pieces of paper surrounding me.

"I'm mapping out our suspect list," I reply. I expect questions, but I'm only met with silence.

Glancing up, I find Penny's concerned gaze on me.

"What is it?"

"I'm just—worried about you. I don't want to see you get hurt."

Her point is valid. Last time, I did almost get shot by the bad guy. Not that I'm going to pretend that doesn't make me nervous as well, but I'm not going to stop investigating because of fear. No one should live their lives ruled by fear.

"Penny, you don't have to worry about me. I got this. I'm stronger as a witch now, and I know a little bit more about all of that detective work. I'll be more careful."

She still doesn't look convinced.

"You have to promise that you're not going to go visit random people on your own or break into any houses." I don't reply right away because I technically almost did that and the only reason I didn't was because Finn sent Dean to babysit me. I still need to talk to Finn about that.

"Cassie!"

"Okay, okay, I promise...To try." I raise my hands as she glares at me. "No, I'm serious. I'll be careful. I promise."

My friend stares at me for another few moments, as if weighing my words, before she sighs.

"Not that I can stop you, right?" I shrug, and she chuckles. "Fine, show me what you got."

She takes a seat beside me, as I wave my hands in front of the papers on the floor.

"We've got Tamara, right in the middle," I begin, pointing to the paper in the middle. It has the victim's name and then a few bullet points about who she was.

"You still don't know why she was here?"

"No. And it's not like anyone is upfront about sharing any information, so what I know is pretty minimal. My next step is searching her room, which has been closed off for the investigation."

Penny sends a look my way and I shrug again.

"What? It's at the inn. I won't be alone with all the people here. Anyway," I turn back to the papers. "These are all the suspects I've been able to find."

Each has the name written on top with their own bullet points, branching out from the middle paper.

"I see you still organize your ideas by mind maps," Penny comments as she leans over to read the papers. It's true, I like having information and ideas visually spread out in front of me. I spent most of today mapping out what I'd do at the mayor's house, so it's not like I haven't been productive either.

"That vendor she was feuding with, Betty, another witch, Justin, Mary—" Penny reads off the papers, "Why are my employees on the list?"

"Because they had the opportunity. And the means, if we're going to be honest. Although, as you can see, they're not really on the list because I have nothing on them."

Penny contemplates for a moment. "Okay, what's the deal with the vendor and the witch?"

"As far as I know, Tamara was having issues with someone at the market. Maybe things got a little too competitive? And another witch would just make sense. Especially since this Betty has called her out in front of everyone. But who knows, she could've said the other "itch" word."

Penny chuckles, but all I can do is stare at the paper. I don't have much to go on. All I've done so far is collect random information about nothing. There has to be something more to it, but I have no idea what. My biggest concern is that Penny keeps experiencing unrelenting problems at the bakery. Thankfully, today it was just that a bit of flour and chocolate chip cookies went missing. It was a nuisance but not as bad as something going up in flames in her hands. Still. I don't like it. But I don't know what to do about it. Auntie Grace hasn't said anything about it to me all day, and my research is stalled. I'm becoming slightly useless at this.

MAYBE THIS WASN'T the best idea, but now that I know for a fact that Tamara was a witch, I'm curious to see why she was in Monroe Cove. And why she needed Auntie Grace's help.

The best way I can think to find out is to see if there's anything in her room that may offer up a clue. Of course, I know that it was cleaned after it was processed by the police. It's still on lockdown though, and I'm not sure when the room will be reopening to guests.

Not that I'm an expert, but I'm hoping my magic could give me a clue. I've been reading Auntie Grace's books, with the help of Birdie, whenever she feels like it, and I'm learning magic isn't all I thought it was. Just like with anything else, I'm learning that I need to keep my opinions open. My relationship with magic is definitely changing because of that.

Making my way to the second floor, I try to look as inconspicuous as possible. When a couple walks by me, greeting me with a smile, I almost slap myself on the forehead in cartoon fashion. I'm supposed to be here, this is my family's inn. I've seen way too many movies.

However, I did have to sneak around the front desk and swipe the key. Master keys are with Auntie Grace and Lucy, and I don't want them asking questions just yet. So, I had to grab a key to the room specifically.

There's no police tape on the door. When I unlock it, I slip through, shutting and locking the door behind me. Immediately I feel weird. There's something here. There's the possibility I'm being slightly dramatic, considering what happened to the last person who occupied this space. But maybe not. I stand near the door, giving myself and my magic time to adjust.

One of the things I read in all those magical books all the time is tip number one: listen to your magic. I've been working for so long and so hard to keep it suppressed, I'm not sure I know how to listen to it. But I'm learning. So, I guess there's that.

Bring on the confetti.

Moving away from the door, I move around without touching anything. I know some witches can really read items, but I've never had that gift. I'm not even sure if I can develop it at this late stage of life. Although, once again, what do I really know?

Okay, I'm annoying myself with this self-deprecating thought process, and I need to stop. Yes, I know nothing about magic. Yes, I'm learning. Now, I need to focus.

I go over to the window to look out and see Monroe Cove

open up in front of me. I do love this little town. It may not seem so, with me leaving and all. But the longer I'm back, the more I realize it's not quite how I remember it. There's more good here than not.

My eyes drift down to our front yard and Dean pulling down two by fours. He's working on a gazebo for the park and using our yard as a workstation. We have plenty of yard, that's obvious. And since he spends a lot of time here already...

Pulling my attention away from him and his nicely fitted shirt, I turn back to the room.

Yes, things aren't how I expected them. Even me playing detective isn't something I signed up for. But here we are.

Goody.

After a careful study of the room, I only have one thing left to try. My magic.

Closing my eyes, I concentrate on the pull inside of me, asking it mentally to come out and play. I need it to sense if there are other magics in use, but I'm not sure how to do it.

Immediately, my magic flares up, running out across the room to look for beacon of other magic. Maybe I don't have to do anything.

Opening my eyes, I concentrate on the unfurling, giving my magic the freedom to sense whatever it needs to sense. At first, I don't think I'm going to find anything. But then, something catches my attention.

Walking over to the corner of the room, I pull up the chair and step on it. Stretching, I reach up to the crown molding, running my hand across the top.

The feeling doesn't go away. Even though I don't think I'm going to find anything, I keep searching. And then, just like that, I find it.

I pull down a crystal. It's a tiny one, the size of my fingernail and darkened. It's as if it pulled in whatever it was supposed to protect Tamara from. This is a basic protection spell. I was going to try a similar one at Penny's. But what did Tamara have to be hiding from?

Because if she had crystals placed around the room, then she was definitely hiding from somebody.

I take the chair to the next corner, and after some searching around, find another crystal. It's just as small and just as blackened. I repeat the process and come away with four crystals, placed in the four corners of the room. From what I remember of my readings, this is a standard protection spell. The only reason I'm able to discover the crystals is because the witch who put them there has passed away.

Studying the four stones in my hand, I concentrate on trying to see if I can glimpse anything from them. Then I stop. This energy, it feels familiar.

And that's when I realize, it's the same energy I felt at Penny's.

13

———

"You're being awfully quiet," Penny comments as we take our seats at Dan's Diner. After I found the crystals, I got a text from Penny asking if we're still on for lunch. I'll be honest, I forgot. But of course, I said yes.

"I may have found—"

"Hello darlin' girls." Sue Lynn announces her presence in a very loud voice as she grins down at us. "What will you have?"

"The special, of course," Penny replies with a smile. Before I can give my order, Sue Lynn is leaning over toward my friend.

"How are you, darlin'?" she asks, her face pinched in sympathy. "What a dreadful time you've had. Are you holding up okay? And with all the bake off stress, that can't be good for ya! I'll add a little something to your order, what do you say?" She winks and turns to leave.

"Umm, Sue Lynn?" I call out.

"Oh sugar, you're getting a special and a coffee. I know," she says over her shoulder before her laugh rings out. And I mean, I could contradict her, but that would be stupid. I do want a special and a coffee.

"Well?" Penny asks when Sue Lynn is clear across the diner.

"I'm not sure this is the best place."

"True, but give me something?" Penny looks so eager, I can't say no.

"There might be some connection... between you and her," I nearly whisper, keeping my head inclined toward hers.

"What kind?"

"I'm not sure. I think—" I stop as Sue Lynn waltzes over with two cups. One full of coffee, the other full of tea.

"Drink up, ladies. And don't let me stop y'alls whispering. My ears are shut tightly." She winks again, but now I'm completely done talking about this. When I glance over at Penny, she nods.

"Tell me about the mayor's house."

Penny is a natural. She changes the subject like a pro. But it's not even thirty seconds later that Sue Lynn is bringing us water we didn't order and taking a seat.

"Did I hear you're decorating the mayor's house? I can't believe that woman lives in that spooky neighborhood. That must be dreary, no?"

"It's a neighborhood like any other," I reply with a gentle smile. It cracks me up that a town such as Monroe Cove has a 'spooky neighborhood' as if we live in a Stephen King novel. "It just needs a little TLC."

"From what I hear, it needs a lot more. We've had all kinds of extra help sent that way lately, so the mayor must be cooking something up."

I know nothing of the sort, but I'm curious.

"What do you mean?"

"Oh, she's been hiring the younger kids to do odd jobs for her for weeks. Haven't you seen them all over town? Busy little helpers. She's planning something." Sue Lynn looks at me like I have the answer to what that might be, but I simply reach for my cup. "She's changing things up. That's a lot for this place.

Even today, she's over there, cahooting with that sheriff. They were just here not twenty minutes ago."

"Sue Lynn, she is the mayor. I'm sure she's not cahooting."

"Say what you will, but I see people in cahoots when they're right in front of my face."

The woman hurries off again, the little tornado that she is. I turn back to Penny and find her eyes already on me.

"What?"

"Don't what me," my friend replies. "You're already cooking up ideas in that head of yours."

"I have no idea what you're talking about."

But of course, I do. I'm already thinking that I need to pay Mayor Moore a visit—unannounced. And unnoticed. I haven't noticed any extra help around the neighborhood, but I've only been there twice. Also, since I'm relatively new to all these people, I can't tell who's supposed to be there and who's not. Thankfully, before Penny can launch into more interrogation, Sue Lynn is back with our food.

"Here you are. Dan is still in his soups and salads obsession. Healthy foods, pfft. I could use a burger or two, if you know what I mean."

"I heard that!" Dan shouts from the kitchen.

"You heard nothing!" Sue Lynn hollers back. "That man. Enjoy the healthiest diner food you'll ever find." She turns away then, speed walking toward the kitchen, shouting. "I said what I said!"

"No matter how much they bicker, she'll never leave him," Penny comments, as we laugh. Sue Lynn and Dan are two peas in a pod. I honestly have no idea how they put up with each other. You'd think they were married but neither is. Instead, they just drive each other bonkers. I'm happy to see that hasn't changed.

I glance down Dan's current special of yummy goodness in front of me. There's nothing like a creamy potato soup served in a bread bowl. And of course, extra bread and butter on the side.

"What part of this is supposed to be healthy?" I mumble as Penny chuckles. When we dig in, I place this moment into my good memory bank, because right here and right now, this feels like home.

But I better eat up. I have some sleuthing to do after.

AFTER LUNCH, Penny heads back to the bakery, and I head back toward the inn. I told her I'm on my way there, but I didn't mention anything about diverting. Driving around the park, I end up on Second Street, and slowly creep toward the alley that'll lead me to the abandoned neighborhood.

I really should stop calling it that. It's just two blocks over from all the hustle and bustle, and it's not even creepy anymore. Still, I know that seeing my car drive down the street will be too conspicuous. Instead, I park near Tatas for Teas, and head for the mayor's house on foot. At least the heat isn't scorching yet like it can get in the summer. Most of the tourism at that time revolves around water. The beach is north of the town and within easy driving distance. I'm putting it on my list of things to do this summer, for sure.

After another two shops down, the alley is on my left. There are a few of these throughout town. I almost think whoever settled here originally realized that the main three streets form a complete circle and they needed ways to cut through. Just like near Trinkets and Things, the alleyway is wide and lined with trees and lights. It would be quite romantic to take a stroll here with a hunny. But oh well.

And don't you be thinking about Dean, you traitorous brain! Really now. I have more important things to focus on.

When I finally reach the neighborhood, there are no cars or

people in sight. It really is an oddly shaped place. It's kind of oval in that the houses face each other, but there's this semicircle happening as the neighborhood attaches to the rest of the town. The other neighborhoods are very square shaped. I guess it begs the question, did this development come first or was it built after?

Mayor's house is to my right. I turn that way without hesitation when I notice the sheriff's car parked in front. I swerve into the first yard and head for the back of the house. As I glance toward the mayor's, I see that there are no fences separating the yards. It must be my lucky day.

Not that I wouldn't have jumped a few fences or walls. I can be pretty adaptable. Although, my skirt probably wouldn't have survived the adventure.

Anyway.

I make my way toward Mayor Moore's house, staying in the backyards of the abandoned houses. My interior designer heart longs to remodel every single one of these historical beauties, but my friend/amateur sleuth/witch heart is on a mission.

Honestly, I'm not exactly sure what I'm looking for. It just seems like eavesdropping on the mayor and sheriff's conversation might yield me a much-needed push in the right direction. Especially if Sue Lynn is to be believed and they are in "cahoots."

Everything really is coming up roses for me because the windows are open, and there are plenty of bushes to hide in. After a quick scan of the street, I get closer and follow the sound of the voices. They seem to be in the sitting room, right near the kitchen.

"There's nothing we can do about that now," the sheriff says, his gruff voice much louder than I expected. "Word will get out."

"You mean it hasn't already?" the mayor asks. It's as if she moved closer to the window, so I duck down even more, lest she sees me. I'm not directly under the sitting room's window, I'm two down, but still. The bushes here are thicker as well and seem to hide me well.

"Everyone has been preoccupied with the murder."

Wait, so they're not talking about that? What else could they be concerned about?

"Understandably so. That poor woman. Still no leads?"

"She had no family that we could find."

"What about the woman you told me about?" That perks up my interest instantly. Did the sheriff find someone who might know Tamara?

The sheriff's voice sounds farther away when he answers, and I don't catch his words exactly. There has to be a way to get closer, but I have no idea how. I'm still crouching in the bushes when I hear a voice behind me.

"Cassie?"

I twist around and come face to face with a very confused looking Dean. Before I can even think about it, I grab his arm, pulling him down beside me. It doesn't go exactly to plan because somehow, he lands hard with me on top of him. I keep as still as possible as I try to see if anybody has seen us and blown my cover.

"Cassie. Wha—"

I slap my hand over his mouth, cutting off whatever he was going to say. That's when I realize I'm straddling him, pinning him down on the ground in the bushes.

With my hand over his mouth.

"I'm hiding, Dean," I whisper, looking down as I retract my hand.

"I can see that."

I roll my eyes, just as a noise comes from the house. I slam my hand back over Dean's mouth, just in case, as I sit frozen.

Yes, still on top of him.

I don't see any movement from the house, and after a few minutes, I pull away.

"Well, are you going to tell me what *we're* doing then?" He gives our position a quick eye raise as his lips turn up in a smile.

I scramble off him.

While still staying crouched down behind the bushes.

"Please don't ruin this for me," I whisper, knowing full well I'll have to explain later.

"Cassie, are you spying on people?" he whispers right into my ear over my left shoulder. My whole body shudders at the sound. I'm pretty sure I'm going to be dreaming about his voice in my ear for the next seventy-five years.

Okay, Cassie, focus. What is wrong with you? This is Mean Dean we're talking about. Just because he whispered in your ear, doesn't mean you should go all mushy. Ugh.

"If you must know." I turn slightly so that I can direct my whisper at Dean. "I am not snooping. I'm investigating."

"Oh, that's what we're calling it?" There's definite amusement in his voice, but I ignore it. This is no time to find him appealing.

"Yes, that is exactly what we're calling it because that's what it is."

"Like the drive over to Hastings was research?"

"Yes, as a matter of fact. Now stop talking and let me listen."

I assume Dean will get up and leave, but he doesn't. He stays right by my side. It's a little distracting having him this close by. I mean, I can feel his body heat and he smells delicious.

And here I go again—digressing. I need to focus.

The conversation beyond the half open window has moved on to cookies. Oh no, did I miss their whole discussion about Tamara?

"So, is this part of your new persona?" Dean asks, thankfully, keeping his voice low.

"You know what, mister?" I glance at him, instantly taking offense. "I do not appreciate that tone of voice. If you're not going to help, you can go ahead and just scoot your butt out of here."

"Scoot my butt. Who talks like that?"

"I do, obviously. Now hush, I'm trying to listen."

But when I turn back to the window, the conversation is over, and they're gone.

Great. My mind is trying to think of what to do next, but I honestly have no idea where to go from here. I can't figure out a way to connect Tamara to Penny at all. Or even to my aunt, outside of knowing she was a witch. What was she doing here?

"What's going on in that pretty head of yours?" Dean asks, still keeping his voice low. I throw a glare his way, and then slowly make my way out of the bushes.

"As if you actually care," I reply without pausing. He falls into step with me easily. I head back the way I came, after making sure the coast is clear.

"I do care," he replies. There's something in his voice, but I can't do this right now.

"Look, I don't need any kind of judgement from you," I say, stopping to face him. It takes me a bit to look up into his eyes, the largeness of him more evident than ever. "I'm concerned about my friend, and I'm trying to help. I just want to do my part."

"You don't trust the police to do their part?" he asks, but there's no judgement in his voice. He seems genuinely curious as to what I have to say.

"I do trust the police, of course," I reply honestly. "But if there's something that I can do, I want to do it."

That seems to be enough for him because he gives me a small smile. That's when something occurs to me.

"How did you find me?" I don't miss the way his hands reach

for his pockets, in his most nonchalant pose. "Dean, did Penny send you?"

He glances at me, but I already know the answer.

"Unbelievable." I throw my hands into the air, ready to storm off. "If it's not Finn, then it's Penny."

"I would've followed you anyway."

Dean's quiet words stop my almost rant. I turn to glance at him and see him shrug.

"Why?"

"Because Finn and Penny aren't the only ones who are concerned for your safety."

I have no idea what to do with that information. And I don't have time to process it anyway. A voice catches my attention.

"Cassie?"

14

"Hello, Mayor Moore." I plaster my customer service smile on and face the woman. She's right outside her house with the sheriff walking down the stairs to join her. He gives me a thorough study. I can see how this may look suspicious. Dean and I random show up, and then stand in the middle of the spooky neighborhood, arguing.

"Miss Duke. Mister Harvey. What brings you here?"

My brain goes blank, but thankfully, Dean is here. Never thought I'd think that type of thought.

"We've been working on a project, and Cassie needed a break. Thought we'd come by and take a look at the house."

"Yes," I jump in. "I usually like to do a walk through or ten. The house inspires me every time. If it's not too much trouble."

I'm not lying. That's actually part of my process.

"Well, come on in then. The sheriff is just leaving."

The man stayed quiet the whole time, and now, he merely nods in our direction, says something to the mayor, and gets into his car. As he pulls away, another car comes down the road.

"Oh perfect. Mary is here. I have some work to do, but you

are free to walk around." The mayor's cell phone rings, and she answers it right away.

Dean and I are just starting up the stairs when the car stops, and a young woman gets out. I realize I've seen her around town more than once. Even outside of the mayor's office.

"I haven't seen you for a while, Mary." Dean greets the girl as she joins us on the stairs.

"Oh hi, Dean. Yeah, I've been busy helping around town with all the festivities. The mayor has been extra on edge with everything." She nearly whispers that last word. Mayor Moore walks past us, still on the phone and waves Mary to her. The girl follows, but I can't take my eyes off her.

"What is it, Cassie?" Dean asks, clearly noticing.

"I'm not sure. She just looks so familiar."

"Well, I'm sure you've seen her at Penny's. She does the cookies. And deliveries."

That makes me pause.

"That's *Mary*? Penny's Mary?" I almost point a finger at the house but restrain myself.

"Yes." Dean is once again confused at my randomness. "You haven't met her?"

"No. She's been pretty MIA from Penny's for over a week now. I think she may have come in once. But I see her every-where. Outside of Penny's."

"That's kind of her thing. She gets bored easily, so busi-nesses around town hire her to do small jobs. She's a good worker, just—"

"Flakey?"

"I was going to say eccentric, but yes. You really haven't met her?"

"No. She was supposed to come in the morning of the murder but didn't show. Before that, Penny was already wondering what happened to her blender, so everyone was on edge. Well, Penny and I were. Justin wasn't aware of anything. And Mary was obviously not there."

"That's weird. She would have at least let Penny know."

"Maybe—" Before I can finish, the mayor and Mary are back out of the house.

"You're welcome to say, but I have a few meetings today. So, the house is yours."

I say thanks and watch as the two women get into the car. A nagging feeling nearly overwhelms me, and I have no idea what it could mean. Maybe I'm just being protective again. It's disrespectful that Mary would show up to the mayor's office for work but not Penny's bakery. Sure, it's the mayor. But it shouldn't matter. All people deserve to be treated equally.

"Cassie?" Dean steps into my line of sight, bringing me out of my musings. He probably thinks I'm losing my mind, the way I zone out around him. I'm just frustrated with myself that I do it in front of him. I don't typically trust strangers with myself enough to do so. But it doesn't seem to matter with Dean.

Luckily, he isn't looking at me like I'm crazy. He's looking at me like he wants to get to know me.

I kind of want him to.

"Anyway." I push all those intrusive and unnecessary thoughts away. "Shall we go in? I mean, we're here, right?" I need time to figure out how all this fits. And also, I'm curious to see if the mayor left behind any useful clues. It's not that I suspect her in anything, but there's a possibility of information. I'm not about to pass it up.

"Am I helping you with this project?" Dean asks, following me into the house.

"I'm not remodeling anything, so I suppose not." I shrug, but he doesn't leave. That's when I think of something, "Wait. Did you work on this house?"

"I did," Dean replies, running his hand over the wall with

fondness. He clearly loves his work as much as I love mine. It's a rare quality, and I can see it. I noticed it when I first came. There's a special touch to the building and the way it was handled.

"It looks great," I say, unable to prevent myself from giving him the compliment. He doesn't reply. When I glance at him, he's wearing one of his smiles.

"Oh yeah? I've got skills?"

"No, I take it back. It's atrocious, " I deadpan, and he outright laughs. I turn away, refusing to fall into that trap. The Dean trap.

Instead, I move toward the mayor's office. For someone who is very organized and put together in every way possible, her home office is a bit messy. There are papers all over her desk, and a few chairs. I do a quick walk around but don't disturb anything.

"She really seems to care about this town, doesn't she?" I ask, glancing up from a paper with plans for renovation on it. Dean is leaning against the doorframe, arms crossed against his chest.

"She does," he replies, and there's nothing more to say. I'm not sure what I was thinking, but maybe the mayor is all she appears to be. If my instincts are off, then I don't even know what I'm doing anymore.

"I NEED you and Finn to stop sending Dean to babysit me," I say when Penny comes out of my bathroom later that night. There was nothing more to do at the mayor's house after Dean and I did our walkthrough. I made notes, he drove me to my car, and then we parted ways. He was supposed to help with the booth setup. There were still a few stragglers coming in. I spent the rest of the afternoon researching and sketching out ideas.

Magic and design, my now two favorite things, I guess. Birdie has been nearby for all of it, opening her eyes every now and then to make sure I'm still making progress. Or something. I can't exactly read the cat's mind.

"We're worried about you," Penny says, as she towel dries her hair, taking a seat opposite me on the bed.

"And I'm worried about you but come on. Dean?"

"What? He's big and strong. He would be a great bodyguard. Easy on the eyes too," Penny adds as if it's an afterthought, even though we both know it's not.

"You really need to stop that." I roll my eyes while she grins.

"I have no idea what you're talking about."

"Mmhmm. Whatever you say."

I get off the bed, taking my sketchbook with me. It's mostly so Penny doesn't see the mind map I've been drawing on it, filled in with all the information I've been able to discover about Tamara.

I haven't found much.

Tamara came here in search of someone specific. That person is still unknown. She was a witch, and she asked Auntie Grace for help but never told her with what. I also know Tamara placed protection crystals around her room, and that she, at least at some point, used magic at Penny's. The reason is still unknown.

My two only true suspects are the unknown witch, which is always a possibility in the magic world, and the vendor that's been in a fight with Tamara for the last few seasons. Neither of them have led me anywhere.

"This whole sleuthing business is exhausting."

"But you're so good at it."

I roll my eyes again, as Penny chuckles. Maybe last time was just a fluke.

"Cassie, please stop worrying. You'll get wrinkles." She reaches over, poking me in the forehead.

"Ah! How dare you? My complexion is perfect. Perfect I tell you!" I grab my face, smoothing it out. We both laugh, and for the hundredth time since I returned to Monroe Cove, I feel like I'm finally where I need to be.

It's a strange conundrum, coming back to something you tried to escape for so long. But as Penny gets ready for bed, I can't imagine not being here for her as she's going through this. Thankfully, whatever was happening at the bakery has slowed down. It hasn't gone away, but it hasn't been as bad.

I wonder if it's because Tamara's magic is fading. I still haven't mentioned to Penny what I found. I think I'll need to talk to my aunt before I do. But tomorrow is the first day of the week-long bake off event, and everyone has been incredibly busy. I suppose there's nothing left to do but wait.

I don't remember falling asleep, but I immediately know I did when I open my eyes. And I'm still sleeping.

"It's about time, Cassandra Duke," the woman sitting on my bed says, her body encompassed in a glow. I'm still in my bed, but I can see that it's like I'm in another dimension or something. Penny is sleeping soundly beside me. Even Birdie is undisturbed at the foot of the bed.

"Wait, you're—"

"Tamara Weber. It's nice to make your acquaintance." The woman looks exactly how I remember her, minus the blood obviously. But she's pleasant, which surprises me for some reason.

"I don't understand what's happening."

"You have my protection crystals, Cassandra. My magic is attached to them. Thus, I can speak to you."

"I've never heard of this before," I mumble, still quite amazed.

"That aunt of yours has really been lacking in the teaching department, huh?"

"It's not really her fault. I did run away."

"I did once too." Tamara looks into the distance, as if she's remembering another time. "Sometimes we have to run from something before we realize we're only running from ourselves."

"Is that what happened to you? You were on the run? Who killed you?"

"Oh, Cassandra. You know I can't tell you that. A witch never remembers her own demise. And even worse, the longer you're dead, the fuzzier your memories become."

Well, that's unfortunate.

"What can you tell me? Why were you in Monroe Cove? You were looking for someone?"

Tamara grows quiet again, that faraway look back in her eyes.

"I was looking for family."

"Family?"

"I only recently found out that I was adopted. I know, what a thing to find out in your forties. My parents were wonderful, don't get me wrong, but they didn't have powers and I did. I had questions."

"Why Monroe Cove?"

"Because this place attracts witches and because your aunt is part of one of the strongest covens in the country."

"What?" That's news to me. Holy moly, I really know nothing about my magical heritage. Tamara doesn't hear me though. She's still reminiscing.

"I thought maybe I could find out where I came from. That bakery called to me, and Penny was always so nice. I wanted to give something back but—"

"But?"

"I don't remember."

"Why did you have protection crystals in place?"

"I always traveled with those. You never know if the witches you encounter are good witches or dark witches. One must always be ready."

That sounds like something my aunt would say. I have so many more questions to ask, but that's when I notice Tamara is fading.

"I heard you get answers once you cross over. Maybe I'll find my family then. My magic is slowly fading though, just like it does when you die, I suppose. I'm ready to get to the other side. Whatever it may be."

"I'm trying to help. I'm trying to find answers."

"You will, Cassandra Duke. You are much more than you think you are."

With that, Tamara disappears. I sit up in my bed, fully awake, and find Birdie staring at me with both of her eyes open.

"Did I really just have a conversation with Tamara?" I ask the cat, because she's the only one I can ask. I'm not hallucinating when I say that Birdie full-on nods, still keeping her eyes on me. "Okay, am I bound to help her like I was with Mabel?"

This time, Birdie shakes her head and then proceeds to lick her paw.

"Well, at least there's that."

I've recently learned that if a ghost asks a witch for a favor, they're bound together until that favor is fulfilled. In my case, the favor was finding the ghost's killer. So at least, Tamara isn't bound to me.

But I guess when Auntie Grace said I'll be developing new powers, she wasn't kidding. I don't think I've ever had conversing with the dead through dreams on my resume before.

Knowing full well I'm not sleeping, I creep out of my room and into the little library. Birdie is quick to follow. There has to be a way to help Tamara. I now want that more than anything.

Suddenly, I have an undeniable desire to pick up a certain

book. Without hesitation, I walk in the direction of the shelf and reach for one.

"That was a little weird," I comment, taking the book back with me to the couch. Birdie jumps up beside me, curling up to watch me in her usual fashion. When I flip the pages open, it's like they move on their own. My eyes scan the page, and I glance up at Birdie in surprise.

"I guess I know what I'm doing tomorrow."

15

The day started off way too early. After my nearly sleepless night, I'm exhausted. I've had absolutely no time to speak with Auntie Grace about Tamara showing up in my dream. I've been running errands and helping out at the bakery and the booths since seven in the morning. Now I'm giving Loretta a break at her booth as she runs to the bathroom.

"Here, please caffeinate yourself." Dean appears beside me, handing me a cup of coffee. I don't hesitate. The smell hits me before the taste does, and I nearly moan out loud.

"You are an angel. I think I want to have your babies."

Dean and I both freeze at my outburst, and I refuse to look at him.

"I'm clearly talking about the coffee," I finally comment.

"Clearly."

"But thank you," I hurry to add. "This was just what I needed."

He gives me a soul searing smile. I'm a little nervous I'm about to swoon fifties-style, when Loretta returns.

"Thank you, sugar. Could you make sure the vendors on the other side have all had a break?"

"Of course."

Apparently, I'm the only one around to give breaks? Not sure how I got volunteered into that position.

"Oh dear, could you give Frank a hand?" Loretta says to Dean. I wave in his direction before I make my way to the other side of the town square. With the fountain right in the middle, and the booths set up around it, it all feels very picturesque.

"Hello there. Anyone need a bathroom break? I am here to be of assistance."

"You are a gift!" a woman who looks to be in her sixties exclaims, and I head toward her. "Please watch the table as I rush over there." She doesn't wait for me to reply before she steps around and is gone. I stay in front of the booth when I notice the one right next to it. It has some of the prettiest crystals I've ever seen.

"These are beautiful," I say, still studying the table.

"Why thank ya," the woman replies. I glance up at her and smile. She appears to be in her fifties and is dressed how I would imagine a witch to dress if I didn't know any better. I've never seen her before, so I introduce myself.

"I'm Cassandra, the unofficial official bathroom break associate."

"Hi, Cassandra. I'm Betty."

At first, the name doesn't register. But that only lasts for a moment.

"You wouldn't happen to be the Betty that has a booth at Hastings?"

"Why yes, I am. Have ya been there?"

"Just recently. I heard they had a few booths with a wonderful crystal selection, but I didn't find one." I smile, but I'm nearly ready to jump out of my skin with anticipation. Betty has got to have some kind of info on Tamara.

"That's strange. There was supposed to be."

"What do you mean?"

"Oh, there is another vendor. This year, she was supposed to be at Hastings, and I was to be here. And then the following year, we were going to switch."

"You had a system going?"

"Only recently." The woman smiles, fidgeting with the crystals on the table. I glance back to see if the other vendor has returned, but no one is in sight. "We didn't always see eye to eye but came to a recent agreement."

"That's strange. There were no vendors there."

"That is strange. I wonder if she's alright. She would never miss an opportunity. She did love the craft, and Hasting is prime real estate, ya know."

"The craft?" I prompt, trying not to sound so eager.

"Oh yes. I'm a practicing Wiccan. No, I don't have any magical powers, before ya ask." She chuckles, not unkindly. "But I am sensitive."

I've heard of people like her before. Those who are aware of the magic but don't quite possess it. Many of them sell supplies such as herbs and crystals, just like Betty does.

I open my mouth to ask more questions, but a family comes over and starts asking Betty questions. She seems genuine in her belief in the supernatural, but she doesn't seem like a vengeful competitor bent on taking Tamara out for a spot at the market.

That means, I'm once again at square one.

∾

SMALL TOWNS really do go all out when it comes to their events. Something as simple as a bake off is a week-long event with basically every kind of activity you can think of. I'm exhausted.

Yet, I'm not sleeping.

Penny is passed out as I get out of bed and grab my shoes and the bag I prepared earlier. Birdie gives me a questioning look, but I only motion for her to stay on the bed. Last night, the book that called to me had a cleansing spell in it. I mean, it had other spells as well, but that's the one I couldn't get away from.

Tamara said her magic was fading. But if all my readings have taught me anything, it's that unchecked magic can cause a lot of havoc. If that is what's happening at Penny's, I need to see if I can cleanse it away. And release some of Tamara's magic in the process.

It would be helpful to do this with Auntie Grace, or during waking hours, but this seems like the only time I'll have the place to myself for the next week. At least. I'd like for my friend to be able to feel safe at work again.

The town is quiet as I make my way toward Penny's. It's a little past eleven at night and there are only a few couples out, enjoying an evening stroll. Must be nice. Not that this is the time for me to be wishfully staring off into the stars, hoping for a special someone to come walk with me under the night sky.

Priorities, Cassie.

I find a parking spot near the park and then make my way on foot over to the bakery. Being the amazing friend that I am, I swiped Penny's keys before she went to bed, so it's easy to get inside. I go through the back, leaving the lights off. Penny has a nightlight near the fridge, just in case she has to come down for a drink or food during the night. That's the direction I head. I don't want to attract too much attention by turning on the lights, so I flicker on only the light over the counter.

As I take out my supplies, my mind runs over all the information I have gathered about Tamara. It saddens me to know that she was just trying to help when she was killed. Every single motive I've come across seems implausible. She wasn't in competition anymore. There were no secrets she was hiding.

The witch angle is still in play, but only because it's always in play. Dark witches exist. That is a fact of life. We can't escape them or their shenanigans.

But this whole thing is different.

Why was she found behind Penny's? I don't think I ever asked that question. There are so many other places a body could be dumped. But it got dumped there. Why?

I never understood that connection, not even after Tamara said she came to give Penny a small gift. I can only assume it was a gift of protection and good fortune. Did Tamara think there was a bad voodoo happening here that Penny needed protection from? That's the only thing I can think of. But what could it be?

I'm so new at this, I can't quite decipher different energies yet. Not the way a skilled witch can.

A noise catches my attention. I pause, trying to listen. It's true what they say, everything is creepier in the dark. Like churches for example. Ever been in one of those when it's empty and it's past ten o'clock? Creepsville.

I listen again, but there's nothing. I can see why Penny has helpers here. At least she's never alone. Although, that only qualifies to Justin. Mary is still a flake.

A strange girl, that one. Now that I know who she is, I've noticed her around town. She seems fine, just on edge. Who wouldn't be in a town full of crime? Okay, I'm being a little dramatic, but I'm tired. I'm allowed.

Still, there's something about her that just doesn't sit right with me.

As I begin mixing two of the ingredients together, some-thing occurs to me.

I know exactly why I don't like Mary. I reach for my phone when a noise catches my attention.

And then everything goes dark.

16

Everything is slanted when I finally come to. I'm half lying on the floor. My hands are tied behind my back, and my legs are duct taped together.

Well, this is fun.

I glance up and see Mary pacing on the other side of the counter. I really am terrible at this sleuthing thing. I figured it out, just way too late.

"Mary?"

"You're awake. Oh no. I thought I might've, but I didn't. Which is good. But it doesn't matter. Because now I'm in trouble. I didn't mean to."

"It's okay, Mary," I say, keeping my voice calm. "I know. You didn't mean to. You're not in trouble."

"I am. I need to figure this out. I don't know. What I've done? It's—I don't know how to get out of this mess."

"What did you do, Mary?" I ask, my mind racing with all the magic spells that could be useful here. A sleeping potion would be helpful, but I doubt she'd drink anything I prepare right now. Plus, my hands are tied behind my back.

"I didn't want to, okay? I just had debts to pay. And I had to pay them. So, I only took a little. I took a bit. Wasn't even noticeable."

Mary was stealing from Penny? That's where all those little things have gone. They weren't misplaced. And Penny wasn't cursed. She just had an employee with sticky fingers.

"It's okay. I'm sure it'll be fine. How about you untie me, and I'll help you figure it out?"

"No!" Mary shouts, rushing over to me and pointing her finger right in my face. "You stay. I need to—I need to find a way—I can't do this anymore."

"Mary." I use my most gentle of voices. "Tell me what happened so I can help."

"You can't help me!" she nearly screams, raking her hands through her hair. "You don't know what I did. I did that. Me. And that's on me forever." She points her finger toward the back door. I don't have to be a genius to know what she's talking about.

Mary was spiraling, and fast. People who spiral are not safe. She's about to become more dangerous.

"Mary, I need you to talk to me."

"I'm the worst. Okay, I am. And there's nothing you can do to fix that. I needed money, and have been working so hard, and I just, I didn't want to steal from Penny, but I had no choice. I had absolutely no choice and then, and then she was here. And I—I didn't mean to. I didn't mean to at all." She's fidgeting with her clothes, pacing from side to side. She's like a powder keg ready to explode.

"Just talk to me. What did you do?"

"No! I know your tricks. I'm not saying. You're not going to make me admit it. No, this is all out of control."

She storms out of the room, leaving me on the floor. I'm trying to figure out if there's any kind of magic that can get me out of here without exposing my powers to her. Unfortunately, I don't know a spell that unties knots or rips up duct tape.

I need to get to my phone, and I need to call the police. I need to call Finn or Dean or somebody. Maybe this isn't the time to have an epiphany, but I've got one coming on.

I'm constantly doing these things on my own. I need to learn that I'm not by myself anymore. I have people in my life. I promised them I would be careful and here I am at the mercy of a very disturbed young girl.

Mary returns then, still just as distraught as she was before. Actually, probably worse. She looks like she hasn't slept in days.

"Mary, whatever it is, whatever the situation. I can help you." I try again, even though I understand that trying to reason with her is useless. I just need to buy some time.

"You can't help me. We've been over this already. Stop—just stop talking."

"Mary."

"No, you're trying to talk me out of this, but it's not going to work. Okay, I have to figure this out, I have to. I don't want to but I have to—I know what I have to do, and it's the only—it's the only choice. The only way I'm going to get out of here." She's mumbling to herself now. I definitely don't like the sound of that.

"Mary. Whatever you're thinking. Don't."

"Don't tell me what to do!" She gets right in my face. "Everybody's always telling me what to do, and I hate it. I can't do this anymore. This stupid town, all these people that are in everybody's business. They're too much. The walls are closing in around me, and I have to get out. I thought I was gonna get out. And now, I just. I'm stuck, and I can't—" She breaks off, moving away to do another walk about the kitchen.

She's not making much sense. Well, except for the whole part where she's talking about this town. I felt like that once. I don't anymore. But maybe I can use that to help her.

"Mary, I ran from this town once too. I ran from everything here, but the world out there? It isn't some miracle cure. You have to figure yourself out—"

"Don't you think I know that? Don't you think I've been trying to do that this whole time? It's not working, okay. And it's not my fault. I did everything right. I did everything that was expected of me, and I still, I don't know, I'm still me and I'm still stuck. I still made the wrong choice. No, not a wrong choice, a choice that I had to make."

She's back to not making any sense. But I know what she's talking about.

"Mary, did you hurt someone?" That stops her. I'm not sure if it's the question or my quiet words. She looks me right in the eye.

"I didn't mean to. She walked in on me taking some of the china. I didn't think, I just acted. And now I have to do it again."

There's a definite resolve in her tone, as if this is her only option.

Well, there goes me trying to bond with her. I guess it doesn't matter what she sees about my magic at this point. I have to do whatever it takes to save myself from the crazy person.

MARY DISAPPEARS AGAIN, this time carrying her backpack. I didn't even see her bring it in, but she picks it off the floor near the back door. I wiggle myself into a more comfortable sitting position, but my hands being tied behind me is very inconvenient.

Sounds are coming from the front. If I were to guess, Mary is cleaning the place out. This is her last Hail Mary—ha, no pun intended—because there's no coming back from this. I don't have much time.

Taking a deep breath, I concentrate on my magic. I've never been in this situation before, and therefore, I have no idea what type of magic could be of help. Not that I know that many. I just have it.

Cheese and crackers, I really need to get to learning my magic.

Cheese. My aunt loves chess. My aunt is great at magic. My aunt does spells!

Okay, maybe I'm losing my mind as well. My way of connecting the dots isn't normal, but this idea has potential.

Typically, spells are read from a book. There are a few I memorized as a kid that I no longer remember. But what if I can create my own spell? It's worth a try, right? I don't have much of a choice anyway. Mary seems to be on a warpath.

Ugh, I'm a terrible detective. Why did it take me so long to realize Mary has been avoiding Penny's on purpose? Or to notice the bracelet she's been wearing every time I've seen her with the mayor? It perfectly matches the necklace Tamara was wearing. The dreamcatcher. It was Tamara's thing apparently, and Mary got her sticky fingers on it.

But no, I couldn't have realized that in the comfort of my own home when I was going over the clues. I'm really bad at this.

Focus, Cassie. You don't have time right now to lament over your shortcomings. If you survive this, lament all you want then.

Closing my eyes, I do a few quick breathing exercises to calm my nerves. Then, I make sure Mary is still in the other room before I start whispering.

"Ropes that bind,
Tape that sticks,
Please untie,
Set me free?"

Okay that wasn't the greatest rhyming but I felt...something. I'm not sure what it was, or how I know it relates to my magic, but I'm certain it does. Nothing happened though. What am I doing or not doing?

Wait, Auntie Grace always says that magic comes from emotion and intention. I have asked, but I need to put my whole intention behind it. Still keeping my voice low, I try again.

"Ropes that bind,
Tape that sticks,
Please untie,
Set me free!"

The moment I say the last word, the ropes snap. The duck tape does not. Crap.

Using my now-free hands, I half pull half crawl over to the counter where Penny keeps the knives. Standing on my knees, I'm pulling one out when Mary returns.

"How—" But she doesn't even bother to finish. She launches herself at me, all emotion and no common sense. I roll out of the way at the last second, but since her feet aren't bound, she's on top of me in seconds.

Wild hair, wild eyes.

I slam my hands into her chest and push as hard as I can. She's not expecting me, so she falls back, which gives me a chance to kick away, using her as the springboard. She screams, sliding back against the floor as I try to get to my feet.

This duct tape is really as strong as they advertise. My eyes land on the counter and my phone. She didn't take it!

I hobble across the kitchen, half hopping, half shuffling my feet. I'm not fast enough. Mary grabs my hair, yanking me back.

"Stop fighting!" she yells, spinning me away as I stumble into the counter.

"No!" I yell back. I wonder for the first time if I can make enough noise for someone outside to hear me. But Penny's is right near a curve in the road. There's hardly any traffic around during nighttime.

I have to outmaneuver her somehow. She's now between me and the knives and my phone. The only thing near me is the rope she used to tie my hands. That's when I remember two things: the protection crystals in my pocket and a video I watched when I lived in the big city and was paranoid about random things.

"You don't get it do you? I have to do this! You won't let me go quietly, and I can't end up in jail."

"Oh honey, you won't end up in jail. Prison is your only way to go."

She looks at me a little confused, but I take that second to reach into my pockets and grab the crystals. In the same motion, I toss them right at her, hoping there's enough magic in them to protect me for a few seconds. Mary appears stunned as the crystals land in front of her.

I grab for the rope. Threading it through the duct tape, I wrap my hand around it and yank up with all the strength I have left. The front of the duct tape rips open, and I pull the rest of it off.

Mary yells again and pushes past the crystals toward me. But that was all I needed. I may not have control of my magic fully, but I do know some self-defense. I was a big city girl for years.

I take a stance, arms raised, feet apart. When Mary is almost upon me, I duck and then move up. Her body trips and then flies back. She lands hard against the counter, wind knocked out of her.

Okay, maybe I also watched a lot of football growing up.

I don't hesitate to grab the same rope she used on me. Jumping on top of her, I roll her over and pin her hands behind her back. Making quick work of the knots, I'm up and going for my phone before she has regained most of her consciousness.

"You stupid witch! You ruined everything!"

"That's Miss Witch to you," I say, grinning against the pain in my side. "And I think it's my specialty to ruin things for people like you." I might not be solving these crimes on time, but I can at least be here to see that the guilty party pays.

I hit the favorites button on my phone and dial Finn.

"Is this just a thing I'm going to be doing from now on?" Finn asks as I sit on the edge of the sidewalk, getting checked over by the paramedics.

"I don't know. Can you make people stop murdering each other in our town?" Maybe it's not a laughing matter, but I deserve this moment.

"If only I could, Cassie. If only I could," Finn replies, reaching over to give my shoulder a squeeze. I place my hand over his, reassuring him with my touch that I'm still here. Everything is good.

He arrived in mere minutes after I called because he was already on the way. He and Dean actually, who is talking to the sheriff on the other side of the parking lot, near the cop car that now houses a very angry Mary. Angry and talkative. She spilled the beans the moment the brothers stepped foot in to the kitchen. They found me sitting on the counter, knife in hand, just in case. Mary was still lying on her stomach with hands tied behind her, throwing mental daggers my way.

Apparently, Birdie woke Penny up, and when my friend realized I wasn't there, she thought something might have happened. So, she called Finn.

And now, they're here, and Mary will not stop talking.

I deduced pretty much everything correctly. Tamara wanted

to show Penny a kindness and give her a protection spell on her bakery. Tamara didn't know that Penny wasn't the family she's been searching for, but it was Tamara's way of giving back to this town that she loved. Obviously, Finn doesn't know about the magic angle. He does know about Tamara searching for her family, so maybe they just assume she came to the bakery for that reason.

When she showed up, she caught Mary stealing. Mary grabbed the first available pan and slammed it against Tamara's head. It would've been fine if Tamara hadn't also hit the side of the dumpster. It was an accident, but it doesn't matter. Mary is going to prison.

She also owes a lot of money to some brokers in the next town over. In her trying to get out of town, she racked up some debt. That is how she came to steal stuff from Penny and other employers she picked up jobs from. She hates this town so much, but the funny thing is, they would've helped her. If only she had asked.

Finn gets called away, and Dean takes his place.

"So, you're really into solving crime now, huh?"

"Not sure if I'd call it that. I didn't figure it out until it was too late." I'm not getting over that any time soon. If only I was a little more observant.

"I think you should give yourself some credit," Dean replies, looking intently into my eyes. "You aided in apprehending a criminal, and you walked away with nothing but a few bruises. That looks like a win in my book."

He watches me steadily. I can't seem to tear my gaze away from him either. I think maybe this is the moment I tell him we can be friends after all. But the moment is broken when the sheriff walks up to us.

"Well, Miss Duke. We find ourselves here again."

The paramedic finishes up, giving me a clean bill of health so I stand.

"Well, Sheriff Bernard, we do." He shakes his head at me, but he doesn't seem angry.

"You're going to be a lot of trouble, aren't you?" It's not even a question really. "You Duke women sure have it in your blood."

"Oh, sir, we definitely do."

He chuckles. I grin, satisfied that I finally got through to him.

"Want to walk me through what happened?"

"It would be my pleasure."

17

___

The last few days have truly been a blur. The final event of the bake off festival is finally here. I have to say, I'm going to be very happy when this is over because I need a vacation. I think my aunt is also ready for me to take a vacation, if only to get away from all the recent mayhem.

After fussing over me after I got home that night, Auntie Grace and I haven't talked about what happened. There are always people around, and I can't be spilling magic secrets willy nilly. I'm waiting until everything dies down. Then, Auntie and I are having ourselves a talk.

If Penny ever leaves my side.

She blames herself for everything, of course. For not seeing what kind of a person Mary was, not noticing items missing besides her baking equipment. Mary was really starting to get desperate by then. Surprisingly enough, Penny might be able to get most of those things back. She might even get the collection of silver bracelets I got her for her birthday five years back.

Penny has been so overworked, she hadn't even noticed Mary took them.

Before my big showdown with Mary, the sheriff was already getting ready to have a talk with the girl. While in Hastings, checking up on Tamara's history, the sheriff and Finn decided to visit the pawn shop there. They had a hunch of non-magical proportions about what was going on at Penny's. If anyone was going to steal items, they'd start selling them in the towns surrounding ours. It's not like anyone here is a criminal mastermind. They lucked into one of Penny's cutting boards, which is carved wood and very distinct. Finn recognized it right away.

That coincidence between the murder victim and the troubles in our town was enough for Sheriff Bernard to start asking questions.

And here we are.

"Miss Duke." Mayor Moore comes up to me where I stand behind the rows of chairs. The park area has been turned into a makeshift theater, with a stage and everything.

"Good afternoon, Mayor."

I smile at her, thinking I'll feel guilty thinking she was involved in this somehow. But that day when I was hiding in the bushes, the sheriff was doing his part in asking about Tamara's connection to the mayor. It began and ended with that purchase of the dreamcatcher.

It's interesting how threads I thought would connect, didn't connect at all. That's why I should never assume things. Lesson learned. I hope.

"Have you recovered well?" the mayor asks now. I nod. "Maybe the sheriff should think of hiring you to assist with his cases. You do have a knack."

"I'm not sure what the knack is for, at this point. Simply getting into trouble, I suppose."

"True." Mayor Moore chuckles. "Plus, I think you'll have plenty to occupy your time soon enough."

"Oh?"

She turns to face me, all business now.

"I know it's presumptuous of me to think you'll say yes, but I would like to ask. I have plans for the spooky neighborhood." I must give an indication of some sort because the mayor smiles. "Yes, I am fully aware that is what everyone calls it. But this town is beautiful and holds so much history within its borders. I want every part of it to be appreciated. I have plans for my neighborhood. I want families to live there, and I want to open up a few vacation homes as well. But I'll need your expertise. Yours and Dean's, actually."

"Dean?"

"He's agreed to help me, in conjunction with working on his other projects, but only if you do."

That's not what I expected. This is a huge deal. I don't see why it would matter to him whether I do it or not.

"I understand it's a lot, and I'd like to give you a few days to think about it. But please do. I think we can make this town even greater than it already is."

"I will."

I'll definitely be thinking about it.

It's close to ten at night before I park near the inn. The day has been long but amazing. Penny won first prize, of course. She made six different types of dessert. My favorite was definitely the cheesecake cake—yes, that's a thing apparently. But it felt good to honor her in that way, after all the work she put into it. She didn't even know her "example" creations were going to be entered, but the whole town agreed. I left her passed out in her own apartment before heading home.

As I make my way up the stairs, a voice calls my name. I turn, coming face to face with Dean.

"Hey," I start, a little surprised. "Everything okay?"

"Yes. I just finished up dropping off the tables we borrowed for the booths."

I can't see the shed and the driveway from right here, so it's not surprising I didn't notice.

"Well, thank you," I say, giving him a small smile. I expect him to leave, but he takes a few steps toward me. He stops right in front of the stairs with me two steps up. It's the first time I've been eye to eye with him.

"I heard Mayor Moore talked to you."

"She did."

"What did you tell her?"

At first, I told her I'll think about it. But before the day was over, I knew I wanted to help.

"You told her yes." He says before I reply, and that makes me pause.

"How can you know that?"

"I can see it on your face. That passion, that spark in your eye. You're already scheming up ideas, aren't you?"

"Maybe." I smile, but my insides are turning mush at his words. There's something about a man who sees and appreciates you for your passions.

"And working with me, you think you can handle that?" he asks softly, his voice full of teasing. At that, I grin. A part of me wants to ask why he needed my yes before he agreed, but I don't think now is the time.

"I guess we shall see about that. I'm a pretty tough boss, so as long as you promise no crying, I think we'll be fine."

"I make no such promises."

When he winks at me, I think I might become a puddle on these steps. There's kindness and intensity in his gaze all at once, and I have no idea what to do with either of those. Or the other emotion I'm not quite sure I'm reading that mirrors my own.

"Hi, Miss Mary Grace." Dean breaks our staring contest with his words, and I turn to see my aunt trying to sneak back into the inn. I didn't even hear her come outside.

"Hi there, darling. I didn't mean to interrupt."

"Oh, no worries. I should be going anyway." He looks at me then. "I'll see you tomorrow."

I nod Apparently, that's all I am capable of doing as I watch Dean leave. It seems I've taken residence on these stairs because I can't make myself move.

"That's one fine looking young man there. If I was a few years younger—"

"Auntie Grace!" I exclaim as my aunt explodes into a fit of giggles.

"Oh, hush, you know I'm just joshing ya. The look on your face, it's worth it." I shake my head, trying to suppress a smile, but of course I can't.

"Come, come. Sit with your favorite aunt."

She takes a step down and then settles herself on the top of the porch. I take a seat beside her, as we look out at the road and the trees beyond it.

"It's been quite a few weeks, sugar plum, hasn't it?" My aunt sighs, and I turn to glance at her. She has that faraway look about her. I'm not sure I want to interrupt whatever it is she's thinking. When she continues to talk, I'm glad I don't.

"I know I've kept a lot of secrets from you. I'm sorry for that. It doesn't excuse anything, but keeping secrets is part of my job."

"Even from me?"

"Even from you, honey pie. There are just some things you aren't ready to hear yet. But don't you worry, my berry pie, I will work on being more up front with you. You ain't no younglin' anymore."

I smile at her and then the words pour out of me. I tell her about what happened, about all the research I've done, and the tiny spell I was able to create when my life was in danger. She listens intently, letting me get it all out.

"Is Tamara at peace now?" I ask, having been thinking about that for days.

"I believe she is, sugar plum. And before you ask, no, there are no Webers here. We have no idea what family she came from, but she will know now. She is surrounded by family by blood and by magic now. She will never be alone or misunderstood again."

Those words ease the heaviness in my chest, and I smile to myself. But my aunt isn't done speaking.

"I've always known you would be a mighty force to be reckoned with. You always have been. But magic choses, and it has chosen you, my sweet girl." Auntie Grace places her hand over my cheek. "Your talents are many, and I will be here, every step of the way, doing what I can to make sure you aren't alone."

There are tears in my eyes as I reach over and pull her into a hug. I've tried so hard to find myself, and all this time, my destiny was waiting for me. I truly believe that now.

"I'd help too, if you'd ever learn to listen."

I pull back suddenly, glancing around at where that voice came from. But it sounded like—

"Well, finally," the snarky woman's voice says, but I still don't see where it's coming from. Auntie Grace looks at me in question. "Down here, darlin'."

I glance down to find Birdie coming up the stairs. She's watching me steadily before I hear it once again.

"It will be a lot easier helping you out, now that you can hear me."

"Umm, Auntie Grace?" I say, scooting away from the cat and toward my aunt.

"What is it?" She's on alert instantly at my tone.

"I think I can hear Birdie talking?"

"Oh goodness gracious me, you gave me a fright. I thought something was wrong."

"It's not? Am I having a stroke?"

"No, sugar plum. You have finally come to terms with your magic and accepted who you are. That spell at the bakery proved it. Your gifts will start manifesting more definitely now."

"Gifts?"

"Each witch's bloodline carries with it certain specialties. We have a few, coming from a strong line."

"And one of them is hearing sassy cats in our heads?"

"Yes." Auntie Grace chuckles. "Among others." She reaches over and pulls me in for a hug. "I am so proud of you, Cassie."

I hold her back just as tightly, feeling that comfort of home. When I pull back, I glance down at the cat once more, filled with mixed emotions.

"It's about time," Birdie says. I roll my eyes, pushing my hair behind my shoulder.

"Keep your sass to yourself, cat."

"Not on your life, lady."

Well, awesome. This is going to be so much fun.

<<<<>>>>

Cassie is going on vacation! And she's bringing her sleuthing with her. Find out what she, and the gang, are up to next.

Preorder today: Third Witch's the Charm

THE SIMPLE AND FAST BUT DELISH RASPBERRY CHEESE DANISH

INGREDIENTS

- 8 ounces of cream cheese
    - 2 teaspoons of vanilla extract
    - 1/2 cup of granulated sugar
    - 1/4 cup of raspberry jam
    - 1 egg
    - 2 tablespoons of milk
    - 1/2 cup of powdered sugar
    - 1 box of frozen puff pastry sheets

INSTRUCTIONS

1. Thaw the frozen puff pastry sheets
    2. Preheat over to 400F
    3. Unfold the puff pastry sheets over lined counter or parchment paper. Cut out the circles using a cookie cutter (or other utensil you might have). Place circles onto a baking pan, lined with parchment paper.

4. In a bowl, combine cream cheese, sugar, and vanilla. Mix until smooth.

5. Place a tablespoon of cream cheese onto the center of the danish first. Place a dollop (or a teaspoon) of jam in the center of the cream cheese, over the top.

6. Make an egg and water wash. One egg to 1-2 tablespoons of water. Gently brush the edges of the danish with the wash.

7. Bake for 15-18 minutes, or until golden.

8. While baking, combine powdered sugar and milk into a glaze.

9. Drizzle glaze over cooled danish.

10. Enjoy!

PS. You are more than welcome to make your own dough. Or choose a puff pastry of your own liking.

INSPIRED BY VARIOUS FAMILY RECIPES

THIRD WITCH'S THE CHARM

CROOKED WINDOWS INN COZY MYSTERY #3

Valia Lind

1

What does one do when their life seems to be spinning out of control? Take a vacation, of course. I have the perfect image in my head. I'm sitting at a cafe, watching the rain fall, somewhere no one knows who I am or about my magic. I'm eating delicious food and walking by the water. It sounds simply lovely. My actual plans ended up a little different, but it's still a vacation. For the past two weeks, that's all I've been able to think about, and the day has finally arrived.

"Auntie Grace, we're only going a couple hours down the road. If anything comes up—"

"Sweetie pie, I have managed without your constant hovering for years, I can do so for a few days." She squeezes my cheeks on both sides, while I roll my eyes at her.

I've been back in Monroe Cove for a little over six months now. In that time, I've managed to help solve two murder cases, usher a ghost into the afterlife, and reunite a witch with her lost heritage. I've also been helping Mayor Moore restructure one of the older neighborhoods and been helping Auntie Grace remodel the inn. But none of that is what's causing me worry.

Magic has been strange around these parts for months, and I don't want to leave Auntie Grace to deal with it herself, even though she's more than capable. I'm the one who's been having problems with my magic, which is why I had to leave my big city interior designer job in the first place and finally come home. Things have been getting better with that, but that doesn't mean that my need for control makes any of this any easier. Leaving, that is. The last half of the year has truly taught me some lessons about my obsession with being the one in control of everything. It makes me a great interior designer but not that great of a witch. Magic isn't science, after all.

"Don't you worry about me, sugar plum. I'll miss you."

"Not if she never leaves." This comes from the grey furball as she jumps on top of the counter and gives me a bored look. Birdie and I are not friends. I've never been a cat person, but I thought we were heading into mutual agreement territory. That is, until I've come more into my powers and recognized I can understand animals. Well, mostly just this annoying one that's my familiar or something along those lines. We're at a standstill right now.

I send a glare at the cat, making sure to remember not to reply to her when there are non-magical humans around. Lucy, Auntie Grace's business partner, reaches over to scratch Birdie by the ear. I roll my eyes again. The cat makes sure to give me one of her condescending looks, and that's it, I definitely need a vacation.

"Are we ready?" Penny, my best friend of many years and the only person besides my aunt who knows about my magic, appears at the front door. She is also more than a little excited about our trip, considering the last case I helped out with involved her bakery and the dead body that was found behind it.

Talking Penny into giving up the reins on her business for a week was not easy, but it's necessary.

"We are ready," I announce. We head to my trusty Toyota Corolla, as Auntie Grace follows us out. I tell myself I'm not looking for him, but I can't help check to see if Dean's truck is here. It's not.

"Are you sure you're okay, sugar plum?" Auntie asks as she gives me a hug. I nod into her shoulder before pulling back with a smile.

"Of course I am. I'll see you in a week."

Once inside the car, I back out of the driveway as Auntie Grace watches from the porch. There's a little bit of worry on her face, and I can't help thinking she knows that I haven't been completely honest.

For the past three days, I've been experiencing strange dreams. Well, actually just the one. No matter what I'm doing or where I'm at, a man shows up, begging for help. He grabs me by the shoulders, yelling straight into my face, before he runs out of the dream. It's not anything earth-shattering, but I wake up exhausted every time. I'm hoping a change of scenery will help with that as well.

"Music?" I ask, shaking off my thoughts as we leave Crooked Windows Inn behind.

"Absolutely," my best friend replies, reaching for the cord.

This vacation is going to be great for the both of us. No magical shenanigans, just two young women on a holiday.

"DID you think we'd actually get out of Monroe Cove?" Penny asks as we walk into our bungalow after checking in. It's taken us three hours to drive up to Williams. It's been a long time since Penny and I did a road trip, as mini sized as this one is. We enjoyed every second of it, but her question is valid.

"No, I really didn't."

The last six months have been beyond unpredictable. Between two murders, a zombie, and my magic being a complete disaster, I've been trying not to hold my breath about actually having a vacation. But now, things—and my magic— seem to have settled, so I will take what I can get.

"We should totally go out to the island tomorrow, instead of this weekend," Penny says, holding up her phone for me to see. "Rain is coming."

Granted, we should've booked a vacation during the summer months, but it was just too busy for both of us. Penny with her business, me with the town's business. Mayor Moore is determined to remodel the whole of Monroe Cove, and I have become her trusted advisor. Well, myself and Dean.

The moment the man's face comes to my mind, I push it away. This is a vacation from everything Monroe Cove, including the handsome handyman who's been bothering me at all hours of the day, including my dreams. Well, when I'm not dreaming about that other strange man I've never seen.

"Let's go over to the dining room," I say, running a hand through my long red hair, trying to tame it somewhat. The color has always been dark and more sunset red than the typical ginger. People have often asked what product I use to color it, and it gives me immense pleasure telling them it's all natural. But it's also a pain in the butt sometimes.

Giving up, I pull out my handy dandy hairbrush and begin to untangle while Penny looks through the brochure.

The place we picked for our little vacation is a witchy dream. Instead of one building, the room and board is broken up into small bungalows. There are about ten, spread out on this side of the property, plus a main house at the front by the entrance. There are rooms inside the main house as well. It houses the main dining room, a banquet hall for events, and spa facilities. It's a combination of modern and past conveniences. But the bungalows make it witchy.

Ours is a two-room cozy haven. The semi bohemian decor, live plants, coupled with pillows and blankets, make this seem like a witch getaway. Or a fortune teller's lair. Your choice.

I like to think it was created just for me, a place where I can recharge and reevaluate.

I have to be honest with myself. The last six months have been a whirlwind of magic and feelings, neither of which I expected or wanted. It's a lot to deal with on a daily basis.

When my suppressed magic went haywire at my last big city designer job, I felt like my life was over. Everything I've worked for, everything I wanted, slipped through my fingers. I had no place to go but home.

Once in Monroe Cove, I didn't disappear into oblivion. The magic that brought me home took me on my next adventure, which is how I ended up solving a murder—and helping a very outspoken ghost on her way to eternal peace.

That was just the beginning.

Since then, I've learned more about my magic than I ever wanted to. And I'm finding out, I actually *want* to know about magic. Being part of Monroe Cove—it truly has been like coming home and finally making a place for myself.

But none of that denies the fact that Penny and I needed a break. Too much of a good thing can be suffocating. So here we are.

"I'm definitely down for food," I finally say, dropping my hands at my sides. Maybe I should start lifting weights, just so I can brush my hair without getting winded. Penny looks up, giving me an understanding smile.

"You'd think in all your magic there would be a spell to help with the hair."

"I know right?" I whine, shaking out my now tired arms. "It's like a full-time job."

But even as I whine, I know I would never cut it, especially not when my hair is the only thing I remember of my mother.

I try not to dwell on the unknown, but the more time I spend in Monroe Cove the more I want to find out what happened to her. She disappeared when I was too young to remember, and no matter how amazing Auntie Grace has been at raising me, that question has never been answered: Where did she go?

Doing another quick run through the hair, I put the brush away and turn to my friend. I'm more than ready to have a break from all things Monroe Cove.

"Let's get food."

Penny jumps up immediately, heading for the door. When we step out into the cool autumn air, I take a second to breathe it in. The air here is slightly crisper because of the water, and I'm eating it up. Just then, my stomach growls. Speaking of eating.

"Do you think—?" I begin, when a prickle of awareness runs over my skin. I turn toward it, just as the door to the bungalow next to us opens.

"Fancy meeting you here." The grin that splits Mean Dean's face is blinding, even in the shadows of the setting sun. I stand there completely perplexed as I gape at him.

"Oh, hey Dean. Finn," Penny greets them, completely unfazed. I turn to my best friend, and she ducks her head down at my glare.

Pigs in a blanket; this is a setup.

2

———

"Penelope Sharks, you better have an ironclad explanation for this." I pull her right into our bungalow, leaving the guys staring after us. "When were you going to tell me?" I place my hands on my hips as Penny refuses eye contact. "Were you even going to tell me?"

"Well, no," she replies, shrugging. "I knew you'd get your panties in a twist, so I figured we'd just run into them."

"Next door?"

"Yeah, that wasn't planned."

"So, this was planned!" Penny rolls her eyes as I point at her. "Also, who says panties in a twist?"

"That *is* the important question here," my friend comments, and that's when I realize she's trying not to laugh.

"Penelope!"

"What?" She raises her arms up in surrender. "You love Finn."

"It's his brother who's the problem," I grumble, but she only rolls her eyes at me again.

"Maybe you don't want to admit it, but we both know that's not so true anymore."

Now Penny is the one pointing at me, as I narrow my eyes. It's difficult not to fidget under the scrutiny, especially because she's right. Things aren't what they used to be. Dean and I aren't truly enemies anymore. That means I have no idea which category to put him in, which is driving me slightly crazy.

"Dean was driving out here anyway, so Finn suggested coming along and being part of our little vacation."

"I thought this was a girl's trip."

"It still is. They're just sleeping next door."

That really isn't the kind of distance I wanted between Dean and me. I need us to be an ocean apart while I figure myself out. It's taking a lot of work, okay? I'm complicated.

"So, are you done being dramatic now?" Penny asks, breaking through my thoughts. "Can we go to dinner?"

"I will never stop being dramatic," I reply, raising my chin. "But yes, we can go to dinner."

I have absolutely no other option at this point. I can't hold Penny hostage with me just to avoid the guys, and that will also raise too many questions. I have to be an adult about this. Plus, my stomach is really hating me at the moment.

When we step back outside, the guys haven't moved. I can feel Dean's eyes on me, but I focus on his brother instead. Finn wears an amused expression. Narrowing my eyes only makes his smile grow broader.

"There are my two favorite ladies," Finn says, coming to meet us on the path to the main house.

"We're the only ladies who tolerate you. Of course we'd be the favorite," I say, falling into step beside him. He throws his arm over my shoulders, pulling me close. His touch is instantly comforting, just like it's been since we became friends as kids. There's something about platonic soulmates that I truly believe in. We all have those people in our lives that just fit in the most perfect way possible. It doesn't have to be romantic.

My eyes find Dean of their own accord as he walks in front and to the left of me. Penny is beside him. They're chatting about cakes—Penny's favorite subject. Even from the back, I can tell Dean is genuinely listening to her. It brings a smile to my face. I make it disappear immediately. What is with my mind lately? I'm all over the place.

Focus, Cassie.

"Are you totally mad at Penny?" Finn asks. I glance up at him smiling down with a knowing gleam in his eye that I don't appreciate. Sending a glare his way, I shake my head. I'm really perfecting my mean face here, people.

"No, I'm not mad at her." Because it's true. Maybe a little suspicious. "Mind telling me why you're here?"

"You've been talking about this place for weeks, and I had some time saved up. So here we are."

I narrow my eyes once more because there's definitely something he's not telling me. I can feel it in my bones. I have no idea if it's my newfound sleuthing powers, or I've just known him long enough.

"Mmhm, sure. Now what's the real reason?"

"There's no real reason, Miss Suspicious of Everything." He squeezes me closer to him, and I shake my head. Before I can prod further, we arrive at the main building. There are a number of people out in the outdoor sitting area. A string of lights hangs low over the tables. Candles are placed strategically across the surfaces, creating a very cozy atmosphere. It looks like what I would stage an outdoor space as, utilizing the placement of the sitting area between the buildings. The gentle breeze plays with the flames, and I can't help but smile to myself. I can feel tension seeping out of me already.

Then my eyes meet Dean's. He's watching me study our surroundings, and he doesn't miss the smile. His own eyes sparkle, as if he's doing his own assessment of the area. We've been working together a lot lately, especially since Mayor Moore came up with her plan for renovating one of the old neighborhoods. It's become evident that Dean and I are on the same wavelength. It's a strange place to be, especially after our childhood history, but here we are.

Strange. Weird. Unusual. I can throw a lot of words at this situation.

Tearing my gaze away from Dean, I give myself a mental shake. I shouldn't let my mind wander back to Monroe Cove. I'm here to relax, no matter how unrelaxed I feel in Dean's presence.

Okay, maybe I'm slightly annoyed with Penny. But I am a grown woman, and I can get through dinner without pouting.

Maybe.

"I REMEMBER when you decided to redecorate my room for the first time," Finn says after we order our dinner. We're sitting in the outdoor space, Finn to my right and Penny to my left, which leaves Dean directly in front of me. Even though it's after seven in the evening, I'm sipping on a cup of coffee. I need something to soothe my nerves. Yes, I understand the contradiction this creates.

Now, I laugh.

"But let's be honest, your love of 80s movie posters was overwhelming."

"Hey, those were classics!" Finn protests.

"And they still are. But you needed order. I gave you order."

I still remember taking down all the posters, uncovering the fact that Finn had pinned new ones over old ones. It was messy and unnecessary. According to my aunt, we discovered that some of the posters were actually valuable, so those went into frames. I rolled up and stored a whole bunch of others.

"I still have all of them, by the way." He sounds proud of that, and I'm not surprised. He's become a collector of sorts.

"Of course you do," Penny comments, taking a sip of her tea. Finn immediately zeros in on her.

"Excuse me, what is that supposed to mean?"

"Nothing," she replies, smiling into her cup.

"No, no. Say what you're thinking. Don't hold back now."

They start bickering back and forth, and I can't help but chuckle. One of these days, they might actually admit how they feel about each other. Until then, I'll sit back and enjoy the show. I glance over at Dean, and I can tell he's thinking the same thing. Not sure when I became adept at reading him, but I think I'm getting there. He throws a wink my way, and it disarms me for a second.

Okay, Cassandra Duke, get yourself up off this floor. No metaphorical melting allowed.

Because, goodness gracious, cheese and crackers, the man can give out lessons on winking. And make a million bucks.

Thankfully, just then, our food arrives, and we dig right in. As I take my first bite of the mashed potatoes, a shiver runs up my spine. Pausing, I give my surroundings a quick scan, but I can't see anything out of the ordinary. Still, the feeling doesn't go away.

Could it be my witchy powers are picking up something?

I wish I could be sure, but with the way things have been going, I'm not definite on anything. You'd think by this time I would be able to handle magical disturbances and read them like an adult witch, but most of my magical journey started six months ago. I'm learning everything for the first time.

It doesn't change the fact that I still pick things up, even when I can't understand them. When I turn back to the table, Finn is talking. Penny gives me a quick questioning look, but I only shrug. It could be possible I'm simply paranoid about everything, especially after the last few murders.

"Didn't the mayor say she wanted to host a party there? Cassie?" Finn's question makes me refocus back on the conversation.

"Sorry, yes. She talked about it, but I doubt we'll be able to do a whole holiday affair like she wants."

"It would be the best way to reintroduce the neighborhood to the town," Dean says, taking a bite of his food. I narrow my eyes at him because we've had this argument before.

"Yes, but the place isn't ready. I'd rather not have people trampling through half-finished rooms."

"That's because you don't think I can have it done on time."

"You really think you can?"

"Yes."

"So, what are you doing here then?"

"Arguing with you, apparently."

We're leaning toward each other across the table, and I can feel fire burning within me at his proximity and his words. We're always just at the edge of igniting, and I can't pretend that I don't like it. That I don't look for it.

"Okay, kids. Back to your corners." Finn waves a hand between us, and Dean and I pull back.

"All I'm saying is that we can find a compromise," Dean says, and I smirk.

"A compromise that benefits you."

"One that benefits everyone. You know you can simply ask for help."

I really hate that he seems to know me so well. Of course I'm thinking of how much work and preparation it would be, on top of everything else I'm doing.

"Cassie doesn't ask for help," Penny says. I turn my shocked eyes on her.

"Whose side are you on?" I ask. She picks up a spoonful of

her mashed potatoes, trying to look innocent while I shake my head. This is a never-ending argument, and Penny is officially taking Dean's side.

"Wait, is this why you're here?" I ask, pieces falling into place. "You think you can wear me down?"

The three of them look down at their food, completely guilty.

"I knew it. You guys are ridiculous."

"Come on, Cassie," Finn says, being the brave one to meet my eye. "We're just trying to make you realize you don't have to do everything by yourself. We can help and will, if you let us."

Just like that, my friend has disarmed me. I've been trying so hard to stay in control of every aspect of my life, taking on this project seemed completely impossible. But they're basically holding an intervention to remind me I'm not an island to myself. I can't fault them for that, which is probably why I finally concede.

"Fine, we can talk about it."

Penny claps her hands together in glee as the guys grin. I'm becoming a softy.

3

Before I realize what's happening, I'm in the dream once again. I don't even remember falling asleep. I was probably way exhausted after having to endure the torture that was dinner with Dean. Okay, my dramatics are at an all-time high, but I'm allowed. Because I say so.

But I can't dwell on that right now. Right now, I'm back in the weird fog filled dreamscape.

These dreams have been coming nonstop for a week now, and I almost expect them at this point. I still have no idea who the man is, and I still know nothing about the actual setting of the dream. I have no choice but let it ride itself out.

"You're here." The voice comes from behind me, and I turn to see the same man step out of the shadows. At least he seems to be done with that whole running up to me and screaming *help* bit. As far as I can see, we're in a forest, but there's not much to make out past the darkness and the fog.

"You've been visiting me. Why?" I've learned—thanks to Auntie Grace's many books—that repeat sightings in a dream are just that: visits. But it's usually from someone you have an emotional connection to. I've never seen this man.

"I've been lost," he says now, his eyes so dark they appear black. He's looking at me, but not quite. I can't figure out if he's a ghost or not. My last run in with a phantom was when a recently deceased decided to ask me for help and then haunted me until I solved the case. Okay, haunted is a little dramatic. She just appeared in random places when I wished she didn't. But I solved that case, and she was able to cross over. This man and these dreams seem nothing like that.

"Who are you?" I ask now.

He doesn't answer right away. For the first time, I give myself time to study him. He's dressed in a plaid shirt and jeans that seem expensive. He's wearing a watch that costs more than my fancy boots. His beard is trimmed, his hair brushed. He doesn't look like he's experienced any distress in life, except for the weird screaming he does. And then he's grabbing my arm—like he always does in these dreams—and nearly yells into my face, "You have to help me!"

And then, poof. He's gone.

I blink a few times and realize I'm awake. A sliver of sunlight peeks through the drawn curtains. Seriously. I think I might need to hold a seance or a cleansing ritual because I think I'm being haunted for real this time.

It's becoming very inconvenient.

"Cassie, are you up?" Penny's voice comes from the other side of the door, and I simply grunt. She chuckles before continuing, "I want breakfast before we head to the docks, so you have fifteen minutes!"

"Stop being so bossy, Mom!" I shout back.

"Not on your life, missy. Now get a move on."

It really is true what they say. A best friend relationship is one person who loves mornings and another person who hates them. And they're stuck with each other. Or maybe that's marriage. Who knows? It's too early for my brain to be making those connections.

With my eyes still half closed, I slide my hand across the nightstand, looking for my phone. I remember a time, back when I was working in the big city, this little gadget wouldn't leave my hand. Now, we're only slightly acquainted most of the time. I can't even complain about that. If I was still at my old job, I would've never gotten away for this fall retreat with Penny.

Plus, Dean and Finn, apparently.

I groan again, this time at the memory of the guys' smug faces as we all headed down to dinner last night. Well, I don't know if smug is accurate. Finn looked slightly apologetic, but still excited. Dean looked—

No, I am not entertaining any thought on how Dean looked or looks or will look. I am getting out of bed and getting dressed because I'm pretty sure my best friend will leave me behind if I don't hustle.

Good job, Cassie. Make a plan. Execute it. You've got this.

Twelve minutes later, I'm by the front door.

"WHAT'S the deal with you and Dean?" Penny asks, raising her eyebrows. But two can play this game.

"I don't know, Pen. What's the deal with you and Finn?"

She flusters immediately, turning away to look out at the water. "I don't know what you're talking about."

"Mhmm, denial is more than just a river in Egypt."

"Did you just quote Auntie Grace to me?"

"I did. Oh my stars, I'm turning into my aunt!" I raise my hands to my cheeks, feeling for a fever as Penny bursts out laughing. We've taken our seats on the ferry, the sharp breeze blowing against our cheeks. I feel refreshed already. It's been a long time since I've been out on the water.

Apparently, there's an abandoned island right off the coast and the locals have turned it into a tourist attraction. It has a few mansions on the land, and I'm eager to explore how the other half used to live. Learning about design from years before helps me with design now. Eventually, I'd like to explore the main house of the resort as well. It might hold a few historic rooms in it.

"I still can't believe you guys ambushed me about the holiday party," I say, as the ferry fills up and we begin our journey toward the island. It's only about a forty-minute ride. The feel of water beneath us is a bit soothing, and the slight wind makes me feel connected to nature. But I can't forget what has happened.

"I'm sorry, Cassie. But you're notorious for not asking for help, and Mayor Moore didn't want to order you to have the party. It was time we had a serious conversation."

"You know I could've done the party by myself, if I wanted to."

"You could've. But the guys wanted to help, and I couldn't exactly give them the real reason why you're being so opposed to this whole shindig."

She's right, of course. The main reason I've been so opposed is because of my magic. Since it's gone haywire, I've been doing my best to work on it. But during days of celebration, there isn't much I can do about control. I'm afraid that if I agree to this party, I would make a mess of things with my magic in front of everyone. It almost happened during All Hallow's Eve. My magic will be much stronger during Winter Festival.

"So now that I've agreed—after the ambush," I point out, and Penny only shrugs, "What are we doing to do?"

"You're going to delegate. With Auntie Grace's help, we'll get contingency plans in place."

"Wow, you're so efficient."

"You're not the only boss woman around here." Penny raises her chin, grinning. I can't help smiling in return. My best friend does know how to handle her business. She started her bakery from nothing and has built it into a favorite of tourists and locals alike.

"It's risky," I say, looking out over the water.

"But necessary."

"What do you mean?" I turn to her, because it feels like she has a speech prepared.

"You can't live your life in fear, Cassie. Your...magic," she whispers, "it's part of you. So, you can't stay at a standstill while you figure it out. You have to be moving forward."

"You have been talking to my aunt," I comment, and Penny shrugs again.

"We love you. We want you to succeed."

It's crazy that once upon a time, I ran from all of that. I thought the only way I could become unstuck was to leave Monroe Cove and everyone I knew and rediscover myself. What I've discovered is that I'm much more than just an interior designer and a witch. And learning those important lessons about myself are invaluable. Also, I have the best support system around me.

"Wait, what's going on?" Penny suddenly asks, and I realize the boat is turning around. Just then, an announcement comes over the loudspeaker.

"We apologize for the inconvenience, but the storm is rolling in much faster than we anticipated. We can reach the island, but we would not be able to come back. We apologize and will be offering other schedule options and refunds at the dock."

"Well, that's a bummer," Penny says. I agree. I was looking forward to it. But I'm not too disappointed. This just means more spa time for us.

4

———————

The rest of the day is spent at the spa. I haven't been this relaxed in ages. The rain hasn't come yet, but the clouds hang low most of the day. Those clear out right before sunset, which made my need to be out in nature too much to ignore. I leave Penny at the bungalow and go for a walk.

It's the kind of night that makes me feel like I can let the magic out to play. The closely guarded secret I have lived with my whole life is almost like a friend I'd like to spend some time with. Auntie Grace has always taught me that my magic and I are companions through life, but it is only in recent weeks that I finally see that for myself.

The moon is so full and close today, it illuminates the garden around me in the most beautiful of glows. It calls to my magic, and for just the smallest moment, I let it out to play. Raising my left hand slowly, I focus on the leaves on the ground below me, sending my intention their way. They raise as I raise my hand and follow the flow of gentle movements as I let my hand sway around. The basic magic brings a smile to my face, and I think it's grateful to be out and about.

A rustle of leaves catches my attention. I drop my hand, letting go of the magic. A second later a person steps out of the woods on my right. Even without the extra glow from the moon I'd be able to recognize Dean anywhere.

"What are you doing lurking in the forest?" I ask, letting my voice carry toward him on the breeze. He freezes for a moment and then his eyes find mine. An easy smile falls to his lips, and I try not to fidget. He really does make me feel like a young schoolgirl all over again.

"And here I thought you'd take this opportunity to throw some jabs at me," he says, coming my way. I turn toward him a little more fully as he stops a few feet away.

"It would simply be too easy to make a dig at you, communing with your ancestors. There *are* flying monkeys in this forest, no?"

I'm teasing him. I'm flirting. *Red alert. Red alert. What is happening?*

"Really, Cassie. Mary Grace would be so disappointed with your manners." He *tsks tsks*, just like my aunt would do, and I roll my eyes.

"We both know she would praise me for my gumption, so the joke's on you," I say, then turn back to stare out at the water. This is the only place in the little clearing that has a break in the forest to oversee the town below and the glistering water beyond it.

I find it easier if we're not making direct eye contact. My insides are definitely forgetting that we're supposed to hate him. It's become harder and harder to distinguish the man I know from the boy I remember. I know we should clear the air eventually, but it seems I can't fully do that without talking about my magic. And there's no way I will do that. It's enough that Penny knows. More people would simply make it complicated.

"Are we going to talk about it?" Dean's voice breaks through my musings. I glance over at him, but his eyes are on the water. He looks pensive almost, and he can't actually mean us because —wait, can he?

"Talk about what?" I ask, since that's safest. He turns to face me then, and I realize he's much closer, with only a few feet separating us. And holy moly, macaroni, the intense way he's looking at me is going to burn this little patch of grass into crispy cinders.

"You hate me."

Like a bucket of cold water his words hit me, and I nearly take a step back.

"I do not."

The words are a reflex, but I'm surprised to know they're true. Well, maybe not surprised, considering I've been in "Confused-land" for months, but still. It's a development. Good or bad, we're going to have to find out.

"But you did." The intensity in his gaze is too much to take. Some type of a vacation this has turned out to be. We came here to escape all things Monroe Cove, and here I am, having a conversation with one of those "things" I was trying to escape.

"Dean—"

"Cassie, I know you well enough to know I'm right." He shrugs, but I simply narrow my eyes.

"Know me? You know me." I say the words, but I can't believe them. There's enough of a tone behind them that Dean stands up a little straighter.

"Let's not kid ourselves. You know nothing about me. Besides how to torture me and make my life difficult every single day when we were in school. And now, always being underfoot. Rescuing me from situations I don't need to be rescued from."

Okay, I'm really lying on that last one. But the rest still stands. He cocks his head to the side, bewildered and maybe something else? I can't tell, it's suddenly too dark. I glance up and see the moon hiding behind the clouds. *Well, aren't you so helpful?*

Great, now I'm mentally yelling at the moon. I need to calm down.

"I was not a nice kid." Dean's quiet words bring all my attention to him. There's a pause and then his eyes are on me, and I can't look away even if I wanted to. Which I don't. But we've been over this already.

"I was angry. I was acting out. And I liked you. There's no excuse for any of that, but I want to say I'm sorry. I don't remember half of what I did, but I remember enough."

My brain is still a dozen words back at the "I liked you." I blink to refocus.

"You liked me?"

That is not what I meant to say, but it's out before I can stop it. I slap my hand over my mouth before I wave it in front of him. "Never mind, it doesn't matter."

"But it does. I tortured you because, well, I had a crush on you." He looks down now, looking almost sheepish. I'm still trying to wrap my mind around it. But I guess it's not that surprising right? Little boys often pull on pigtails if they like a girl. It's the other stuff that I don't understand.

"You thought putting mayonnaise all over my final project for the science fair was going to make me like you? I failed that whole project because of you." The words and the hurt rush out of me all at once, and Dean's eyes fly up to meet mine.

"I never did that."

His words, and the way he says them leave no room for argument. He believes what he's saying. But how can that be true?

"I remember it. I cried for hours. It was my ticket—" But

then I stop. He's looking at me in disbelief, and I suddenly don't know what's true and what isn't.

A few months ago, I found out my aunt had magically altered my memories to protect me. She hasn't been able to tell me more than that, not yet at least. But is it possible that some of my experiences are different from what I remember?

I glance up at Dean, at the confusion and apology in his gaze, and I decide that it doesn't matter. We're not the same people we were as kids, and I can't hold this over him forever. No matter how much that project set me back. Or ruined my acceptance into the school of my dreams that my mother attended. It doesn't matter anymore.

As I stand there, processing all of this, Dean takes a step toward me. I glance up, as he fills my personal space with his scent, his eyes intense on mine.

"Can we start over?" he whispers, holding out his hand toward me. "I'm Dean, Monroe Cove's handyman. I used to have trouble expressing my emotions, but I have really matured since then. I like coffee, pie, and road trips."

I stare at him, and his crooked smile, then down at his hand. Didn't I just decide to put everything behind us?

Well, get to it, Cassie. Haven't got all night.

Taking a deep breath, I place my hand into his. His half smile becomes a grin, and I can't help smiling back.

"Nice to meet you, Dean. I'm Cassie, part time interior designer, full time Auntie Grace's babysitter. I don't like pie, I'm partial to eclairs. But I do love coffee and road trips."

We stand like that, hands clasped, grinning at each other.

I've been acting like a child when it comes to him for way too long. Maybe it's simply a protective mechanism, a way for me not to accept the ever-growing feelings I have toward this man. But it's time I've stopped being childish. It's time I gave us a new start.

⌇

WE MAKE our way back toward the bungalows shortly after, walking a little slower than usual. Maybe I'm romanticizing this situation, but it almost feels like he's not ready to say goodbye to me either. We don't talk, but there's a new sense of *something* here. I would call it friendship, which is not a place I ever thought I'd find myself.

"I'll see you tomorrow," Dean says, stepping up onto the little porch at the bungalow beside mine.

"See you tomorrow."

He waits until I'm inside before reaching for his door. I shut my own softly, hoping not to wake up Penny. Leaning against it with my back, I think of how different things appear all of a sudden. It's true what they say, I suppose. Everything can change in the blink of the eye.

I push away from the door when something stops me. An uneasy feeling rushes over my skin, and I search the darkness to try and figure out what it could possibly be. This feels similar to how I felt at dinner. It's definitely my magic, that much I can tell. Since I've begun working on learning more about it, I'm more attuned to it. And I know not to ignore the pulls.

That's what is happening now. The magic is tugging on me, pulling me back outside. Glancing over to make sure Penny is fast asleep, I step back out. The night is quieter than before, with only an occasional owl or a rustle of leaves. The bungalow next to ours is dark, so Dean must've gone straight to bed.

I close my eyes, centering myself and my magic. The man from my dreams suddenly fills my mind, his face in panic, his mouth open, as if he's trying to say something. My eyes spring open. I almost expect him to be right in front of me, but I'm still alone. And now I'm more concerned than ever.

Scanning the night once more, my gaze latches onto a little glow coming from the direction of the pool house. Because it's so dark out, the sliver of light is more visible. It's also gone before I can pinpoint what's making it. But the moment I focus on it, the magic inside of me tugs me in that direction.

Alrighty then. I guess I'm going to the pool house.

My feet carry me across the pathway, passing the silent bungalows. It must be after midnight at this point. I'm sure most people have an early day here tomorrow. I strain to listen to any unnatural sounds, but there's nothing.

When I reach the pool house, I find the door cracked. All my internal alarms were already going off, but they are even more so now. One of the things this place is known for is how careful they are with everything. They would never leave the door open, not when there are children on the premises. In fact, the manager made sure to mention that to us when we arrived. She did a quick overview of the resort with us, and I remember her saying so.

Without touching the door, I push it open with the tip of my shoe and slip inside. It's slightly darker in here, and I give my eyes a second to adjust. As I peer into the shadows, I don't see anything or anyone. Deeming it safe, I pull out my phone and turn on the flashlight. That's when I notice something in the water.

Stepping closer, I shine the light over the calm surface when I see it.

A body, floating face up in the pool. His mouth is open, as if he's trying to say something.

It's the man from my dreams. And he's dead.

Without a moment's hesitation, I open my phone and dial the police. This vacation has become anything but.

5

T he police are on scene within ten minutes. I was told by the nice dispatcher to step out of the pool house and wait on the lawn. They also called the manager, Lizette, down from the main house. I'm still on the phone with the police when she shows up.

"Is it true? Someone is dead in there?" She looks distraught, her shirt wrinkled as she moves toward the door.

"Don't go in there. The police are on their way."

Just as I say that, I see lights pulling up to the front of the main house. The dispatcher asks if they have arrived, and only when the officers step out of the vehicles do I hang up. They kept their lights on, but sirens off, as a courtesy to the guests. Even so, I see people peeking out of their bungalows.

"News travels fast, huh?" I comment. Lizette doesn't hear me. The officers reach us at that time, and I point them in the direction of the body. Auntie Grace is going to have a field day with this. The whole point of me leaving Monroe Cove was to get away from all the murder. Yet, here we are again.

One of the officers comes back out, walking over to where Lizette and I are waiting.

"Which one of you found the body?" he asks. I raise my hand. "Are you able to answer a few questions now?"

"Yes, of course."

"What do I do? I have to get in there and see who it is, no? I mean, this happened under my watch. I just don't—" Lizette begins rambling, and the officer gives me an apologetic look before turning to the manager.

"Ma'am, it's going to be okay. Can we take a seat over here?"

I let him fuss over her as I watch people coming in and out of the pool house and all around it. It seems that while I wasn't watching, another fifty people arrived. My eyes are cataloguing everything, and I itch to take out my phone and start making notes. It's one of the things that translates from my interior design business to solving murders. The devil is in the details.

Just then, my eyes land on a man on the other side of the lawn. He's dressed in a suit and a long coat, very big city detective vibes, as he speaks to the officer who arrived first on the scene. Both men look up toward me, and the well-dressed man nods. Definitely a big city detective. I have no idea how he got here so fast though. I stay where I am, waiting for him to approach.

"Hello, I'm Detective Ames with the state police. I was told you found the body?"

"Yes. I'm Cassandra."

"Cassandra...?"

"Duke. I'm here on vacation with my friend." I know how this works. He's going to need every little bit of detail, no matter how irrelevant it is. It never looks good when I find a body, but especially like this. I had no business being in the pool house this late at night, and I can't exactly tell him my magic led me here.

"Why were you in the pool house this late, Miss Duke?" the detective asks, just like I expect him to. He looks to be in his late forties, well-groomed but sad around the eyes. I always feel for law enforcement personnel. They don't get called when there's good news to share.

"I was a bit restless and decided to go for a walk. I saw a light in this direction, so I came here and found the door ajar. I didn't touch it, by the way. I stepped inside and found the man floating."

"You didn't touch the door?"

"What?"

"You mentioned you didn't touch the door. Why wouldn't you? It's a natural thing to do."

He's right, of course. But I guess I've been around crime scenes one too many times now that I automatically stay extra vigilant. I'm a little nervous to tell him that though. It might look bad. But it might look bad not saying anything either.

"It's not the first time I've found a dead body," I admit and watch his gaze turn more curious.

"So, it's a habit of yours to stumble onto homicide investigations?"

"I've been...misfortunate enough to aid in a few."

"Aid?" But before I can reply, one of the officers calls his name. "Stay close, Miss Duke. I think we're going to have to have a more in-depth conversation about that."

"I'm not going anywhere, except to my bungalow, if that's alright?"

"Yes."

He leaves me then, and I turn toward the houses. I want to stay and poke around more, but I don't need to look any more suspicious than I already made myself look.

He's going to be watching me like a hawk, I can feel it already.

As I make my way back to the bungalow, I glance over at Lizette, sitting on a bench with an officer hovering beside her. My heart goes out to her. This is not the kind of thing anyone should be dealing with, but I can imagine how stressful it may be when you have a whole campus full of people depending on you.

More of the bungalows have lights on now, and people are looking out behind the curtains as I walk back. When I reach our bungalow, Penny pulls the door open before I can.

"Hi," I say, a little surprised.

"Don't you even "hi" me like that, Cassandra Duke. What have you gotten yourself into now?"

PENNY BRINGS me a cup of tea, and I wrap my hands around the warmth, inhaling deeply. It's past one o'clock now, and I'm finally feeling it.

"Are we just going to ignore the part where you have stumbled upon yet another dead body?"

Penny is clearly not having a good time with this. Not that I am either, but at least the whole dream haunting makes more sense now. Somehow. Or it will. Maybe? I'm still not sure how I was dream-haunted before the man was even dead. The next time I see him, I'll be sure to ask. There has to be something he can tell me, considering this isn't a typical ghost interaction.

How funny is that? I now have typical ghost interactions. Ha.

"Pen, I honestly think this is just my lot in life now." I shrug as Penny nods, sitting down on her bed.

"I think so too. But I don't like it. I don't like it one bit."

"I can't say that I'm a fan either."

I take a sip of the tea, letting it warm me from the inside as my mind races through the night. I've already pulled out my phone and made a bunch of notes, just so I don't forget anything later on. Or when I'm questioned next.

Feeling restless, I make my way to the window and pull

back the curtain. There's an array of activity on the lawn now. A few deputies stand around talking to the guests, but I don't see the detective. He really seemed not to like me. Or maybe I'm just projecting. Sheriff Bernard doesn't like when I interfere in his investigations. Maybe that's how the detective is feeling too. Or maybe I'm making stuff up. I don't even know anymore.

"Was it really the man from your dreams?" Penny asks, pulling me back to the present. I drop the curtains into place and walk back over to sit down on the couch. She's the only one I told.

"Yes. It's so strange. I know he seemed to have called me toward the pool house, but I still have no idea how. I'm hoping he'll show up in my dreams again and will be able to offer some information, but we both know that's probably not going to be the case."

I'm referring, of course, to the uncanny way ghosts seem to forget everything the moment they die. It's like a reset switch is flipped or something. It makes helping them so much more difficult. I mean, I've only had two instances with them. And with a zombie. But once you're dead, your memories are no longer there. At least not in any useful way.

It's kind of like talking to an amnesia patient. They remember how to talk and walk and read but can't remember their own name. That reminds me, I need to find out what this man's name is. Maybe that will shed some light on him.

"So, what's our next move?" Penny asks.

"I would say try and get some sleep?" I take another sip of tea. "Tomorrow is already here, but we both could use some rest."

"Won't they be coming around to interview people?"

"I think they'll hold off until morning. They're mostly talking to those who have stepped out of their bungalows on their own. Or so it seems."

Just then, the resort phone rings, making us both jump.

"Okay, that was not helpful to my heart rate," Penny says before picking it up. I sip my tea as I watch her listen to whoever is on the other line. She agrees with whatever is being said and then hangs up.

"That was the resort staff. They're asking everyone to meet in the main dining hall in the morning. No one is allowed to leave the premises until after they've been spoken to by the police."

"Makes sense," I say, standing up. I really need a good shower and some sleep. Today has definitely been a roller-coaster of a day. I'm not sure what will happen come sunrise, but I do know that I will need to do my best to stay ahead of the game. Since my magic is the one that brought me to this man, I have to be the one to solve the murder. I don't think it'll be an easy one.

6

———

The next morning, I'm up before the sun. I'm pretty sure I won't be getting a good night of sleep until this murder is solved, and I can give my dream phantom some "rest in peace" so that I can rest in peace. He didn't show up this time. Because of course he wouldn't the one time I actually need him to. But I know he'll be back. Those are just the rules.

Leaving Penny in the room, I grab my jacket and boots and tiptoe outside, shutting the door softly behind me. The cool air hits my skin. I breathe in deeply, taking in the quiet morning for a second. I've never been a morning person, but that doesn't mean I can't appreciate the beauty of it when I am awake.

Sitting down on the steps, I pull on and zip up my boots before tugging on my jacket. As far as I can see, there isn't a soul in sight. That works in my favor. I need to go study the scene of the crime before the *charming* detective shows up.

Okay, yes, that charming was way too sarcastic, but seriously. Just because I don't have a badge, doesn't mean I can't think like a cop. I have to give him the benefit of the doubt though, I'm sure he's dealt with plenty of meddling do-gooders. I just have to prove to him I'm an asset, not a hindrance. And maybe then he'll let me take a look at the medical examiner's report.

Ha. Even as I think it, I'm laughing at myself. I sound so official, and I know better than to expect him to share anything with me.

When I reach the pool area, police tape is wrapped over the door. But the door is open. I crouch down, making sure not to touch the tape or the walls, and slip inside.

It's just as warm in here as it was yesterday, but a chill still runs down my spine. It has nothing to do with the actual temperature. I know that, which makes it all the more ominous.

I give the room a quick scan, but no one is there. Not even my dream phantom. I don't expect him to show up, but just in case. It seems that I have no actual knowledge on how the whole dead thing works, because each time, it's been different. Partially, I wonder if it's because my magic keeps growing and developing, so I'm getting bombarded from every side, but that's just guess work. As much as Auntie Grace has promised to be more open about magic with me, it's still a work in progress.

I walk over to where I stood yesterday, glancing down at the water. My memory is sharp when it brings up the image of him floating face up.

This has really become a situation I find myself in way too often, but it also feels right somehow. I have no idea what to think about that.

I take my time walking around the pool area, looking for anything I may have missed yesterday. As far as I can see, there's nothing out of the ordinary here. No splashes of blood or anything else, no scuff marks, no forgotten towels. Logically, I'm sure the police have picked up anything that might've been discarded. They would've looked for the same things I'm looking for.

I'm getting ready to head back to the door when something occurs to me. This place is too clean.

There aren't any pieces of dirt or dust anywhere. I know this resort prides itself in keeping things clean, but shouldn't there be something?

"Why am I not surprised?"

I turn just as the detective walks into the pool area, hands in his pockets. I stand, where I've been crouching to study the floor and shrug.

"Because you're perceptive?"

His lips curl up in an almost smile before he shuts that down. I still feel like I just won a tiny victory.

"This area is off limits," he says. He doesn't come farther in, and I don't move from my spot.

"You know, this pool is the cleanest I've ever been to. Not a speck of dust to be seen. Curious, isn't it?"

I'm watching him like a hawk, so I see the way his eyes work at staying focused on me. He's trying not to give anything away, and in doing so, he's giving me just enough. Of course he noticed that, but I still want him to admit it.

"It's a very good resort."

"Oh, it is. But we both know the resort wasn't the one to clean up the scene."

This time, I swear his eyes flash. I think it might be with respect or something along those lines.

"Look, I know you've been involved in a few cases recently, and have even been—"

"Helpful? I think that's the word you're looking for, Detective."

This time, his eyes do flash, and I know it's with amusement. He takes a step farther into the room, trying to appear as nonchalant as possible. But I also know how to play that game, so I recognize it.

"And what do you think you can help me with here?"

"I think it would be good to have another pair of eyes around." I shrug, pushing my hair over one shoulder. "I might be able to glean information from guests that they're not willing to share with law enforcement."

He narrows his eyes, but I can see the wheels turning. He's considering it. So, I wait him out.

He walks farther into the room, heading to the opposite side of the pool with slow, steady steps. Even though I'm not an expert in these types of techniques, he's doing something similar to what I used to do when designing. He's giving me ample opportunity to break the silence because most people are uncomfortable with it. Little does he know, two can play that game.

It's another full minute at least before he looks up, meeting my eye. Then he chuckles. I cock my head to the side, raising my eyebrows.

"You are something else, Cassandra Duke."

"So I've been told," I reply, smiling. He studies me for a moment longer before coming to a decision. Almost resigned, he stands up straighter, not breaking eye contact.

"What is it you think you can bring to the table?"

"Ah, detective. You can just ask me for help, you know."

"That will not be happening."

This time, I'm the one who chuckles. But I also finally abandon my place at the opposite end of the pool and head toward him.

"This couldn't have been a crime of passion," I say, coming to the same place I found the body.

"Those kinds of offenders are messy. They don't take the time to clean up. And whoever he or she is, they didn't just clean up. They scrubbed the place down. Did you find traces of anything?"

I look at him expectedly. After a moment's hesitation, he shakes his head.

"No, we haven't found anything."

"And I don't think you will."

"You don't suppose it was an accident?"

"I mean, it could be. Then the person panicked and cleaned this room top to bottom. But it—"

"What?"

"It doesn't feel right." The moment I say it, I know I probably shouldn't have admitted it out loud. I can't tell if the dream phantom is affecting my judgement or if my witchy senses are picking up on something. But I know it's true.

"Unfortunately, in police work, we can't go on feelings." He doesn't say it unkindly, so I don't take offense. But I do face him squarely, giving him a thorough study.

"You mean you never follow your gut? Your instincts?"

"That's not the same."

"Isn't it? You're relying on something other than cold hard facts."

"I have years of learned behavior and experience. You're telling me your gut has the same after two cases?"

"You have been checking up on me."

"It's only the right thing to do."

I nod at that, turning back toward the room, trying to pinpoint what it is that's bugging me. But of course, I can't. If I had a way to do a searching spell, maybe I would find some evidence. But I doubt I can sneak in here with my crystals and potions.

"I can't explain it, detective." He would think I'm insane if I mentioned magic. "But I'm willing to listen to my instincts. What about you?"

This time when I turn to him, he's studying me intently. I

have no idea what he sees, but I don't squirm under the scrutiny. I wait for him to say whatever it is he needs to say.

"My instincts are telling me to let you help."

That is absolutely not what I expected him to say, but I try not to show outwardly just how happy it makes me. Not just for myself, but for the fact that I will be able to help my dream phantom sooner rather than later.

"You can talk to the guests, see if they saw anything or noticed the man around."

"I can do that. What will you do?"

"I'm going to talk to the suspect."

That stops me in my tracks.

"You have a suspect already?"

"Yes."

"Come on, can you at least give me more than that?" We turn toward the exit, and I think he won't answer, but then he does. And everything in me stops.

"Dean Harvey. He knew the victim."

7

"Dean knew the man?" Penny asks, sitting up in bed as I pace inside our little bungalow.

"His name was Arthur Gilla, by the way. I asked."

"You and the detective are friends now? I thought he completely shut you out last night."

"Well, he came around this morning."

I stop pacing, my mind racing with possibilities. Dean didn't say he knew anyone around these parts. My suspicious mind is taking off faster than I can follow it, so I need to slow it down. And breathe. There has to be a rational explanation about this. If I'm going to learn how to trust Dean, I have to trust that there is a rational explanation. How many times am I about to remind myself of that fact? My mind really is my best and worst friend in this.

"Cassie, don't go getting into your own head. I'm sure Dean would've told you."

I give Penny a look, as she climbs out of the bed.

"Okay, fine. I don't know if he would've, but it's Dean. We have decided we were going to trust Dean, remember? You can't go back on that without talking to him." Everything that's happened poured out of me the moment I got back to the bungalow, and now Penny is using that logic on me. She's right. I can't go making up stories in my head.

I need hard facts, so I can figure out what's going on. But I don't add that last part, I just nod. Because of course she's right, but Dean is out there talking to the detective, and I wish I was there to hear what he has to say.

Wait a minute.

I twist around, looking for where I discarded my phone.

"What are you doing?" Penny asks, as I find it on the desk and grab for it.

"I'm calling Auntie Grace to see if there is a spell that will help me eavesdrop."

"Cassie, I hope you realize how nonchalantly you just said that," Penny comments, heading for the bathroom. I don't reply as the phone begins to ring.

"Good morning, honey bun. You're up early." My aunt answers on the second ring. She's always up before the sun.

"I need your help."

"What do you need?" There's no hesitation in her response, and that makes me feel calmer immediately. So of course, the words rush out of me in one breath.

"I found another body, Auntie Grace. He was floating, face up, in the pool. The state police are here, the detective is letting me sleuth around. Dean is a suspect. He apparently knew the man. The man in question is the same one who's been invading my dreams for the last week. I didn't tell you that part, and I should've. I don't know what's going on, but I want to see if there's a spell that will help me eavesdrop on the investigation. Can you help?"

There's a slight pause, and then an exhale, before Auntie Grace speaks up.

"Oh, sweetie pie, I'm sorry."

"I'm okay really, I just—I need to help, Auntie Grace. I need to."

"I understand." And I know she does.

"Will you help?"

There's no hesitation in her voice when she replies, "Of course I will. Let's start at the beginning. The dreams. He's the man from your dreams?"

"Yes. I've never seen him before, and I have no idea how he was showing up before he was even dead. It started about a week ago, he would show up, scream at me to help him, and poof out."

"There are a few possibilities here. I'll have to do some research."

"Auntie Grace, what aren't you telling me?" I can hear it in her voice. There's definitely something.

"I don't want to mention something that might be wrong, honey bun."

I narrow my eyes, even though she can't see me. Auntie Grace is very good at only giving me pieces of information. I can understand she wants to protect me and my magic, but considering I'm not a little kid anymore, it's making me a little crazy.

"Okay, I'll wait. But what about the eavesdropping spell?"

"You know using magic for your own personal gain isn't what we're about."

"This has nothing to do with personal gain, Auntie Grace. This is to help a ghost and my friend."

Just then, Penny walks out of the bathroom, freshly dressed, her eyes big and round.

"Friend?" she mouths, and I shrug. Right now is really not the time to get into my stance on Dean. Or what he and I decided last night. I can't really think about that right now anyway.

"There is something that I think will help," Auntie Grace

says. I can hear her rummaging around, her voice distant before she comes back to the phone. I put her on speaker and reach for my notebook. "There is an opening the senses spell that may be able to help you. It would allow you to hear better than usual. You'll have to be close to overhear what you want to overhear."

"You're trying to find a spell to eavesdrop?" Penny asks, looking from me to the phone.

"Good morning, Penny dear," Auntie Grace greets her.

"Good morning, Auntie Grace. Can I have a moment with your niece please?"

"Sure thing."

Auntie Grace goes back to turning the pages, as my friend turns to me.

"What?"

"You know, I think I may actually be able to help with this. In a way easier way."

"What do you mean?"

"I mean, we have a phone that can listen in."

"What?" Auntie Grace and I exclaim at the same time. Penny chuckles.

"You magical ladies think there's only one way about things. While I love you embracing your magic, Cassie, this is something that doesn't require an ounce of it."

"Auntie Grace, I'm going to have to call you back."

"You do that, sweetie pie. I'll do the dream research for now." There's a smile in her voice as we hang up. Then, I turn my full attention to Penny.

"Well, don't keep me in suspense."

"You know how you've been sleuthing—"

"I suppose—"

"And reading investigation books when you think no one is watching."

"Hey, now."

"I think you're very proactive by learning more about your calling." I roll my eyes at her, but she's not deterred.

"Anyway, I've been doing my own research. And did you know, you can set your phone up as a listening device? All we have to do is be close enough for our earphones to be hooked up and we can listen in."

"Show me!"

She pulls out her phone, scrolling down from the corner to pull up the hidden menu.

"Here, if you push the ear-shaped button, it becomes a listening device. All we need are our wireless headphones, and we can listen in. Getting the phone into the room with the detective will be the challenge."

"It won't." I'm already thinking, my head spinning with ideas. "First of all, you're a genius. Second of all, if I go in there with a piece of information, or..." I snap my fingers. "If you volunteer to be the first one interviewed.

"Yes, let's go!"

We both turn toward the door when I stop.

"It's early. He's probably not going to start interviews until breakfast."

"So let's go to breakfast. Most people will be showing up early." Which is true. Human nature is very curious. And morbid. Hopefully the combination of the two will give people the loose tongue syndrome. We grab our jackets, and head toward the main dining room.

EVEN THOUGH IT's before seven in the morning, people are already mulling around. Penny and I exchange a look as we step into the dining room. My eyes do the mandatory crowd survey and land on Finn. He sees us immediately as well, but I don't see Dean anywhere. I wonder if the detective is already interviewing him, and I missed my chance.

But no, there's the detective. He walks into the room from the main house. Our eyes meet, and I give him the slightest of nods before I pivot toward Finn.

"You ladies doing okay?" He stands to greet us, pulling me into a hug.

"Yes, we're okay," I reply against his shirt. He holds me tighter for a second before stepping back and looking down at me.

"This is becoming a habit," Finn says, his eyes somber.

"So I've been hearing."

We turn at the voice as the detective stops at our table.

"Good morning, detective." After I greet him, he inclines his head.

"Where is your brother, Mr. Harvey?"

"He stepped out to the restroom," Finn replies, and I send a quick glance toward Penny. She takes it as a cue and steps forward.

"Detective, if you don't mind, could I be interviewed first? I would love to not miss my designated breakfast time, if at all possible."

Finn keeps a completely impassive look on his face, but I can feel slight tension in his body, since I'm still standing at his side. The detective glances at my friend before he gives me a look that's a mixture between amusement and warning. I don't give anything away as I look back at him.

"Sure, Miss Sharks. Right this way." He motions for her to follow him to the side of the hall where a set of doors stand ajar. A uniformed officer stands beside them. As soon as Penny and the detective step through, the officer pulls the doors shut and steps in front of them.

"Okay, what's going on?" Finn turns to me immediately, and I shrug.

"I could ask you the same thing. Where is Dean?" Finn looks away for a second, and I squeeze his upper arm. "What aren't you telling me?"

"Nothing. He just needed a moment. It's not every day his friend dies."

I nod, but that raises more questions. How close were they? If they were friends, would Dean know who could hurt him? And what was he doing here?

"Were they—" I want to ask Finn, but maybe it would be better to wait for Dean.

"We met when I lived in Boston." Dean's voice comes from behind me. I turn as he walks up to the table, and I have the sudden impulse to reach out and hug him. I don't, but the impulse is definitely there.

"I'm sorry for your loss," I say and mean it. There isn't a doubt in my mind that Dean had nothing to do with this. I can't explain it, but I feel it in my bones. Somehow. I'll need evidence to prove it to the detective, but that's another story.

"Thank you, Cassie." He sits at the table as Finn takes a step back.

"I'll go get us some food."

For a second, I offer to go with him to the buffet, but then I look at Dean and take a seat instead. We don't speak as we watch the people coming into the dining room. I want to pry, and this would be the perfect opportunity, but something stops me.

"You can ask, you know." Dean is the one to break the silence. I turn to see him watching me.

"I don't know what you mean," I reply.

"Mhhm, as if I don't know how that brain of yours works, Cassie," he says, with a small smile. I try not to let those words get to me, but they do. They burrow straight in toward my heart, because there's conviction there. He has proven, more than once, that he understands me. Even when I didn't want to believe it.

"I didn't know you lived in Boston," I say, and Dean smiles.

"For about five years. I worked for a firm there before I realized I would rather build with my hands than with computers. Arthur and I met at the company. We always said we'd start our own eventually. That's when I started my construction company, and he did landscape. He was good with plants."

"Is that why he was here?" I'm trying to be gentle, but I can't just not ask.

"Yes, he's been working at the resort for the past five years. He'd landscape for people in towns near, but they had a running contract with him to be here twice a year for upkeep. And if they wanted updates."

The sadness in his voice is real, and my hand moves toward him on the table before I can stop it. There's just a brush of fingers against his before I pull back. His eyes fly up to mine. There's an emotion there I'm not prepared to deal with, so I look away. But even I can't ignore the imprint of heat left on my skin after touching him. I try to settle my too-fast heartbeat by breathing in through my nose and out my mouth.

"Do you know of anyone who would want to harm him?" I ask, knowing it's the hardest question, but I have no choice. Dean is silent for a moment, and I glance at him from the corner of my eye.

"I know he had some rivals in the business, but nothing a few compromises couldn't fix."

Just then, the doors to the side room open, and Penny steps through. Her eyes zero in on mine, and she raises her eyebrows. She left the phone behind. I transfer my gaze to the detective, who's now looking at Dean.

"I guess that's my cue, huh?" Dean says, standing up.

"Hey," I say. "Answer truthfully. It's the best thing you can do."

Dean nods, and then he's off, weaving around the tables. Dean doesn't know he's a suspect yet, but he might after he talks to the detective. And I'm about to be in there like a fly on the wall.

8

The moment Dean is in with the detective, I fast walk over to Penny. She's leaning against the wall, near the doors, half hidden by one of the decorative trees. When I stop beside her, she hands me one of the cordless headphones. The moment I put it in my ear, I hear Dean's voice.

“We've kept in contact, but not enough that I would have any information on what he's been doing recently.”

“But you did see him last night?”

“Yes, we were going to meet up for lunch today.”

“So, you didn't have an argument?” Dean doesn't reply right away, which makes me stand up a little straighter. I wish I could see his face. I glance over at Penny, but she simply shrugs.

"Yes, we had an argument," he finally replies.

"About what?"

"His business. He was in the midst of making some kind of deal, and he wanted me on board. I told him I needed more information than vague promises of profit, and he got upset with me."

"How so?"

"He thought—" Dean pauses, and I can almost see the sadness in his eyes, "He thought I should just trust him and not ask questions."

"What did he want from you?"

"To invest."

"You mean money?"

"Yes, money. We were going to discuss it at lunch today."

There's another pause, and I strain to hear anything, but they're both silent. I have so many questions. And now I need to find a way to ask them without raising any kind of suspicion, since I shouldn't have these bouts of information.

"Do you think he was in trouble?" Detective Ames asks, breaking the silence.

"Yes." There's no hesitation in Dean's voice. "He sounded desperate when we talked."

"And talking is all you did?"

There's definitely something there, the detective is fishing. But what, I can't even think of it. I'm missing a major piece of information.

"Yes."

Another slight pause, and then, "So how did your finger-prints end up on his skin?"

"What?" Penny mouths, her eyes rounding as she stares at me. I shake my head, because I have absolutely no idea what the detective is talking about.

"Mr. Harvey, why did the deceased have your fingerprints on his skin?"

My heart drops. This is why the detective wanted to talk to Dean. There's actual evidence that puts him at the scene of the crime. I have no idea what to think about that.

Get your feelings under control, Duke. You have a murder to solve. Yes, I'm yelling at myself in my mind. I think it might be working.

"We got into an altercation."

"A fight?"

"An altercation." There's hardness to Dean's voice, and I wonder if he's staring the detective down. I can imagine him doing so. Even though Detective Ames is probably at least fifteen years Dean's senior, the handyman can hold his own. Both men are intimidating in their own way, and if I know anything about them—even after such a small amount of time—I know they will not back down.

"Explain, please." There's a note of hardness in the detective's voice too, and I smile. Dean got to him. I shouldn't feel as proud as I do. What is happening in my brain?

"He was desperate," Dean replies. It sounds like he turns away from the phone's direction, because his voice gets quieter. Or maybe it's the sadness. There's a touch of it there; I can hear it even across electronic waves.

"He came at me, grabbed my shirt, I had to pry his hands off me. I didn't want to hurt him, but—when you're desperate like that, you're not thinking straight. So I took him by the wrists and I pulled him back."

Arthur coming at Dean sounds a lot like Arthur coming at me in my dreams. Curious. There's a ruffling of papers before Detective Ames speaks up again.

"And what time was that?"

"Around eleven, I suppose."

Eleven. Wait. That's about the time I saw him. And he was coming from the direction of the pool house. My brain truly does not want to think Dean has anything to do with the murder, especially now that we've decided to reconcile. But I can't ignore the fact that now Dean is probably the last person who saw Arthur alive. Well, besides the killer. Unless Dean is one and the same.

I have got to stop this spinning in circles.

There's more noise over the headphones and then the door opens and Dean steps through. He doesn't notice us but walks quickly past everyone and out of the dining hall. The detective follows him out, his eyes on me immediately.

"Lose something?" he asks, holding up Penny's phone. I glance at my friend, but she's a pro at this somehow, because she's not even fazed.

"Oh, my goodness, thank you, detective! I was just looking for it."

He nods and hands it over, but he's not fooled, that much I can see.

"Miss Duke, mind if I have a word?"

He doesn't wait for a reply, but heads back into the room. After I exchange a quick glance with Penny, I follow him in.

"You have a history with him, don't you?"

I guess we're not beating around the bush here. Detective Ames walks me over to the other side of the room, away from the officer who's sitting at the interview table. Well, I'm assuming that's what it is.

"Yes, we're friends." When I say it, I realize I mean it.

"Can you be objective?"

"Yes."

The detective pauses, studying me in that calm way of his. There's a strange sort of connection between us that I can't seem to deny. It's almost like if this were another life, he could be my father. At least, that's what I think a father would be like, considering I've never had one. That's probably why I blurt out my next question.

"Why are you letting me help? You're not obligated by any means. You don't know me."

He takes a second before replying, as if really thinking over the question.

"I talked to a few people back in Monroe Cove this morning.

You have a good head on your shoulders, Miss Duke. And my gut," he smiles a little, "is telling me that your potential is not to be wasted."

Interesting. I think there might be more to it than that, but the way he says this rings true to me. Maybe he truly sees something in me. And if that's the case, I don't want to fail him.

"Thank you," I reply.

"Don't thank me yet. You have to be careful. If anyone else found that phone, they wouldn't be so nice about it."

I nod in understanding because I know he's right. Sheriff Bernard would've possibly stuck me in jail just to teach me a lesson. But then I think about what the detective just said and how there are people back in Monroe Cove who spoke highly of me. I don't want to fail them either.

"How can I help you, detective?" I ask, standing up a little straighter.

"What can you tell me about Dean Harvey?"

I guess I should've expected the question, but it still takes me a little bit off guard. It makes sense why the detective would want a character witness on Dean, especially after that interview. I focus on staying objective before I reply.

"Dean owns his own company in Monroe Cove. He's well liked and respected in town. We've been working together on a few projects for Mayor Moore recently."

"Are you...friends?"

I wonder why the hesitation, but I don't ask.

"We're new friends. We knew each other when we were young, but we didn't exactly run in the same circles."

"Why not? You're friends with his brother, yes?"

My eyes fly up to meet Detective Ames, curious at this line of questioning. He's fishing for something, but I'm not quite sure what. It makes me feel like I should be more careful around him. I don't like that feeling. I want to trust him, not suspect him of who knows what.

My brain is truly taking itself on a rollercoaster ride. I have to chill.

"I'm friends with Finn, yes. But Dean wasn't part of that friendship. He had his own friends and activities."

"So he and his brother are not close?"

"They are." I narrow my eyes. "What is it that you're getting at, detective?"

"Just trying to build a profile."

But that's not it, is it? I can tell, even with my small knowledge of how this whole investigating thing works.

"Detective Ames?" This comes from the officer and we both turn in his direction. "The next staff member is here."

"Thank you." The detective nods at the officer before motioning me toward the door. Even though I have a bunch of questions, I leave without asking any of them. On the way, I pass a woman dressed in a suit. Her blonde hair is pulled back into a low bun, not a strand out of place. She looks put together in a way I will never be. She doesn't meet my eye as she passes me, but I know I've seen her before.

I step out and head toward Penny.

"What did he want?" she asks as I take a seat at the table.

"Honestly, a character sketch on Dean, but that's not all."

"What do you mean?"

"I have no idea. But he was fishing for something. Did you see who went in there just now?"

"Oh, yes." Penny glances at the closed door. "That's the head maid, I think."

"Priscilla Janson." Finn appears beside us offering a plate and a name.

"How do you know?" I ask, reaching for a piece of toast.

"I asked around while you were in there. I figured you'd need all the information you can get." He glances over at Penny, and I study the two before I sigh.

"Penny."

"What? He guessed, okay? It's not my fault you're Miss Investigator over here," Penny replies, taking a bite of her piece of toast and I simply shake my head.

"I don't want you guys involved in this. The detective is already suspicious—"

"Of Dean, I know. I talked to him." I look at Finn and notice the concern in his gaze.

"How is he?"

"Sad. And frustrated. He blames himself."

"Finn."

"Not like that. He just thinks if he went along with Arthur's plans, the man would still be alive."

I let that sit and marinate for a second. Arthur was definitely into something. I need him to show up in a dream, so I can ask. But if he worked here, there will be people who can point me in the right direction. It's time I started asking questions.

9

———

My first order of business is Lizette, the resort manager. Last night, she seemed as distraught as anyone would be, but this morning, she's running around, throwing orders at anyone who will listen. I watch as she power walks across the dining hall, heading to the kitchen. I jump to my feet, motioning for Finn and Penny to stay put as I casually walk in the same direction.

The tables in front of the kitchen door are full of food. I watch as Lizette checks over each portion. Grabbing a plate, I slide up to her, and when she notices me, I smile.

"Oh, hello there," I say, watching as she puts on her customer service smile.

"Hello, Miss Duke, are you doing alright?"

"I was going to ask you the same thing. And please, call me Cassie."

"If you call me Lizette." I smile at that and pretend to look through the breakfast options before me.

"To be honest, Lizette. It's been a rough morning. It wasn't like I was planning on discovering a dead body when I came here."

"Oh, please know this is not a regular occurrence in these parts." She turns to me immediately, her manager hat on as she talks. "Of course, we would be happy to provide any compensation for your misfortune, but we truly hope this doesn't tarnish our reputation in your eyes."

I know this tactic, which is why I knew mentioning the resort as a whole would get her to pay attention to me instead of dismissing me. I need to get her to open up to me, so I'll take any avenue I can.

"It's such a tragedy," I say, turning my full attention to her. "Have you worked with him long?"

"Oh yes. Arthur has been here longer than I have."

"You've only been here—?"

"Four years. I came to take over for the owners. They were at retirement age and needed someone to live on the property and make sure everything was running smoothly."

"That's a great opportunity. Have you run a resort before this?"

"Never." She chuckles. "I've been a manager at a few hotels, moving around a bit, but nothing like this."

"Were you a world traveler before you settled here then?"

"Oh, I wouldn't call it that." She chuckles again, and her gaze turns somewhat distant. "I just wanted to live in a few places, that's all."

I nod, but something about that seems vaguer than not. It's probably because she doesn't want to spill her life story to a total stranger, but I'm being extra suspicious. Understandably.

"Has running this resort been everything you ever wanted?"

"It kind of has," she replies right away, her eyes still in a faraway gaze. "It's so beautiful here, and the people are great. It's definitely the best place I have lived."

"So, you haven't had any major issues with anyone?"

"No, we're like a big family around these parts. It's why Arthur's death is going to hit us so hard. Excuse me." She moves away then, turning her attention to the elderly couple on the other side of her. I leave as well, but I've only taken two steps when a voice reaches me.

"Oh please, no one is going to miss Arthur. Not after the hassle he's become." I turn toward the voice and find a woman in her early sixties, sitting at the end of one of the tables. Gray hair piled on top of her head, wearing expensive jewelry and a sweater combination straight out of those rich old timey movies. She looks at me expectantly and then at the chair near her. I don't hesitate to take a seat.

"What do you mean by that?"

"I mean that I've been here every year for the last ten, and I can tell you that in the last few months I have heard more arguments than ever. It was like this place became its own soap opera, with scandal, and now apparently, murder. Goodness gracious me, this is the best vacation ever."

The woman is lost in her own glee, so I hope she misses my look of surprise before I mask it.

"You're the one who found him, aren't you? I heard some whispers."

"You find me at a disadvantage then. I'm Cassandra."

"I'm Victoria. I've been friends with the Sanchez's for a decade now. It was such a shame they decided to hand over the reins to that woman. Between her and that Priscilla, this place isn't what it used to be."

It's like I don't even have to ask the questions. Victoria is playing both parts here. She leans closer to me, lowering her voice.

"If I were you, I'd have a talk with Priscilla for sure. She's a hard woman, but she tells it like it is, instead of sugarcoating it like Lizette here. She's been kissing butt since she arrived."

"You don't think that's part of her job? In customer service?"

"Pash, no one wants to be lied to. You tell the truth, that's how the world works. And if you lie, you get burned. Now run along and ask your questions. I've been watching you make your rounds. I like you. You have a sharp mind."

I don't hide the smile as I nod at Victoria and stand.

"Oh, and that boy toy of yours." Victoria stops me with a hand on my arm. "I'd go check on him if I were you. He seems to be having a difficult time with this."

She nods in the direction of the main hallway, and I don't bother correcting her on her assumption. I have been concerned about Dean, and it's probably time I go check on him.

I FIND him outside on the patio. There are people pretty much everywhere. The officers are still taking statements. I can only assume the detective is interviewing those he knows will have information before he moves on to the rest. I'm still feeling the weird connection to him, but I file that away to think about later. Right now, I have to ask Dean the hard questions.

"I figured you'd come find me sooner or later."

"How are you doing?" It's not the question I should be asking, but it's the first one I blurt out. Dean looks over at me, a small smile on his lips. He's leaning forward, his hands wrapped around the top of the railing as he watches people walking by.

"I keep thinking if only I took him up on his offer, if only I had helped him."

"You can't really think it would've changed anything," I reply. This earns me a confused look.

He stands up straighter, turning fully to face me. We're much like we were last night, only a few feet apart, unsure of our foundation.

"How can you say that with such confidence?" he asks.

"Because I think whoever did this? They had a plan long before you showed up here. Arthur was into something, something that got him killed, and you can't blame yourself for that." There's a touch of passion in my voice, and I realize I want to protect him.

Well, this is news to me. I'm really just pulling out all the stops here.

"You are right," Dean surprises me by saying. "I should really listen to your expertise." His lips curl up in a smile, and I know he's not mocking me. He's actually telling me he trusts what I have to say.

"Dean, I have to ask you some tough questions."

He stares down into my eyes, as if searching for something, before giving me a firm nod.

"Fire away."

"The altercation you got into with him—"

"You know about that?"

I shrug, "I'm getting good at the investigating."

"Of course. Sorry, what about it?"

"Well, you said you pulled him off you. What happened after?"

Dean doesn't break eye contact and he doesn't hesitate.

"He said he would do anything to make things right, but he didn't think he had the time. I told him we could talk in the morning. And then—then I left him."

"Where was this?"

"In the gardens near the pool house. He was in there, working. At least I thought so."

"What made you think that?"

"The ground around him and in the flower beds was turned up. Like he'd been digging."

What gardener would be working at eleven at night, digging up flower beds? He may have just been doing busy work, to keep his mind off things. He was definitely in the middle of something after all. In any case, I make a mental note to see if the detective found anything in the gardens.

"And after you left?"

"I found you."

The intensity in his gaze doesn't escape me. It's like I'm holding my breath too. We reached new ground last night, a new level in our relationship, and we both feel it. I can see it in his eyes like I can feel it in my heart. But this whole murder thing is really complicating my outlook. And it's also making it difficult to stay objective. What a lovely time I've decided to have feelings.

Focus, Cassie. Focus.

"When you left him, how did he seem? Was there anyone else around?"

"No, no one. Arthur was distressed and maybe a little frantic, but I left him working."

I remember Dean coming out of those woods. He didn't seem frazzled or like he'd been in an altercation. We stare at each other once more, and I'm really struggling to stay objective here.

"Is there anything else you're not telling me?" I ask, breaking whatever moment we were having. I mean, I know it was a moment, but I'm uncomfortable with the moment. Also, now is not the time, so here we are. With me breaking the moment. My mind is officially a jumbled mess.

Dean doesn't answer right away, and when he does, he doesn't really meet my eye. Only a fleeting glance.

"No, there's nothing else."

Now, why don't I trust him?

10
______

The police are still conducting their interviews, but I need a moment to get my head straight. The moment I step inside our bungalow, my phone rings. Glancing down, I see it's Auntie Grace and answer right away.

"Good morning, honey bun. How are you doing?"

"I've been better, Auntie Grace," I reply honestly, taking a deep breath and letting it out slowly. "Dean is the prime suspect, it seems. And I think he really is holding things back from me."

"Oh, I'm so sorry sugar plum. But I do have some good news that will hopefully help. I think there is a way for you to talk to your phantom."

"You mean outside of him invading my dreams and disappearing when it's convenient for him?"

"Yes. There's a spell that can call forth a spirit. It's typically done over the body, right after passing. Sort of like a last goodbye before the person moves on. But since these circumstances are different—"

"It's worth a try," I finish for her.

It does feel a little like cheating, getting information from the deceased himself. But it's not like I'm a real cop, right? It doesn't matter how I find out my information. Except if the detective asks. Then I'll have to come up with a story, but that's a problem for another time.

"Okay, what do I need?" I ask.

"Me."

The voice comes from behind me and I'm a little ashamed to admit that I jump off the bed with a little squeak. I turn to watch Birdie push her way into the room, my eyes narrowing.

"Umm, Auntie Grace, why is your cat here?" I glare at the feline, and I swear she glares back.

"The cat can hear you," Birdie replies, stretching her back a little as she slowly makes her way farther into the room. "And is this the kind of thanks I get for hauling this dumb pouch all this way?"

That's when I notice a small bundle around her neck.

"Birdie brought you a pouch with all the ingredients you need for the spell," my aunt says while Birdie and I have a mini stare down. We're constantly coming to terms with each other and clashing. I think it's just a thing now.

"Thank you," I say, stepping up to the cat. I swear Birdie throws a glare my way before jumping onto the bed. I'm almost positive she wants to snip at my fingers as I reach for the pouch, but thankfully she doesn't. I unwrap it carefully, letting the items drop into my hand.

A crystal, a rolled-up piece of paper, and some charcoal sit in my palm.

"All the instructions are there, honey bun. Let Birdie help as well. She'll amplify your powers."

I swear Birdie heard that and is now looking extra smug. I simply roll my eyes.

"Also, make sure you have at least an hour of no interruption. It might take a moment longer than usual to call him out, and you don't want to be disturbed halfway through."

"Thank you, Auntie Grace. Have you been able to find anything out about why I've been seeing him?"

"Not yet. But I'm still looking. Blessed be, Cassie."

We hang up, and I stare down at the cat.

"Alright, should we do this?"

"You're the witch. You tell me."

I swear, this cat is way too snarky for her own good. But instead of engaging, I pull up the favorites tab on my phone and dial Penny. I'm going to need a bit of help with this one.

ONCE I'VE EXPLAINED to Penny what I'm doing, she agrees to stand guard, so to speak, to make sure I have the bungalow to myself. Pulling all the curtains tightly closed, I set out the items on the floor in front of me before sitting down cross-legged. Birdie takes her place across from me, watching expectedly.

"I really wish you wouldn't stare like that," I say.

"Tough luck, witch. I have to pay attention to make sure you don't mess things up."

"I liked it better when you didn't talk."

"Oh, I could always talk. You just didn't know how to listen, witch."

"Are you sure you're a cat and not just a cranky old lady who was turned into one?" I mumble. I'm pretty sure Birdie's gaze narrows, but I ignore it. I need to focus on the task at hand.

The instructions are pretty simple. I light a candle, then I say a little chant while holding the quartz crystal in one hand and charcoal in the other. Between the light and the dark, it's supposed to cleanse and balance the vibrations out.

It's also a little bit intimidating and scary because I don't do magic like this. Most of my magic is intuitive. Now I'm required to be intentional. Part of me thinks I'm not ready for that, but then again, when is anyone ever ready for the things life throws our way?

"Are you planning on sitting there all day?" Birdie's voice breaks through my mini freak out, and I turn my attention to her, making sure to glare extra hard.

"You should really work on your bedside manner, cat."

"You should really work on your magic, witch."

We stare at each other, unblinking, for a solid thirty seconds before I realize I'm having a battle of wills with a feline. What has my life come to? Shaking my head, I glance down at the paper in front of me. Picking up the crystal and the charcoal, I place my hands on my knees, palms up. I can still hear people outside the bungalow, but the moment I focus in on the spell, that all seems to fade away. I take a deep breath, focusing my energy on the task at hand, and begin to recite.

"Mother Nature, hear my plea,
I am seeking a guarantee.
Help and guide, like seasons past,
Bring this spirit as a guest."

I close my eyes, breathing the words in and pushing them out of my body on a sigh.

For the longest time, I fought against my heritage. I thought magic was nothing but a nuisance, something that made my whole life difficult and unnatural. But in recent months, I've learned magic is the most natural thing to me and that I can trust it. It has saved my butt more than once already. But it's more than that. The more I learn and practice my magic, the more I feel like myself. Leaving Monroe Cove was my way to try and find out who I was, but I was only running from what was right under my nose. I'm trying to be better about not doing that.

Taking another long breath, I curl my fingers over the items in my hands and close my eyes.

At first, nothing happens. But then, it's like a veil is lifted and the space around me comes into focus. Once again, I'm in a large room, but this time, I can see past the immediate area and what I find are walls of trees. It's like the room turns into a forest, with no doors in between. Looking around, I try to see if the man is here, but there's nothing but the darkness. Making sure to stay in the moment, I do my breathing exercises as I wait for the spell to work. For some reason, I know it will.

When I hear a slight noise in front of me, my eyes spring open and there he is. He's standing in the middle of the room that's not really a room, looking confused.

"What did you do?" he asks when I meet his confused gaze.

"I called you here for a little one on one. We need to talk."

"I don't know what you mean."

"What do you mean you don't know what I mean?" I take a step toward him, cocking my head to the side. "You know you're—"

"Dead. Yes."

"Okay, then we need to talk about the fact that you were haunting my dreams, even before you died. How do you explain that?"

"If I could, then I would," he replies, studying the mist that's gathering around us. It's moving closer. I've also noticed, but I don't take my attention off Arthur, afraid he'll disappear.

"Fine. What was it that you were involved in that got you killed? Let's start there."

"I have no idea what you're talking about."

I throw my hands up in the air, completely exasperated.

"You're seriously going to tell me that you haunted me for a week before you were murdered, with no reason, and you don't know why we have the kind of connection that allows you to do so. And that whatever you were involved in just happened to get you killed the week I'm here for vacation?"

"Yeah, that's what it appears to be," he says, raising his

eyebrows. Okay, this man is officially getting on my nerves. I mean, he has been since he started this haunting of his, but this is another level.

If he wasn't dead already—

Okay, Cassie, calm down, and we're going to have to keep that train of thought from forming because we are supposed to be nice to people, even dead people these days.

"Let's think of this logically. You were a gardener with your own business, who came out to the resort a few times a year to redo the gardens..." I trail off, trying to organize the different points of information. From everything I've learned, Arthur was in a bad place. But how do I make a ghost realize that and admit it? Or even remember it? Ghosts are notorious for forgetting basically everything once they die. But he visited me before his death, there has to be a connection there.

"Should I leave you alone?" Arthur says, interrupting my mental ramblings.

"No, do not move, we are figuring this out." I point at him, another list of questions forming in my mind. "Have you ever experienced anything weird in your life? Maybe supernatural?"

"Not that I can think of."

"Except where you showed up in my dreams," I raise my eyebrows at him, and he shrugs.

"As far as I know, that's it."

"How did that work for you?"

"I went to sleep, and then I was in your dream."

"Always screaming at me to help you," I point out.

"It was an impulse; I couldn't control it." He shrugs again.

This is truly going nowhere.

"Okay. How did you get the job? Are you from these parts?"

"No, I moved from out west. I wanted to work with my hands and live somewhere where there are seasons. I started in Boston, now I'm here."

I can understand that. We do have the prettiest seasons

around here. It would be especially appealing to someone who loves nature.

"While you worked at the resort you didn't have any problems with anyone? Any arguments you can recall?"

Arthur opens his mouth to reply, but then stops. I feel like he was about to deliver another one of his flippant remarks, but something stops him. He seems to actually be thinking over my questions now. The gears are turning as the mist creeps closer and closer.

"There was something. But I can't really grab onto the memory enough to remember it. Why is that?"

My heart softens a little at the way he looks at me. It must be so scary. He seems to be aware of his death, but I still tread carefully.

"When someone passes, their memories become jumbled. It's almost like the reset button has been hit and the brain has to rebuild itself. Except now that you are no longer living, the brain doesn't rebuild the same way."

"That's not very helpful, is it?"

"No, I suppose it's not. But we'll figure it out. Someone knows something."

Arthur is quiet for another minute as I approach the question I've been eager to ask. The mist is almost upon us, and I know our time here is short.

"Arthur, you knew Dean." The man looks up at me, slightly surprised. "You saw him last night. Could you tell me what happened?"

"Are you asking if he's the one who hurt me?"

Ghosts may not remember a lot of things, but they sure hit it on the head when it comes to these inquisitive questions.

"Did he hurt you, Arthur?"

There's a pause, as his gaze gets far away.

"I mean, you're the detective here. I'm just the dead guy." And with that, he disappears.

11

———

"So did he say it was Dean or not?" Penny asks a little while later. She's sitting on the bed, petting Birdie while I pace. After Arthur disappeared from the room, the spell kicked me out. Birdie said I was only under for about a minute, even though it felt way longer than that. Something I made a mental note to ask Auntie Grace about. I always seem to be missing some rules about how it all works.

"He didn't. But I think maybe he would've if Dean was involved?" I'm not sure if I'm grasping at straws here or not.

"Dean didn't do it."

I glance over to where Birdie is stretching out under Penny's hand and narrow my eyes.

"How would you know that, fur ball?" Penny looks up at me, startled, before she realizes who I'm talking to.

"It really is super weird and cool that you can talk to Birdie," Penny comments.

"Yeah, that's only because you can't hear Birdie talk back," I reply. The cat hisses a little, before rolling over and getting to all fours.

"Dean didn't do it."

"But why do you keep saying that?" Penny waves her arm.

I translate. "She keeps saying Dean didn't do it."

"I would be inclined to agree with Birdie." Penny shrugs, and I don't admit that I do too. But that's more of a feeling than fact. And there's no way Detective Ames is going to go off feeling.

"Dean doesn't have a dark heart. He would never."

"A dark heart? What are you talking about, cat?"

But Birdie is clearly done with me, because she jumps off the bed and heads toward the window.

"Really?"

She's up and out of it before any of us can do anything else.

"That cat—"

"Is adorable."

I glare at Penny but don't comment further.

The whole conversation with Arthur gave me absolutely nothing but a practice run at my spell casting. I'm grateful for that, of course, but I would've liked it more if I came away with some kind of information I could use.

"So, what's our next move?" Penny asks. I turn my attention back to her.

"I wish I knew. I should probably go see if I can talk to a few more people. The more information I gather, the better my chances of figuring this out. But—"

"But what?"

"It's hard to stay objective when Dean is involved."

And of course, I had to circle back to this. Because it's causing way too many problems in my brain. Penny doesn't comment, so I glance over at her, noticing she's trying to hold back a smile.

"Okay what?"

"Nothing."

"Spill it."

"It's just that—I'm glad you're not running from this anymore."

Whatever I thought Penny was going to say, this isn't it. I stop pacing and turn to her more fully. She gives me a sheepish smile and shrugs again.

"What is that supposed to mean, Penelope?"

"It means," Penny doesn't hesitate, getting off the bed and walking to stand in front of me, "that whatever happened in your childhood can finally be left there. You're trusting your heart and your friends over the memories that may or may not be true, and I think that's amazing. I'm proud of you."

Being the only person, besides Auntie Grace, who knows about my magical powers, Penny is in a unique position to understand me better. I told her all about how my aunt messed with my memories to protect me. Well, not "messed." That sounds so bad. Basically, not everything I remember is how it happened. A side effect that she is beyond remorseful about. I've been trying to work through the memories and the information I'm receiving from people to piece together what actually happened, especially the part where my mother disappeared.

But now is not the time nor place to be thinking about any of this. Just then, a knock sounds on the door. Penny rushes over it, pulling it open. Pricilla Janson stands on the other side, as prim and proper as ever.

"Good afternoon," she says. "I just wanted to come by and remind you personally that the game night dinner is happening tonight."

"Even with everything going on?" I ask.

"Yes, it has been approved by the detective. Hope to see you at seven."

With that, she turns on her heels and walks back down the steps. Not wanting to miss my opportunity, I dash after her.

"Excuse me, Miss Janson?"

She stops, spinning around to face me. There's no pretense of a customer service smile on her face. Her face is blank as she watches me.

"I'm sorry, I just wanted to see how you were doing. I know Arthur was like family around here and I—"

"You do not need to concern yourself, Miss Duke," Priscilla interrupts with no emotion on her face. "We are all grieving, but we are fine. We will see you for game night tonight."

She doesn't wait for a response, cutting me off completely. I watch her retreat, narrowing my eyes. As I make my way back to the bungalow, Penny shuts the door slowly, turning to me.

"You know what this means, right?" I ask.

"What?"

"Detective Ames is putting everyone under one roof. We're about to play games with a killer."

FOR THE REST of the day, I'm restless. Birdie has disappeared, and Penny is simply trying to keep me from walking up to every guest and bombarding them with questions. I can't be one hundred percent sure, but I think performing the spell was like a caffeine boost. I have way too much energy inside of me right now.

We haven't seen Dean or Finn since this morning, and Detective Ames only nodded in my direction when I went back to the dining area for lunch. I've asked a few guests the basic questions about seeing Arthur or anything suspicious, but most didn't even know there was a gardener on the premises. None of these questions lead me anywhere, and I would like to find at least one person who would be willing to talk to me. I tried cornering Priscilla and Lizette again but both have been side-stepping me. Who I do find is Victoria, still at the same table she was at when I met her, watching people walking by.

"Hello Victoria," I say, stopping by the table. The woman looks up at me, a small smile on her lips.

"Hello, meddling girl. Is this your trusty sidekick?" Victoria points to Penny, who curtsies.

"Sorry, I'm not sure why I felt like I had to do that," She giggles as I try to hide my smile. "I'm Penelope. But my friends call me Penny."

"It's nice to meet you, Penny. Take a seat, you two. You're hovering."

Penny and I sit immediately as Victoria reaches for a cup in front of her and takes a sip.

"So, what have you learned, meddling girl?" She looks eager and aloof at the same time. I should really be taking notes because I've always wanted to be able to balance that expression on my face.

"Honestly, not much. I don't believe Dean had anything to do with it, but I haven't been able to find any information to back that fact."

"And the good detective won't go off feelings," Victoria comments, taking the words out of my mouth. I nod before leaning in a little closer.

"Have you heard anything?"

"Oh, I hear all kinds of things, but I do wonder why you're so invested in this. Is it because of your boy toy?"

Penny's eyes bug out so much, she looks like a doll.

"He's not my boy toy," I reply. "Or my anything actually."

"You say that like I don't have two perfectly good working eyes in this head of mine." Victoria huffs, and this time, Penny is for sure trying not to laugh. I send her a warning look, but she's having way too much fun. That's it, I've got to stop bringing her as backup.

"Dean and I are...friends." I try again to steer the conversation in the right direction. Both Penny and Victoria give me a look like they know I'm full of it, but they don't comment. Much.

"Mhhm, sure, honey. It's so nice to live in denial." Victoria reaches over and pats my hand before picking up her cup and taking another sip. "But to answer your earlier question, I heard that Walter and Lizette were getting into all kinds of arguments earlier."

"Walter?"

"The Sanchez's grandson, of course. Try and keep up, meddling girl. He's been working as a cook here for a few years now. He had some grand plans to be a chef in the big city, but then grandpapi asked him to come and oversee the food at the resort, and he packed up and showed up. But between you and me, I think he's been quite bitter that Grandpapi Sanchez didn't hand over the reins to him but chose Lizette instead."

I let myself mull that over before I lean forward, lowering my voice.

"You don't seem to like Lizette much?" I leave it as an open-ended sentence and Victoria doesn't disappoint.

"I don't like anyone who comes in thinking they know better than years of tradition." Victoria huffs, her eyes shining. She might be older than I initially thought, pushing seventies at least, but there's a fire about her that I find charming. "The new staff all wanted to shake things up, but that's not the appeal of a place such as this. It's the old way of life. That's what people who come here are looking for. No television in the rooms or bungalows, no internet, and only a landline to reach the main town. People come here searching for peace."

As Victoria talks, I realize that was partially why Penny and I picked this place. We wanted to be cut off from the rest of the world, if only for a few days. But in that, I also realize why this place is such a perfect place for a murder. It took the police ten minutes to reach the resort when I called. The campus is spread out with the forest weaving in and out, and there is plenty of room to hide.

I make a mental note to find Walter and talk to him. Maybe he'll be more talkative than Priscilla. Actually, now I really want to hear what both of them have to say about this place.

"Whose idea was it to host the game night?" I ask next, as I watch people walking out of the dining room after lunch is finished.

"Oh, that is an old tradition of this place," Victoria says, sitting up a little straighter. "The Sanchez's started it when they opened this resort. Back then, we played bingo and such. Now, there's an array of games available. It's such a delight."

"Is everyone required to come?"

"Of course they won't make anyone come, but the staff gets pretty into it usually, so most of the guests show up."

It does sound fun. But it also sounds like a great opportunity to observe and maybe talk to those pesky people I've been missing.

12

I try to catch the detective's attention a few times, but he's completely avoiding me. The one piece of information I don't have is the cause of death, and it's been bugging me. Personally, and I'm not sure if it's a gut feeling or what, I don't think Arthur drowned. I need to know the other sides of the story to build a solid narrative.

"Are you ready?" Penny asks later that night. Game night is starting any minute now, and I'm eager and nervous. Not sure why I'm feeling that last emotion, but here we are.

"Sure. Have you seen Birdie at all?" I ask. Penny shakes her head no. I called Auntie Grace to go over the spell a little bit ago, and she also hasn't seen Birdie. That cat better be staying out of trouble. Not that I'm worried or anything.

"Let's go."

The ballroom has been converted into a casino type setup. When we step inside, following the signs and directions, I'm amazed at how much energy I'm feeling in the room. Maybe I expected everyone to be more subdued, but there's general excitement here. People really do bounce back from tragedies faster than we give them credit for. I scan the faces as we make our way around the tables, trying to pinpoint any glimpse of sadness or guilt or even fear. But everyone seems to be just fine. I'm not sure if I'm supposed to feel better about that though.

"There's Finn." Penny tugs on my arm, pulling me to the corner of the room. Finn is standing beside the table. When we're almost there, I notice Dean sitting behind him. Dean's eyes find mine immediately, and he's displaying all the emotions I've been looking for in these people. My heart squeezes at the sight. I have a desire to reach out and hug him. Which obviously I don't.

Chill, Cassie.

"There you ladies are. How goes the sleuthing?" Finn asks as soon as we take our seats at the table. I roll my eyes at him, and then throw Penny a look.

"I am innocent of any wrongdoing," she comments, shrugging.

"Cassie, I have known you for most of my life. Don't you think I know how you think by now?" Finn raises an eyebrow at me, and I try to play it off nonchalantly.

"Maybe you don't know me as well as you think."

"Really? You're going to tell me that you've given up?" The way he's looking at me is making me squirm in my seat. It really is a bother sometimes, having people who know you this well. Okay, okay, not a bother. I am blessed. But also annoyed.

"I'm just trying to help."

"Have you—" But before Finn can ask whatever question he has, the crackle of a microphone sounds over the speakers. We turn as one toward the small stage setup on the opposite side of the room. Unable to help myself, I glance over at Dean and find his eyes on me. He looks tired and sad. I offer him the tiniest of smiles, which he returns.

"Good evening, everyone." Lizette's voice comes over the speakers, and I turn back to the front of the room. "Welcome to the annual game night! In light of recent events, please make sure to follow all the posted and spoken rules. Detective Ames and his officers are here to make sure we are safe for the night."

My eyes scan the crowd, focusing on where each officer is posted, before they land on Detective Ames. He's standing to the left of the stage, near the double doors that lead out into the main house. As if he can feel me watching him, his eyes find mine. Even though he's been here since around one in the morning, he still looks sharp. From this distance, I can tell he's not missing anything. That makes me think I probably am.

I go back to scanning the crowd, looking for any signs that will give me a clue. But I've only done this a few times. I'm still a newbie. I wonder if the detective would be willing to share some tips on how to spot suspects. Lizette is still rattling off instructions, and once she announces the games to commence, I get to my feet.

"Where are you going?" Finn asks.

"I'll be back. You can start without me."

Our table has the game of Clue on it, which I find a little too appropriate. I wonder if that's why the guys chose this spot.

It's something Finn would do. I ignore their inquisitive looks and weave around the tables to where Detective Ames is making his rounds.

"Miss Duke," he says when I come up to him. "Enjoying your evening?"

"Yes, thank you." I glance around to see how many people are in the direct vicinity of our conversation and see that it's too many. If I'm going to ask him questions, I can't do it here. "Mind taking a walk with me?"

"Are you sure your friends would be okay with that?" I glance over my shoulder to where he's looking and see all three of my friends watching me like a hawk. I can also see a lot of other people have their attention on us now. Maybe I should've been more subtle about coming over here.

"Maybe we should talk later."

"No, it's okay. Let's make it look official." He motions to the officer closest to us, and the man steps up to escort me out of the room. Detective Ames follows.

When the doors shut behind us, the officer moves off, and the detective and I step across the hall.

"It wasn't all that smart for me to do that," I admit, because I know how it can look. People will be less willing to talk to me now if they think I'm working with the police. Although, I haven't been able to talk to that many people anyway.

"It could've been better." The detective smiles. It's the kind of fatherly smile that makes me feel better about my mishap immediately. "What have you found out?"

"Not much, actually. Everyone I've spoken to didn't even know there was a gardener on site. I've been trying to talk to Priscilla, but she's been running around, too busy. The only other thing I know is that Walter Sanchez had an argument with Lizette Bats about the way things are run around here."

That seems like new information to Detective Ames.

"Tell me more."

"I only know what I've been told, but according to my source, there's bad blood between him and the rest of the staff. He was probably thinking he'd run of this place. Did you talk to him?"

"When I talked to him, he only had the nicest things to say about the people here."

I mull that over.

"I suppose that makes sense, right? People want to put their best foot forward when they're being interviewed by the police."

"There's a lot to this case that doesn't add up." I'm almost positive I wasn't supposed to hear him mumble that. But he did, and now I want to press him for some answers.

"How did Arthur die?" I ask, not beating around the bush.

Detective's eyes snap up to meet mine, but there's not an ounce of emotion there. He's giving nothing away.

"I can't disclose that information."

"But it wasn't drowning."

"Miss Duke—"

"It wasn't right? There's something about this that seems like—"

"Like what?"

"Nothing." My mind just keeps going back to this. For some reason, I think if I knew how he died, something would actually fall into place. But what? I can't be sure.

"That's not something I'm willing to share, Miss Duke."

Just then, a movement catches my eye down the hall, and I nod.

"That's okay, Detective. Thanks anyway. I should visit the ladies' room while I'm here."

With that, I pivot and head to the bathroom. I already have a new plan in the works.

WHEN I STEP inside the bathroom, a tiny black shadow sneaks in behind me. I flip the fan on and then turn to Birdie. She's perching on top of the counter, staring at me.

"Where have you been?" I ask.

"Around."

Seriously, this cat is full of attitude. She's a mix between a cranky old lady and a hormonal teenager. That's the best description I can come up with and no one can convince me otherwise. But I can't say it, because I need her help, which might be physically painful for me to admit.

"Birdie, I need you to help me with something."

"I figured you'd be hopeless without me."

I bite the inside of my cheek to keep back the retort. I really need to stop arguing with a feline.

"Detective Ames won't share information with me, like how Arthur died. Do you think you can sneak into the room they used for the interviews to see if there are any files there?"

"I suppose that's a possibility."

She jumps down and heads for the door immediately, and I pull it open so she can sneak through. Leaving the door partially open, I wash my hands and make my way back to the ballroom. The buzz of people talking and laughing hits me before I step through the doors. The energy in the room is so different from what I'm feeling and thinking.

I find my way back to the table, to see the group playing Clue. Penny and Finn seem to be arguing, as usual. Dean sits, watching quietly. I take a spot beside him, and he smiles up at me.

"Are you done sleuthing?" He keeps his voice low, leaning close to me.

"Never," I reply, with a genuine smile. He chuckles at that, and the sound warms my heart. It's clear he's sad, and carrying guilt on his shoulders, but if he can still laugh, then there's hope for healing.

"You're good at it, you know," Dean says, his eyes still on me. I scrunch my face up a little in question. "The sleuthing. You have a knack for seeing things in a way others wouldn't."

"Why Dean Harvey, is that a compliment?" I place one hand against my heart, while the other fans my face.

"It most definitely was. But now you're being all dramatic, so I take it back."

"Nope, too late. No take backs."

I bump my shoulder with his and feel lighter somehow.

A sudden bang echoes through the room and everyone jumps at once.

"What was that?" Penny whispers right before it comes

again. That's when I realize what it is. The wind. It's rattling the windows.

"Everyone please stay calm." Lizette is once again up on the platform, microphone in hand. "A storm has rolled in unexpectedly. We are taking precautions and barricading against the gusts. There's no need for alarm."

"Should we go back to our rooms?" someone calls out.

Lizette shakes her head. "It would be best to stay in the main house. The bungalows are built sturdy, but they don't have as much protection as the main house. We will watch the storm closely, but it would be best to prepare to spend the night here. It's not the first time this has happened. We have cots available and will be setting those up in the foyer, as well as this room. Those who have rooms in the main house, it will be up to you if you would like to share your space. We will not mandate that from anyone."

I look around at the people, the shaken-up faces now showing the fear and comprehension I expected earlier. Staying in the house is probably the best choice for all of us, considering it's built a little higher and sturdier in case there is any flooding.

"Is it fair to keep us here while others have the comfort of their own rooms?" another person calls out, bringing my attention back to the crowd.

"I understand the inconvenience, but they paid extra to stay at the main house. Please understand, we are doing our best to ensure the safety of our guests. If you are absolutely determined to wait out the storm in your bungalow, we will not stop you, but we advise against it."

"Safety?" A man stands up, and even from the side, I can see he's outraged. "Like you made sure that gardener was safe?" Gasps resound all around the room. Finn turns to me, concern plainly on his face.

"Things are going to get out of hand," he says. I can see his law enforcement mind working out scenarios. I notice it too, the signs of panic.

"Should you offer to help?" Penny asks, but Finn is already shaking his head.

"I have already offered. The detective is very insistent on letting his people handle things. I won't overstep my bounds."

Good thing I don't have those restrictions. I know I need to be careful, but I also know I need to ignore some parameters in order to reach my goal.

"What happened to Mr. Gilla is a heartbreaking tragedy." Lizette's voice is calm, catching on the last word. It immediately seems to pacify the man who stood up. "The main building is secure, the officers from the state police are here to make sure it stays that way. But we will leave the decision up to you." She takes a deep breath before continuing on. "We have already begun setting up cots in the main foyer. We will need to clean up this room, and we can set up a section in here as well."

She continues to give out information as Finn and Penny turn back to me. I glance at them, then at Dean, and realize they're all waiting for me to make a decision.

"If you're waiting for me to tell you where to sleep, that is not my job," I say with a smile.

"But it is," Dean says, and my eyes fly up to meet his. "We'll follow where you lead."

The way he says that—I can't seem to look away or form any coherent responses. The intensity in his words matches the intensity in his gaze. It turns me to a puddle of mush.

I think I fell for this man when I wasn't looking.

The thought slams into me with the speed of a bullet. I tear my eyes away. This is not the time and place for life changing revelations. I glance at my other friends and find them still watching me.

"Okay," I say. "We stay here. I would rather be in the foyer where I can have a better vantage point of who comes in and out."

"Got it." Finn stands, extending his hand to Penny. "Shall we go find ourselves a resting place?"

"Why must you make it sound so ominous?" Penny stands, grabbing his hand and pulling him after her.

"It wasn't. It was grand and exciting."

"No, it made us sound like we're picking out a spot in the cemetery."

They continue to bicker as they walk, and I smile. One of these days, those two will realize they're meant for each other. I glance over at Dean and find him watching them with his own smile. He looks over at me, and that intensity that's reserved just for me is back in his eyes.

I open my mouth to say something, anything, when a tiny prickle on my calf makes me jump.

"What is it?" Dean is immediately reaching for me as I grab my leg. My arm brushes against soft fur, and I bend down to look under the table.

"Stop making eyes at Dean. I found something," Birdie announces, looking way too smug.

"You're ridiculous," I mumble.

"What?" This comes from Dean. I straighten quickly, pushing the hair out of my face.

"Nothing. I—I just need to go to the restroom, that's all."

"Are you sure you're okay?"

"Peachy keen, jellybean. I'll be back."

Then I stand and bolt out of the room as inconspicuously as I can manage.

13

I head for the bathrooms once more. These people are about to think I have a real bladder problem. But it's the only place I can think of where I can talk to Birdie without people also thinking I need to be locked up.

When I slip inside, Birdie is already sitting on the counter.

"Did you have to claw at me?" I ask, keeping my voice low.

"Yes. You don't pay attention to anything when Dean is around."

I—I'm not sure how I feel about a cat noticing such a thing. Note to self, be a little more discreet around prying eyes.

"I have no idea what you're talking about," I say.

"Of course not," Birdie replies, and seriously, having this conversation with a cat is crazier than me having magic.

"What did you find?" I sigh, because I think she's going to argue with me for the rest of the night if I let her. She gives me a look—this cat is way too expressive—before raising a paw to give it a thorough cleaning. I try not to fidget, waiting her out, but I can't help it.

"Really now?"

"Patience, witch."

"I need buckets of it when dealing with you."

I really truly thought we were getting to be friends—almost, after the last fiasco. She's been helping me after all. But no. This cat is here to drive me mad.

"Anyway," Birdie says, placing her paw back down on the counter. "The detective didn't leave any files laying around in the interview room."

"You could've just told me that in the ballroom."

"But—" Birdie narrows her eyes at my interruption. "He has checked himself into one of the rooms upstairs, and there, he does keep his files."

Of course, that makes sense. All his suspects are here, why would he leave? It's true that the killer could've left before I found the body, but it seems like that's not the case if the detective is sticking around. There also has to be a way Detective Ames could tell the killer is still here, and now I'm wondering what information he's not sharing. Well, at this point, he's not sharing anything.

"You're welcome," Birdie says, breaking through my thoughts. I focus on her.

"Thank you, Birdie. Now, which room is his?"

The cat glares again, as if my thanks weren't good enough, but she replies, "1507."

"1507? The house has that many rooms?"

"No. But all the rooms start with 15."

Birdie jumps down from the counter and heads for the door, staring at it expectedly. When I don't open it right away, she looks over at me.

"Hold on." I hurry to flush the toilet and then wash my hands before I shut the light off and open the door. I step out first before I feel Birdie's fur brush against my legs. When I look back down, she's gone. I will never admit it to her, but she's been extremely helpful. I turn back toward the ballroom, my mind racing over possibilities.

Now would probably be the best time to head upstairs and find room 1507. But I need to make sure I know where the detective is first. When I step into the ballroom, the tables have been all but removed. Beds are being set up in their places. I scan the crowd, but I don't see my friends or the detective. Making my way back out, I head for the main foyer, and I spot him before I step out of the hallway. He's on the opposite end, talking to Priscilla. My friends are there too, near the staircase, in the perfect position to see the front door and the stairs heading up. I smile to myself. It was probably Finn's idea because he's just as cautious about seeing all the exits as I am.

The next problem is how to get upstairs without being noticed. I step back into the shadows of the hallway, thinking over my options. Then, it clicks. The kitchens. There's the main one and a smaller one to the side. There has to be a staircase in there for the food to be brought up. In an old house such as this, there are probably multiple servant passageways from the olden days. I just need to find one.

Hoping no one notices my absence, I head toward the kitchens. The place is busy with activity, just like the rest of the house, as everyone prepares for the storm. It's not the first time one of these showed up unannounced. They even mention it in their brochure, just to make sure people are prepared.

I watch a few people coming in and out and then I notice the door at the back. No one pays me any attention when I sneak around people and to the door. It opens suddenly, and I step to the side, holding it.

"Thanks!" one of the women says as she carries in a tray, not sparing me a glance.

"You're welcome," I reply before heading through the open doorway. The hallway is small and there are stairs going up and down. Without hesitation, I go up, hoping I don't run into anyone else. Luck must be on my side because I don't. When I reach the second landing, there's a door there. I push it open carefully. I find myself in a small room with countertops on both sides. Stacks of napkins and sets of silverware are laid out on one side. This must be the in-between room where they place food before distributing it to the rooms.

There's a door on the opposite end, and I head toward it. When I crack it open, I see a hallway stretch beyond it. After looking both ways, I step out, walking over to the first room. 1518. So Birdie was right. The rooms all start with 15. I wonder why that is.

But now is not the time to think about that. Who knows how much time I actually have? Quickly, I move door to door until I find the one I need. 1507. I try the doorknob first, but of course, it's locked up tight. Thankfully, I have a spell for this.

Well, more like a trick I've learned.

Closing my eyes, I focus my intention, placing my hand against the metal and pushing intention into it. There's a moment of stillness and then I hear a click. After another quick glance around, I slip inside.

There's one lamp on in the corner, and I let that be my only guiding light. I don't want to tip off anyone that I'm here. There are stacks of papers everywhere. As much as possible, I look over the papers without disturbing them. Detective Ames seems to be meticulous about keeping notes. That's a quality I can admire. It would take me way too long to go through this information. I wonder if there's a spell I can use to help me out when the paper in front of me catches my eye. It's beneath stacks of other papers, so I pick those up, keeping them hovering over where they lay so I can put them back exactly.

Bingo.

It's the medical examiner's report. Scanning it quickly, I nearly gasp out loud. Arthur wasn't drowned. He died by bleeding out. The medical examiner didn't seem to know how that happened. The only indication on the body were three puncture marks on the neck. Well, and he has bruising on his head, as if someone hit him first. The marks on the neck only bring one possibility to mind.

Wait, are vampires a real thing?

That's something I will have to ask Auntie Grace. They have no idea on the actual murder weapon, so a supernatural killer makes sense. Except, no. Vampires aren't real. Are they?

While I'm lost in thought, a noise comes from the direction of the door. I have absolutely no time to react before Dean is slipping inside the room.

"What are you doing here? Besides giving me a mild heart attack," I hiss at him, keeping my voice low.

"I saw you sneaking off. I figured you'd get yourself into trouble."

"How am I in trouble?"

"Detective Ames is on his way up. He said he needed to grab some folders."

I drop the papers into place immediately, and walk to the door, but Dean stops me. Yanking the door to lock, he grabs me by the arm before pulling me after him and toward the closet. It's a very small armoire type of closet.

"Dean, what are you—?" He clasps a hand over my mouth and pulls the doors shut. My back is plastered to the wall, but still, our bodies are touching. Dean leans down just a bit, his lips at my ear.

"He's almost here," Dean says, and right as he does, the keys rattle in the lock. I gasp, but then go quiet. Some from fear, some from proximity. Dean and I are sharing the same air now, our bodies brushing ever so slightly every time we take a breath. I turn my full attention to the spot on his shoulder, hoping Detective Ames doesn't have super hearing and can't tell just how loudly my heart is beating. When Dean's hand settles on my back, I nearly jump out of my skin at the sensation the small touch sends through my body, even through the clothes. My hands grasp his shirt, curling into him as I hear the detective come farther into the room and begin moving the papers around. If he opens this door, we're in trouble.

Well, I think I'm already in trouble.

I HAVE no idea how long we stand like this. The detective continues to move through the room, and I can hear the shuffling of papers. He sighs a few times, and I can almost feel the frustration. I've only played investigator twice, and I know how frustrating it can be not getting the answers you want. He's been doing this a long time.

Dean tightens his grip on me, bringing me even closer. My eyes find his in the darkness, and then, I can't look away. It's as if he's radiating his own glow, or maybe it's my magic playing with my vision. But he's all I see—in this moment, it's just him.

I think of all the time we've spent together recently, working on the Crooked Windows Inn remodel, then helping Mayor Moore with rebuilding the forgotten neighborhood. He's been there every step of the way, patiently waiting for me to heal from my past. Not pushing, just being a friend. And then, when I wasn't watching, he became more.

"Cassie."

The barely-there whisper of my name on his lips stops all sense of time, and I suddenly forget that we're hiding. His eyes are still on me. My hands curl into fists, pulling on his shirt. He doesn't hesitate to bend down. Now, our lips are barely inches apart, and I can feel his breath on my skin.

I'm not sure which one of us moves next, but suddenly we're reaching for each other. I hold my breath as I wait for the sweet touch of his lips on mine.

Something bangs on the closet doors, springing us apart.

The doors swing open. I'm terrified to have been discovered, but when the room opens up, no one is there. Well, no one but Birdie. Sneaking under the bed. The detective is gone.

Without meeting Dean's eye, I step out of the armoire, tugging on my shirt. I can't believe I almost kissed him. Or he kissed me. Or—I'm not sure what I was thinking.

"Cassie?"

"We need to get out of here," I say quickly, making a beeline for the papers I was reading before Dean came in. Quickly, I take pictures of everything with my phone before rearranging them back how I found them. There's also a map of the main house, and I snap a picture of the floor plan to study later. This will come in handy. I know Birdie is watching me, but I can't exactly talk to her now. Hopefully, Dean didn't notice her at all.

When I straighten, he's by the door, his eyes on me. I look in his general direction as I walk toward him. Placing my ear to the door, I try to hear if there is any movement out there, but there's nothing.

"Do you think it's safe?" I ask, still whispering.

"I think there's only one way to find out," Dean replies. I step back as he reaches for the doorknob and pulls the door open. He steps out first before motioning for me to follow. I glance back into the room, only to find Birdie already slipping between my feet and down the hall. She moves in the opposite direction of where Dean is looking. This cat is truly something. Maybe she was a spy in another life.

Shutting the door quietly behind me, I hold onto the doorknob for a second longer than necessary, sending my intention into it. The lock clicks into place and then we're moving away.

"No, not that way," I say when Dean heads toward the stairs.

"What do you mean?"

"The detective is probably at the bottom of those stairs, keeping watch over the people in the foyer and the front door. Follow me."

In a very Dean fashion, he doesn't hesitate to follow. That brings a tiny smile to my face, but thankfully he can't see it.

I'm all kinds of unbalanced as it is. That almost kiss is going to haunt me longer than Arthur. I'm sure. I have no idea what possessed me to give in to the moment, but I really need Dean not to bring it up. I don't think I'm ready to talk about it.

We step into the tiny kitchen and thankfully it's empty. Everyone is probably still downstairs, setting up against the storm. Even being somewhere in the middle of the house, I can hear it raging outside. It was probably a good idea for everyone to stay in here for the night. Dean is right behind me when we descend the stairs. When I open the door, one of the staff members looks at me confused.

"We got turned around," I say, shrugging. The woman looks over my shoulder at Dean and then her confusion turns into a smile.

"Of course. Right this way."

I dare a glance at Dean and find his half smile in place. That's when I realize the woman probably thought we were up to nothing good, which she technically would be right about. But I don't feel like correcting her. She leads us back out into the main hall with a little shake of the head.

"Cassie—" Dean tries again, but I really can't have this conversation right now.

"I have so much information to go through," I say, turning to him. "I need to find a quiet place to read over it. You should probably go back out into the main foyer. We wouldn't want Detective Ames getting suspicious. Cover for me if he asks."

Dean studies me for a long, tense moment before nodding.

"Please, be careful."

He doesn't wait for a response, but pivots and heads back toward the front of the house. I stand there for a moment longer, watching his retreat. I wish he knew how mistimed his words are. He should've warned me to be careful a long time

14

———

After some looking around, I realize getting alone time is going to be difficult. While the upstairs is mostly empty, the downstairs area has people mulling around everywhere. I could go hide in the bathroom again, but I'm pretty sure I'll just bring unnecessary attention to myself. Finally, I find one of the smaller sitting areas nearly unoccupied and decide this is as good as it's going to get. Grabbing the sitting chair in the corner while the others sit in front of the fireplace, I open my phone and start scrolling through pictures.

I read over all the information twice before coming back to the medical examiner's report. Arthur had puncture wounds on his neck. That has to be the way his blood was drained. But that seems so specific. If it's not a vampire, is it someone pretending?

Opening the messages up, I type out a quick text to Auntie Grace asking about vampires. But as I watch the bar on top, I realize it won't send. I have no signal all of a sudden. It must be the storm. That's the only explanation I have. This is the time it would be super helpful to know if I could send messages with my magic, but I'm definitely not there in my studies yet.

I click over to the notes app where I've been keeping information about the case and read over that next. I'm still going to talk to the Sanchez grandson and Priscilla. Maybe right now is as good a time as any.

"I heard this place has been losing money," I hear as I leave my chair to head to the door. Slowing down immediately, I pretend like I got a text as I eavesdrop.

"For sure, I heard them arguing about it when I first arrived. I guess business hasn't been great since that woman took over."

I take a step toward the three people sitting on the couch near the fire, ready to play my role.

"Are you talking about...the manager?" I mock whisper, perching on the arm rest. The two women and a man turn to me immediately, and I lean forward. "I heard the Sanchez's grandson is so unhappy."

Finding a kindred spirit in me, the three lean toward me immediately.

"Oh, he most definitely isn't happy. When he first came back from the big city, he was running the show. We stayed here that year, like we do every other year, and this place was starting to thrive again. But then that woman came, and she brought her right-hand woman with her, and the whole atmosphere changed. I heard the gardener wasn't going to be coming back next season."

"Lizette brought Priscilla with her?" I whisper, and the woman nods excitedly.

"She most certainly did. It was a big deal around these parts because they booted poor Walter right out of his position and took over. Everyone has been on edge since then."

"Wow. Everyone seems to get along so well though!" I pretend to be shocked, but also, not really pretending.

"They have to put on a good show for the guests, but trust

me, I've been coming here long enough that I have felt the tension. I wasn't even surprised one of them ended up dead. God rest his soul."

The woman pauses, like she's saying a silent prayer and then the others are talking to her about other resorts and how maybe they should check those out next year. I won't get anything else from them without looking suspicious.

Leaving the sitting room behind, I think over what I just found out. If the gossip mill is to be believed, this place was like a powder keg waiting to go off. If that's the case, that means the suspect list is probably a lot longer than I first thought. The one thing I need to do though is talk to Walter. I've been putting that off for way too long.

Pivoting, I head for the kitchens. It's now or never.

When I reach the main dining room, workers are still going in and out, now carrying trays with cups and kettles on them. Auntie Grace has always said that tea is good for the soul. We've used the same tactic at the Crooked Windows Inn when we're trying to keep people calm. There's something about sitting around and sipping tea that feels homey enough that all your worries go away.

I slip into the kitchen, this time from the main entrance rather than the side one I used earlier. This front area is much larger, as it houses most of the burners on one side.

"I'm sorry," I say with a smile as one of the staff stops beside me, clearly about to ask me what I'm doing in here. "I'm looking for Mr. Sanchez. Is he in here?" The man smiles back at me and then points me toward a man at the corner of the room near the burners.

I'm not sure what I was expecting of Walter Sanchez, but it wasn't the barely 40-something, six foot one, body builder type. When Victoria mentioned him before, I thought I'd seen him already. But I guess not, because this is the first time I'm laying eyes on him.

"Mr. Sanchez?" I say, coming up to where he's looking over papers on the counter near the burners.

"Walter is fine," he replies before glancing up and giving me a distracted smile. "Can I help you?"

"I hope so. My name is Cassandra Duke, I'm—" I was going to say one of the guests, but he would know that. "I'm the one who found Arthur Gilla. I was wondering if you had a moment to talk?"

He studies me for a moment. I'm not sure what he sees in my eyes, but he nods.

"Let's talk in here." He leads me back out into the dining hall, moving away from the busyness of the kitchen. "How can I help you Miss Duke?"

"Cassandra, please." I give him a small smile, reminding myself to go gently. "This whole situation has been so sad. I guess I'm just trying to make sense of who Arthur was when he was alive."

"I'm sorry you were the one who had to go through that," Walter says. Right away, I can tell there's genuine emotion there, not empty words. That's when I notice he also looks tired. "Arthur wasn't a bad man, I think he was simply a little lost."

"What do you mean by that?"

"He was always getting into these schemes, always looking for the next best thing, instead of focusing on the business he already had. I could understand that, since I went through a similar phase. But since coming here, that has changed."

"You really care about the resort." It's not a question, but Walter replies anyway.

"I do. My grandparents have spent their life rebuilding it, nearly from the ground up, and turning it into a place where families can feel safe. It's important I uphold that legacy, but I guess I didn't in this case."

Even though it's not his fault, I can see him taking the

murder on personally. Well, granted, it might be his fault. I'm trying to stay unbiased here. It just doesn't feel right to put him on the suspect list. Not now that I've met him.

"I traveled a lot in my twenties." Walter continues as if I'm not even here. "I had to find myself. It's how I became a chef in the first place. I stayed with this elderly couple in Italy for a few months, and they taught me everything I know about food. When I finally felt like I had my feet under me, I came home."

"But not to take over the resort?"

His eyes fly up to meet mine, as if he just remembered I'm there.

"No, Lizette was already hired, running the place even before she arrived. I was barely allowed to do anything." I'm trying to pick up the underlying emotion in his words, but I can't quite place it. The information is slightly different from what I received from the guests. I wonder why that is. He rubs his hands together, and I notice how callused and strong they look. He's someone who works hard.

"May I ask why?"

He sighs, running a hand over his hair as he watches the kitchen door for a moment.

"It had to do with money. Lizette brought a marketing plan to my grandparents which was going to take the resort to the next level. So, we made an agreement. She stays on for five years and implements her business plan. If I prove that I can work at the resort in the meantime, it goes to me at the end of it."

"How many people know about that deal?"

"Only those directly involved with management, Lizette, Priscilla, and myself, of course. Also, Helen, who's in charge of the marketing department for the resort and the reservations. And Arthur, I suppose. He was the on-sight groundskeeper, even when he wasn't here full time. It's funny actually. He was going to become full time when I took over. I wanted someone on the premises over the course of the year and to help out with some maintenance work."

"Arthur was going to get a full-time gig here?"

"Yes. I guess that's not happening now."

"Where was Arthur living while he was here?" I ask, knowing that my luck is probably running out when it comes to Walter. People only like to share so much.

"He stayed in one of the bungalows behind the pool house, near the gardens."

He says goodbye then, heading back to the kitchen. I did come away with one piece of information though. This place really is a tight knit community. So what did Arthur get into to get himself killed?

THE STORM IS STILL RAGING outside two hours later. It's about a quarter past nine now. Some of the younger kids are already in their cots in the foyer and the ballroom. A hush has fallen over the whole building. Those who are still awake are keeping their voices down as parents whisper comforting words to their children. I haven't seen Birdie since she caught Dean and I—doing absolutely nothing! I refuse to go down that road.

"Where have you been?" Penny whispers when I find her, Finn, and Dean sitting in the corner of the foyer a little while later.

"Snooping around, I'm sure." The voice comes from behind me, and I turn to see Detective Ames making his way over to us.

"I've just been keeping busy, that's all," I say with a smile.

"I'm sure your busy and my busy are two different things," he replies. "Please tell me you haven't been doing anything that may compromise my investigation."

"Of course not, Detective. But if you're willing to share some information, I would be more than happy to make some suggestions."

Detective Ames gives me a thorough study, as if he's thinking it over. I nearly hold my breath. But of course, disappointment is the name of the game.

"Keep yourself safe, Miss Duke. I will see you in the morning." With that, he turns to walk away.

"Detective?" I call out, because I need to know something. He turns, waiting for me to ask. I take a step closer and lower my voice.

"Is Dean still a suspect?" Detective Ames watches me for a moment, because I know telling me is sharing parts of the investigation, when he already said he won't. But then, he shakes his head, ever so slightly.

"No. Good night, Miss Duke."

My heart feels lighter as he walks away, even though I don't have the exact details.

"I can't tell if he actually wants to mentor you or just keep you on a leash," Finn says. I swivel toward him.

"What?"

"Come on, Cassie. You can't pretend you don't notice the special interest he has taken in you."

"It's not like that!" My whisper has risen a few octaves.

"Shhh." The sound comes from behind us, and I mouth *sorry* in the general direction.

"I didn't say it like it was a bad thing," Finn comments. "I sometimes think Sheriff Bernard would love to use your unusual set of skills, but he's too proud to ask. Detective Ames is definitely curious."

"Well, I did find the body, after all."

During this whole exchange, Dean has stayed completely silent. I have refused to look in his direction. Penny has been eyeing the two of us like she's watching one of her favorite K-dramas. If I didn't know any better, I'd think she was an empath witch because she can always pick up on whatever is getting put out there.

The thing is, I should probably lay down and go to sleep. But I'm too restless, and there's one place I would love to check out while everyone is huddled in the main house. Since I promised nearly everyone in my life not to do dangerous things alone, I need a backup.

"Penny, can I borrow you for a second?" She stands way too eagerly, and now, I can feel Dean's gaze on me like a physical imprint. He's basically ready to stand and follow me wherever I go at this point, if only to keep me out of trouble. But I can't deal with myself when I'm around him, so that's not going to work.

"Cassie, what are you up to?" His voice reaches me as Penny and I turn to go. If I ignore him, he'll just come after us. So I make myself turn to face him.

"I need to check on something, and I need you guys to cover for us." I glance between him and Finn. Neither of the guys like that I'm leaving them behind, I can tell that much with a single look.

"Cassie—"

"Please," I interrupt, before Dean can launch into any kind of speech. His brother is just as ready to rush after me. While I love the fact that I have two strong men on my side, I think better when I'm not around them. Well, not around Dean. I really need to stop digressing.

"We'll be fine. We won't go far. Trust me." I give them each a long hard look, and only after each of them nods do I grab Penny's hand and pull her into the shadows with me.

"What are you up to, Cassie?" Penny leans over to whisper as quietly as she can. The hallways are mostly deserted, but I'm not taking any chances. Detective Ames is clearly watching me a little more closely than I thought. I take out my phone and pull up the picture I took earlier of the floor plan. Scrolling through, I know when I've found exactly what I'm looking for.

"Here." I show it to Penny.

"We're going outside?" she mock-whispers, and I hush her.

"Yes. I need to get to the bungalow at the back of the pool house. The storage area behind the kitchens has a door to the pool house. And that will take us outside."

"Cassie, if you haven't noticed, there are hurricane-like winds outside. It's not that I don't want to help, but isn't that dangerous?"

"It is. I won't make you go outside. You can stay in the pool house and keep an eye out."

"Really? As if I'm actually going to send you into a storm alone?" She huffs, shaking her head. "I'm still going, I'm just pointing out the obvious. As in danger, Will Robinson."

I smile. I can't help it. She may be small, but she's mighty. I couldn't have asked for a better best friend.

"If I can get to Arthur's place, I might be able to find something that will make sense of this whole mess. Or maybe I can find something that will jog his memory if he ever ends up in my dreams again. I don't know, Penny. I feel like I keep getting all this information and it's not fitting in anywhere. I need to do something."

"Don't you think the detective has already searched the place?"

"I'm sure he has," I reply as we begin walking again. "But I need to see it with my own eyes. I wish I could get Auntie Grace on the phone for a spell or something, but I've had no bars all night."

"Same here. It's probably the storm."

It is. But how convenient is it that Mother Nature decided to bring a storm right when a murder investigation is going on? If I didn't know any better, I'd think another witch was making this happen. Just as the thought enters my mind, I nearly stop

15

W e slip through the kitchens and the back storage area without any problems. People are simply too exhausted and preoccupied to pay us any mind. That is great for us, but also a little concerning. If anyone was going to do anything sneaky or suspicious, now would be the time.

Okay, my brain needs to chill with the conspiracy theories before I give myself an ulcer.

"I have to say, the storm is way scarier in here," Penny says as soon as we step into the pool house. I agree with her immediately. The glass roof is not exactly hurricane proof, and the dark clouds that hang low seem like they're laying right on top of it.

"It's holding so far, so let's just hurry," I say, hoping my faith in this building structure is not misplaced. I'd send Penny back inside in a second, but I know she won't leave my side.

"Just distract me, somehow," Penny says as we make our way around the chairs, staying far from the pool itself. There are no lights in here, just the occasional lighting. My phone's flashlight is the only guidance we have. I'm slightly thankful for the storm because I know no one is outside walking the perimeter and would be able to see it.

"Have you seen Birdie at all?" I ask.

"No. I hope she's okay. The storm must be scary for her too. Oh." Penny grabs my arm suddenly. "You don't think she went back to Monroe Cove and got caught in the storm, do you?"

"Don't worry. She was just banging on the closet door Dean and I were hiding in."

I know the moment the words leave my mouth I have made a mistake.

"I knew it!" Penny slaps me on the arm, and I shine my light in her face for a second.

"What was that for?" I grumble as she pushes the light down.

"For keeping things from me. I could feel the tension between the two of you. I could see it. A blind person could see it! What happened? Tell me, tell me."

"Okay, first of all, don't hit me again. Second of all, nothing happened."

"What do you mean nothing happened? Why is your face so red then?"

"There is no way you can tell my face is red in this darkness!"

"I don't have to see it to know it is!"

We're whisper-arguing now, and we have reached the outer door. I place my hand on the doorknob and unlock the deadbolt on top.

"Cassandra Duke, we are not going out there into our near death until you tell me what happened!" Penny is standing so close to me I can feel her body vibrating in excitement. I think it over for a second before I blurt out the truth.

"We almost kissed." And then I push the door open, and the wind nearly takes it off its hinges. Penny grabs onto me, and we step out into the crazy weather. My long red hair whips around us, slamming into my face painfully. I really should've put it into a braid before I came out here, but it's too late now.

"Do you know where we're going?" Penny shouts. That's the only way I can hear her over the roar of the storm. At least there's no rain right now. But I know all about these storms, and the rainfall comes suddenly and randomly.

"Come on!" I take her hand and lead us to the left where the map showed a path. The gardens are spread out all around the resort's grounds, but I'm hoping since Walter said Arthur was at the back of the pool house, this is the right direction. It's also the same direction Dean would've been walking from that night.

Once we're between the trees, the wind quiets a little, and I breathe in a sigh of relief. We follow the small path on the ground. In the next minute, we're in a small clearing with two bungalows. They're identical to the one Penny and I are staying in and both dark.

"Do we know which one?" Penny asks. We come closer, and I study the two buildings.

"The one with the yellow tape?" I point to the scrap of tape barely hanging on to part of the doorframe. We step over to the door. I can see that it's been sealed off, but the storm has ripped most of the tape away. I try the door, but it's locked. Once again, I'm grateful I've been practicing my magic. Sending a little bit of intention into it, I breathe in and out, and the door clicks open.

"Such a cool trick," Penny whispers over my shoulder. I grin as I push the door open. Just as we step inside, the rain comes. Shutting the door behind us, I give the room a quick scan with the flashlight.

"Do we turn the light on?" Penny asks. I think about it for a moment before walking over to the light switch and flipping it on. Just like in our bungalow, only the bedside lamp switches on. The rest of the lamps need to be turned on manually.

The room is nearly identical to ours, except it only has one bed. The rest is basically the same, right down to the generic sheets and comforter and almost no personal items.

"You said Arthur lived here? Did the police take all his stuff?"

Penny and I begin moving through the room. She reaches for the dresser, and I stop her.

"Use your shirt if you need to touch anything. Just in case."

I'm sure this has already been processed, but I don't want to take any chances.

"And to answer your question, yes, he lived here. Maybe he packed light because of his short stay?" I open the closet and find clothes still hanging, so I know the police didn't take his stuff. "The only thing I can see them taking is his computer or planner or journal, if he kept one."

"So, what are we looking for then?"

"I'm not sure, Penny." I sigh, because I really am not. Everything I've been doing, I've been doing on instinct. If I had more experience, like the detective, maybe I would be able to see things differently. But I just know that I needed to come in here for...something.

"I don't think I'm good at this sleuthing stuff, Penny," I say, turning to where my best friend stands on the other side of the room. She looks up at me, a question in her eyes. "I've been trying to read books and learn because I keep getting put into these situations. But I'm not like the cool mystery solvers on TV. I don't automatically just know what to do or say. Or what questions to ask. I talked to Walter today."

"Walter?"

"The cook. The Sanchez's grandson. I'm sure there were a dozen questions I could've asked him that I didn't. I just didn't know what I was looking for. Just like now. I made you go out into the storm, and I've got no direction."

"Isn't that how we all start out? Do you think when I started baking I knew how to make your favorite cheesecake or the danishes that are so popular in Monroe Cove? I didn't. I made a lot of mistakes, and I tweaked it until it was my own. I think maybe that's what you're doing. You're figuring out your footing. With magic, with being home again, and with this. As humans, I think we're all trying to figure things out. You're doing the best you can and that's all you can do."

I let her words settle in my heart because they're exactly what I need to hear. It's so easy for me to be hard on myself or to feel like a failure when things aren't going exactly according to plan. And let's be honest, since my whole magical fiasco with my last boss, nothing has been going according to plan. But I am trying. And I'm going to keep trying until I figure it out.

"Plus, you have that hot handyman that you almost kissed —don't think I've forgotten about that particular bomb. I'll get the whole story, even if I have to torture it out of you. Or bribe you with my raspberry cheesecake."

"Let's not get carried away," I say, turning back to shuffle through Arthur's clothes. "It wasn't that exciting of a story."

"Mhhm, so tell me about it then. I need to know!"

"Penny, I—" I pause as I pull out one of the hanging shirts. My eyes go to the label, and if I'm being honest, I'm more than a little shocked.

"Come on, Cassie. Just spill it already."

"Penny, come over here please." My friend doesn't hesitate, walking over to stand beside me.

"What is it?"

"Can you tell me if this is Burberry?" She glances at the label before whistling.

"Umm yes. And that's Dolce & Gabbana."

We ruffle through the rest of the dress shirts, pants, a coat, and a few jackets. Except for the first four shirts, every other item in the closet is from a fancy brand.

"Okay, how can a gardener that is having money trouble afford all of this?" I ask out loud.

"Well, maybe you found that missing piece you were looking for?"

And that's when the light blinks out.

"Cassie!"

"It's okay." I'm already pulling out my phone and turning the flashlight on. Walking over to one of the other lamps, I try to turn it on manually, but there's nothing. "I think the power might've gone out."

The storm sounds even more fierce now. When I peek outside, the rain is still coming down.

"I don't think we should be going out there right now," I say. I hear Penny agree with a resounding yes. I try not to show it, but the sudden loss of light has also spooked me. The timing was impeccable.

"The guys will wonder what happened if we take too long," Penny points out. She's not wrong. I'm sure Dean is already pacing while Finn is trying to make sure they don't look too suspicious while they worry. The two brothers might be different in some ways, but their protective streak is very simi-lar. I'm honestly surprised they didn't just follow us out here against my orders.

"What do we do?"

"We'll wait it out. If it gets too much, we might have to brave it, but let's give it a few."

I lead Penny to the wall, and we sit with our backs against it. I'm not exactly comfortable sitting on Arthur's bed. Glancing at my phone, I see that my battery is getting close to twenty percent. I shut the flashlight off.

"I'm going to save it for when we head back," I say into the darkness and hear Penny exhale.

"I guess this is as good a time as any for you to tell me what happened with Dean."

"Penny!"

"What? I'm curious."

I chuckle, but I know I can't keep not talking about this. Maybe the shroud of darkness will help put some of my feelings into words. A girl can hope at least.

"I went up to Detective Ames's room. I needed to take a look at the medical examiner's report."

"Cassie!"

"Hey, no judging. If you want the story, you keep your opinions to yourself."

"Fine!" I can't see her, but she definitely just pouted at me.

"Anyway, Dean figured it out and came to warn me about the detective coming back, and we hid in the closet." I pause, my mind immediately conjuring up the memory of being pressed against his body.

"And? Don't leave me in suspense."

I shake the intruding images away and focus.

"And Birdie caught us. Thankfully, Dean didn't see her. Can you imagine me trying to explain that to him?"

"You're skipping over all the good parts, Cassandra."

"You're relentless, Penelope."

"That's true." We both chuckle at that, and I take a deep breath before I put into words what I've been trying to ignore.

"I think I was the one who almost kissed him."

"What?" Penny grabs my arm, scratching me a little.

"Dude, you're so violent." I slap at her grip and feel her body shift in my direction.

"You almost kissed him? You've been running from your feelings for so long and you almost make a move now?"

"And then I actually physically ran as well—wait what do you mean running from my feelings?"

"Oh, come on Cassie. I've known you for nearly twenty years. I know when you're lying to yourself. I also know that Dean and you have a history, and it wasn't the greatest one. But he's grown into a very nice man, and he's clearly into you."

"First of all—wait, wait, into me?" I sound like a parrot.

"Cassandra." I can hear Penny trying not to laugh. Maybe I really am a complete idiot when it comes to love because none of this is making sense in my mind. "The guy has been crazy about you since you yelled at him in the driveway of the inn. But he's been giving you the time you need to come to terms with that, instead of being pushy."

I think back to all our interactions. Maybe if I put this new information alongside the information I already have, I can see it. Maybe it's not just me who's having these feelings. And if it's not just me, is that better or worse for me? What do I do with this information? I may possibly be having another existential crisis while sitting in the dark bungalow of a deceased man. What is my life even?

"Speaking of men in our lives, what's the deal with you and Finn?"

Good job, Cassie. Way to divert attention.

"I have no idea what you're talking about."

"Ha! I'm not the only one in denial here, am I?"

"This is not about me."

"Well, it could be. We could definitely be talking about you."

"You're not getting out of this that easily, Cassandra," Penny says, nudging me with her shoulder. Maybe I'm being a little sappy because of everything that's been going on, but I can't help but think that even though I'm in the middle of yet another murder investigation, I'm actually right where I'm supposed to be. My friends have truly stood by me while I figure myself out, Penny more than anyone else. I can't help but feel grateful for being so incredibly blessed. Even though she often threatens to withhold raspberry cheesecake from me.

"Wait!" I exclaim, sitting up. "That's it, Penny."

"What?"

"How does a man, who has no good income, afford such expensive clothes?"

"Am I supposed to answer that?"

"There are only two ways," I continue, excitement fueling my words. "He either steals it or he blackmails someone. Think about it. His business wasn't doing great. He was looking at other avenues of income. That's what Walter and Dean both told me, in different ways. He had to either be stealing the money from someone, which would get him killed if the person found out. Or he had some information that allowed him to blackmail, and that got him killed because the person didn't want to live under his control anymore."

"It's possible."

"It's more than possible. It's probable. There are only three reasons people commit murder. For love, money, or to cover up a crime. With Arthur's expensive lifestyle, I can see it being the latter two in a mixed kind of way."

It really does make sense. Unfortunately, it doesn't get us any closer to figuring out who that person might be, but I have a motive now. I'm eager to talk to Detective Ames and see if my motive matches his.

"Are you ready to brave the storm?" I ask. We really do need to get back to the main house. Penny stands, and I can almost hear her steeling herself against what needs to be done.

"Lead the way, fearless leader," she says, and I grin.

16

———————

We only get a little soaked on the way back. The rain lets up once we step outside, and I'm thankful Mother Nature seems to be on our side. It doesn't take us long to make it back to the pool house. Once we're back in the kitchens, we realize the lights are out here as well.

"This must be really fun for everyone," Penny says, and I agree. This vacation hasn't been the kindest to anyone. The kids are probably scared because I'm sure the majority of them are still awake. It's just how these things work, isn't it?

"We need to clean up a little. We look like we've been outside," I comment.

"How do we do that?"

"Come on."

I lead Penny to one of the bathrooms and we slip inside quickly. After washing our faces and braiding our hair, we look a little more put together. Our clothes are damp, but hopefully, since it's pitch dark, no one will notice.

"Thank goodness!" Finn is hugging me the moment we reach them and then he pulls back. "Why are you wet?"

"Shh, keep your voice down," I say, pushing him down onto the cot. There are enough candles in the foyer for me to make out people's faces, and I can see concern on Finn's. Dean stands up from the bed beside us, and the next thing I know, his arms are around me, pulling a blanket over my shoulders.

"Thank you," I mumble as he takes his seat near me. Penny is wrapped in a blanket as well, taking the place Dean vacated on the other side of Finn.

"Cassie." Dean leans toward me, keeping his voice down. "Did you go outside?"

"Yes." I see no point in lying to him. Finn opens his mouth, but I stop him. "We're fine. I wanted to see Arthur's bungalow."

"And?"

"And the man had very expensive taste for someone with money trouble."

Dean pulls back at that, mulling over my words. Then he nods.

"You're right. He has been dressing differently. I don't remember him ever owning slacks before now."

"That's what I figured. Burberry, Dolce & Gabbana. I'm sure if we looked further, we would've found Armani in there as well. It didn't seem like something that would be part of his regular wardrobe, but that's mostly what he had."

"So, what do you think?"

"I think he got in over his head about money, and that's what got him killed. I want to talk to Detective Ames and see what he says about that, but I'm not sure how to approach the subject and still get an answer. He said I could help with the investigation, but he hasn't exactly been forthcoming with information."

"Did you expect him to be?"

"No, but I wanted him to be."

There's a moment of silence while the others think about this new piece of information. I scan the room, but I can't see into the shadows, so I have no idea where the detective is.

"He came by to check on you a little bit ago." Finn brings my attention back to him. "I just said you were in the bathroom."

"I doubt he believed that."

"I doubt he did."

Taking a deep breath, I stand once more.

"I think it's time I had a talk with him. Dean, would you like to come with me?" I'm not sure what possesses me to ask, but I'm immediately glad that I do.

"Yes, I would." Dean doesn't hesitate. I give the others a quick smile before Dean and I make our way between the cots and candles, looking for the detective. When we finally find him, he's near the front doors, talking to Priscilla. He notices me right away, and says a few more words to the head maid before walking over to us.

"Miss Duke, I hope you aren't getting into any more trouble."

"What a way to greet a friend," I say, and Dean chuckles beside me.

"How can I help you, Miss Duke?" I think the detective is trying not to smile either, and I take that as a victory.

"I know you won't share specifics about the case, but I was wondering if you have come up with a motive."

"There are a few theories."

"Isn't that what cops say when they have no idea?" Dean asks. I kind of want to high five him for that. The detective looks over at him and then back at me before motioning us farther away from the people.

"We're still going through a list of suspects," Detective Ames admits. "And I will be honest, Arthur had a few enemies around here."

"Did that have something to do with money?"

"In a way." Detective Ames cocks his head to the side, eyeing me curiously. "What are you thinking?"

"I'm thinking Arthur was having money issues, but was living a lifestyle of the rich and famous. Something wasn't adding up."

"What do you mean rich and famous?"

"His clothes, his accessories, they were all much too expensive for a man of his means," Dean says, and now the detective is looking at him.

"How would you know that?"

"I recognize a Dolce & Gabbana suit. I may not wear it now, but once upon a time I did."

Well, this is a piece of information I didn't know about Dean. It would make sense, considering he worked in the big city. I used to wear a lot more heels as well.

"You're very perceptive," Detective Ames says, but now his gaze is on me. "We found some discrepancies in his finances. He was definitely getting money from somewhere and was making small, unsuspicious deposits very often."

"Is it possible he was stealing? Or maybe blackmailing someone for cash?"

"Those are both solid theories, Miss Duke." If I didn't know any better, Detective Ames sounds a little impressed. But I'm not about to comment on that, lest he stops being impressed. "We did recover a laptop, but it was locked. I sent it to our lab, but with the storm, I have no idea if they've been able to get into it already."

"So, what next?" I dare to ask.

"Next, we get some rest. This storm isn't letting up and tensions are high in here. If the killer is among us, he or she will be spooked. That makes them more dangerous."

"Do you think they are, among us?" Dean asks. I watch the detective for any kind of tell of what he's truly thinking. He glances over the group of people laid out on the cots before turning back to us.

"I do. I think the killer is someone within these resort walls. So, I ask you to please be careful."

~

OF COURSE, I can barely sleep. Is anyone really surprised by that? The power doesn't come back on, and the candles make an already eerie situation more...well, eerie. Every time someone moves, my senses are on alert. I keep watching the shadows dance on the ceiling, my mind filled with a hundred different scenarios.

Detective Ames clearly knows something I don't. That's to be expected. I feel like I only have bits of information from all sides with no definite leads. I've checked over the notes I made on my phone about all the pieces I've been able to gather, but it isn't as much as I would like it to be.

The only definite information I have is that Arthur wasn't as innocent as he appeared to be when he first visited me in my dreams. I tried falling asleep earlier, just to see if maybe he'd show up, but no dice. After that spell, I doubt I'll be seeing him again. Then again, who knows. I sure don't. Not when it comes to my magic.

It would be helpful if I could use said magic to help with the storm, but I can't do that either. All in all, I seem to be quite useless at this. Sighing, I lay on my back, staring up at the ceiling.

"So dramatic."

I jump a little, twisting my head to the right and then to the left. My friends seem to be sleeping no problem, and I wonder what time it is. My phone is getting low on battery, so I'm trying not to reach for it every chance I get.

"Birdie?" I risk the whisper, trying to see her tiny shape somewhere in the shadows of the room.

"Under here," she says. I lean over the side of my cot,

hanging down to look under it. There she is. "You look great from this angle."

I roll my eyes, even though I'm glad to see her. I won't admit it out loud, but I was a little concerned about the cat. It is a bit scary out there.

"Where have you been?" I whisper as softly as I can. I don't need Finn or Dean waking up and thinking I've officially lost my mind, talking to a cat. Also, I have no idea how I would explain Birdie to them.

"Doing your work for you, of course."

"What?"

"Detective work, witch. I've been around, eavesdropping, and learning all kinds of fun information." Birdie raises one of her paws and begins to clean it thoroughly. I swear she does this just to annoy me. I'm still hanging over the side of the cot like an idiot, so I sit up carefully, before pulling the blanket back. There's no way I can have a conversation with a cat where someone might see me. As I bend down to put my shoes back on, I whisper, "Bathroom?"

"Our favorite place."

The cat leaves before I do, already halfway across the hall by the time I weave through the sleeping bodies. No one pays me any attention, and I'm glad. It's easier than trying to explain myself. From what I can see, the detective is nowhere to be found. He's probably up in his room. I wouldn't blame him. He needs rest to stay sharp. Picking up one of the candles, I walk slowly, making sure the flame doesn't go out.

I reach the bathroom and find Birdie sitting near the door. Pulling it open, I step inside with the cat and shut the door behind us.

"You know, you can make light. You don't need that fire hazard," Birdie says, jumping on top of the counter.

"We both know I'm not good with magic," I point out. "What if I set the whole building on fire?"

"Fair point."

Birdie stretches out her back before turning to face the mirror. She seems to admire herself for a moment, completely forgetting I'm even here.

"Birdie, we don't have all night. Mind sharing what you found?"

"You witches and your sense of urgency." The cat huffs before getting up and turning her whole body to face me. "There has been a lot of chatter around these parts. The main woman—"

"Lizette."

"Yes, her. She seems to have thrown herself entirely into work. The other woman—"

"Priscilla."

"Yes!" Birdie hisses, frustrated with my interruption, and I try not to smile. "She came in to where the main woman was, telling her to stop controlling everything. She was folding towels. Lizette was," Birdie hurries to add when I open my mouth. The cat really doesn't like using people's names. I've noticed that. She calls me witch almost every time.

"They're not getting along," Birdie continues. "Priscilla." Oh there's real bitterness in Birdie's voice now. "She thinks Lizette needs to loosen the reins a little. And Lizette thinks Priscilla should mind her own business."

"So, they are clashing. They presented such a united front at the game night."

"It's their job, isn't it, witch? They have to keep up appearances, since all the money problems have brought them nothing but grief."

Walter mentioned that too. This place looks like it's doing great, but in reality, there is a lot underneath the pretty exterior. I remember when I used to stage apartments. We always had to make sure the foundation was solid. It seems the resort doesn't have a solid foundation anymore.

That's when it hits me. The money problems, all the high

tensions between the staff, Arthur's expensive taste. It all makes sense if I consider that maybe Arthur was stealing from the resort. Detective Ames mentioned small money deposits regularly. This was probably to keep the bank from raising any questions. But what if—

"Mind sharing with the class?" Birdie's voice penetrates my thoughts, and I glance down at her watching me.

"I'm just trying to put the pieces together. Everything I've found out points to Arthur stealing money. What if he was stealing from the resort? And his other jobs? It would explain the frequent cash deposits. He would just break them up. But if he was stealing from all his contracts, that would explain the weird behavior and the expensive taste."

"The dead guy was stealing?"

I guess she didn't hear about that in her eavesdropping, which makes me feel way too smug. I'm literally competing with a cat. Giving myself a mental shake, I focus.

"He was. And I think the high tensions just put Lizette and Priscilla back to the top of my suspect list. I wish they would talk to me. Priscilla has completely sidestepped me every time I've tried to approach her."

"You can try cornering them upstairs. They both have rooms up there."

"What? Do you know their numbers?"

"1563 and 1501. Lizette is the one at the end of the hallway."

Well, this is actually helpful. Birdie goes back to grooming herself while a plan starts forming in my mind. I need to get ahead of this thing. I need to be more proactive. And I think I know just where to start.

17

———

That's it. I'm putting my foot down. I need to get this show on the road and solve this case before the storm lets up and all the suspects scatter. But I can't do this alone. I check my phone and see that it's barely four in the morning. I'm sure people will be waking up soon, so I need to make myself rest. For at least a few hours.

Birdie leaves without a backward look as I head back to the main area.

Reaching the cot, I lay down, closing my eyes immediately. My mind continues to race over all the things I must do, but I force myself to do some meditation exercises, focus on my breathing, and relax.

After a few moments, exhaustion catches up to me and I'm thrown into dreamland. I land in the same weird forest room I've been to before, but there is no sign of Arthur. I call out to him a few times, but all I see is fog. A lot of it.

There's much more than the last time I was here. I want to look around more, but then someone is calling my name, and the room begins to fade.

When I open my eyes, I find Dean looking down at me.

"What's going on?" I ask, sitting up slowly. Dean pulls back, his eyes still on me as I push my hair out of my face.

"We're heading over to breakfast," Penny announces. I look over to see her standing next to Finn. "We didn't want you to miss out."

"What time is it?"

"After eight."

Wow, I guess I did sleep. And hard. That dream felt like a minute max, and yet, it's been nearly four hours. I do feel much more rested than before though. So success.

"Thanks," I say, getting off the cot and straightening my clothes. I also discreetly look around to see if Birdie is anywhere to be seen. She's not. Then again, it's not like I expected to see her. She's the best at staying under the radar.

We make our way to the dining room, passing a few lines in the hall.

"The storm is really bad outside," Dean says from beside me. "They've provided towels and toothpaste for people to clean up, but the bathrooms aren't big enough to accommodate everyone at once."

I nod, giving him a tentative smile. Things have been a little weird between us. Well, mostly because I've been avoiding him. But sue me. I'm in run-from-my-problems mode. I can only handle so much at a time.

The dining room is bustling with activity, and we find a table in the corner with four seats still available. Finn and Dean head off to the line immediately, saying they'll bring us back food. The moment they step away, I pull Penny close, lowering my voice.

"I need your help. And theirs."

"Oh, you woke up with a mission?" My friend's eyes are shining, and I smile.

"Absolutely."

A few people walk by, so I pause before continuing.

"I have three solid suspects," I say. Even though I don't want to rope Walter into that group, I know I have to. "And none of them will talk to me."

Of that, I am sure. The tensions are too high, and everyone is on edge.

"So what's the plan?"

"Since I can't talk to them, I was thinking my best next move would be to look through their stuff."

"What?"

"Shh, Penny." I tug Penny back down, since the outburst made her sit up straighter.

"I mean I know we just did this to Arthur, but it's not like he could've walked in on us, and you know, murdered us!"

"Yes, I know. That is why I'll need everyone's help. You and I will go through the rooms, and the guys will stand watch. We'll have backup. I promised Auntie Grace I'd stop putting myself in dangerous situations. So this is half true. I'll at least have someone watching my back."

Penny listens carefully before slowly nodding.

"Okay, that makes sense. Do we know where?"

"Yes, Birdie was very helpful in that regard."

I still haven't seen the cat, but as long as she's in the building, she'll be safe. From the storm at least.

The guys come back, placing the plates of food in front of us. As Dean takes his seat beside me, he's looking at me curiously.

"What?"

"Just wondering what shenanigans you're about to get into." He shrugs before taking a bite of his bagel.

"First, did you just use *shenanigans* in a sentence?" I place my hand over my heart in mock outrage. "Second, I have no idea what you're talking about."

"Sure you don't." He smirks. "I can see the gleam in your eyes."

I—have absolutely no idea what to say to that because he can tell from the look in my eyes? He keeps doing that to me, showing me that he knows me. He's been paying attention.

Hold on, heart. You've got to stay calm. And in my chest.

"Are you planning something?" Finn asks, leaning forward. I study my friends' faces before letting my lips curl up in a smile.

"I knew it." Dean's words are but a whisper, but the grin he gives me can probably be seen as well as heard from space. I can't seem to look away. I think I'd stare at him for forever, until a slight nudge under the table jerks me back to attention.

I glance over at Penny, who gives me a knowing look before proceeding to eat her bagel.

"I have some—shenanigans planned," I finally say, keeping my voice low. "And I'm going to need your help."

AFTER WE'VE EATEN, and go over the plan of attack, it's time to get a move on. The backup generators have finally come on. People seem to be a little calmer now, even though we're all still stuck inside.

"Miss Duke." Detective Ames stops us when we're exiting the dining room. I glance at my friends, and they keep going, giving the detective and me some privacy.

"Good morning, detective," I say, keeping my customer service smile in place. He's wearing the same clothes as yesterday, but he looks showered. I envy him for a moment. It would've been nice to clean up after going out into the storm. It'll take me days—and some magical powers—to untangle the mess that is my hair.

"How did you sleep?" Detective Ames asks. I guess we're doing the polite thing now.

"Good. You?"

"Interestingly enough, not well. It seems I had an intruder in my room yesterday, so I had to be on high alert."

"Oh?"

Detective Ames gives me a look as if to say, "really Cassie?" But it's not unkind. He doesn't even seem annoyed.

"Mind sharing what you've discovered?" he says instead.

"I'm not sure what you mean," I reply.

"Please, Miss Duke. Give me some benefit of the doubt. I do this for a living."

The fact that he did notice someone being in his room really does prove he's good at it. What would be nicer is if he shared the information he knows, but I know that's not happening. If there was a magic spell for this kind of a thing, it would've been on top of my to-learn list. But magic doesn't work like that. I still have to do the hard part myself.

The hard part being the actual conversation and back and forth question and answer that I have to do. I basically have to "people." Suppose I'm about to test that skill.

"Have you been able to find anything out about the cause of death?"

Detective Ames studies me for a moment before he motions for me to move out of the direct hallway and to the side.

"I'm not supposed to be telling you this," he prefaces. I don't dare make a sound lest he stop. "But the victim has a gash on the head that was made with something sharp and ragged. And then he bled to death."

"But not from the head wound."

"No."

"Any idea what caused that?"

"Only the marks we found on the neck. Whoever this killer

is, he or she knows exactly what artery to pierce in order to inflict the fastest amount of damage."

"But that could be anyone, couldn't it?" I say, my head spinning with possibilities. "All they need is a working internet connection and they can look it up."

"True. But the way the medical examiner calls it is that it was too practiced of a move to be spontaneous."

"So whoever killed Arthur went into this knowing exactly what to do. Which one of the suspects has a medical background?"

"No one so far. We're still checking, but the storm is making it difficult to get anything done."

This is why my plan of digging through the suspect's rooms is looking better and better by the second. I could honestly see all three of them having some kind of medical knowledge. Both Lizette and Priscilla have worked with the public long enough to know basic first aid. And I'm sure Walter had to learn when he was traveling. Maybe I can find something that gives me something more definite.

A girl can hope, after all.

"Whatever it is you're thinking, you have to be careful," Detective Ames comments, as if he can see the thoughts racing through my mind.

"Careful and legal, you mean?"

"If you're thinking of entering any more locked rooms—"

"Detective, I think it's best that we keep our investigation methods to ourselves. In case it ever comes up, for any occasion." I grin at him as he sighs. It's the most parental sound I have ever heard, and it kind of makes me want to grin even bigger. I'm getting to him, but in a good way.

"Just be careful," he says, right as someone calls out his name. I turn to see Priscilla waiting by the doors, which only solidifies my plan.

"Always am," I say, before I leave him to his official business

18

————

I t doesn't take long before the guys are in their designated spots and Penny and I are making our way upstairs through the back kitchen. In my pocket is Dean's phone. Apparently, he and Finn have an app that allows the phones to turn into walkie talkies. The service seems to be spotty, so we can't just keep each other on the line. We tried. But the app is working, so we're going with that.

"Where do we start?" Penny asks once we're through the waiting area and back in the hallway. A few people head down the main staircase, a family that appears to be staying up here in one of the rooms. I turn us in the opposite direction.

"I'm thinking—Priscilla. She's first." And we saw her downstairs before we came up here. She should be occupied for a little bit.

We reach the door number Birdie indicated to me last night, and I try the door handle. Of course it's locked. I give myself to the intention, pulling up my magic, and then the lock clicks.

"I'm never getting over how cool that is," Penny whispers

beside me. I smile as I push the door open and we step inside. This is mostly why I told Dean *no* when he said he'd come with me. I can't explain to him how I keep getting into these rooms, and there's no way he'd believe I'm lucky to keep finding all of them unlocked.

I find the light switch and flick it on. This room looks way more lived in than Arthur's did. I'm surprised any of the staff members stay in the main house, but maybe that's just the easiest. Sure helps me out with the investigating when I don't have to venture back into the storm.

"What am I looking for?" Penny asks. I experience a sort of déjà vu after our excursion last night.

"Anything that ties Priscilla to the money situation or to a medical background. I'll explain later," I hurry to add when Penny gives me a confused look about that last part.

She takes one side of the room, I take the other, and we start our search. Is it weird that we have a system for this now? It feels a little weird. But I also know it's necessary.

"Hey, look at this," I say, pulling out an album from the bottom of the dresser. Flipping through it, I see that it goes back quite a few years. Priscilla looks much younger in some of these.

"Wow, she does know how to smile," Penny says from beside me as I turn the page to a group shot of her and five other people all scrunched inside the frame. She's front and center, grinning like I've never seen her grin before. They're all wearing matching t-shirts with a familiar looking symbol on them, but I can't really place it.

"Penny, look!"

I point at the man in the back left corner, and it's none other than Arthur. Even without the beard, I'm sure of it. There's no date on the picture, so I flip a few more and find one that has Priscilla looking similar, from nine years ago.

"Priscilla and Arthur knew each other before he came to work here," I say, glancing up at Penny.

"So why did she appear so cold before when you tried talking to her?"

"Maybe that's how she deals with grief?" I say. Who am I to judge how someone handles something like that? Everyone grieves differently. But what I don't get is why she lied.

"Penny, she told Detective Ames she barely knew Arthur. I'm sure of it."

"Why would she do that?"

The only reason I can come up with is if she was hiding their relationship from everyone, which needs a reason. And since there's been a murder, that reason isn't an innocent one.

"Maybe they were scheming and stealing money from the resort together," I say out loud, mulling it over. "It's possible that's how Arthur had access to the books. Priscilla is in charge of all that. Especially—"

"Especially what?"

"Especially their marketing budget! She's in charge of all their promotions. I mean, that woman, Helen, helps, but she hasn't even been on campus lately as far as I can tell. What if that's where the money was being taken out of? No one would know how much an ad or a website placement would cost but her right? She could be taking extra off the top."

"And that would in turn create issues elsewhere."

"Priscilla was also brought here by Lizette, so they could all be in on it."

"And Lizette is in a perfect position to cover for all of them."

Penny and I look at each other in shock. We really are getting all conspiracy minded up in here.

"Okay, did you find anything else?"

"No, not really. She's very clean and organized."

"She would be the type of a person to clean up a crime

scene," I muse, replacing the album where I found it. "We should check out Lizette's room next. We don't have much time."

Grabbing Dean's phone, I push the talk button.

"How's our favorite manager doing?" I ask. There's a crack of static and then Dean's deep voice comes over the line.

"She's schmoozing the locals," he says.

"Perfect." I glance up at Penny. "Let's go."

LIZETTE'S ROOM is at the end of the hallway, tucked away in the corner. Once we step inside, I'm surprised by how different it looks from the others. While Priscilla's room looked like a typical resort setup, much like the one Detective Ames is staying at, Lizette's room is entirely different.

"Wow, it's like stepping inside of a different house all together," Penny comments. I nod.

The ceilings in this room are higher, decorated by a crown molding that is probably at least a hundred years old. The whole room is painted in a dark blue and gold, making this room darker than the others as well. There are paintings in gold frames on the walls and plush furniture with velvet covers. Everything looks classic and pristine.

"I think this is what the resort might've looked like before," I say, walking slowly through the room. It's kind of how the Crooked Windows Inn looked a few decades ago, and a bit of what I want to bring back to my home.

"Look at these," Penny calls. I turn to see her opening a trunk at the foot of the bed. All kinds of colorful materials sat inside. I pull out a decorative throw with beautiful stitch work all over it. The designs look vaguely familiar, but I can't place them.

"Lizette is quite the seamstress," I say, looking through the rest of the material. I leave Penny there as I make my way to the dresser, pulling out the drawers carefully to look inside. Maybe I should feel like I'm violating their privacy, and I am, but also, if one of these women is involved, the other will just have to forgive me.

Penny and I move in silence, making sure to place things exactly like we found them. It's not until I reach the dresser on the opposite side of the room that I find something useful. There are a few lanyards in the top drawer, along with passes and pieces of movie tickets. I sift through them all before something stops me. The same design I saw on the stitching is on one of the lanyards. Sigma Theta Charter. And then right under the big letters, some small print. Honor Society of Nursing.

Twisting around, I walk back to the trunk, pulling it back open. The stitching on the throw is the design for the nurses logo, two snakes twisting around a staff with angel wings. The caduceus. It's the staff from Greek mythology carried by Hermes, the messenger of gods. It's a universal insignia for the public health organization.

"Penny, I think I found something."

That's when my eyes land on the top cover of the trunk. There's a piece of material attached to the top with metal snaps. I pull on one of the snaps, revealing a whole set of stitching tools beneath. Lizette isn't just an amateur hobbyist, she's serious about this.

"What is it, Cassie?"

"Look at this." I point to the logos, both on the lanyard and the throw.

"It's the medical symbol?"

"Yes, although technically it should be the Rod of Asclepius, but that's a whole different story." And it's from a lifetime ago when I thought I was going to study history. "But you know what this means."

"Lizette is a nurse?"

"She at least participated in the honor society. I'm not sure how that works, but she would have to be, right? But this is the symbol Pricilla has on her shirt in that picture. She at least volunteered too."

"Oh. How does that help us?"

That's right. We haven't really discussed what Detective Ames and I talked about.

"The way Arthur was killed—it wasn't a sloppy job. Someone knew what they were doing. It had to be premeditated, and it had to be done by someone who knew where to strike."

"A nurse would."

"Yes. But what's the motive? With Priscilla, it makes more sense if she was the one helping Arthur with the money. If Lizette was helping them with the money theft but decided to pull out, she could've just fired him. She has the run of this place. It would make more sense for Walter to take Lizette out so he could have the resort back to himself. And he's a big dude, he could do it too. Although, he'd probably be messier. Then again, he's a chef, so maybe not?"

"Honestly, Cassie," Penny says, her eyes big. "Sometimes your brain scares me."

"Yeah, same here." I chuckle. The phone in my pocket buzzes, and I pull it out in time to hear Dean say my name.

"What is it?" I reply immediately.

"We've lost sight of both of them. Get out now," he says. Penny and I glance at each other before we rush to opposite sides of the room, to place things where we found them. We're at the door, pulling it open, just as a noise catches my attention. I glance back into the room as I'm shutting the door, and something clicks into place.

19

"These near...*something* experiences are not good for my heart," Penny says as we take our seats on the cots. The guys are there, both looking at us with worry.

"It's usually near *death*," Finn points out.

"Very helpful, Harvey." Penny rolls her eyes. They're cute and all, but right now, I'm nearly bouncing out of my seat with excitement.

"Cassie, is there something you'd like to share with the class?" Dean asks, his eyes on me. He hasn't really looked away from me since we met them in the hall outside of the side kitchens. Apparently even sneaking into other people's rooms is giving the poor man anxiety over me.

"We found out some things."

"Okay."

"I think the only way to be sure is to—" I stop, thinking over what needs to be done.

"To what?" Penny exclaims, "Don't keep us in suspense."

"Is to get them talking about it. Hold on, I'll be back."

Now that I think I have figured it out, I need to talk to

Detective Ames. Jumping to my feet, I leave my friends gaping after me as I weave in and out of the cots toward the dining room. As far as I know, Detective Ames was going to hold more interviews today, so it's only natural he'd be using the same room. He's standing outside it, talking to none other than Walter. Perfect timing.

"Detective, can I have a word?" I ask, coming up to the two of them. Walter gives me a clipped smile and goes to step away when I stop him. "And can I talk to you about something as well? In a little bit?" I put on my best Bambi eyes look, and it works.

Walter watches me for a moment before nodding.

"I'll be over there." He points to the buffet.

"Nicely handled, Miss Duke," the detective says.

"It's taken years to perfect," I reply, turning to face him.

"As long as you don't use those on me," he says, and I grin.

"No promises. But what I can promise you is that I know who killed Arthur."

All sense of humor goes out of Detective Ames's eyes as he narrows them on me.

"Explain yourself."

So I do. In hushed tones, I tell him what I found. He listens without interruption, and then muses over my words before finally replying.

"It makes sense, but—"

"But it's all circumstantial," I finish for him, because I already know this part as well. "You can't take anything I found into evidence because it wasn't obtained legally. And you need more than this to get a warrant."

"You really have taken on this persona, haven't you?"

"I'm going to take that as a compliment and run with it," I say. "We need them to admit it."

"How do you suppose we do that?"

I smile, glancing back to where Walter is waiting before looking at the detective once more.

"With a little help. First, I need you to check on something for me."

IT TAKES us about an hour to set everything up the way I want it. The plan is truly simple. We have a sit-down with our three main suspects and discuss the crime. Sure, it can go up in flames about a dozen different ways, but with the detective not having direct contact with his precinct, we have to do something.

Detective Ames has arranged the upstairs meeting room as the designated place for our meeting. Dean is sitting on one side of the room as Lizette, Priscilla, and Walter walk in. I'm standing near the left side of the room while Detective Ames is at the front.

"What is the meaning of this?" Lizette asks when her eyes land on me. "I'm in the middle of preparing lunch for the guests."

"Yes, we all have important jobs. Like actually cooking the lunch," Walter says. Lizette sends an array of glares his way. Priscilla looks between the two before rolling her eyes and taking a seat.

"Can we get started?" she asks.

It's an interesting dynamic. I've never seen the three of them interact before. Each holds a high position within the resort, and they're the three people in the whole place who should be getting along the most. And yet, they're not.

Detective Ames looks at me before nodding his head. The three glance between the two of us as he walks to the back of the room. I take his place at the front.

"I know you have a lot of work ahead of you, but this couldn't wait," I begin. It feels weird to stand in a meeting room like this, with a white screen behind me. It brings back memories of when I presented design ideas to our clients. But now, this is a whole different set of skills that I'm using, and I'm kind of glad I get the opportunity.

"I don't understand what any of this has to do with you," Priscilla comments, ever the expressionless one. I smile at her before I reply.

"As you all know, I found Arthur's body. It seemed such a strange situation, right from the beginning. The pool house was spotless, a body was floating in the pool. Most of his blood drained, but not where he was found. It was odd."

"We are all saddened by Mr. Gilla's passing, but I don't understand how that pertains to this meeting," Lizette says, ever the businesswoman.

"Well, we need to talk about who killed him. But Miss Bats, some of you are more saddened than others. Isn't that right, Miss Janson?"

I turn my gaze to Priscilla, and for the first time, I see her shift uncomfortably.

"I'm not sure what you're insinuating."

"No? You knew Arthur before you came to the resort, did you not?"

Walter and Lizette both turn to Priscilla like they've never seen her before.

"You knew him?" Walter asks.

"Okay, fine. Yes. We worked on a volunteer trip after college. That's all."

"Is that why you had my grandparents hire him? You pushed pretty hard." She shifts in her seat once more, straightening her blouse.

"He wasn't in a good spot, okay? I wanted to help him out."

"But it was more than that," I say, and everyone once again turns to me. "You were in love with him. It's why you helped him."

"Helped him?"

"To blackmail."

"What? Blackmail who?" Lizette asks.

"You, of course." Everyone gasps, but I don't give them the chance to continue. It's important that I build a narrative strong enough that the guilty party has no choice but to burst out with a confession. "You, Miss Bats, have been the one skimming off the books. You brought Priscilla on, thinking she'll be an accomplice, but she wasn't. She, in turn, brought Arthur. And Arthur found out. So, he blackmailed you to share."

"I have no idea what you're talking about."

"You don't? Because the expensive taste that you've acquired says otherwise. How much do those velvet covers cost?"

"You've been to my room?" The outrage is there, and now everyone is shifting uncomfortably in their seats.

"The door was open, I looked inside."

"The door would never be open. I never leave it unlocked."

"Hmm, I think it might be unlocked now." I made sure it was. A quick spell and I left the door ajar. It's all I needed to convince the police to walk by and see what's inside.

"That's not true. I make sure to lock it."

"So you can lock away all your secrets?" Walter bursts out, the outrage clear on his face. "My grandparents trusted you. They gave you the resort and you let them down."

"Oh please, don't start with shifting blame. We all know you were the first to let them down."

"Now, listen here you—"

"Excuse me, I'm not done," I interrupt before they really get into it. There's only bad blood between this trio. That much is obvious.

"You're only making up stories," Priscilla says. I can see that I got to her. There's emotion in her eyes for the first time. It was the love comment. I know I hit her where it hurts. My eyes find Dean and his are shining with silent encouragement.

"So which one of you decided to get rid of Arthur first?" I ask. That sends them into complete silence. "No comments on that?"

"What are you talking about?" Walter asks, so I finally turn my attention to him.

"You said you wanted to prove yourself to your grandparents. But when you found out money was going missing and Arthur was making bank, it wasn't hard to figure out what happened. So you had to get rid of him. But first, you wanted the money back."

"I don't—"

"Know what I'm talking about? But you do. I noticed a little bruising on your right hand. It's from where you punched him in the face, isn't it?"

"Walter, what did you do?" Lizette whispers, looking at him in shock.

"Fine. We got into it, okay? But I didn't kill him. He said he'd return what he took. I told him I'd go to the police if I didn't have the money by the end of the week. It took some physical force to convince him, but he promised. I didn't lie before." Walter looks at me. "I do want to do right by my grandparents. I wanted to restore this place to its former glory."

"So you killed him?" Priscilla asks, and now there are tears in her eyes.

"No, I didn't!" Walter snaps. "Why would I kill someone who was getting me my money? That makes no sense."

"That's what I thought too," I comment, and they turn to me once more. "Which is why it made more sense for Priscilla to be the one to kill him. Out of a jealous rage."

"What?"

"You loved him. He didn't love you back. But you saw the way things were between him and Lizette, and you couldn't stand it. You didn't know he was blackmailing her. All you knew is they were whispering and going behind your back."

"That's not true."

"It's not? So if we test the rock you used to smash over his head they won't find your fingerprints all over it?"

The gasp is so loud it echoes in the room. Everyone turns to stare at Priscilla, as she bursts into tears.

"I didn't mean to hurt him. I just got so mad. And he didn't care. Not even a little. He was just working on those stupid flower beds."

"So you grabbed a rock and you hit him in the head."

"But I didn't kill him. He was breathing when I left him!" She turns to the detective, jumping to her feet. "You have to believe me. I didn't want him dead. I just wanted him punished."

She advances on him, begging for forgiveness. With our attention shifted, no one sees them move. I turn to Lizette, and my heart stops. She's holding a gun and it's trained right on Dean.

20

"You figured it all out, didn't you?" Lizette says. I stare at her with my heart in my throat. "Don't you even think about it, detective," she warns. I glance over and see the detective raise his hands away from his gun. Priscilla distracted him, and he didn't draw in time.

"Let's take a walk, pretty boy." She motions for Dean to stand and points him to the side door. Dean's eyes are on me. I couldn't look away from him even if I tried. The moment they're through the door, the detective rushes out the back door to cut her off, but she fires off a shot. My feet carry me toward them before I can think about the fact that I'm running into gunfire. There's screaming, and the detective is near the wall, slumped over. My eyes zero in on Dean, who's back is to the top banister with Lizette still pointing the gun at him.

This is not how I pictured the conversation going. I just wanted to spin a tall tale to get her to confess.

"Please, Lizette, be rational about this."

"What's there to be rational about?" she snaps as she takes a step forward, pushing Dean farther back against the banister. "I gave my everything to this place, and I was getting fired? Because I couldn't make ends meet. It wasn't my fault Arthur was stealing from the Sanchez's. I shouldn't have been the one punished!"

I was wrong on that. He was the one stealing, not her. But then her money situation doesn't make sense.

"You're right," I keep my voice calm, inching closer to her and Dean. "You've only been trying to do what's right for this place. I'm sure the Sanchez's will understand."

"I didn't mean to hurt him." She's not listening to anything I'm saying, lost in her own mind. "He found out I sold some of their art. I bet it all on black and lost. I didn't know how I'd repay. He threatened to go to them and tell them I was the one stealing, unless I gave him a big payout."

"He blackmailed you."

"What was I supposed to do? I went to the garden to confront him, and I saw Priscilla hit him on the head. He fell down, unconscious, and I—I took the opportunity. I had to protect myself. And the Sanchez's. They should be grateful I stopped him! They would've been ruined. I only took a little, but he took so much! I saved them."

The logic is definitely skewed, but her aim holds true on Dean. I glance at him, and he's already watching me. He shakes his head ever so slightly, but he's crazy if he thinks I'm just going to back away.

"You can tell the police that, Lizette. You can tell them the truth."

"No one is going to believe me." She's beyond gone now. I can see the manic look in her eyes. "Just let me get out of here, and I'll disappear. I will."

"Lizette—"

"No, you don't understand. This place was my last chance, and he ruined it. He ruined me. There's no going back now."

"Lizette, we can talk—"

Before I could say anything else, a small black form comes out of nowhere, dropping straight onto Lizette's chest. The gun goes off, and then, as if in slow motion, Dean is going over the banister.

"No!" I scream. My hands thrust in front of me as if I can reach him. All of my intention goes into this one moment, my heart and my magic on the line. Lizette is also screaming, but then an officer is there, pulling her down to the floor so he can cuff her. I only see that out of the corner of my eye as my heart threatens to beat right out of my chest. Rushing over, I expect to see him gone, but then I gasp.

"A little help?" Dean asks. Somehow, he managed to grab onto one of the banister's uprights.

"Oh my." I reach for him, but I'm not strong enough to pull him up. He slips a little farther down. My hands latch onto his wrists and then I put all my intention into my magic and pull. There's a second of hesitation, but then I'm lifting him up—or maybe it's my magic—and in the next moment he's tumbling over the banister. He twists at the last moment, so I end up on top of him as we land.

"Oh, my goodness gracious," I mumble as I let my hands roam over every part of him, checking for injuries.

"Cassie, Cassie, I'm okay!" He reaches for my hands, stopping their progress over his chest and our faces are barely inches away and everything I'm feeling is probably written all over my face. I'm entirely on top of him, as close as I've ever been, and everything I'm feeling just pours out. I don't think. I act.

My lips are on his and there's no hesitation on his part. He wraps his arms around my waist, pulling him fully flush against him as he devours me just like I devour him. We kiss like we've been doing it all our lives. We kiss like we can't get enough of each other. He's filling my lungs with his breath, giving me life with the touch of his lips. There are no reservations between us, no awkward fumble of the hands.

He holds me like I'm precious and I hold him like he's mine.

"Well, that's an interesting development." Finn's voice cuts through the euphoria, and I pull back. Then the gravity of what I've done hits me, and I'm scrambling off Dean as fast as I can.

"Yeah, he's fine. Dean's fine. Lizette is in custody. It's a win win," I rattle off, refusing to meet anyone's gaze. "I need the restroom."

And then I bolt.

"So the whole bullet proof vest thing really works, huh?" I say, coming up to where Detective Ames is getting his ribs looked at a little while later.

"Right down to the fact that it still hurts."

I smile at that, glad that no one was hurt. I still can't believe how close I came to losing Dean. I should've insisted he stay out of it when I decided to do my little presentation.

"Well, I'll keep that in mind for the future," I say.

"How did you know?" Detective Ames asks as he stands, shrugging his jacket back on.

"That it was Lizette? The stitching tools. She made the puncture wounds with the awl. It was in the trunk, but upside down. Not like the others. It stood out to me."

"So you put it together from that?"

I couldn't exactly tell him about the magical conversations I had with my cat—kinda my cat.

"The last time I was involved in one of these situations, I didn't recognize the threat in time because I wasn't looking at the whole picture. I tried to do better this time. And when I started putting the pieces together, I knew there's no way only one person was involved."

"It was my first thought when I came here as well."

"Why didn't you tell me?"

"Because I'm an officer of the law." He smiles fully, maybe for the first time since I've met him. It makes him look ten years younger. The nagging question that I carried with me from the beginning comes up again, and this time, I ask it.

"Why did you decide to let me get involved?"

"What do you mean?"

"You know what I mean. You checked up on me, sure. But then you didn't really ask questions. You just trusted me. Why?"

Detective Ames is quiet for a long moment, and I think he might not answer at all. But then he does.

"You look like her, you know," he says, making me completely baffled.

"Who?"

"Your mother."

It's like a hole has opened up beneath my feet and has swallowed me whole. I can't seem to make myself move or form a coherent thought.

My mother. The woman who disappeared when I was only a child, one who's memory I barely carry anymore because magic and time has taken it all.

"You knew my mother?" I finally manage. He inclines his head.

"I did. She helped me out on a case when I was only a rookie. She was an incredible woman."

"You don't—" I clear my throat. "You don't know what happened to her?"

"I'm sorry, Cassie." It's the first time he's used my name, and it feels familiar somehow. "I wish I could give you more than that. I've looked into her disappearance more than once over the years, but there have been no new leads."

That stops me. My chest feels too heavy, my lungs too full, but those words give me something I didn't have before. Hope.

"So there were leads?"

"A few."

"I need to see what you have."

"Cassie—"

"Please. I don't have any answers, but I also don't have any memories to go off of. I need closure."

He studies me for a long time before finally nodding.

"I'll see what I can do."

21

"How long exactly are you going to avoid Dean?" Penny asks, as we pull up to the Crooked Windows Inn. Home sweet home. Auntie Grace is waiting on the stairs, her hands over her heart. Birdie is the first out of the car when I open the door.

"Good riddance to that pile of metal," she mutters.

"You're welcome!" I call out to her, receiving a strange look from one of the people walking by on the sidewalk. Oops. "And I don't know what you're talking about," I say to Penny. She just groans at me. Grabbing my bags, I head up the stairs toward my aunt. She rushes down the stairs, pulling me into her embrace. I drop the bags so I can hug her and it truly does feel like home.

"You, my sweet sugar cookie, are in need of a protection spell and a karma cleansing and whatever else I can find to keep these dreadful dealings away from you," Auntie Grace says, pulling away to give me a thorough once over.

"I think the time for that has passed, Auntie Grace." I reach down and give her cheek a kiss. "It's my calling."

"A calling!"

"It's what we decided on the way back," Penny says as she gives Auntie Grace a hug as well. "She can't escape."

"Oh, you poor dears, not much of a vacation, wasn't it?"

Penny begins the rundown of the events, up to the part where the storm let up about ten minutes after Lizette was in custody. I guess Mother Nature was doing me a solid. As we step inside the inn, Lucy greets me with a warm welcome. Birdie is already spread out on the counter, giving me a side stare. I roll my eyes but don't even bother calling the cat out on her unbecoming behavior. I gave her treats and drove her home. She should be a little more thankful.

"I'll catch you up on my side of the story later. I could really use a shower."

Penny and I left as soon as we were free to go. We just wanted to get home. Dean was still being questioned, so I haven't had a chance to talk to him. Not that I'm ready, after what I pulled. Penny gives me a quick hug before grabbing her keys and waltzing back out the door. I'm sure she'll be coming back as soon as she's done checking up on Penny's bakery. The whole Dean conversation is definitely not done.

I still haven't told her about the bomb Detective Ames dropped on me. And I'm not ready to talk about it to Auntie Grace just yet.

Instead, I do what any self-respecting person who's hiding from everything in her life does. Take a shower and then a nap. The moment I close my eyes, I'm one hundred percent in the dream. At first, it's a pretty normal one, not in the room with the fog I've grown used to, but a comfortable sitting area, and then Arthur is there.

"You did it. You figured out what happened."

I nod, looking at him in a new light. He was the victim, but he also inflicted a lot of pain.

"Why did you do it? Any of it?"

"I'm not sure." He shrugs, but I don't think he's deflecting. I think that's an honest answer. "I wish I could've turned out to be a better person."

"Maybe you can do that now," I say, because I know this is a goodbye. I still have no idea why he came to me, but I'll figure that part out as well as everything else I have on my list.

"Thank you, Cassie Duke," he says right before he disappears. I open my eyes to see Birdie sitting on my bed, staring at me.

"Your lover boy is here," she says, right as a knock sounds on the door. I narrow my eyes at her, getting out of bed. I smooth my hair down as I pull the door open.

"Hi," Dean says. The way he shifts from one foot to the other makes me smile.

"Hi, yourself. You made it back."

"Yeah, they know where to find me if they have more questions."

I motion him to come in before I shut the door. He seems to fill the whole space of my room. Birdie watches from the bed, and Dean walks over to give her a scratch behind the ears. The little traitor actually purrs.

"I'm sorry," Dean and I say at the same time and then chuckle.

"What do you have to be sorry for?" I ask.

"For getting you involved in all that."

"Oh, come on, Dean. I wouldn't have it any other way." I shrug it off, and he smiles as he watches me.

"I believe that actually. So I guess after I'm sorry comes the thank you. Because thank you. You really, truly saved me."

"Just doing my side job." I chuckle.

"You're good at it."

As we talk, we're moving closer and closer to each other until there's only a few feet separating us. The pull I've felt toward him since I came has intensified by thousands. I'd be lying if I said I haven't been thinking about that kiss nonstop.

But I have no idea where that leaves us. We just decided to be friends, and suddenly, we're something else.

"Where do we go from here, Cassie?" he asks. I kind of wish Birdie wasn't here to witness this. She's going to give me so much grief about it later. I can feel it.

"Forward?" I ask, and Dean chuckles again.

"I would very much like that, which is why I'm officially asking you on a date. A winter wonderland stroll through the Christmas village, with dinner and hot chocolate."

"And snow?"

"I'll see if I can get Mother Nature on our side."

We grin at each other, and my heart feels lighter than it has in years. Which is probably why I say what I say next.

"Dean, I'm going to try to find my mother."

NEXT IN THE CROOKED WINDOWS INN
SERIES

The new year brings new possibilities...and murder!

Cassandra Duke has officially accepted her dual role as
witch and amateur sleuth. Life settles into a new rhythm—

until a body is discovered in one of the houses she's renovating, plunging Cassie right back into sleuthing. It looks like murder, but no one can tell how the man died.

Now, it seems her services are once again needed. But discovering a corpse isn't her only problem. A fog has rolled into town, putting everyone on high alert. When a new witch shows up unannounced, Cassie's magic is put to a new test, and it's clear that something otherworldly is going on in Monroe Cove.

And, of course, it happens right when she and sexy handyman, Dean, were finally taking a step forward.

Between juggling a new relationship, her snarky furball familiar, a murder, and a magical mystery, Cassie has her work cut out for her.

It seems that anywhere she turns, someone she loves is in danger. Cassie must do whatever it takes to protect the town she calls home—even if it might mean giving up her magic forever.

If you love a little magic and wit with your murder, you'll love this fast-paced paranormal witch cozy mysteries series from USA Today bestselling author, Valia Lind!

NOTE FROM THE AUTHOR

Thank you for reading my book! If you have enjoyed it, please consider leaving a review. Reviews are like gold to authors and are a huge help!

They help authors get more visibility, and help readers make a decision!

And, if you'd like to stay up to date with all of my shenanigans, sign up for my newsletter today!

CLICK HERE TO SIGN UP!

Thank you!

DO YOU LIKE ACADEMY ADVENTURE ROMANCE?

Get the complete series here:
Thunderbird Academy Boxset

I'm losing control of my magic... and a wolf shifter has to keep me in check.

An Ancient evil is spreading throughout the land. When it knocks on the door of my school, everyone expects me to fight it.

But I'm hiding a secret....my magic is on the fritz.

Not only that, but the headmaster forces me into combat training lessons with my nemesis.

Aiden Lawson, wolf shifter. Did I mention he's ridiculously gorgeous and impossible to ignore? Our lessons are explosive, and I never seem to come out on top. He won't go easy on me. He's as ruthless as he is loyal.

If I can just get my magic under control, then I can be rid of Aiden for good.

But when the Ancient evil breaks through the school's defenses, Aiden and I have to fight.

Whether we're ready or not.

Welcome to my year at Thunderbird Academy.

Full of magic, adventure, and enemies-to-lovers angsty romance, Thunderbird Academy is an addicting young adult paranormal romance series by USA Today bestselling author Valia Lind that will keep you reading late into the night!

ABOUT THE AUTHOR

USA Today bestselling author. Photographer. Artist. Born and raised in St. Petersburg, Russia, Valia Lind has always had a love for the written word. She wrote her first published book on the bathroom floor of her dormitory, while procrastinating to study for her college classes. Upon graduation, she has moved her writing to more respectable places, and has found her voice in Young Adult and cozy mysteries.

Sign up to receive updates, behind the scenes, & more!
CLICK HERE

ALSO BY VALIA LIND

Crooked Windows Inn Cozy Mysteries

Once Upon a Witch #1

Two Can Witch the Game #2

Third Witch's the Charm #3

Witches Four the Win #4 - coming Spring 2022!

The Skazka Fairy Tales

The Scarlet Rose (A Beauty and the Beast Retelling)

The Golden Slipper (A Cinderella Retelling) - coming Spring 2022!

Blackwood Supernatural Prison Series

Witch Condemned (#1)

Witch Unchained (#2)

Witch Awakened (#3)

Witch Ascendant (#4)

Hawthorne Chronicles - Each season can be read as standalone!

Season Three

The Complete Trilogy Boxset

Shadow of the Fae (#1)

Blood of the Fae (#2)

Revenge of the Fae (#3)

Season Two

The Complete Trilogy Boxset

Of Water and Moonlight (Thunderbird Academy, #1)

Of Destiny and Illusions (Thunderbird Academy, #2)

Of Storms and Triumphs (Thunderbird Academy, #3)

Season One

Guardian Witch (Hawthorne Chronicles, #1)

Witch's Fire (Hawthorne Chronicles, #2)

Witch's Heart (Hawthorne Chronicles, #3)

Tempest Witch (Hawthorne Chronicles, #4)

The Complete Season One Box Set

The Skazka Chronicles

Hardcover Omnibus - 4 books in one

Remembering Majyk (The Skazka Chronicles, #1)

Majyk Reborn (The Skazka Chronicles, #2)

The Faithful Soldier (The Skazka Chronicles, #2.5)

Majyk Reclaimed (The Skazka Chronicles, #3)

Havenwood Falls (PNR standalone)

Predestined

The Titanium Trilogy

Pieces of Revenge (Titanium, #1)

Scarred by Vengeance (Titanium, #2)

Ruined in Retribution (Titanium, #3)

Complete Box Set

Falling Duology - YA contemporary romance

Falling by Design

Edge of Falling